THE COAL BOAT

SAM KIRK

First published 2018

ISBN-10: 198038777X
ISBN-13: 978-1980387770

'Let us leave the heavens
To the angels and the
sparrows'

'While you do not
understand life, how can
you know about death?'

Confucius

To Loraine,

Glad you enjoyed the
journey.

With love,

Carolyn

Prologue

Cambridge, May 1962

Dear Norman,

It's hard to write the first line when I'm not quite sure how to describe the pages that follow. Do they constitute an apology? The word itself has enough syllables to convey a certain gravitas but we both know that the consequences of my actions will last a lifetime, so I'm not sure mere words can justify seeking your forgiveness. I feel like a weasel even asking for it. So, then, is this a confession? Perhaps, though there is no church, or priest sitting behind a screen to hear it. Is it an account of how I found salvation, not via religion, but via the peace I've finally found within myself, living a disciplined life through my work? No, that all came later. Interestingly, Freud tells us that every culture is based on compulsory labour and instinctual renunciation – ultimately a libertine existence is doomed to failure. I learned that the hard way, but learn it I did, without false promises of divine pleasures or retribution.

Apology, confession. If that sounds a scarily serious proposition then let me put your mind at rest. I had a huge amount of fun along the way: bad girls usually do, don't they? But I would be doing you a disservice if I didn't give you the full picture. Some of it you will have been told, some of it you even feature in. And as the years roll by, I feel more strongly than ever that this is all I can ever give you.

First, let me set the scene for you: two desks facing each other in the tiny and tired-looking but much-loved garret room we call our office on the fourth floor of an old limestone building which sags and lists with age, not a straight wall in sight. Sloping ceiling, one high window. If you crane your neck far enough you get a wonderful view of the Cambridge spires and the sun sparkling on the river Cam, which weaves its way through the city, carrying carefree students and tourists who are taking time to fail comically at punting. This spectacle is like a film with which one never gets bored, but my worry is that these charming surroundings lend the whole writing process a sanitised feel, which I must and will not let lull me into any false sense of security. What I have to tell you cannot be portrayed in soft focus. You deserve to hear the truth, and though the truth itself is something to be endured, I cannot bear that you know only lies about me from the Clayton-Reids.

On my desk is my prized early model third-hand typewriter, and the stillness of the office is punctuated by a noisy and robotic *click-clack* of keys striking paper. Sadly, my typing is still execrable so there are lots of false starts. The walls are covered in newspaper cuttings and a framed picture of Sigmund Freud. I share the office with my colleague, Dr Sarah Mead. We are child psychologists – she much more eminent than I – and we divide our time among academic work for the university, our work for the National Health Service and our stalking of our favourite psychologist *du jour*, Donald Winnicott (of course, I'm joking). I met Sarah during the long, dull, pain-filled months in hospital. She was working there, but on a different ward. I suppose you could say she took pity on me. First, by bringing me books to read. Then, by the many hours she spent talking to me. And finally, by giving me not just a job, but also a career. I've come to believe that sometimes guardian angels do take human form after all.

I do my writing after Sarah has left for the day; although she is in many ways still my mentor and continues to guide me in my career, in this task I have no need for company and, of course, at a practical level the typewriter would disturb her. During long evenings that span many seasons I press on with this task, allowing the present to give way to the memories of the past. At the end of the working day, a new kind of day starts for me; I watch the light turn a creamy yellow and start to cast long shadows across the room, highlighting energetic dust particles carried on tiny pockets of air. The hours spent alone with the typewriter and the endless cups of tea I make to break up the time are as comforting to me as a heartbeat, and, latterly, just as necessary. I am quite at home with my own company here. I sometimes imagine myself as one of the particles of dust, carried on a strong wind and entering an open window, landing in a room where you happen to be. But I am getting sentimental, and must concentrate on my story.

I tried to contact you many times over the years. Did you receive any of my letters? After I was sufficiently recovered to be able to leave hospital, I resolved to make the journey back to the last address I had for you. But the war was on and the house was locked up, everyone long departed – to a kindly aunt in Cumbria, perhaps? The government sent me up to Lincolnshire to work in the fields for the war years. The hard, physical work and superficial bustle of life with the other girls provided a wonderful, if temporary, distraction from my emotional pain. During that time, I was not able to return to London at all. After the war, I moved to Cambridge to take up working for Sarah. Once again, I made the journey down to London, hoping to see you. My stomach was full of butterflies as I walked up the pretty driveway in Hampstead that warm summer's afternoon, the wisteria and ivy claiming even more of the entrance than I remembered. I could hardly believe it was the same place in which I had last seen you all those years ago when the snow was on the ground. But this time Mr Clayton-Reid came to the door, his face full of the kind of fury that has festered and fed on itself and grown organically over the years. He grabbed me roughly by my arm, telling me that if I were to show my face again round there he would call the police and I would be put away for a very, very long time for what I had done. And anyway, what benefit or advantage did I really think I could bring to your life? I was devastated and, looking back, my intent was far more subdued by this threat than it ought to have been, but there you go. This is only something you can see when enough time has passed to allow for hindsight.

I left and went on my way, my pride hurt and my longing to see you only heightened and made more painful. If there is no way of seeing you to tell you my side of the story, then writing it down is the only means at my disposal. I have no idea if you are still at 34 Westfield Drive, or whether you have long since moved on. I will send this journal to that address and hope for the best. The chances appear to be slim that this might ever reach you, but I have limited options.

You'll forgive me, I hope, for not transcribing the story in the wonderfully guttural pitmatic that is the near-dialect of my birthplace; too much distance and too many years have passed for me to trust myself to give it a faithful representation. And if I occasionally lapse into describing you in the third person … well I hope there will be some tolerance for that too.

I'm not going to use the 'L' word, Norman, but I hope the pages I'm about to send will let you know how I feel. The next steps will be up to you, but I'll be here, daring to hope that we may meet once again.

Yours,

Nancy.

Chapter 1

My name is Nancy Thompson. I was born in 1919, just after the end of the First World War, and, by the way, just after they began to chlorinate our drinking water, which was pumped out of the mine. My mother was a typist and my father a shaft sinker who hailed from Tyneside. They met at a Salvation Army dance. As far as I can tell, these dances were a kind of sober, chaste dating service for working-class men and women of marriageable age, conducted under the paternalistic gaze of the Methodist-led Oslington Coal Company and to the soothing tones of a Salvation Army brass band.

My father travelled all over the north-east with a team of shaft sinkers. This was, of all the precarious vocations which existed within the mining profession, both the best paid and the most hazardous. After their wedding, my parents moved into one of the prestigious shaft-sinkers' cottages at the top end of Oslington and started to make their own way in the world. My father avoided conscription in the First World War and made it right the way through to the end of the conflict, but then, in a gesture of abiding irony, managed to plop head first into a mineshaft and perish, just as I was growing inside my mother's belly. This earned him the posthumous title of 'daft bugger' from my grandad. My mother, about whom I know embarrassingly little, was undoubtedly traumatised by her loss. Suddenly, she found herself widowed, pregnant and living back home with her parents, and died heartbroken while giving birth to me.

I was entrusted to the care of my maternal grandparents, Ada and William Thompson, and to avoid confusion I was also given their surname. We lived in a second-from-end purpose-built colliery house on Acacia Street, one of several long terraces built to a grid system for speedy construction and named alphabetically in order of increasing distance from the pit.

Grandad was a hewer and was paid relatively well for his job, which was to hack away at any part of the coal seam that had not been blasted successfully by explosives. Nana kept home, you could say, though it often felt like it was the other way round. Anyway, Norman, in case you were starting to make assumptions about a beautiful baby being a kind of consolation prize for this pitiful pair, please don't. I was not, as the cliché would have it, a bundle of joy. I was born with an apparent allergy to my surroundings: cold-eyed, unsmiling and preternaturally quiet. I watched and analysed, like a predator stalking an unfamiliar animal – unsure whether to attack it or walk away. My childhood personality was like a bucket of ice, sucking the heat out of a bottle of wine. In the one or two photos of me from my childhood that still survive, I am sporting a narrow-eyed, ponderous look, as if I might rather be chatting with Jean-Paul Sartre in a Parisian cafe, smoking a Gauloise, and trying for the umpteenth time to understand Existentialism – *Just explain it to me once more, Jean-Paul, I promise this time I'll get it.* My grandparents, in turn, were also not the grieving clichés you might mark them down as. Life had undoubtedly dealt them a very unlucky hand, but they spent their remaining time looking forwards, not back. They lived their lives with good grace, turning my strangeness and every other egregious twist of fate that befell them into something that could be made light of, or at least given a sprinkling of the ridiculous. And you can't really say fairer than that.

My first ever memory is sitting in an enormous perambulator in the backyard in the shade of a hot sun, sucking with my first few teeth at that most nutritious and well-regarded of baby foods, the cheese pasty. The reason I remember this, is that at some point a huge, ballsy seagull swooped down, stole the greasy feast from my tiny fingers and flew off with it. Naturally, I bawled the place down and was apparently inconsolable for some time afterwards. But then, I never was very good with injustice. Gastronomically speaking, the cheese pasty remains a high point: it really was all downhill from then on. There weren't many cooking utensils in Nana's kitchen, so it's not surprising I remember keenly the one frying pan, covered in unspeakable grimy filth and cleaned after each use only by means of a quick wipe, or 'a lick and a promise', as Nana called it. Perhaps I was the only one who noticed that the frying pan offered up a little bit of its past, like an eager historian, during each use.

Imprinted on my memory is a carefully catalogued nightmare of carbon-crusted, lard-fried uneatables: Spam, fried mince and onions, tripe, eggs, Fray Bentos pies, dumplings, black pudding. These were all stroked with jet-coated horrors from that frying pan's vaults. The only other dish of note was the dreaded home-made pea soup, frothing and bubbling in the pan like some salty primordial swamp. Once this voluminous orange gloop had made the journey down the hapless, groaning gullet into the stomach, it then began some sort of laws-of-physics-defying expansion. I'd seen the little kids out in the back alleys slowly filling balloons with water until they exploded, and I've no doubt that anyone eating an uncontrolled amount of Nana's soup could undergo a similar experience. Pretty soon I found myself beached on the sofa, unable to move, until the feelings of extreme discomfort passed – only to be replaced by The Great Unquenchable Thirst – and certainly long after my elders had had a chance to wag their fingers at me peevishly and call me an ungrateful little brat.

Food was my first disappointment, and that perhaps explains why eating has never been a priority for me even to this day. This has been both an advantage and a disadvantage in my life so I mustn't complain. But even so, Nana's lack of interest in culinary matters grated on me. Apart from the scary Mitfords next door, we lived back-to-back with others who seemed to run a much tighter ship than us. As I grew older, my nose grew highly tuned to baking smells emanating from our neighbours' houses. Cheese scones, Bakewell tarts, sponge cakes – all made by proud, industrious miners' wives. It seemed, although I know this cannot be true, that it was only in our house where such application was lacking.

Grandad was tall and, although in his late-forties when I was born, still considered to be something of 'a dish'. He had enviable olive-brown skin which he attributed to his Welsh heritage. Indeed, he only needed to glimpse the watery north-east sunshine to turn a beautiful bronze colour. His hair, once dark brown, had now with the help of a bottle bought from the chemist begun to resemble the coal he hewed out of the ground all week. A light-extinguishing shade of black. This was his only concession to vanity, and he did it only to maintain his looks so that he could continue his singing act; on Saturdays, Grandad performed as Al Jolson, his all-time hero, at working men's clubs all over Northumbria, sometimes performing in blackface make-up. Grandad not only possessed the comely looks of his hero, but he had also perfected the singer's kindly, paternalistic gaze – as rumour had it, when he sang 'You Made Me Love You' and 'That Haunting Melody' there was, among those rough, broken old miners, never a dry eye in the house. At home, Grandad was quiet and almost totally sedentary, delivering the occasional pithy one-liners but more often than not quite content to hand the chatterbox mantle over to Nana. He had become an expert in the art of half-listening.

Nana was small and rotund with large, pendulous breasts. She wore a beige housecoat dress, a pinny and her famous brown tartan slipper-bootees, with sheepskin trim and a red pom-pom on the top. But this homely, domesticated pat-on-the-head exterior belied the reality of the situation: Nana was bored, frustrated and, quite frankly, uninterested in matters of the home. I could see it each and every day on her face, which was fixed in a happy smile when walking up the street or going to the shops but would settle into a frown as she entered the house. I could see it in her shoulders, which hunched up like the stiff Roman blinds of the Oslington Institute library whenever the subject of the next meal was discussed. Countless disappointments in the areas of cooking and cleaning had led her to a kind of trench warfare, if you can describe such a thing as existing between a person and a load of inanimate objects. Nana began to regard it all with caution until eventually she didn't regard it at all.

The inanimate objects, in turn, steadfastly refused to give up the secrets that might have led to a more successful outcome of their application. In order that the home did not become a place of conflict for her, Nana decided it was better to let it all go. I was as likely to come home and find her painting a picture, or writing poetry or an article for the colliery magazine, as I was to find her involved in less satisfying domestic occupations. This behaviour imbued in me a horrible oil-water non-mix of delight at such evident female emancipation, and shame at the state of the place. Nevertheless, it did not occur to me I had the power to help out or improve the situation by doing some cooking or cleaning myself.

I was given the second bedroom in our two-up two-down house, and I enjoyed a panoramic view of the pit. The wide pavement and railway lines were merely the sideshow; looking further, my gaze was drawn upwards, to some forty or so feet in the air, where the two winding shafts, with their spinning wheels at the top, pulled coal out of the ground all week long and Saturdays, too. Below, was the manager's office where the men queued, laughing and joking, on a Friday morning to collect their wages. To the right, almost out of view, was the junior school, a plain building with separate classrooms for boys and girls. To the left were the sidings, where I could watch as the tankeys arrived to collect giant tubs full of black diamonds, before they departed again for the coast; the Oslington Coal Company had its own ship which carried the coal to London and beyond.

The brick buildings around the pit were covered in a thick coat of tarry black, as were the men leaving the pit as their shifts finished.

Grandad said that there were new showers in the colliery but the men were too embarrassed to use them. I liked to see their blackened faces light up with the first puff of a hand-rolled cigarette at the end of their shifts. From the distance of my room, I shared their sense of relief that another working day – or night – was over. Behind were the coal heaps, sloping gently upwards towards the sea. Sometimes they caught the sea fret in the early mornings, and gave off a magical misty silver-red hue.

In any event, the scene outside my window drew me throughout my early childhood years to sit like a cat, curled up on the window ledge, wrapped in blankets, watching out of the draughty window. It is, of course, those little events that one is not expecting which are remembered: Mrs Percy running across the railway bridge to the entrance to the pit with her husband's forgotten bait tin, trying to catch him before he descended underground for his shift; the proud but sinking feeling I felt when watching the St John's volunteer ambulance service, headed up by my grandad – his First Aid Certificate stood proudly above our mantelpiece in its own frame – carrying off Geordie Johnson on a stretcher to be taken to the hospital, the blood from his leg leaving a trail of its own along the way; Terry, the halfwit boy, running behind a departing tankey along the tracks of the siding, whooping and shouting for the train to stop and let him on, followed by his long-suffering mother who was yelling back at him and trying to pull him to safety. But, of course, the vast majority of the time the scene was unexceptional and repetitive, time marked only by the background whirr of the winding shafts. I spent what felt like geological timeframes sitting at that window watching the coal dust gather around the frame and industrial life unfurl in front of my eyes. But mine was an eye searching for beauty, for fineness, just as my brain was searching for intellectual stimulation. So you can probably imagine my near-constant disappointment, which sometimes bordered on hysteria. For some reason, I could tolerate the sight of the pit as long as the clouds above it were grey, or when the rain peeled down from heavy, ash-white skies. What I could not tolerate, however, was when the sky was blue and the smoky walls were lit up with sunlight, and the sooty smell became so sharp that you could taste it on your tongue. I had got into my head a strange notion that only beautiful things deserved sunlight, therefore the pit bathed in a yellow, warm glow was a scene I really could not stomach. Those days were the most unbearable, my ennui taking on a desperate, maniacal undertone, which found no physical expression, except what I can only describe as a horrible feeling of being sick of my own self. Actually, Freud had plenty to say on *that* subject, but I digress.

I became unhealthily preoccupied with the belief that my intended life was happening elsewhere, that this was all a huge mistake and that one day a *Great Expectations*-style correction would take place. My real parents would waltz in, my mother dripping with furs and jewels, dabbing her eyes at the sight of the long-lost me, my father some sort of rich-but-principled merchant banker. They would make a large donation to the institute library, buy Nana a new frying pan, and then my parents and I would drive off into the sunset in their chauffeur-driven limo. I would spend the rest of my childhood in a beautiful, ivy-clad Georgian tenement overlooking Regent's Park where we would mingle with royals and writers. My mother and I would idle away the days shopping in Selfridges, and I would spend the evenings playing chess and … I don't know … learning Cyrillic script with my father. Allow me to blush at the inherent male chauvinism in this slightly nauseating little fantasy.

In any case, sadly or not, it became apparent that Dickensian-style corrections only happen in books and in children's imaginations. I lived the first years of my life like a homing pigeon on a route between school, home, a few bars and pubs in town where I helped Grandad perform his singing act, and the Oslington Institute, where I was an eager if officious library volunteer; in fact, I performed my role as Junior Cataloguer – Non-Fiction and Large Print – with the graveness and attention to detail of a heart surgeon about to perform a major operation.

The institute was situated just behind the junior school; it had two sizeable rooms and a tiny scullery out the back. The largest room was widely used for a number of different purposes: Monday evenings were for the Women's Institute; Tuesdays were for the Oslington colliery band to meet and practise; and Wednesdays to Fridays were for men to meet after work and play billiards, darts and whist, chat to each other and read the free newspapers provided by the coal company. Saturdays would depend – the room was sometimes used by the Salvation Army for their dances, sometimes by couples for their wedding receptions, and sometimes by the Scouts. If nothing else was on, then the men were free to come and use it.

The unofficial town library was situated in the second and slightly smaller room, and this is where I gravitated to at some point most evenings after school, even though the library only officially opened to the public on Thursdays and Saturdays. I could usually be found poring over a book, wrapped in the yellow glow and heavy shadows thrown off by a paraffin lamp. Sometimes I would check the book inventory, or I might tidy up the aisles if I was feeling particularly energetic. The library was run by a retired miner called Mr Pearce. Mr Pearce had been the victim of some unspeakably bad luck – he had been involved in a catastrophic mining accident in 1922 which had claimed the lives of some twenty-five men at the pit. He had worked on and off after that, but ended up unable to continue through bad nerves. Initially Mr Pearce turned to the church, but then he threw his energies into building up the library, and you were most likely to find him reading Darwin or Freud late at night. Once, I saw him reading a leaflet about rationalism, which he kept hidden under a pile of other books. We talked a lot about religion, in a quiet, abstract kind of way, without revealing our own views. But in spite of our polite obfuscations, I could tell that Mr Pearce's heart was full of science and reason and that his views were his own and not filtered via the prism of religious doctrine or context. The library became his *raison d'être* and I admired him for it.

The Pearces were kept from the hard card by community donations. I remember the foreman calling by once a fortnight to collect 'for the Pearces', and everyone gave what they could. But the accident took its toll on the whole family and led to the son dropping out of grammar school after only one year.

Let me tell you more about Oslington. A small mining town in the north-east of England. Row after row of orangey-red-bricked colliery terraces, slate roofs nestling upon one another like the plates on an armadillo's back. Washing lines strung across cold, windy back-alleys that were thick with boot-eating mud. The ever-present stench of sulphur and soot, which hung like a fog about the place and settled tangibly in lines on every possibly surface. The shift foreman walking the streets at five thirty in the morning, Monday to Saturday, ringing his bell to wake up the workers.

For years the Methodists and the Oslington Coal Company conspired to prevent any pubs being built in the town, until around 1920 when the first working men's club, the Soot, opened. Alcohol arrived in the town like a cartoon baddie with its fists up ready for a fight. The Soot quickly gained a diabolical reputation, which was made worse by its decision to introduce a monthly Saturday 'Special' featuring a stripper and a drag double-act called Sodom and Gomorrah. There were rumours that our next-door neighbour, Mr Mitford, performed the role of Sodom, but that was never confirmed. By 1932 the town had twelve working men's clubs. As the Methodists had predicted, once the artery had been cut, the blood flow could not be contained.

Oslington during the time I lived there could be described as being in her prime: cohesive, and well removed from big-city slums, mass unemployment and the Great Depression that was just around the corner. But I could never understand why the Oslington Coal Company appeared so solicitous to the miners' needs above ground – providing a workers' institute, schools, tennis courts, rugby and football pitches – yet seemed so utterly untroubled by what was going on below it. I supposed this was one of those things that adults just got, but children weren't supposed to understand. The mine took in boys and spat out diseased old men: injured, hunched over, panting for breath, lungs solid with coal dust, knees gnarled up with rheumatism and arthritis. And not in their fifties and sixties as you might think, but in their thirties and forties. Did no one at the Company notice? And I watched this unfurl in front of my eyes, and happen to people I knew. The men lived out their lives like a horror film played at speed. Their illnesses and injuries terrified me and, although I felt some sympathy, I was certain that I wanted no part of it.

Retirement was a tenuous concept. Many felt they could not live on the ten shillings a week pension, and had no desire to give up their houses to move into an Aged Miner's Home between so-called formal retirement and earthly departure. So they just kept on going till they dropped. Irritatingly, it seemed to me that there was never any other kind of departure from Oslington, unless you were a lump of coal, of course.

In our home in Acacia Street we were uneasily ensconced between a number of Wesleyan and Primitive Methodist families and, at the very end of the terrace, right next door to us, the Mitfords. A feckless bunch of eleven partially-shoed urchins and their gravel-voiced, man-faced mother, Mary Mitford, whose near-continuous pregnancies and fondness for ale had bestowed upon her the body of a fully-grown bear. The father, to whom I have already alluded, was largely absent: absent, that is, from the home. Largely present in the

Soot, unfortunately. Mrs Mitford played the victim card very well. A poor lonely woman, left alone to bring up a swathe of unruly children while her husband went out drinking away all their money, leaving her with not enough to even feed the poor little creatures. This was, of course, until the Soot opened a backroom that allowed women; then she was off as well, shouting at her husband and drinking all the men under the table from behind the hatch. From that point on, no more talk of being a victim was heard, and the children were left to bring themselves up.

I guess I would have known their individual names when I was young, but they seemed to me to exist as a single, interchangeable, atomic unit of terror, a sea of feral warriors charging around laying claim to various local territories. I both feared and looked down on their noses coated with semi-dried lacteous mucus and their tatty old clothes. As neighbours, we felt constantly besieged by them and the stunts they pulled in their parents' absence. An average afternoon consisted of the children, one by one, leaping out of the upstairs backyard window, down onto the outside nettie roof, where they skidded and bounced their way down onto the bones of an old sofa, carefully placed below to break their fall. This could be accompanied by squeals of laughter if all went well, or howls of pain if it did not. If this were not bad enough, it could then be followed by hours of tedious local in-fighting, conducted loudly in the backyard. Not as much as an average monotheistic religious text might contain, but definitely significant. Who was going to bray whom, and for what misdemeanour. What sorts of levels of violence and injury could be expected, etcetera. There was also a lot of laughter, shrill and menacing. As I fancied myself to be of a delicate constitution, I lived in perpetual fear of them laughing at me or coming after us in some undefined manner. In fact, my main aim in life for a long time was to make myself as inconspicuous as possible so that I wouldn't attract their attention in any way. I was pretty successful at this for many years – none of them ever came near me in the places I frequented. I do remember that Elsie Mitford was in my class but, luckily for me, she had a vacant look about her and seemed to struggle to remember who *she* was never mind work out who I was.

Next door in the other direction were a family of Wesleyan Methodists – Mr and Mrs Weightman, and their sons John, who was a quiet boy the same age as me, and Terry, the halfwit. They took their love of hard work and sobriety to almost orgiastic levels and also lived in fear of an encounter with the Mitfords, who in their minds represented the kind of moral abyss one could plunge into if one did not follow the teachings of both the good Lord Jesus and the father of Methodism, John Wesley. Since we were godless but sober and Grandad was a hard-working and well-respected miner, we became a kind of uneasy buffer between our incompatible neighbours. Opposite us lived a family of Primitive Methodists; I later heard this branch of Methodism being unkindly described by Mr Weightman as 'a load of lower-order types romping around in the countryside, folk whose concentration span does not lend itself to actual church sermons'. Grandad simply called them the 'Singy Songies'. Ouch. We often saw them trooping out to the fields in their terrible knitwear, braving the biting north-easterly wind, for their

Sunday love-ins. These, I can assure you, Norman, were more innocent affairs than they might sound.

In any case, there was little love lost between the Wesleyans and the Primitives. But I should not overstate all of this; the community was happy and tolerant in spite of these differences. It was more a case of sibling rivalry than clash of creeds. When I think of what was happening in Europe at that time it hardly even warrants a mention, except for completeness.

I waited for many years in that existential antechamber. I could never have predicted the whirlwind that would rip through this extended siesta of a childhood, or from how close to home it would come.

Chapter 2

I wonder, Norman, what have been the punctuation marks in your life, those points when your life has changed direction? At the time you may not even have been aware of the transition, but looking back you will notice that – actually – *that* was the point when a seismic shift occurred and things were never the same thereafter. For me this happened gradually, like the pit winding shafts rolling into life with the first light of day. At thirteen, my own life began to roll into focus, overcoming inertia, gaining momentum. I had made it that far without being noticed by the Mitfords, or found out as being a secret rationalist during my occasional attendance of Sunday school, or kicked out of the institute library for being female during the men's sessions, or turned to stone on my bedroom window ledge on account of extended periods of sulky inactivity.

I awoke one Thursday to the sounds of floorboards creaking in the room next door and a theatrical yawn, which turned into the first few bars of a Gilbert and Sullivan song, possibly something from the *Pirates of Penzance*. This was followed by some hearty and prolonged coughing. My grandparents were stirring; Nana was shushing Grandad and cursing him for waking up the whole street with his antics. It was time to get up. My room was already suffused with a weak lemon sunlight which peeked through the netting, throwing grey shadows across the room. It was mid September but it was already chilly. The last thing I had done the night before was to bank the fire, and the first thing I would do that morning would be to revive it. I stretched, psyching myself up to brace the plunge in temperature I would experience on emerging from the blankets. I had placed my hooky mat underneath my bed so that my first step would not be onto a freezing floorboard, but it seemed to make little difference. My bedroom defied all seasons and seemed to be locked into a single year-round temperature of biting cold.

I lay still, closing my eyes. From next door came the sound of drawers opening and my grandparents talking in hushed tones.

'They don't think it'll be long now, Bill. The bairn …' said Nana.

There was a pause, then more rattling of drawers. 'Have ye seen me stockings? I swear to God …'

'I said, that bairn doesn't have long now, Bill.'

More creaking of drawers, and a whiff of frustration muttered under his breath. 'Which bairn?' said Grandad, in a bored voice.

'Next door. I told you the other day?' Nana sounded irritated. 'Your stockings should be in there. I haven't moved them.'

'Oh, aye. Next door's bairn.'

'Mrs Mitford. The baby has the measles, Bill. It's very poorly. They don't think it will last much longer.'

The baby, as I recalled, had also been born with a small head and 'various other problems', whatever that meant. The Weightmans had made a special visit to tell us that it was a punishment from God to the Mitfords for their debauched ways, a meeting that, shall we say, didn't end well. As soon as the Weightmans had had their little gossip, Grandad had pointed out their own halfwit son: 'If God can do owt he likes, why is he making halfwits at all?' he had asked, and

Nana, with customary directness, had told them that sort of Old Testament stuff was all a load of tripe anyway. They had shuffled off home shaking their heads and giving off a condescending air of regret at our blasphemous ignorance. Nana had waited until the back door clicked shut, then scandalously shouted, 'Kiss My Árse!' through the letterbox at them.

'Well, there'll be another bairn along next year.' The drawer rasped shut. 'There's rabbits can't reproduce as fast as that lot.'

'William! Now that is uncharitable of you. A bairn is a bairn. It didn't ask to be born to them lot.'

'Aye, you're right, Ada. But, look at it a different way. The eldest laddie – what's his name now?'

There was a pause. 'Norman,' said Nana. 'I think, any rate? Yes, I'm sure that's it. Norman.'

'Well, the word down the pit is that laddie is working day and night, either side of a regular school day, to keep all them bairns fed. He's doing all sorts, Ada. *All* sorts ...'

'What d'you mean?'

'Let's just say he's been in a lot of bother with both the polis and Mr Shaw.'

Mr Shaw was the colliery manager; a staunch Methodist, he was unmarried and lived an apparently frugal, pious and teetotal life with two spinster sisters. He had a finger in every pie, though – he was also the local magistrate, Chairman of the School Board, and of the Hospital – and you would most definitely not want to get on the wrong side of him. I wondered, briefly, via which of these lofty contexts Norman Mitford had fallen foul of him.

'Oh,' said Nana. 'Well the laddie doesn't have any choice, does he? At least someone round there sounds like they've got a bit of sense. Those parents should be ashamed of themselves. Feckless pair, indeed. Still, I canna help myself; it still upsets me about that bairn.'

'Aye, I agree, pet. But the way I look at it, and the way you have to look at it to stop yersel gettin' maudlin, is that it's one less mouth for the laddie to feed.'

Nana clucked a bit more, but I got the feeling it was mainly for show. 'I'll get the porridge on and make your bait up,' she said, and then I heard her footsteps descending the groaning stairs. 'Nancy,' she shouted up from the bottom, at a frightening level of decibels that assumed I had apparently turned deaf overnight. 'Time to get up and do the fire.'

Next door, Grandad was closing the remaining drawers and getting ready to follow his wife downstairs. 'Aye, that's right,' I heard him mutter. 'Tell me off for a bit of singing, and coughing, which I canna help, then wake up the whole street by shouting up to the little'un. Welcome to the logic of the female species.'

I grinned. How much longer was Grandad going to call me little'un? Already I was towering over Nana.

'Oh yes,' continued the whispered monologue from next door. 'Ah canna wait for that porridge. Yum yum. I swear there's more movement in the cement they use to hold the pit props in place.'

I wondered in a lazy kind of way whether all men were prone to such vocalisations when their wives were out of earshot. On the plus side, it certainly seemed to help my grandparents' relationship;

grievances got to be aired cathartically without offending the other party.

I pulled on my dressing gown and clogs and wandered downstairs and out to the nettie – our outside toilet, which also served as a store for coal and wood – to gather some materials for the fire. The morning air was sharp and gusty, and the wind blew the fabric against my legs. My thoughts drifted back to the bedroom conversation; my interest in this boy from next door had been piqued. Wracking my brains, I tried to remember when I'd seen him around; it struck me that although I had of course seen him a few times over the years, I had rarely seen him walking to or from school. He seemed to just appear at the entrance in the morning, and float off afterwards at the end of the day. He had a bicycle, I think, and a noisy jackdaw named Jackie – clearly a flurry of imagination taking place there – which lived outside in the yard in a wooden box that I believe Norman had made in a woodwork class. When the children were playing their frenzied leaping-out-of-the-window game, this poor, hapless creature gave loud, terrified caws of protest and flew dementedly in and out of other people's backyards.

Once, during an afternoon of severe stress, Jackie had flown into our house and started to peel off strips of wallpaper with his sharp, black beak. Nana that day moved faster than I had ever seen her, her large breasts flopping up and down as she chased Jackie round the front room, swatting at him with a shawl, cursing him for damaging our property. Grandad, when he returned, made no comment except to say that the bird had a talent and should take up decorating, and that he'd never liked the wallpaper anyway. Nevertheless, Jackie was banned from our house from that day forwards. I'm not sure anyone ever told him, though.

What of Norman himself? Nothing terribly exciting came to mind. He was tall and under-nourished, as you might expect, with dark hair that fell down in a lock from his cap. He wore the same as every other man and boy in Oslington: white grandad shirt with the sleeves rolled up, waistcoat, cap, wide trousers, black boots. He was, I guessed, about the same age or slightly older than me, with a face that might be called handsome once he'd grown into it a bit more.

I remember a frame held in my memory, a reference point, from a few years earlier. I'd been asked to take some books over to the boys' section of our junior school, and had entered the main assembly hall, where desks and chairs were arranged in rows. Norman had been there, slowly setting out exam papers, grim-faced. He had looked at me briefly, then looked away as if he'd just seen any old stranger – the postman, or the man who sold fruit and vegetables on a Friday outside the pit. And as I knew him as a Mitford, I had been mightily pleased not to have been recognised. The papers, I later realised, were for the eleven-plus exam, an exam which would determine our future: off to grammar school to study for one of the professions, or stay in the regular school and become mine-fodder (the boys) or housewives (the girls). I had been about to sit the equivalent over at the girls' school.

I had passed the eleven-plus, and I now attended Oslington Grammar School for Girls. The sense of ennui of my earlier childhood years was still present, but I was happier at the grammar school, where I excelled at mathematics and the sciences. I saw less casual violence by the teachers against the pupils there. My personality had begun to thaw a little too; I was getting used to dealing with the rest of the human race, and perhaps it was true the other way round as well. Moreover, I sensed a path opening up for me, something I had discussed at length with my form teacher, Miss Trott, who responded enthusiastically and encouragingly to my proposals. I intended to work as hard as I could, then in just a couple of years I would sit the Oxford School Certificate exam. With luck and hard work I would matriculate and stay on at school until eighteen. After this, I would embark on a career as a teacher. This would involve one or two years at teacher training college in order to gain my certificate. Miss Trott said our nearest one was in Newcastle, and that I would have to live there under their very strict rules while I was studying, but that it would be worth it; I would have an excellent qualification and job at the end of it.

There was no solid logic behind this choice of career, other than I had but the dimmest awareness of the limited and dire range of other jobs available to me. In my plan, for the first few years after gaining my certificate, I'd remain in Oslington, saving money for my escape. Then, in a move that would take my life into glorious technicolour, I would move to London and teach in a friendly school on the edge of Hampstead Heath. In a few years, I'd be running the place. Then I would marry. I didn't want children, but surely a place like London, stroked by the graceful hands of the Enlightenment and bristling with modernity, would be able to prevent this from happening. Nana and Grandad would visit twice a year and be terribly impressed at my sophisticated London existence and urbane ways. I would translate from pitmatic to the King's English for T. S. Eliot (whom I would, of course, have befriended) when he came to afternoon tea. I would own different types of tea, and would eat delicate cucumber sandwiches with their crusts removed for lunch.

My husband would be very liberal in countenance, but also commanding in a physical sense; his hobbies would include boxing and helping out with the suffragette movement. The school board would boast that the school had never before achieved such academic success, and I would be interviewed by the *Daily Sketch* about my groundbreaking new pedagogic techniques. In fact, I had already practised a demure but wise pout in front of Nana's crackled bedroom mirror for the accompanying photograph. I would not return to Oslington, not even for a visit, feigning work commitments as an excuse.

It was 1932. I knew nothing of the laws of the land and of the Great Depression that was already underway, sweeping remorselessly across England and the rest of the world, nor of the Nazi party about to accede to power in Germany. All I knew was that right then, the enfranchisement of women had become a reality, and I was ready to take on the world. It all sounded so easy.

The fire was coming along nicely. The coal glowed red and the wood burned brightly, though I fretted that the hissing and sizzling meant that the wood was wetter than it should be. I sighed, and put the tongs back in place. I returned upstairs and put on my grammar school uniform of white shirt, school tie, navy tunic and black stockings. There was also a school hat, panama style with navy velour, which I despised with a vengeance – I thought it made me look at best like a gangster, and at worst just plain ridiculous. The back door clicked shut: Grandad off to work. I lay on my bed, picked up *Jane Eyre* and read quietly for ten minutes. Nana came up to try to persuade me to eat some porridge, but I wasn't hungry. At eight thirty, I pulled on my boots and coat, said goodbye, and strode out to school.

***

'Nancy, will you cover Miss Dungait's class again, please?' said the headmistress, Miss Elliot, upon my arrival. She tutted. 'She's ill with the migraines. *Again.*'

Miss Dungait was a pretty woman with fair hair and freckles. She was afflicted with crippling migraines during her monthlies, and in those days it was not thought unusual to ask one of the more trustworthy and, dare I say academically able, pupils to take a class. Miss Dungait took the children in the first year of grammar school, so technically these girls were only two years younger than me, but I'm ashamed to say I applied the same tyrannical techniques I had learned from my junior school teachers. I also flouted my status as Monitor and used a frightening scowl – that came far too naturally to me – to suppress any insubordination. I told myself that when I was running my own school in London, things would be different.

'What shall I teach today, Miss?'

Miss Elliot indicated for me to follow her to her office, where she proceeded to list out all the topics to be covered in today's class. Rain started to tap on the window, gently at first, then more insistently. By the time I got to the classroom, it had started to lash with rain and the morning sky had turned as dark as evening. I loved that feeling of being indoors at school while it poured down outside. The class was warm with the glow of paraffin heaters. I settled down to take Miss Dungait's class. A smell of vinegary disinfectant emanated up from the linoleum floor.

The morning passed uneventfully. The girls had settled down after the long summer break and were getting into the rhythm of the term. I set some algebra problems on the board and asked my pupils to complete them on their chalk boards. While they were doing that I wrote a list of spellings, and some prose to be turned into indirect speech. But my thoughts kept wandering back to the earlier conversation; I was intrigued. Looking back, I think Norman Mitford interested me because, in spite of everything I might have told myself about not fitting in, I was at heart, absolutely, deeply conventional. And here was a boy on the fringes of our community, doing things his own way and getting on the wrong side of the authorities. He was a risk-taker, whereas the riskiest thing I'd ever done was to misappropriate a copy of *Jane Eyre* from the library, remove its listing from the catalogue and keep it at home, under my pillow. Even that small act of theft gave me many sleepless nights.

Looking over the agenda for the afternoon, I saw that I was due to take a Religious Education class. Initially, I panicked. What on earth would I say? I had already decided I was a rationalist, and that religion fitted into the same category as astrology and tarot-card reading, but one could go to still go to prison for blasphemy, so I would need to be extremely careful what I said. Then I remembered; there was a book we'd used in my first year at grammar school, called something like *Religions of the World*, a huge and weighty hardback. I resolved to hunt out a copy during the morning break. When the first class ended, I popped into the library but could not find any copies, so I went to the staffroom and enquired there. I was kept waiting at the door while Miss Powell, the Religious Education teacher, was summoned.

'Sorry to bother you, Miss Powell,' I said, insincerely, 'but I need a copy of *Religions of the World* for my afternoon class. Miss Dungait's class. Would you happen to have a spare one, please?'

Miss Powell did not seem very pleased to be bothered during her morning break. 'I don't have any spares, child,' she said. 'I've got enough for my own classes and that's it. You'll need to go and fetch a spare from the senior school.'

Marvellous, I thought, crossly. That meant a lunchtime trek through the muddy backstreets to the other side of town. There was no canteen at the school, so we all went home anyway, or brought in potted-meat sandwiches, but I was now looking forward to no lunch and a long walk. Seeing my annoyance, Miss Powell relented a little. 'Wait there,' she said, 'I'll write you a note.'

I wonder now why I didn't just do something else for that lesson. Looking back, it strikes me as interesting how linear children can be; I'd been taught using that book, therefore I assumed that was the only possible way to teach others the same subject matter.

The rain had stopped when I left at lunchtime and made my way through the colliery rows. The mud was all stoked up, and my passage was laborious. A terrible, overpowering stench wafted up from the drains, and long rivulets of rainwater flowed along the edges of the road towards the grates. The streets were ugly, with poverty emanating from every brick. It all reminded me, all over again, how I couldn't wait to get away from the place.

The senior school was, like the junior, segregated by gender, even to the point that the playgrounds were not shared. I wandered into the reception, my ears and fingers cold and my stomach rumbling. I explained to the secretary that I was here to borrow a book, if I may. She looked at me quizzically, as if I'd just asked her whether she'd like to relocate to Mars, so I handed over Miss Powell's note.

'We are not a charity you know,' she said, irritably, reading the note over her half-spectacles. 'I honestly don't know who you grammar school lot think you are.' I thought she might refuse, and turned to leave. 'Wait,' she continued through pursed lips. 'Wait here. I'll see if we have a copy. But tell your teacher not to send you or anyone else again.' I sat down and started absently reading notices on the table and walls. Football and netball fixtures, Sunday school outings to the coast, baking competitions for the girls, term dates. Initially, everything looked mundane until one caught my eye and caused my heart to start racing. On the wall was a list of exam leagues for the past academic year for English, Science and Mathematics, showing top performing boy and girl. There it was, right in front of me; Norman Mitford's name was listed there for everyone to see, consistently top across nearly all subjects. His marks, I noted, had not dipped below an impressive ninety per cent throughout the entire year. I looked out across the playground and back, somehow mistrusting my own eyes, but the information had not changed.

The secretary returned, her permed hair as tight as her clenched-up face. She thrust the book at me, with a note saying that the book must be returned promptly by the end of the school day, and then she opened the door and stood there wordlessly with her arm facing outwards to indicate in no uncertain terms that it was time for me to leave.

I felt suddenly weary, humiliated and nauseated due to lack of food. I was also incredibly angry, as I realised I'd have to make yet another trip back to that damned place later on. Wandering slowly through the playground, I heard a burst of laughter in a classroom to my left. I think I already knew what I was going to see, just sort of knew without even looking; but as I turned my head slowly, yes, there he was: Norman Mitford, taking a class. Smiling and pointing to something on the blackboard, though I couldn't see what it was.

Turning out of the school, I headed back the long way through town, up the high street, past the Oslington Hotel, with its grand entrance and maroon curtains, past Bowers' Department Store, where I saw Mrs Pearce coming out; she even stopped to exchange a few pleasantries with me for a moment, expressing concern that I looked awfully pale. I carried on past Thompson's Fruiters, Brown's Butchers and finally past the Soot, which smelled, even from the outside, of stale ale and cigarettes and lost afternoons. All around me were people: women in headscarves chatting conspiratorially; men walking up and down in their caps and waistcoats, nodding the time of day to each other; and finally, the notorious 'Bad Man', as he was called by the children of the town, with his thick grey beard and old sou'wester, and his eyes narrowed suspiciously. Limping towards me, he was pushing his barrow-contraption thing which looked like it had been made out of several old prams. His barrow was full of old bottles today, which jangled and clanked as he walked along. He came closer and closer, until I could see the thread veins on his nose, and a flea crawling up his neck into his beard, happy as you like. I shuddered and looked at the floor as he walked past.

It all became like a dream-sequence, with smudged edges, the sounds fading out gradually like the end of a record. I had never felt so lonely, so alienated, so ridiculous. Choking back sobs, I pulled my hat down firmly, tucked the huge book under my arm and ran back to school.

***

'There you are. I've been worried about you,' said Nana, standing in the scullery doorway as I finally slunk back home after my second trek across town and back that day. An acrid, metallic smell of fried liver and onions filled the air, which did nothing to help my ongoing nausea. I knew, though, that if Nana saw me gagging I would be in trouble. 'Where've you been?'

I looked at the clock; just after five already. 'Taking Miss Dungait's class,' I said, yawning. 'Miss Elliot had me marking the girls' work and preparing for tomorrow as they think Miss Dungait will be off again. And then I had to return a book to the senior school.'

Nana followed me into the sitting room, wiping her hands on her pinny. 'Well that's all very well for them,' she said, 'getting their teaching done for free and sending young lasses on long journeys when they should be home having their dinners. And what about your own work? When are you supposed to get that done? Sit down, good god, before you fall down. Have you seen yourself in the mirror?'

I sighed, and sank into Grandad's chair. 'I already knew about you having to go at lunchtime,' continued Nana. 'Mrs Pearce called by to tell me. She said she'd seen you in town looking as pale as a ghost. But I didn't realise those buggers would have made you go again. Wait there – I'll make you a cup of tea. And don't be complaining about the sugar.'

Tutting about the school 'taking a lend of their pupils', as she put it, Nana disappeared off into the scullery. I closed my eyes. I appreciated Mrs Pearce's concern, but it was impossible to blow your nose in Oslington without someone knowing and having an opinion about it.

After a few minutes Nana returned with a cup of tea and a huge piece of Victoria sponge cake, delicately frosted with icing sugar. 'Here,' she said, 'I made this for you. Eat up.'

'Thank you, Nana,' I said, surprised. I couldn't smell any baking, so surmised that she must have made it earlier. The cake was excellent – rich and moist, and just what I needed. I took a long drink of the sweet tea and felt much improved; I could feel my body refuelling itself and replenishing its depleted stores. Nana had excelled herself and I wondered, feeling suddenly brighter, whether this was the start of a new culinary era in our little house. 'This cake is lovely,' I said. 'Can I have another piece please?'

Nana looked at me with narrowed eyes. 'As long as you still eat your tea.'

'Can I have my tea later, Nana?' I said, hurriedly. 'I need to be getting off to the library in a minute. After I've got changed.' I had developed a number of tactics for meal-avoidance over the years, and that one was a trusty favourite. Nana would be fast asleep on the couch when I got back from the library, and the limp horrors sitting on a plate in the scullery with my name on them would be forgotten, ready for me to carefully manoeuvrc to the bottom of the Weightmans' dustbin first thing in the morning before anyone else was up.

'Do you want me to top us up with water before I go?' I asked, gulping down a second piece of cake and capitalising on my earlier successful diversion tactics. We had no running water in the house; all our water had to be collected from a tap at the other end of the row. I was usually 'Chief Pail Operator' for the household; Grandad had made me a wooden balancing contraption with a pail hanging off either end, sort of medieval stocks meets a pair of scales. This device sat across my shoulders and I wrapped my arms over it to hold it steady. Not only did it kill off any remaining hopes I had of appearing sophisticated and debonair, but it also made me look as if I should be taking part in a strongman competition, until you looked closer and saw that I was in fact shaped like a stick of liquorice that would blow away in a strong wind.

‘No, we’re good, pet, thank you,’ said Nana. ‘Let’s look at you now. Yes, I think the colour is starting to return to your face. Take care tonight, though, and don’t be overdoing it, alright?’

I took a long drink of tea. ‘What, in a library?’ I said, though I knew what was coming next. It was Nana’s favourite story, and I heard it at least once a week. It was the comedic equivalent of perpetual motion, never losing its ability to make Nana laugh. I had played my part, the quiet enabler with my innocent-sounding question, and now I could relax.

About a year earlier, partially-sighted Mr Davis had tripped over me in the large-print aisle, breaking his wrist and demolishing an entire section in the process. I came off relatively well, suffering only a black eye when several hardback botany books fell down on me. But the part that really made Nana laugh was that Mr Davis’s glasses were so thick they didn’t even crack, even with his full weight on top of them. The story had to be told in stages to allow for Nana’s chortles and what-a-bloody-menaces. I nodded and closed my eyes. A trace of disdain fell across my lips.

‘Anyway, *you*, next time a teacher asks you to go halfway round town cos they can’t be bothered to make two of their own pupils share a book, you stand up there, you hold your head up high and you say “No, it’s not fair, I’m not prepared to do it.” D’you understand?’

I considered this for a moment. ‘I can’t do that,’ I said, in a lofty voice that suggested that someone of her limited education could not possibly hope to understand the delicate conventions of a grammar school education system.

Nana came over to me, then, and rested her wrinkly hands on my cheeks, bringing her own face close. Her skin was old and dried out from the carbide soap, but her eyes were still bright and pretty, and I saw the young girl that she once had been. 'No, Nancy, you can, and you will. Shy bairns get nowt, do you hear me? Repeat that after me.'

'Shy bairns get nowt,' I said. The fire crackled behind us softly, as the clock struck the half hour.

'Now, off you go,' she said, walking back into the scullery.

***

That night, I lay in bed, eyes wide open, staring up at the ceiling. I lit a candle, to relieve the monotony if nothing else, enjoying the sight of the flame casting strange shadows across my room. After a time I decided to read a few pages of *Jane Eyre*, and told myself rather haughtily that when I did have my first crush, he would be just like a pre-fire-damaged Mr Rochester. This was such a blatant lie in the face of what was actually going on that even my subconscious was embarrassed for me. My thoughts continued in a circular pattern and the night stretched on interminably.

Finally, the stop-clocks outside gave a short 'click' and the gas lanterns switched themselves off. Darkness was replaced by the wan sunlight of the autumn dawn. I looked at the clock; four forty-five. My mouth felt dry. I put on my dressing gown and went downstairs to the scullery for a glass of water, and to turn 'Liver Surprise' into a new kind of surprise for the Weightmans: a bin that smelled like someone had died in it. On the kitchen table, peeping out from under the sponge cake, was a handwritten note from Mrs Pearce: 'I made this for your Nancy. Hope it puts some colour back in her cheeks!'

Oh, Nana, I thought, shaking my head. *What are you like?*

Looking up, I noticed that the yard gate was open; one of us must not have closed it properly when coming back from the institute last night. Pulling on Grandad's pit boots, I clomped my way through the yard to the gate.

'Morning, Nancy,' said a voice in the alley, suddenly. I nearly jumped out of my skin, and looked round. There he was, wheeling his bike out of his own yard, that same old lock of dark hair hanging down from his cap and eyes looking right at me. I could not believe he knew my name. Without another word, Norman Mitford tipped his cap, swung his leg over his bike and cycled off down the street, taking my breath with him as he went.

***

We awoke on Saturday morning to the sound of knocking at the door. Nana went down first to answer it, then came back upstairs, ashen-faced.

'The Mitfords' baby has died,' she said, grimly. 'That was Mrs Mitford.' Then she sat down on my bed and began to cry, silently. I sat up sleepily and put my arm around her. 'It's never easy losing a bairn,' she said, and it didn't even occur to me she was talking about my mother.

I visited the institute that morning and went through the motions, and for several hours I was lost to my duties there. But I felt strangely removed from reality, as if I were an actor playing myself in my own life. I felt very sad for the Mitfords, but also relieved that it was one less person for Norman to have to worry about. At the end of the session, I locked up the back entrance, washed up the teacups then walked slowly home via the baker's, where I bought myself a cream horn. I found a park bench near the recreation ground – the 'rec', as it was known – and sat there, eating slowly. A few children were playing nearby, shouting happily on the swings and slides and shuggyboats, glad to be away from the muddy backstreets.

'Nancy, pet, run next door to the Mitfords and take them these scones,' said Nana, when I returned. I ignored her and went straight into the sitting room. Grandad was sitting in his armchair, reading a newspaper.

'Finished for the week, eh, Grandad?' I said.

'Aye pet, smashing it is too. A wonderful feeling.'

'Nancy!' shouted Nana again. 'Did you hear me? Can you take these cheese scones next door?'

'Why are you baking them scones?' said Grandad. He put down the newspaper and began to peel an apple with his penknife. 'You know what happens if you feed rats.'

'More rats?' I ventured.

'I honestly think you're losing your memory, Bill,' said Nana, walking into the front room with a griddle of scones, setting them down on the table and waving her hand in front of her face. 'Eee god, I am *so* hot, standing in that scullery. I'm not used to mass catering. The Mitfords' baby has died, Bill.'

'What, and you're trying to add to the tally?' said Grandad, nodding at the scones. 'Anyway, don't worry.' He winked at me then began to carve out slices of apple onto a plate. 'They'll have added another six by this time next year.'

'That's physiologically impossible,' I said, grinning, taking a piece of the fruit.

'Well that's a mighty big word, little'un, but even so, I'm not so sure. I tell you, that lot are part rabbit. Tek them some carrots instead and we'll keep the scones. Beggars can't be choosers.'

'Ignore him, Nancy. Here – take these and give them to Mrs Mitford. Don't go in, though. You don't know what kind of germs are lurking in there. Tell her: we're very sorry about the bairn,' she said, slowly, as if I were some sort of halfwit who might not quite understand what was going on.

'Will do,' I said, as I pulled on my coat and picked up the griddle holding a slightly flat, sorry-looking array of scones.

It was the first time I had ever been in the Mitfords' yard. It felt strange seeing the same configuration of house as ours repeated just a few feet away, but in such a parlous state. There were piles of wooden planks, old bicycle wheels with all the spokes missing, old clothes sodden with rainwater and, near the gate, a large purple stain that looked very much like blood. From the corner, a rat watched me closely before disappearing through a protrusion of dandelion leaves into a crack in the wall. An aura of neglect hung about the place and something else, too – difficult to describe, except as a kind of tainted hope, a cloud of wayward possibilities and adventure that comes from a place with no rules. A waft of cigarette smoke hit me and I turned round, heart thumping.

'Hello again,' he said, bouncing a scruffy ball against the wall with one hand, and taking a long drag of a cigarette with the other. 'Early start for you the other day.'

I hesitated, afraid I might tremble if I started to speak. A clamp pressed at my throat. 'We're very sorry about the bairn,' I squeaked, imaginatively, my voice breaking mid-sentence.

'Thank you,' he said, in a non-committal way. 'Are they for us?'

I nodded. 'There's enough for two each.'

'Whee is it Norm?' called a gravelly voice from somewhere inside, thick with grief and slurring slightly from something else entirely. I looked back at Norman; a lean face that had not seen many cheese scones in its time, a gaze that told you he'd already worked you out before you even opened the gate, and eyes that looked like they could get you both in and out of trouble.

'It's the lassie from next door,' said Norman, shouting back towards the house. 'She's brought us some scones.' There was a loud, violent sob from inside the house. 'Sorry, me mam's not up to seeing anyone.'

'Of course,' I said. 'My nana says, if there's anything we can do, just to ask.'

'There is one thing,' said Norman, gulping down a scone like a snake trying to swallow a goat. 'Just for me personally, I would like to know what you do up there in your room all the time.' I was amazed at this boldness, and at the fact that I'd not been as invisible to the rest of the world as I'd hoped.

'Well, not much,' I said, blushing. 'I read. I mean, I like reading. And lots of looking out of the window.'

'Well, that's all very well but you know what they say: all work and no play makes Nancy a dull girl,' said Norman, tucking into a second scone. 'These are very nice, by the way.'

'I'd better go.'

He looked at me, taking a long drag on his cigarette. 'Why don't you come out with me tomorrow? I'm digging tetties down Thornton's Farm. It's just up the road. It will be fun. Might even put some colour into those cheeks.'

Just then a girl popped her head round the door. *Damn it,* I thought.

'Oh,' she said, coolly, 'it's her. The queen of Acacia Street.'

'Don't be like that, Pearl, she's come to say how sorry she is about Tommy.' Pearl – an ironic misnaming of biblical proportions – took a scone and appeared temporarily mollified, like a lion in its pen who has just been fed a load of meat and does not need to stalk its keepers for another day.

'I really better get back,' I whispered. 'Like I said, we are so sorry to hear about your brother.' Pearl nodded, took another two scones, and disappeared off to a quiet corner of the yard. Norman looked at the rest of the scones, then reluctantly gave a loud whistle. The back door opened and a flurry of tiny Mitfords started to push and kick their way past each other. After just a few moments all the scones were gone. I lifted up the empty griddle and scuttled back home.

***

Walking back into the sitting room, I saw that Grandad had already fallen fast asleep in his armchair. His head was back, his mouth was fully open, his shirt was unbuttoned at the top and he had begun to snore gently. It suddenly struck me how old he looked, those famous good looks being replaced by sagging jowls and wrinkles that seemed to have developed their own offshoots, like a river with a rich valley of tributaries. Why had I ever assumed that Grandad would be immune to the effects of ageing? Soon we would have to rename his performance act 'Al Jolson's Dad'.

I poked about at the fire for a bit and collected new timber and coals from the nettie to last us the rest of the day. Then I fetched some more water, trooping up and down the street with my water-carrying-strongman-device, ignoring the muffled shrieks of laughter from the children out playing. My new ruse for protecting my dignity during water-fetching was to go out heavily disguised, wearing Grandad's overcoat, my own hat and Nana's headscarf pulled right over my face. The disadvantage of this, of course, was that it limited my field of vision to that of a horse with blinkers on. On the way back, one of the little shitbag children took aim with his football and hit a bullseye right on one of the pails, which tipped its contents all over the alleyway and my boot. I had to make a second trip to the pump, but not before I'd grabbed him and had given him a good kick up the backside.

Finally, I returned to the safety of the house, cursing my life and vowing for the millionth time that, once I left, I would never return to this feral place. I settled crossly into my chair, sighing at the world. I picked up my new library book, *Heritage Sites of Arabia*, and started to read about Carthage. Nana wandered in from time to time, rebuking Grandad under her breath for doing nothing to help out. I felt it might be churlish to point out that Grandad had just put in five and a half days of hard physical labour down a mine at the age of sixty-two …

'Shall we go to the pictures, Nancy?' she said, out of the blue. 'I don't see why we should be the ones doing all the work round here while he sleeps like a greet big bairn over there.' I nodded, feeling cheered up. I loved going to the pictures. 'C'mon,' she said. 'I have no idea what's on, but who cares. Grab your coat and let's just head off and try our luck. And how about fish and chips on the way back?'

We were just about to leave, Nana tying her headscarf and hunting for change, when there came a knock at the door. She approached the door, cursing under her breath. Outside were two very smartly dressed, fresh-faced young gentlemen, in clean suits that did not look second hand.

'Good afternoon, ma'am,' said one, smiling, and presenting a Bible to us. 'We are God's witnesses. And we would like to ask you today, do you think the dead can come back to life?'

Nana took a quick look back to the sitting room. 'No, pet,' she said, shaking her head. 'I don't even think I'll be able to wake him up later for his tea. Now if you'll excuse us, we've a film to watch.'

The men looked at each other, confused, as we stepped past them and out into the street.

***

The next day, early in the morning there was another knock on the door. I didn't hear the conversation but Nana came up afterwards, laughing, to tell me the eldest Mitford boy had called for me, and he had actually thought I would have wanted to go potato digging with him. Nana had sent him away, as if it were the most ludicrous proposition ever. *Well, that one's over before it's begun*, I thought, miserably. But I had underestimated Norman. An hour later, there was another knock at the door, and this time it was Pearl who had been sent to fetch me.

'Does your Nancy want to come out and *play*?' she grunted. This ticked a few more boxes in Nana's mind and so this time she called up for me. I came to the front door to find Pearl waiting, legs and arms as thick as tree trunks and nostrils flared, her body already starting to show signs of inheriting her mother's ursine shape.

'Yes, I'll go,' I said. Nana nodded in semi-approval, balancing the normalising benefits of playing outside with the negative effects of hanging out with a fire-breathing Mitford. As we walked out of our backyard, I saw Norman waiting on the street, grinning. He handed Pearl a coin. She took one last glance at me, scoffed slightly, swore profusely, and loped off in the opposite direction. *Classy,* I thought. *How classy and ladylike.*

'Come on then, Nancy,' said Norman. 'Let's go and do something useful.'

***

Though it was still just September, the air was biting cold as we walked away from the colliery rows and out onto open farmland. We must have passed a dozen or so other kids picking up conkers and gathering the last of the blackberries into pails along the hedgerows as we walked down to the farm. I was unused to being outside and was starting to regret my decision to come, but Norman's easy chatter soon put me at my ease. At first, he asked me lots of questions; about my parents, my grandparents, and how I felt about it all, whether I was lonely. I felt a rush of gratitude towards him that made my cheeks colour. We could easily have descended into a sombre conversation but somehow Norman managed to make me laugh with just about everything he said. He was a master of impressions, and it wasn't long before his ale-swigging parents fell prey to his mimicry. He had his mother's gravelly voice off to a tee. He was equally merciless towards his siblings and it wasn't long before I had to stop walking and sit down; I was consumed by heaving laughter.

As we reached the farm, I could see the farmer walking behind two handsome shire horses which were pulling a plough. Behind the farmer were two children, on their haunches gathering up the potatoes into pails. Another seemed to be emptying his pail into a large sack. It all looked more than a little back-breaking. I sighed, pulling my cardigan closer and tying my scarf tighter.

'Well, my queen,' said Norm, 'for your first honest day's work, you shall be paid thruppence, plus you will receive a bag of finest tetties. Come on, or I'll do an impression again.'

'No,' I said, shaking my head. 'Please. My sides are still aching.'

And so we set to work. After ten minutes or so I forgot I had been cold and took off my scarf. My borrowed pail was already about a third full and I realised I was having lots of fun. The low autumn sun rose steadily until it was midday, and we stopped to eat. Neither Norm nor I had any food, but the others shared theirs and the farmer tore large chunks of bread for us from a loaf he had brought with him.

The rest of the day flew past, with us filling and refilling our pails several times, emptying them each time into the large sack at the side of the field. At the end of the day, the farmer gave us our wages, shaking his head at Norm and me who did not even have our own pails to carry our spuds home in. He created makeshift bags for us out of spare sackcloth. I felt something I had never experienced before – contentment mixed with liberation. It was only when we turned into Acacia Street that the familiar ennui began to flood over me once more.

'Thanks, Norm, I've really enjoyed myself today,' I said. I was desperate to know about the activities that had got him into trouble with Mr Shaw and the polis, but I was not yet brave enough to ask.

'I'm glad, Nancy. And listen, you know what you were saying about feeling lonely?'

'Yes?' I said. He pulled me to the entrance of the Mitfords' backyard. I wondered if this was how the gates of hell might look. Even at that distance I could hear the screams coming from inside. In the outside yard, some of the younger ones were playing a sort of wrestling game that appeared to consist of squashing each other using as much body weight as possible. There was a fresh trail of vomit on the ground that had projected far enough to reach several siblings and an old bike. The din was deafening. There was no sign of Mr and Mrs Mitford.

'Well, Nancy, whenever you feel a little lonely, do think of me now, won't you?'

'All right, Norm,' I said. 'Now you've made me feel bad.' We stood for a while, looking at each other. 'You were the one who asked me about it in the first place,' I continued, huffily. 'Now I feel as if I'm full of self-pity, which you know I'm not.'

'I know, Nancy, I'm only joking. I only meant for you to realise there's loneliness in places you might not expect to find it. I don't mean that what you experience is any less valid. Look – will you come out with me again?'

That was Norm, right there, in a nutshell. He read almost nothing but just seemed to get things, how things really were. Whereas I, for all my reading, saw very little at all. I suddenly felt like crying. I said a hurried goodbye and ran into my yard. Nana was delighted with the potatoes, though suspicious about the company I'd been keeping, but insisted I keep my thruppence in any case. That evening, I felt proper, honest exhaustion and fell into a slumber next to my grandparents in the sitting room, *Heritage Sites of Arabia* across my lap.

Things were a little weird between Norm and me for a few days after that. We experienced a shyness that comes from revealing one's hand too quickly, the joker having been played too soon. But again, Norm's maturity won through and he instigated a detente. Cycling up to me on my way home from school, with Jackie perched on his shoulder, he told me in a serious voice that I needed to make sure next time he called at the house that Nana wouldn't send him away. He couldn't afford to pay Pearl each time, he said. I was glad he had found me, and reassured him I would talk to Nana. I knew she couldn't resist a good story, so I laid it on pretty thick. The next time he called at the house, after school a few days later, he asked me to go down to the river with him to catch minnows. Nana wasn't particularly happy. How is a jar of minnows going to feed ten bairns, she asked? Nevertheless, I was allowed to go. Once again, I started off cold and reluctant, and ended up laughing, leaping around in a most unladylike fashion, sweating and throwing off my jumper and scarf, excitedly clambering up trees behind Norm. We even built ourselves a den next to the spot where we sat to catch the minnows in our jam jars, a few yards from the stepping stones that we used to cross the river back towards Oslington and the colliery rows. Some of the boys from school arrived, and we chatted to them for a while, then I fell asleep as they gathered wood to make a fire. Later, I returned home, feet wet and arms and legs covered in mud, but with a tight, coal-shaped block of happiness firmly lodged in my chest.

***

The following Sunday, I met Grandad as I walked back from the tap at the end of the row with my pails. He was in a chirpy mood, having just played a clandestine game of Pitch and Toss in a dark corner between two pit heaps, in a zone whose periphery was manned by child lookouts specially trained to spot Mr Shaw or the polis at fifty paces. I was in a reverie all of my own, though still in denial about it.

But as we turned into the yard, there was Nana, banging her fist on the scullery window. 'Look at the time, Bill,' she shouted, her eyes full of fury. 'Where the hell have you been? We're due at Aunt Flo's in ten minutes.'

'Oh no, please tell me you're joking, woman,' he shouted back. Then under his breath to me, he added, 'Not that bloody old bat again. Shoot me now.' We looked at each other, smirking, and Grandad rolled his eyes.

'No, I'm not. It's your memory again,' shouted Nana, still banging on the window.

Being brought up by one's grandparents is an interesting experience. Sometimes I felt like I was ageing at an enhanced rate and bypassing my youth entirely, involuntarily adopting their old-person mannerisms and colloquialisms. This is why the grammar school was such a relief for me. Much of our home life passed with conversations like this and sometimes I felt like I could scream with the brain-cell-eroding tediousness of it all. However, after visiting great (great) Aunt Flo in her Aged Miner's Home, which smelled of pease pudding and worse stuff I didn't even want to know about, Acacia Street felt like a bastion of modernity, and our conversations seemed like they'd come straight from a university debating society.

Aunt Flo's home was a small bungalow with a front room, a tiny scullery and a bedroom, in a colliery row situated in a little village a couple of miles outside of Oslington. Part of the fixtures and fittings was Aunt Flo, with her white shawl in the style of half a doily, her grey hair piled up on top of her head in a bun, and more hairs on her chin than your average pubescent boy. Over the years, she had pretty much merged into her armchair and now seemed to be part of it; her legs were spread to reveal knee-length stockings and giant white drawers which sat just above her skirt, daring you to look. Worse, one was guaranteed the same dreary stories of hardship each visit: her first home, which had a ladder running up to the top floor, no stairs; how the ash heaps came to within just three feet of their back door; how the Wesleyan and Primitive Methodists requested a chapel each in the tiny village, which the landowning and pious Duke allowed, but then the same Duke wouldn't allow a shop or a school, so the children were forced to walk two miles to Oslington and back each day; how the mail was delivered by horse and cart; how there was no proper sanitation, with the drains running straight into the nearby burn –which was also being used as a water supply. And so forth.

You may not feel, Norman, that I have spared you the details of Flo's tedious rhetoric, but I can assure you that this is a mere taster of what we had to listen to, time after time after time. In the interests of our fledgling friendship, I will leave it there for now.

Except for one teensy, weensy detail. Let me try, now, to remember what was said … The afternoon passed in such a horrid blur. Aunt Flo asked Nana for an update about Grandad's 'situation'; Nana looked quickly at me and tried to change the subject. But Flo pressed on. There was a letter. Grandad was being forced into retirement by the Oslington Coal Company. We would all have to move out of the house.

I wasn't aware that miners were being forced to retire, in fact quite the opposite, but the housing shortage for workers had grown so bad that the coal company was now forcing their men to retire at sixty-five. In Grandad's case, there was also some hint at loss of productivity due to arthritis, and coal dust on the lungs. Nana added that yes, a date had been set, in about three years' time when Grandad turned sixty-five. Aunt Flo exclaimed, showering herself with Battenberg cake, that there was a seven-year waiting list for the retirement cottages, the only ones for the area, and that we would all, therefore, have to move in with her. Family is family, she said. Nancy and I can share the bedroom, she said, flashing me a row of rotten brown teeth, *all girls together*. It will be cosy, but families look after each other and didn't we know about the family of twelve in a one-roomed shack next door to where she grew up?

What about all our savings from the performing, I asked, weakly. Aunt Flo looked at me as if I were mad; didn't I know that had all gone to the grammar school fees and the uniform. Didn't I know that the fees alone were nearly ten pounds a year? How else could they have afforded to send me?

Nana and Grandad exchanged quick looks with each other – clearly there had been conversations to which I had not been privy – and reluctantly agreed that, yes, us all moving in together was a possibility. My eyes filled with tears – all that money spent on me, all those sacrifices. Not a word to me about it.

Sometimes the roof just caves in on your world; the walls turn black and start folding in on themselves. You are forced to reappraise everything, as your mind is ravaged by shockwaves that keep on hitting you, over and over. That evening, back in the safety of my bedroom, I looked out of the window at the winding shafts and the pit, quiet and still and eerie, and suddenly realised that this was nirvana compared to what my life aged sixteen might look like.

The terms of my escape plan were going to have to change.

Chapter 3

An uneasy silence descended on us in the days and weeks following our visit to Aunt Flo's. Nana's usual continuous chatter, which in the past seemed to come to her as easily as breathing, was replaced by quiet spells spent staring into the fire, or by wandering around frowning and sighing. Grandad, too, seemed to have lost his taste for humorous one-liners. Norm called round for me a few times, but I declined each invitation. Sequestered in my bedroom like a hedgehog holed up for the winter I felt some comfort; I could control my thoughts if nothing else. I ate even less than before.

My grandparents had managed to rebuild the walls around the site of the devastation caused by the giant boulder of fate that had crashed its way through their lives nearly fourteen years earlier. But now they felt those precious walls crumbling away. All our previous certainties – the house, the pit, Grandad's wages, my place at grammar school – were suddenly all about to go head first over the edge of a cliff.

I almost confided in my form teacher, Miss Trott, and even hung back to speak to her one day after school, but she was in a ratty mood and wrongly pre-empted the nature of my query by stating, quite haughtily, that we had already talked about teacher training college and she didn't want to have to go over everything again as she had a mountain of marking to do. I lost my nerve after that. I should have confided in Norm, but for some reason I didn't want him to know.

It is all very well knowing the opposite of your goal. No way and under no circumstances whatsoever was I going to be moving in with Aunt Flo, and what would life mean for me if I couldn't continue at grammar school? My stomach churned over and over at the thought that mine would be a life like Nana's, trapped at home in some sort of domestic version of a Mexican standoff. Or perhaps, I considered miserably, worse still, mine would be a life like Mrs Mitford's, squeezing out a new brat every year for an errant husband, drinking my way through it all just to remain sane. But I was bereft of any ideas or solutions, and cursed my brain, so alive with, yet constrained by, the written words of others that it had little room for creative problem-solving when I most needed it. I watched the winding shafts turning for hours on end, hoping to inspire my own neural cogs into action. But to no avail.

Life went on outside my window with a new twist: on Fridays, a market had sprung up next to the pit entrance with all sorts of weird and wonderful characters and goods. There was a blind man selling yeast and eggs – amazingly he never seemed to break any – who brought his goods on a trolley, his milky eyes rolling about wildly. Another chap, known as The Oil Man, sold oil, candles and giant blocks of green carbide soap that we had to saw down into usable pieces. Another stall sold fruit and vegetables and was run by two robust sisters wearing fingerless gloves. Nana and I often ambled down to the stalls after school on Fridays. It provided a welcome relief from the thoughts that were troubling us both and for a few minutes we could pretend that nothing had changed.

Over time, my swirling thoughts began to thicken into a coherent sauce. One Saturday afternoon after my morning session at the library, I wandered slowly down to the rec and found an empty swing to sit on. I sat there for some time watching the breeze flatten the grass and weeds, kicking at dirt with my boots. Some little kids came up to me, telling me to get off the swings because I'd had my turn; I swore at them and told them I would set the Dickensian nightmare that was the 'Bad Man' on them if they came near me again.

The solution was not even that complicated, or exciting. Unusual though it was, I would rent a room from my form teacher, Miss Trott, who I knew lived alone in a large stone farmhouse just outside of town. For all her bluster, I knew she had a soft spot for me and I decided that I would employ Nana's 'Shy bairns get nowt' mantra to use this to my advantage. I already had my sob story worked out. But she would not welcome me into her home for free so, whether I moved in with her or took my own lodgings, I would need money. But I had no money. Ergo, I would need to either steal or earn money. And quite a lot of it too. Because maybe I would have to pay for my own grammar school fees, too, if poor Grandad was retired and was no longer able to perform due to the coal dust on his lungs and the arthritis in his knees.

I twirled round on the swing, tightening up the squeaking chains until they could be twisted no more, then sprang round, legs straight out in front of me, the orange and black of the colliery rows blending into one horrible flash of colour.

My mind wandered back to a conversation with Norm of a few weeks earlier. It was the day we'd been catching minnows, and we'd bumped into some other boys down by the river. I hadn't thought much to the conversation at the time. They had been talking about the fact that they wouldn't be able to meet after school for much longer, since they would be starting down the mine once they turned fourteen. John Weightman and Geordie Gallon had been skimming stones across the river, talking excitedly about leaving school and earning money. The others had wandered around, collecting wood for a fire. I'd found a comfortable spot on a luxurious bed of pine needles and catkins, where I'd settled down, wrapped up in Nana's cardigan, reading. Norm had said something mysterious, like, 'The miner's life is not for me. I've been saving up for a long time. Off to North Shields, get an apprenticeship as an electrician down the shipyards.'

Trevor, Mrs Pearce's son, who had been cleaning his spectacle lenses with a dock leaf, said, 'I thought you spent all that money on your brothers and sisters?'

Norm gave him a wink. 'Not all of it, my four-eyed friend. Some of it gets put to one side into a little tobacco tin, which is used to keep the growing proceeds of the Norman Mitford Evacuation Fund. Actually, I've already got two full tins and I'm going to need another soon.'

'As riches increase, so do pride and anger and lustfulness, especially for the meek,' John boomed, in a fire-and-brimstone voice straight from the pulpit. I thought about this, twirling a catkin between my fingers. The message was clear: if you're poor, you're poor for a reason, sunshine. The worst thing you can do is get ideas above your station. The best thing you can do is stay poor, avoid temptation and let the church look after you.

'There's nowt meek about *him*,' Geordie suggested, laughing.

'You Methodists. Honestly. Money gives you choices. What's wrong with that?'

'Nothing's wrong with that, Norm. Be a good boy now, tell uz where you keep it. I'll keep it safe for you.'

'Sure you will, Geordie, sure you will. You'll keep it safe, right up to when you bet the whole lot on a horse that gets flattened before the first fence. But guess what? When you idiots are down that mine, filling up your lungs with dust and hoping you get through your first two years with your arms still attached, I'll be far away.'

'North Shields is not that far away,' Trevor said, somewhat pedantically.

***

I reflected on the afternoon. 'Those are merlins,' Trevor had said, lost in his own world, 'and those are bitterns.' He'd pointed to the birds on the horizon that were settling around the patchworks of tiny lakes within the marsh beyond the river. His eyes would not meet ours. We knew that he had had to leave grammar school after one year; he wasn't clever enough, so the rumour had it. The shallow water had reflected up a blue haze which had drifted upwards into a light grey sky, through which a pink sun was making a lazy descent into evening. Around the tiny lakes grew grey scrubs of reeds and delicate, tall yellow wildflowers. The air had had a pleasant aniseed smell from the cow parsley that grew in bunches around our den. I remember that I had fallen asleep right there, out in the open, and had thought no more about the conversation, other than to reflect that Norman Mitford was full of talk.

But, on examining the conversation again, I found that I had probably misinterpreted things. Whatever Norm was doing, I would have to be brave and confront him about it. And I would have to ask him to let me in on it.

***

At a quarter to five the next morning, I slipped downstairs, put on Grandad's overcoat and pit boots, placed Nana's thick black scarf over my head, and went to wait in the Mitfords' yard. The air was biting cold. I waited over half an hour, and my fingers began to go white and stiff. I was about to go home when the back door opened and Norm stepped out.

'Norm,' I murmured, stepping out from the shadows, causing my new friend to jump in fright and emit a sort of strangulated 'Argh' sound.

'Jesus Christ! What the hell are you doing here, dressed as the Grim Reaper?' he said, shaking his head, and leaning on the yard wall while his heart attack subsided. 'I don't hear from you for weeks and then here you are, lying in wait for me at five o'clock in the bloody morning. Strange, strange girl.'

I told him the outline of the story about Aunt Flo and having to move out. How my future at the grammar school was now possibly in jeopardy. How I needed money, and how I was prepared to do anything for that.

'Can you help me, Norm?' I pleaded. 'I've heard that you earn your own money, but I honestly don't know any more than that. Is there room for someone else where you work?'

But Norm shook his head, manoeuvring his bicycle out from behind piles of wood.

'It's not lassies' work,' he said, and somehow I managed to refrain from punching him at this point. 'You would end up angry with me for letting you get yourself mixed up in it.'

I thought about this. The previous Sunday we'd been back to Flo's. Although still a couple of years away, the plans for us to move in were gaining momentum and something worse – a sort of inevitability, like a swollen river about to burst its banks. After discussing practicalities, Aunt Flo had fallen asleep, legs akimbo, as Nana cut her toenails. Meanwhile, Grandad had stood outside in the yard, stroking his temples and smoking silently.

'I won't be angry with you,' I said, decisively. 'I want this more than anything else. I'm not joking. You have to take me, Norm. Seriously, I'll run away if you don't.'

'You are an absolute lunatic, do you know that?' he said, finally, and I knew I had won.

'Thank you, Norm,' I said, shivering in spite of the coat. 'I will never forget this.'

'Do me a favour. Don't thank me till you've made it through your first week, ok? I must be mad,' he said, crossly, putting on his trouser clips. 'I'll have to introduce you to the gaffer first, okay?

And I can't guarantee that it will go any further than that. Meet me here on Saturday at four.' And with that, he leaned over and, in a move that I think surprised both of us, kissed me fully on the lips. Then he cycled off into the dark.

***

The fair was in full swing as we wandered in. Gaudy colours, spinning lights and the smells of chips, candy floss and motor oil. Screams of delight from children on the rides. A Wurlitzer, a huge and ornate attraction in its own right, belting out tinny organ music. Caravans with drawings of buxom fortune tellers on the front, wooden tassels hanging from the door, the smell of joss sticks emanating from inside. Dark-skinned, handsome gypsies milling around, feigning insouciance but in actuality watching everyone like hawks as they came and went. A large banner stretched across the entrance that read 'Roman Fair'. To the left were the dodgems, then in the centre there stood a tall helter-skelter and a merry-go-round. Norm and I walked quickly past the rides, over to the back of the fair where the smaller stalls were laid out.

'Are you working for gypsies, Norm?' I said, incredulously.

Norm laughed, pulling his cap further down over his face. 'No,' he said, 'and neither is the gaffer. He just works here when the fair is in town.' In front of us, a small boy with ginger curls tripped over a cable and stuffed both himself and his candyfloss into the mud. He began to wail miserably.

We walked past the hook-a-duck and the football range, and on further to a rifle range. A queue of people snaked round the side of the stall, waiting their turn. I spotted John Weightman, as well as Geordie Gallon and Trevor Pearce, in the front of the queue, and nudged Norm, who waved to them. I wondered what kind of rifle range this might be, as I couldn't see any punters holding guns.

At the back of the stall, Terry Weightman was taking his turn. He was standing against a sheet of red-and-white striped, heavily pock-marked linoleum, facing sideways. A cigarette had been placed in his mouth. It wavered around as Terry jerked and ticked, his body betraying his desire to stay still.

'Keep still, you fuckin' idiot,' shouted a commanding voice from a covered booth at the front of the stall. 'I can't shoot at the fuckin' cigarette unless you stay still.'

'Oh my god,' I said, looking over at Terry. Suddenly, there was a tremendous bang and the linoleum behind him flapped furiously backwards and forwards and the cigarette from his mouth disappeared. Poor Terry jumped about a foot in the air, gave a loud scream and ran off whooping, his hands above his head, back towards the dodgems to the sound of applause.

'.22 rifle,' said Norm, under his breath. 'Most accurate gun from that distance.'

'Next victim,' shouted the commanding voice, drolly, from inside the box. 'Have your penny ready and drop it into the tin as you pass.' Norm took my hand and led me round to the front of the booth.

'Mr Turner,' said Norm, knocking on the wooden door, also painted red and white. 'It's Norman. Sorry to interrupt you, sir, but I need you to meet somebody.'

'I'm busy, lad,' said the voice. 'They've let the funny farm out today. Nearly took that lad's nose off. Come back later.'

'We can't,' said Norm. 'It's urgent. Please come out. We'll only be a couple of minutes.'

I'm not sure exactly what I was expecting; of course, I had worked out by now that I was about to meet the famous gaffer, but when I saw who was standing there, my heart sank and my legs threatened to buckle beneath me. The Bad Man stepped out from the box, a tall rifle in his hand, and a cigarette hanging out of his mouth. He was every bit as horrible close up as I remembered, veins visible across nose and a big grey beard that wobbled as he talked. He smelled of long-dead bodies. He looked at me quizzically and reluctantly stuck out a filthy hand for me to shake.

'I'm so sorry to interrupt, Mr Turner. I promise we'll be quick. This is Nancy. She needs some money, quite badly, and wants to help me do my work, and help you, too. She wants to know if you've got any extra work for her.'

'Huh?' said the Bad Man, aka Mr Turner, with a horrible laugh. 'You think this is the Girl Guides, do you? You think I'm running some sort of church book club?'

Behind us, the crowd started to chatter in frustration.

'Hold up,' shouted Mr Turner to the crowd. 'Won't be a minute.' He turned to us again. 'I can't have anyone knowing about what we do, son. I helped you out cos of your family situation, but I can't help every Lady Muck out who crosses my path.' He turned back towards the booth.

'Wait,' I said. 'Just give me a chance. I promise on oath that I won't tell anyone about any of your activities. I'm in a plight myself, sir, and I need money in a hurry. It's really important.'

'You in the family way?' he said, stroking his beard and eyeing me suspiciously.

'No!' I said, blushing. I had not even started my monthlies yet, and one kiss hardly moved me up the scale of sexual experience. 'Good grief, no, Mr Turner. I just need the money. I'm not going to be like a *girl*. I'll do whatever you need me to do just as if you had another boy working for you. I'll make money for all of us. And when I've made enough money, we'll part ways and no one will know that we ever worked together.'

'Nancy is an orphan, sir,' said Norm, hanging his head. I looked at Norm, surprised and impressed, making a mental note to trot that one out in future if I needed to.

'Hmmn,' said Mr Turner. 'Well you certainly know how to pick your time, lad. Busiest time of the week, this is. Let me think about it.' He looked at his watch. 'Saturday teatime. Time for you to collect the bottles. And no scamming me, okay? I'll be checking with the Co-op what they paid you. A penny a bottle, so it is.'

***

And so, at five o'clock on Monday morning, I found myself out for my first day of proper, paid employment. I left a note for my grandparents saying, simply, that I had to go in early to school. I sat awkwardly on the back of his bicycle while poor Norm peddled standing up, and we slogged down the backstreets, passing row after row of shoddy, identical houses designed on a shoestring by the gods of homogeneity. After a couple of minutes we emerged from the oppressive housing zone onto the Roman road and the going got a little easier. It can't have been comfortable for Norm. I clenched my buttocks, as if that might make me a bit lighter. Norm said, before he ran out of breath, that we were heading for Mr Turner's house. A light rain was falling and a light mist sat just above the shrubs and bushes. I could see my breath in the morning air. With one hand I held on to Norm's waist as he rode, which made me feel both embarrassed and exhilarated. With the other I held on to my panama hat, for I was dressed for school and feeling not a little ridiculous.

A ball of anxiety had knotted itself into my stomach. Norm had been cagey about the work we were about to do, saying he preferred to just show me 'on the job'. When I had quizzed him about whether Mr Turner had formally acquiesced to the new arrangement, he simply shrugged and said that he hadn't said no. I realised that the timing of our fair visit, something that initially looked like madness, had been intentional on Norm's part. Norm, I was learning, did not do things in a haphazard way.

Mr Turner's house was situated in Barring Tye, which made him, ironically, a neighbour of Aunt Flo. His was a large stone house, though, in a part of the village I'd never been to before, with a vast garden to the rear and a huge lumpy shed at the end of it. The garden stretched right down to the river, sloping at the end into a wooden fence that notionally signalled the end of the garden and the start of the reed-covered bank leading down to the water.

As we let ourselves in quietly through the side gate, Norm paused and looked at me. 'Welcome to the Garden of Eden,' he whispered, and we both grinned. A path led down towards the shed, past rows of empty flower and vegetable beds. The sound of the river began to crescendo the further down we walked, lapping and gurgling as it turned sharp left past the end of the garden.

Mr Turner grew all sorts of vegetables here in the summer, Norm said: potatoes, carrots, beetroots, cabbage, radishes, green beans. We continued down, past apple and pear trees which hung bent over, heavy with overripe fruits, past more empty beds covered in carpet which, Norm said, were used for growing sweet williams to make into posies to sell to day trippers in the summer.

All around were heaps of the most basic forms of stinking manure, no more than soil into which what looked like offal and intestines had been crudely dug. Rats wandered openly and mingled with crows and flies over the bloody heaps.

The shed was unlocked, and we walked straight in. Norm kicked amiably at a mouse on the dirt floor, missing, and we watched as it slunk quickly into a tight hole in the corner, away from our gaze.

'Sorry about the smell,' said Norm. This was no understatement; there was a thick, heavy, nose-affronting smell like rotten chicken mixed with a damp smell coming from the shed itself. I covered my mouth with my scarf and tried not to gag. I had promised not to act like a girl, though, and simple pride kept me from giving in. Along the back wall were nailed three long animal pelts, each at least three or four feet in length, with a silky brown-black fur, and covered in a white powder. A grappling hook on a long rope hung next to them.

Next to these was a table covered in linoleum, on which was piled all sorts of junk: large baskets full of hunting knives, catapults, balls of raffia, metal box traps, a box of bullets, paraffin lamps, a bottle of whisky and a row of bottles with home-made labels which simply read 'Parsnip Wine'. In the centre of the shed was a stand with an ominous looking sharp metal hook on the top. Underneath it stood a large wooden pail. To the side was a tin bath with a cloth and a bottle of vinegar inside it. On the right-hand wall hung several guns, and next to them Mr Turner's sou'wester and some other coats, home-made fishing rods and a walking stick. Next to the bath were two wooden stools. The beams of the roof were covered in big, thick cobwebs, some abandoned but still holding insects that had long since turned to ash. Living flies buzzed around, and their dead compadres lined the window ledge, the table and the floor.

I looked out of the rotten, greasy window onto the river, feeling relieved that Mr Turner was not there and, I hoped, would not be joining us. Some moorhens were swimming against the flow of the river and a heron stood at the other side, eyeing us uninterestedly. *Some Garden of Eden,* I thought. And yet there was a blissful charm about the whole place which even now is difficult to put into words.

You probably think that a strange statement, Norman, with me standing there, before eviscerated animals and guns and knives. And I can't really give much of an answer, to be honest, except to say that what I could see was life stripped back to basics, and the kind of joy and honesty which can only be found in self-sufficiency, in producing from the earth and using whatever else nature provides.

'You ready?' said Norm. I nodded. 'You need to get changed first. Here – these are my overalls. Get these on, then get a coat and wellies and pick up a sack.' Norm dipped out of the shed to wait outside while I got changed inside, reluctantly leaving my uniform hanging up next to the pelts. For a split second I wondered if I was mad, and should just leave before I got embroiled in something I probably shouldn't, but then I thought of Miss Trott, and the grammar school, and the London technicolour transfiguration, and my boxing husband who seemed to be turning into Mr Rochester who seemed to be turning into Norman Mitford … and I pulled on Norm's sou'wester and cap and stepped out again into the morning air.

We set off down to the edge of the riverbed, stepping over the wobbly fence, and continued along past all the houses until the bank cleared into open fields, with woods and marshland around the edges. Light jutted down patchily from round holes in the clouds.

We had wandered so far that the houses were no longer in sight, when Norm motioned to us to stop. 'There's the holt, over there,' he said, pointing to a flat muddy bank a few feet away. 'Get your sack out ready.'

'I'm sorry. I don't understand what's happening. You're not telling me anything, Norm. Can you start from the beginning? I'm willing to help and do anything but you need to talk to me first and tell me what's going on.'

Norm sighed and motioned to me to copy him sitting down on his sack.

'Sorry, Nancy. All right – here's what's happening. We are here to see if we have caught any otters in the traps that I laid yesterday afternoon. If we have caught an otter, you will need to drag it back while I carry all the rest of the traps back to the shed. Do you see the traps?'

I nodded. Down among the reeds were two open flat-spring traps, with jagged edges and a piece of rubber in the centre.

'If you can still see the trap open like that, it means that we haven't caught an otter. Keep away from them or you might lose a hand. I'm not joking.'

'What's the rubber for?'

'It's to stop the trap taking the otter's leg off. If he loses a leg,' he continued, matter-of-factly, 'he's going to limp off and die somewhere. Then he's no good to us.'

'Oh,' I said. 'I can't see any animals anywhere. So does that mean you haven't caught anything?'

Norm got up and wandered over to where the traps were staked. He looked around, his eye following a stake whose long metal chain led into the river. There was no trap, or none that I could see at any rate.

'I think we've got one,' he said, grimly. 'You all right about this?'

'Yes,' I lied, frowning at him. A horrible feeling of dread bubbled up in my throat.

'We can't have the animals dead out here. We'd get caught out straight away.'

'So how do they die?'

'They drown, I'm afraid,' said Norm, looking at me guiltily. He sighed and looked at me plaintively. 'There's one in there right now. Are you sure you're ready for this?' I nodded, not feeling very sure at all but thinking of Aunt Flo's brown toenails to gee myself up.

'So, Nancy, start by pulling that chain out of the water.' I waded down to the water's edge, the river easily lapping over the edge of my wellies, the cold water sending me into a kind of shock. The chain was extraordinarily long and the poor otter at the end of it was tremendously heavy. With some effort, I heaved it out and we moved it up onto the riverbank and onto my sack. Norm pulled the trap off its front leg. It was still beautiful in dcath; its fur brown-black and oily and shiny. Delicate white whiskers sprung out next to its nose. A tear trickled down my cheek, which I quickly wiped away before Norm could see.

'Are we going to get the barrow Norm? So that we can bring it back?'

'Can't get the barrow over this clover field, Nance. Got to drag it back. That's your job, while I retrieve all these traps. It's great to have some help I must say,' he added, happily.

I watched while Norm activated all the remaining traps by picking up a long stick and applying pressure to the rubber-covered plate in the centre, an extremely precarious operation even though I could see he was highly practised in the art.

'You know,' said Norm, as I emptied my wellies and we began to head back, 'when I was little I couldn't open these traps by myself. Mr Turner had to make me a wooden stake to get them open with.'

I shook my head. 'How did you get mixed up in all of this, Norm?' Progress was slow as I pulled the sack along. Norm carried the traps on his shoulder. They clanked noisily as we walked.

'Long story. My nan lived two doors away from Mr Turner and she sent me there one day for a penn'orth of carrots. Think I must have been about eight or nine at the time. Well, we all know about the Bad Man, don't we?' I nodded, and Norm chuckled. 'Christ, I was shaking like a leaf. Standing there at his gate, ringing the bell. But Mr Turner ... now, everyone thinks he's a bastard, but it's just his manner, you know? When I went for those carrots, he was growling as usual but he gave me an extra helping because, he said, I came from a big family. He was kind, like. I still legged it back home though, once I had those damned carrots in my hand. I went a few more times after that, for different things, and one day he just asked me outright if I would like to help him and earn some money at the same time. He said ask your mam if it would be all right, but I knew she wouldn't care so I just made up that I'd asked her.'

'You were trapping otters aged eight?'

'God, no. Tying posies of sweet william all day on the weekend for half a crown. He takes them down to the station in the summertime for the fishermen to buy for their wives after they've been out fishing for the day. Grows the whole lot in his garden. Only started trapping a couple of years ago. And the otter season is short – October, and November, too, if you're lucky.'

'Blimey,' I said.

'Do you know how much Mr Turner gets from the furrier for these pelts, Nancy?' said Norm, suddenly.

'Of course not.'

'Have a guess.'

I thought for a moment. 'Ten shillings?' I said, finally.

'Not quite, Nance. Three pounds each, my lovely. Three pounds.' I gasped, and let go of the sack in amazement. 'Ah yes, but for the first year the old goat only gave me half a crown for all this effort, and it worked for long enough, until I spoke to the furrier myself one day and found out what he was making. Mr Turner's knees have gone, so he can't do this by himself any more. He needs me as much as I need him, so I got myself a little pay increase.'

'What do you get now?'

'One pound,' said Norm, proudly. 'It's still a shitty deal when you think about it but for someone my age, it's pretty bloody amazing.'

'Honestly. It's unbelievable.'

'Well I think it's time to start asking Mr Turner for half the proceeds, Nance. Then I can give you a good cut of it all. How does ten shillings sound for your cut? Sure, he'll bitch and moan about it but he hasn't got any choice. God, I love capitalism,' he said, laughing. 'And I must say, you are slightly better looking than Mr Turner as a work colleague. And you definitely smell better. You don't know just how bonny you are, do you?' he continued, flirtatiously. 'There you are, in an old coat, old man's wellies, pulling a dead otter along behind you in a sack. Seriously, I never saw anything finer.'

'Hardly,' I said, laughing, but secretly delighted.

Back at the shed, we pulled the otter out of the sack and hung it on the hook in the middle of the shed.

'You might want to look away for this,' said Norm, and I gave no fight to this suggestion and stepped quickly outside, helping myself to one of Norm's cigarettes en route.

I found a nice spot, down by the river, and sat cross-legged on a spare sack, smoking contentedly. I'd had a few puffs on a cigarette before. On Sundays, Grandad would disappear off to the nettie for some 'proper business' as he described it. Alarmingly, it was his only bowel movement of the week, something he blamed on Nana's cooking. He would give us a ridiculous bow, a sort of final salute, like an Artic explorer off on a dangerous expedition, unsure whether he would make it back alive, or at least with all his digits intact. In protest, Nana and I would surreptitiously slope off in the opposite direction, outside the front of the house, and share one of his cigarettes between us. He must have known, but he never said anything.

But this felt even better because I'd earned it. I felt the smoke filling up my lungs, giving a rush to my head. I sat there on that bank, thinking of everything and nothing. I remember thinking that one day I would feel nostalgia for that place. How true that sentiment has proved to be.

Twenty minutes passed before Norm came out, wiping his forehead. Sure enough, when I went back into the shed there was a fourth pelt hanging up on the wall, covered in the same white drying agent. The bucket in the middle of the room was full of crimson offal and disgusting tubes of intestines. It smelled like death. The cloth and vinegar had been removed from the tin bath. This was now full of slabs of bone and meat.

'What happens now?' I asked, pretending I saw this sort of thing every day.

'All right, we're nearly done. You're doing great. That lot,' said Norm, pointing to the bath, 'is going to the butcher for your sausages.'

'You're kidding.'

'Nope. But don't worry. Mr Turner is very proud of the cleanliness of that bath. I tried to put the meat in there once without cleaning it out beforehand and he nearly took my ear off. I did pick up fleas from the shed, however, that same time. Kind of ironic. Anyway, he cleans it every day, no word of a lie.'

'With those filthy hands.'

'Oh yes, indeed.'

'The whole thing is disgusting.'

'What's your issue with it? The fact that the butcher is putting otter meat into sausages, or the fact that it comes from Mr Turner's Medieval Torture Chamber?'

I shook my head. 'I don't even know. But I'm never going to eat sausages again.'

Norm sniggered and started to lift up the bucket. 'Yes, you will,' he said.

***

We lifted the carpet off the rows of soil and began to chop up the contents of the bucket and dig it all in. I can't even recall how disgusting this task was, suffice to say that I gagged several times but managed not to be sick. When we were done, we carefully replaced the carpet then went down to the water's edge for a wash. No soap, said Norm, bad for Mother Nature, for whom he had suddenly developed a selective solicitude. Then we left as quietly as we'd arrived and, with two bags of bone and meat hanging off the handlebars, we cycled to school via the butcher, who was delighted and gave us sixpence, reminding Norm as we left that he owed him some rabbits too.

We'd gone a few yards past a pet shop with large bowls of animal food out the front, when Norm suddenly swerved into an alleyway and told me to alight. He ran back to the shop, and returned a few seconds later, proudly handing me two dog biscuits that he'd liberated from their bowl outside the shop.

'Breakfast,' he said. Then we set off for school.

***

'Have you not had a wash this weekend, Nancy?' said Miss Trott, brow furrowed, during the morning registration. 'When you start your monthlies it's important to take care of your personal hygiene.'

'Yes, Miss,' I said, meekly, picking up my slate and walking off to my next lesson. Suddenly I put down my slate and turned back to the teacher. 'Miss Trott?' I said.

'Yes, child?'

'How is it that some really clever children don't get to go to grammar school? They don't even sit the exam?'

Miss Trott peered at me over her pince-nez. 'Well,' she said, 'when it's time for the exam, the school writes to all the parents and asks them if they want their child to be put forward for it. There is a cost to it, so the parents need to be able to fund it. It all costs – the fees and uniform and books and such like. Some parents haven't the means to pay for their children to come to grammar school. I've also seen it that children come here but have to leave halfway through, if their parents can no longer afford it. It's not completely fair, but then nor is life.' And with an aphoristic shrug she turned back to her book, indicating that the talk was over.

That's what must have happened to Trevor Pearce, I thought, sadly. We all thought he wasn't clever enough but it must have come down to the fees. I began to walk away, when she said, 'Take me, for example. Living a lovely, simple life in my little house. Pottering in my garden, singing in the church choir, enjoying a thoroughly peaceful life. And then my sister goes and gets herself widowed, and suddenly she's moved into my house with my three young nephews and nieces who do not appear to know that children should be seen and not heard. What a vexation, all in all! I never asked for that, did I?'

'No, Miss,' I said, heading for the toilets in search of soap, a wave of sadness and panic flooding over me at the revelation of this most dispiriting news.

***

After school, I'd agreed to meet Norm in an alleyway just past the Soot to return to Mr Turner's house to do the trap setting. This time I was slightly alarmed to see that we were to be joined by Jackie, who was perched proprietorially on Norm's shoulder. 'Don't worry,' said Norm. 'He'll leave you alone if you leave him alone.' I watched as Norm gently fed Jackie a nut from his pocket and said something ridiculous about being its daddy. And so off we went – me on the back of the bike again, Norm peddling hard in front and Jackie flying along beside us like something that could have come from another favourite book of mine, The Wizard of Oz. Among the many things I was realising about Norm was the fact that he lived his life in the present tense. Which sounds like a ridiculous statement. But what I mean is that he was always on the go, always doing, creating, taking, providing. Living on his wits. His was a subsistence existence and he simply got on with it. An aura of possibility surrounded him, exciting and slightly dangerous. By proxy, he was speeding up my dry, crusty old life too – shattering my previous nun-like existence of silent contemplation into thousands of pieces with each new move. It was thrilling.

When we arrived at Barring Tye, I was dismayed to see Mr Turner sitting on a stool next to the shed. He puffed rancorously on a pipe, as if it were an enemy he needed to keep a close eye on. At his heels sat a stately but insipid-looking whippet.

'Brought the Girl Guide, I see,' he said, peevishly, spitting at some unseen object to his left. 'You think you're so clever, laddie, but you won't get the better of me. Get more work out of that damned bird, I'll be bound.'

'Ah, quite lovely to see you Mr Turner. I trust all is well in the Turner household?' said Norm, brightly.

'Haway, lad, you think I can't spot sarcasm? Young love. Makes lads go daft, it does. Never turns out well.'

'We got a good'un today,' Norm said, ignoring Mr Turner and patting the dog on the head. 'Hello, Sid. Who's a good boy?' he said, putting his nose to the whippet's. Jackie flew up to the shed roof, where he hopped around, hesitantly.

'Yes, I saw. And a bloody good job too, with your head all over the place at the first bonny lass that crosses your path. Yes, Cupid has well and truly nabbed you with his twelve-bore.' I wondered if Mr Turner wasn't a little jealous. *How childish,* I thought. But what would Nana have said right now? *Don't lower yourself to his level*, and so I decided that I wouldn't.

'That's a good smell, Mr Turner,' I ventured. 'What is it?' Next to Mr Turner was a small contraption with smoke coming out of it, emanating a weird fishy-methylated-spirits smell. Mr Turner himself smelled of vinegar and old, damp clothes. Sid looked mournfully across at the smoker, drool falling helplessly from his jaws.

'Trout,' said Mr Turner, proudly. 'Caught them this afternoon. It was a canny day for fishing, in the end. I've gutted them all ready.'

'We've an excellent spot for fishing, Mr Turner,' said Norm. 'Haven't we? Just down from the sewerage pipe. Trout love it there. Especially when she blows. Two o'clock every afternoon.'

Mr Turner chuckled, displaying as many gaps as he had brown teeth. 'Ah yes, son. The fish aren't proud. Sit yourselves down then. Might as well have something to eat before we crack on.'

Norm and Mr Turner both disappeared into the shed, Norm returning with two small stools. I sat down, looking up at Norm who smiled and gave me one of his 'don't worry' winks. Sid began to whine softly, as the aroma of smoked fish reached unbearable levels. Presently, Mr Turner returned from the shed carrying two tin mugs of tea which he handed to Norm and me. He shuffled back in, cursing something undefined and returned again with tin plates full of buttered bread.

'Righty-ho,' he said, lifting the lid of the smoker. 'Let's see how we're doing in here. Shut it, dog, else I'll give you a kick right up your skinny backside.' His hands were black and grubby as he poked a long fork into the smoker and lifted up a trout for each plate, and a fourth one for the long-suffering Sid.

'Tucken Sie in, as they say in Germany,' he said, with a frightful grin, slapping the trout in between slices of bread then biting voraciously into the sandwich. 'Didn't have time to get any more. What are the rest of your lot doing for food tonight, boy?'

'Our Elsie is doing chip butties for everyone later on,' said Norm, fiddling with Sid's ear, as the dog watched him silently with its mournful eyes.

'Mam and dad out?'

'Yes, they'll be out,' said Norm, frowning, 'as the day's got a "Y" in it.'

'Ha!' said Mr Turner. 'And Mr Shaw? Been in any bother with him recently?'

'No, not this week. We've cycled past him a couple of times and he looks like he's just seen the Devil when he sees me.'

'If he comes near Sid he'll get to know what the Devil looks like when I come after him with my .22, the swine,' warned Mr Turner, wiping his bread in the melting butter and juices on his place.

I looked at them quizzically. 'What do you mean?' I said.

Norm explained that they believed Mr Shaw had poisoned Mr Turner's old dog, though he had no proof of it. One day, Bentley, a poor, hapless whippet was quite well and catching rabbits on the Duke's land, the next he was flat and stiff as a pit prop out in the back garden. Poisoned meat was suspected, but no proof was ever found.

I forced myself to tuck in, too, knowing instinctively that my relationship with Mr Turner was at a delicate stage. 'Very nice,' I said, trying not to think about trout swimming delightedly – if indeed trout are capable of such emotions – in a load of effluent and finding it just a little hard to make myself swallow.

We sat there eating and drinking our tea in a comfortable silence, watching a group of cabbage-white butterflies fluttering around a buddleia shrub to the right of the shed.

'Delicious,' said Norm, presently, wiping his mouth on his sleeve. 'Thank you very much, sire. That hit the spot.'

'Yes, thanks very much, Mr Turner,' I added, genuinely. The fish had been surprisingly good – a lovely pink flesh, no scales and a slightly sweet, smoky taste. What a mix of traits this man was. I couldn't work him out at all. Tall and imposing, a giant of a man, with huge hands, a wide face, and a big fisherman's beard. But just the right side of the fence when it came to the man-versus-tramp divide. Not so filthy that you wouldn't buy a posy of flowers for your wife from him, but then again filthy enough that you wouldn't want him across your doorstep. At some point in his life, his speech had turned into a low, menacing growl, which ostensibly held nothing fearful, and actually quite a lot of humanity.

'Right then, Romeo and Juliet – what have I got for you to be doing now?' Mr Turner put down his plate and took a long, last swig of tea, after which he let out a raucous and satisfied burp which was, in my opinion, more than a little gratuitous in length. Some starlings up in the apple tree flew off, squawking with fright.

'You can start by washing up. I've cleaned the tub out, ready. You could carry out an operation in that tub, it's that clean. Then I need *you,*' he said, pointing at me, 'to pick off all the apples and pears – Norman will find you some tubs – while *you,* son, go back and set the traps. And you better watch out with your head all doolally and all. I'll remind you that you cannot grow any limbs back that you may lose as part of this exercise. He's told you, has he, that we've only a few weeks to make our money on the otters? Don't want any of the young ones, you see. Quite a precise art, this is. You gotta respect the animals.' Then he stood up, cursing, and began to shake his left foot around. 'Damned foot's gone to sleep again,' he growled, leaning on his stick.

'Oh, and before I forget – you'll need to prune back the trees after you've done the picking. If you don't prune them enough,' he continued, to me, 'then next summer the sun can't get at them properly. Get all brown and undersized. You won't get all that done today so you'll have to come back. But I'll be watching to see how fast you work. This isn't a charity and I can't carry folk that won't pull their weight round here. Fluttering your eyelashes won't work on me. And Norman – make sure you get that fruit all sold at the weekend. Probably down at the railway station will be the best place, d'you think? Catch the fishermen on their way out in the morning and coming back at the end of the day. You can do the bottles after.'

'Yes, sir', said Norm, with a mock salute, at which point Mr Turner growled a horrible oath then limped back into his house, leaning heavily on his stick, and with Sid at his heels. We watched him go, then Norm stretched out and yawned loudly.

'I do believe you are on your way to passing your probation, young lady,' he said, grinning.

'Er, thanks, I think?'

He pulled his stool towards me and, thrillingly, put his bony arm around me. We didn't smell too great, to be fair. Olfactory memories of the morning's activities lingered over us like, well, an eviscerated otter. I didn't care, though. The block of happiness in my chest suddenly bloomed into an overripe tomato, ready to burst.

'Do you know something?' said Norm, turning my face towards his. His eyes were a deep blue, almost grey, and his dark hair hung down from his cap. 'This afternoon, in fact *right this very second,* we're as both happy as we've ever been. What else is there in life, Nancy? You, me and terrestrial plenty.' I looked at him intently, not knowing what to say. 'And you know what else, Nance? We will never live normal lives, you and I,' he said, and I felt his breath on my face. 'Our lives are going to be an adventure. How many people round here can say that? We're going to have such a time together. Our lives will be whatever we want them to be.'

I replay my memory of that moment often, Norman. I hold it away from me and cover the edges in sepia, for it is tinged with a fragile nostalgia that I fear would break if I bring it too close, or hold it too tight. In the end, my friend was only right on a couple of points. That was the thing about him: sometimes there was just no filter. An emotion popped into his head, he would share it with you. But the sentiment was beautiful and accurate – I didn't have a clue why this garden, next to this river, with these people and this silent dog and crazy jackdaw should make it so. It just was.

A window back at the house opened. 'You can stop those bloody shenanigans right now on my land, you pair of wastrels. Get on and get some bloody work done now else I'll find someone else to do it!' Then the window slammed shut.

***

The days and weeks rolled on that autumn. My learning curve was huge; I went with Norm to Barring Tye before school most mornings and back again after school. Norm had found me an old bike that one of his dad's friends had given to him for sixpence. It was meant for an adult man, something that brought its own challenges in terms of riding it, but I was tall and Norm sawed off the bar between seat and handlebar to make it more suitable. In any case, it was a huge improvement versus the uncomfortable baccas of the early weeks.

We each earned two shillings a day on Saturdays and Sundays, but usually just thruppence on weekdays. In addition, Norm had, as promised, successfully negotiated an increase in the amount he was getting for the pelts, and gave me a cut of two crowns per pelt. I felt this was reasonable enough, given that I left the really horrible part to him and he continued to do all the negotiation with the furrier. Each bottle we collected earned Mr Turner one penny; we never saw any of this money because we did the bottles at the weekends and were simply paid for the whole day. We got paid after school on Fridays, just like the miners of Oslington.

Not all our work was regulated by Mr Turner. I soon realised that Norm had many other means of making money and he pretty much used Mr Turner's shed as his own workshop to facilitate this. Pubs wanted a steady supply of pheasants, which could net us a crown for each bird. The butcher was also keen on rabbits – though he would not take anything with shot in it – and pheasants. Norm also had a tacit agreement with several families to bring them rabbits. After he had killed them, he would make a slit in one of their legs, thread the other leg through, then hang the dead rabbit on the family's back door like some gruesome mafia warning. Money would make its way to him silently via the most surprising means: little children in the playground squeezing thruppence at him from their chubby little fingers, women passing him on the street and depositing payment via a handshake. Not a word was ever uttered.

As part of a process of assimilation into this other world that Norm inhabited, and throughout autumn and winter, I learned how to trap pheasants. Sitting on stools in Archie Turner's shed at the long table, we took sheets of paper which we then painted with flour, water, sulphur and cayenne pepper. These were made into finger sized rolls and left to dry next to a paraffin lamp. After dark, we headed off to the Duke's land. I soon learned that our friend the colliery manager, Mr Shaw, owned the hunting and shooting rights to this land, and had gamekeepers patrolling the area so we had to be careful. This also explained the festering animosity between the colliery manager and Norm.

When we got to the trees where the pheasants were roosting, Norm would tie one of the paper rolls onto the end of a fishing rod, set it alight and let it smoulder. It emitted a curious blue-yellow glow, and of course a pungent sulphurous smell. We woke the pheasants up – a dangerous endeavour in itself with gamekeepers on the prowl – by stamping our feet and coughing. We then lifted the fishing rod up to the trees where the birds were roosting and held the smoking compound under the pheasants' chins. Sure enough, the birds duly passed out and fell with a thud to the ground. Norm then gave their necks a sharp twist, killing them instantly. It was genius, and it made us a lot of money.

Mr Shaw knew what was going on, of that I have no doubt. Occasionally we passed him in the street as we were cycling along. As Norm had already indicated to Archie and me, Mr Shaw's eyes narrowed when he saw Norm, and he sometimes froze to the spot as if he were looking at a ghost. As well as having had a hand in the murder of Bentley, Norm also suspected Mr Shaw of negative intervention over his grammar school entrance exam debacle. Norm said he was simply told to put the papers out for the others. There was no question of him ever sitting it, even though he was leagues above the other boys in his class and he was often called upon to help others with their work. No letter was ever sent to his parents asking whether they wanted him to be considered.

'How could that be allowed?' I asked.

'Miss Shaw was my teacher – you know? That bastard's dried-up mangy old sister. And the other Miss Shaw was a dinner lady. Remember her? With the white crusty bits on her eyelashes?'

I nodded in nauseous assent.

'They were all in on it together. They hated me. Miss Shaw, the teacher, kept on giving me the cane when I'd done nothing wrong. And her sister gave me smaller portions than everyone else at dinnertime. When I asked her for more she said to me "be quiet you'll get what you're given." I said to her, "you'll regret that." Got the cane for that, too, but I meant it.'

On Saturday afternoons in between our work we spent our time rummaging around second-hand clothes sales held by the Women's Institute or the church. I acquired a large poacher's jacket with enormous 'hare pockets' as Norm described them, which did the trick right enough – we lined them with waxed paper and then I was able to carry rabbits in the pockets within the jacket. I had also acquired a cap, and tucked my hair up into it and stuck a few strands out of the front. I bought some men's trousers, braces, white shirt and Land Army girls' boots. Dressing up was also the most enormous fun, with Norm sometimes bent double laughing at me in my baggy male attire, and making the most atrocious jokes about it all. One day, coming back through town together, I pulled Norm into a barber's shop and insisted they cut my hair like a boy's. The barber, a small man with a long-suffering look on his face, was not keen. He shook his head and made a few comments about what was the world coming to … but in the end he gave in and cut it all off.

This completed the boyish look, my hair sticking up all over the place with a thin, urchin face peering out below it. I was delighted, put my cap back on and headed out into the world to share a cigarette with Norm and show off my transformation. To anyone looking on, we looked like two lanky lads out for a stroll. Many times in the high street I walked past my grandparents or Mrs Pearce or Miss Trott without them ever realising who I was.

I also learned how to fish, that autumn, though I was not a natural fisherman, and hated all the waiting around. Norm even made me my own fishing rod from an old tank aerial, reel, thread, a safety pin and wire. We got fishing hooks from the garage, which we kept in our own tobacco tins. For trout fishing, we dug up large lobworms from Archie's garden and carried them in a bucket down to the water's edge. If we were upriver a bit, catching roach, we made little balls of dough and aniseed. The roach went absolutely mad for those, nudging the line almost as soon as we dropped it in. We roamed for miles, covering marshes and fields and woodland, up through bracken-covered paths to find the sites where the effluent was released, or to our other productive spot down by the weir. Norm showed me how to cast in front of the trout, and then made me count to fifty after the first bite before reeling in the fish: 'The trout has to swallow the worm completely,' he said. Once we had landed it, he would hit it on the head and then on to the next. We didn't earn a lot of money for the fish, but they certainly kept the Mitford household fed a few times a week.

I explained my absences to my grandparents in a way which contained a few sediments of truth. I told them I was working on a farm up in Barring Tye earning good money and I proudly offered them some towards my keep and grammar school fees. This was refused with some vigour. They would not take a penny off me but told me to keep it for the future: 'It's always good to have some spare, as you never know what the future might bring,' they said.

But my grandparents seemed to have become old and tired overnight. Nana and Mrs Pearce had started going to the bingo a couple of evenings a week; this was Nana's treat, as Mrs Pearce didn't have a bean to her name. But it also provided a distraction. Grandad's cough was worryingly persistent and, perhaps sensing trouble, he seemed more determined than ever to enjoy himself and often took refuge up at the institute in the evenings, still smoking his roll-ups and playing cards or billiards or bagatelle with the other miners. In any case, they seemed confused as to whether I was at the farm or up at the library, and after a while simply stopped asking. I moved about freely, day and night, without any kind of rigorous questioning from them.

Grandad had begun to cut back on his performances and I felt it was only a matter of time before these stopped altogether. Then they would need to accept help from me. Having money was beautiful, I decided, without guile.

The other thing I learned that autumn was the Art of Torment. Norm kept on returning to the notion he had that Mr Shaw and his sisters had it in for him, and so he devised a cruel but thrilling and hilarious – or so I unthinkingly thought at the time – method of drip-drip torment that was devised to have devastating effects. It was simple, when I came to think about it. The daily hour of torment we inflicted on those siblings took place right at the end of the day – after we'd set the traps, and caught, plucked, trussed and delivered the pheasants, and after everything else had taken place and we were on our way home. Their old stone house was on the outskirts of Oslington, with the main road running in front of it and a dense copse of bushes and trees on the other side. We would take our place in those bushes, then Norm would sneak up and thread a safety pin and white button into the gap between the window and the frame. He would reel the thread right out to the other side of the road where I would lay waiting on my sack, and he would lay down next to me. Luckily there was no traffic to break the thread. By and by, Norm would start tapping gently at the thread, which caused a much greater tap-tapping of the button on the window. After a few minutes, one of the sisters or Mr Shaw would come out and look around, puzzled, shining their torches up and down the street in search of the source of the tapping. Then they would retreat inside. Norm was faithful to his process – he forced us to wait fifteen minutes each time, which would pass at a glacial pace with me yawning and moaning throughout – before he would start up the tapping again. The whole thing could be repeated several times. I often got bored, and cycled home by myself. Word got out that the place was haunted and, six months later, one of the sisters, who was by now suffering with her nerves, moved out and went to live with her uncle in Scotland.

***

By the end of October, we'd added another five otter pelts to the four I'd seen hanging in the shed during my first visit. I was surprised at how low the success rate was; I guess the success of my first-time trapping had increased my expectations unrealistically. In any case, old Archie – as Norm and I called Mr Turner behind his back – was not displeased with the productivity. One day when we were arriving after school, he limped down the garden to ask us, shyly enough, whether we'd like to come to dinner at his on the Friday night. Norm and I agreed, smiling with surprise, and giggled all the way home, imagining various dubious scenarios for the evening. We arrived as usual after school on the Friday and Norm teasingly asked old Archie what was for dinner.

'You're about to shoot it,' he growled in reply. I followed them down to the water's edge where Archie handed Norm a twelve-bore shotgun and pointed to a bevy of swans swimming gracefully down the river. 'You want that one there, see, the one with the dark feather in its tail. Nice and tender. Get it in the eye if you can.'

Norm looked at me somewhat furtively and with heavy eyes, like a solider faced with the dilemma of either shooting an enemy he does not want to kill, or being executed himself for being a conscientious objector. He stood up tall and took aim, catching the swan on the third attempt. Mr Turner immediately threw his grappling hook out into the river and snared the poor lifeless swan, pulling the body in to us as the others took flight, squawking loudly in despair. I was dismayed but arranged my face in a nonchalant way, a skill that I had been getting a lot of practise at that autumn.

'Better keep this between us,' he said, looking directly at me. 'Good god, I swear you look more like a boy every time I see you.' I had changed into a dress and combed my hair. Suddenly I felt cross that my efforts had gone unappreciated, feeling also that Mr Turner was giving me mixed signals. He now wanted me to work like a boy, but look like a girl.

'Norm, get her ready then put her on the spit – it's all laid out for you in the shed.'

'Can you bring us a corkscrew, please, Mr Turner?' said Norm, shakily. 'I need a drink.'

'All right, son,' said Mr Turner. 'I'll fetch you one from the house.'

By seven o'clock, the swan was plucked, trussed and roasting nicely over a long spit in the shed. Coals glowed and burned in a large tray underneath, steaming the shed windows and giving out an honest kind of heat. We'd placed a tray of salted potatoes, carrots and parsnips – which Norm and I had had to peel earlier – on the coals to roast. Drops of swan fat fell onto it from time to time. A wonderful smell of roast meat filled the shed, making our mouths water. Next to the spit was a large wooden bowl of naked dandelion leaves. Various tin accoutrements had been placed on the table ready for the evening – plates, mugs, cutlery, wonky little salt and pepper cellars. Norm and I were already feeling relaxed; my inaugural taste of alcohol had been a very pleasant glass of Mr Turner's parsnip wine. Norm and I had been drinking since five o'clock and I was now on my third glass of wine. It was becoming difficult to feel my legs. Everything was much funnier, I noticed. Even the way Norm was sitting down, spooning the swan's fat from the tray below back over itself, was hilarious.

Presently, Mr Turner appeared, with a fresh shirt, combed hair and a trimmed beard. We greeted him with cries and shouts that this was the best dinner party ever in the history of the world, and he chuckled, and said 'Madame, please bring me a glass of finest whisky.' While I was pouring the whisky, old Archie bent over and spat on the swan. 'I'm just checking whether it's ready,' he said, somewhat guiltily and as if by way of explanation.

This sent Norm and me into further conniptions, which by now were getting harder to control. Luckily, Norm made an unrelated joke, and we were both able to laugh freely, even though it was simply a decoy. Mr Turner seemed pleased too, and supped his whisky as happily as a gnarled old chap can do, occasionally telling us to 'pipe down', which only made us worse. He spat on the swan once more and announced that the meal was ready, and we all sat down to eat. Archie started telling tales in lurid detail about the courting couples he regularly saw on the far side of the riverbank, as he watched via binoculars from the dark stillness of the shed. Sometimes, he said, he shot at a spot nearby just for fun and to see them pull their clothes back on in a tearing hurry and zigzag away through the fields in terror. Norm and I continued to honk with laughter until tears started streaming down our faces.

The wine and whisky continued to flow, until two of everything started to appear.

'I need to go,' I said, suddenly, with a new-found homing instinct.

'Well, I'll be blowed,' roared Archie, 'if the Girl Guide is not as drunk as a skunk. You'd better take her home, son. Off you go, hinney, get home safe now.'

Norm nodded, and helped me to my feet. I crashed into a pail then stumbled out of the shed. Once outside, the cold night air hit me like an iron bar, sobering me up slightly. Mr Turner disappeared into the house and returned with a large glass of water.

'Thank you, sir,' I slurred. 'Thank you for a lovely evening.'

'Many thanks to you, sire,' said Norm, waving goodbye to Mr Turner and helping me to my bicycle.

Once we were back on the road, I tried to mount the bike, but my stomach suddenly convulsed in protest at the evening's activities and a wave of nausea washed over me. I let the bike fall away as I threw up vigorously into the gutter.

***

There are too many stories to tell from that first year, Norman, but I feel that this one is significant enough to need to be shared.

It was late afternoon one Saturday, and a beautiful marigold-coloured dusk was beginning to descend on the day. Norm and I were fishing down at the weir. It had been a good day; we'd caught several trout and a couple of roaches and we were deliberating packing up for the day and treating ourselves to a steak and onion pasty. Suddenly, a child emerged from a dense copse of juniper trees, breathless from running. I recognised him as the youngster from the fairground who'd stuffed his candyfloss into the mud.

'Well, hello there, Fred,' said Norm, standing up and setting his fishing rod down beside the buckets. 'What's up?'

But Fred, pink in the face and ginger curls sticking out wildly, was still unable to speak. He bent over, clutching his knees, panting.

'Take your time. Tell us what's the matter.'

'It's Mr Turner,' said Fred, finally, straightening up. 'He said to run to you as fast as I could. He said to tell you he's found a floater.'

Norm looked at me sharply. 'All right, Fred,' he said. 'You've done well. I'll tell Mr Turner what a fast runner you are. Did he give you some money?'

'Tuppence,' said Fred, his nostrils flaring proudly.

'Run back and tell Mr Turner we're on our way.'

Fred turned to leave. 'What's a floater, Norm?' he said, hesitantly.

'Never you mind, Fred. Just get yourself home and don't tell anyone about this, else we'll be back to collect that tuppence and give you a clip round the ear. Got it?'

'All right,' said Fred, disappointed, and jogged off less enthusiastically through the trees back towards Barring Tye.

I looked at Norm. His eyes shone with cruel intent, like a fox who has spied a rabbit. 'Get the things up, Nance,' he said. 'We're heading back to Mr Turner's right now.'

'Another one of your dubious enterprises?' I ventured, pulling out the line slowly from the water. I wondered if this was how people who had been married for hundreds of years felt.

'Do you want the money or not?' said Norm, crossly, reeling in his line. A plump, dead lobworm dangled from the end. 'Hurry up.'

We picked up our things and hastened down the mud path, back through the woods and bracken down to the village. It was impossible to run with a bucket full of water and fish, though, and our journey was laboured.

'What new joy awaits me?' I continued, irritably. 'Don't tell me. Mr Turner has done a shit so big that it won't flush away, and he needs to get even greater height on the water flow, so he needs me to sit on your shoulders and tip a bucket down?'

'Nope,' said Norm, chuckling, in spite of his frown. 'Not even close.'

'All right. Let's try again. The rumours about Mr Turner are true and he has murdered someone in his bath?'

'That's a little bit closer,' admitted Norm. 'But still quite far off. Mr Turner hasn't murdered anyone. That I know of, anyways.'

'There's a dead body in his bath?'

'No. I said it wasn't that close.'

By the time we got to the house, Norm was still being evasive – and openly enjoying this ridiculous power over me. I still didn't know what was in store. The paraffin lamp glimmered eerily through the windows of the shed, lighting our way through the reeds. Archie was standing by the table, the grappling hook and rope looped several times over his shoulder.

'You heard?' he said.

'Yes, we did. From Fred. You think he'll keep his mouth shut?'

'Yes, I do. I gave him the evil eye,' said Archie, showing us exactly how he'd done it. It was frightening enough, even in this vicarious context.

‘So, is someone going to tell me what’s going on?’ I said, sitting on the side of the bath.

‘Get off that bath!’ growled Archie, suddenly. ‘You’ll get germs all over it. All right, lass, here’s what’s occurring. We got ourselves a dead body from the river. Washed up into my garden. It happens a lot, doesn’t it, boy?’

‘Yes, Mr Turner. We’ve done three or four of these now, I should think? Do you know who this one is?’

‘No. Never seen him before. He’s completely black though, poor bugger. I would say, judging by the way he looks, that he’s been in there a good couple of weeks. I think he looks about forty or fifty in age. Dressed for fishing. Probably fell in up in Stanningfield – they always do. I don’t know why they always end up at my place. Must be something about the way the river curves round a bit past my garden, I think. Anyways, the thing is, if he washes up on private land then you don’t get paid owt. If he washes up on public land, you get ten shillings for reporting it to the polis. So, all in all, we gotta move him over to the other side of the bank.’

‘I see,’ I said, feeling tired all of a sudden. A feeling of dread and self-doubt bubbled up inside me. The appalling nature of some of the jobs I was having to do to earn money was approaching the awfulness of the default alternative – a life with Aunt Flo and her toenails.

‘Gotta wait till it’s dark,’ said Archie, wistfully. We looked out into the sky, which was now charcoal against a huge full moon that hung low and accusing in the sky. ‘She looks about right to me now, though. So, for the lassie’s benefit, here’s what we’re going to do.

You two are going to run to the other side of the river, the public side that is, with this grappling hook. You're going to hoy it back over here to me, I'm going to stick it into his clothes, then you two are going to pull him over and arrange him nice and natural like he just washed up there all by himself. Ted Bray over at the station gets funny if he thinks a body's been moved. The lassie is going to go to the station to report it.' He looked directly at me, unblinking. 'You can't mention knowing me or Norm. All right?'

'I do have a name, Mr Turner,' I said, growing bold. I was fed up of being referred to as the Girl Guide, or the lass or the lassie or girlo or whatever. 'Please use my name when you're talking to me.' Mr Turner looked so shocked at this that for once he said nothing.

'Nancy and me, we want three shillings each,' said Norm. 'That's fair enough, between friends.'

'Friends, my arse!' said Archie. 'You two would have the clothes I'm standing up in if you could.' I looked at Norm and thought I might burst out laughing; whatever you could say about our motives, stealing Archie's manky old clothes would not be on the list. The only way I would go anywhere near Mr Turner's rags would be if they'd been fumigated, burned to a cinder, and the ashes put in a Toby jug that had then been placed out of reach on a very tall shelf. 'But it doesn't look like I've got much choice. Help me move him down a bit first, though, he's a big bugger, this one. And he's washed right up onto my cabbages, the inconsiderate bastard.'

A giggle, unable to contain itself any longer, freed itself in exuberant fashion. Archie glared at me. 'Oh, that's nice, that is. Very respectful,' he said, shaking his head. 'Giggly girls – that's all I need. Why don't you both stop your bleating and come and give me a hand. He stinks, by the way. Probably want to wrap something round your nose and mouth.'

I can now recognise that there was a hint of hurt in Archie's voice. He was lonely. He wanted to believe we were his friends, and I honestly think in a weird way that's what we had become. I should have said as much, but I didn't. I was thirteen years old and, unfortunately, when Norm was around an irrepressible giggle was never more than a goofy joke, or even sometimes a glance, away. Even the very *thought* that this might be something we'd laugh at later, that Norm might mimic, could send me into paroxysms. But increasingly I have come to realise that an unwitting kind of pathos was seeping through the cracks in that grubby, grumpy veneer, as well as a kindness and humanity that, whatever the ethics of what we were doing, basically prevented a whole family from starving and gave me options for my future; sadly, I just couldn't see it at the time.

The corpse was a frightful, bloated, stiff mass and the stench was unspeakable. Under the moonlight he looked black, but when you shone the torch over him you soon noticed a kaleidoscope of colours, horrible shades of black, brown and green. The scarf round my mouth seemed to perform little more than an aesthetic function. Still in a sou'wester, the poor chap was lying on his back on the lower banks of the garden, cabbage leaves sticking out comically from underneath him – these made him look as if he had large, round ears and gave him the appearance of a giant mouse. Brown leaves and other debris from the river were strewn all over his blackened face and neck. Archie stood at the corpse's feet. He lifted them up and motioned to us to get the arms. Norm went over first and knelt down, cursing the smell. But then in a move borne of unspoken but joint stoicism we decided to just get on with it and placed ourselves either side of the man's shoulders. Norm pulled at an arm to try to lift his side up but, horrifically, the whole thing came away in his hand; the arm released with a terrible snapping noise, right out of its socket, and slid out of the jacket sleeve. Norm staggered backwards and fell onto the cabbages with a high-pitched shriek, still holding the renegade arm.

'Hell's bells,' growled Archie.

There was a horrified silence, then time slowed to a crawl and we were all busy thinking what to do next. Presently though, Norm sat up slowly and waved the blackened arm at us. 'Ello boys and girls,' he said, teeth clenched in a ventriloquist grin. I squealed and stepped away in horror, giggling, though I believe I was closer to hysteria by this point.

'Quit that, you two,' said Archie. 'Get him by the head.' So Norm jumped up again, leaving the arm in the cabbage patch, and lifted the corpse up by the head, and this time we were able to manoeuvre it down to the water's edge. Mr Turner stood with his foot placed possessively on it and lit a cigarette, his hands shaking.

'Let's go, Nancy,' said Norm. He handed me the grappling hook and a torch, and picked up the arm. We set off to the crossing point, a little footbridge a few hundred yards upstream. Norm seemed to think that the situation would be improved by some terrible, macabre jokes or by poking me with the arm at regular intervals. We wound our way to the other side of the bank, stumbling around with freezing feet and muddy legs, full of adrenalin. Once we had arrived at the point opposite Mr Turner's house, Norm whistled loudly and I flicked the torch on and off to show that we were ready.

'Hoy it over,' said Archie, with a shout that was trying to be a whisper.

It took about three or four attempts to throw the grappling hook to the other side of the river, but eventually it landed at a spot near Mr Turner. He opened the corpse's sou'wester and secured the hook underneath the dead man's waistcoat. Against the pull of the river, we jerked the poor chap over then laid him out on the bank away from the water's edge, careful not to tug at any limbs for purchase. Then Norm attempted to push his arm back up into the sleeve; an operation that was not as easy as it sounds. The shirt inside the sou'wester was wet and flat; it was difficult to see how to get the arm back in.

'Run and fetch the polis, Nancy,' said Norm, frowning, 'and I'll see if I can do something to get this damned arm back in.'

***

Ted Bray looked like a man who had seen a few things in his time, but even he was puzzled with this one. I walked him back to the spot where the corpse was laid out all relaxed like he had perhaps been sunbathing, his left arm unconvincingly inside the sou'wester but not inside the shirt, and therefore extending out a good few inches lower than the right.

'Hmmn,' said Ted Bray, stroking his impressive moustache. 'You were just passing by, you say?'

'Yes, I was apple picking but I got lost.'

'Where are the apples then?'

'I tripped over my bucket when I saw this poor man. I lost my bucket and all the apples; the whole lot tumbled into the river. My nana is going to kill me.'

'Hmmn,' said Ted Bray again. He walked round and round the corpse, shining his torch all over it. Presently, he noticed the arm length differential, and started to tug gently at the longer arm. 'Arghhh!' he shouted, as the arm came away in his hand. 'It wasn't even attached!'

'Must have been, sir,' I said, innocently. 'What other explanation could there be?'

'You're within a few yards of Archibald Turner's house, lass. Things don't happen by chance near him. You want to keep away from this place, don't come here again else next time someone'll be finding you here the same way.'

He fussed a while longer, measuring and lifting, and writing in his little notebook, making occasional sighing noises as if he wasn't convinced at all but *what could you do*?

'I'm cold, sir,' I said, truthfully. 'Please could I take my token and go?'

'How'd you know about that?' he snapped.

'Oh, everyone knows about that. My uncle got one for finding a body upstream in Stanningfield.'

And so, after more tedious deliberation, I got my token. Lies had flown out of me like honey pouring onto a bowl of Nana's porridge; I was impressed with my performance. The ten shillings was to be collected from the Post Office, and I remember swaggering up there the next day thinking that among the broken old faces (an image which I have subsequently recast in memory as a line of Orwellian proles) queuing for stamps, sending telegraphs and collecting their old-age pensions, I was almost certainly the only one queuing to be paid for finding and reporting a dead body with one arm already detached.

A few months later when we found another floater, I was mortified when Sergeant Bray introduced me to the whole station as the 'Angel of Death'. This time I was hauled in for questioning and kept in the station for several hours. After that, feeling thoroughly rattled by the experience, I refused to be the one to report any bodies we found.

From time to time, Norman, Sarah has asked me whether I think this event has caused me any lasting psychological trauma but to be frank, at the time, the body registered as a human being no more than a sack of potatoes might. I upgraded my bicycle with that money, if my memory serves me right.

***

Autumn turned into winter, and then into spring and Norm and I both turned fourteen. By now, sadly, I could only fit one bum-cheek on my bedroom window ledge, which kind of spoiled the whole ambience of the experience. But I still liked to look out on the pit and the winding shafts, especially at night when they were unmoving and bathed in pockets of streetlight. The little tobacco tin under my bed contained a princely sum of nearly five pounds. It was hard-earned, and I was immensely proud of it. If I could double it, that would mean a whole year of grammar school fees paid.

We stopped fishing in March for the breeding season, and with otters and pheasants no longer in season we concentrated on rabbits. But with Norm set to move in with his cousin over at North Shields in September to take up a seven-year-long placement as an apprentice electrician at the shipyards, an aura of finality hung over us – a sort of *fin de siècle* mood, which was both liberating and sad at the same time. He assured me he would be back every weekend to see me, and praised my new-found skills, saying that I would be able to continue hunting and trapping now even if he wasn't around.

The unsolved puzzle of where I was going to live at sixteen hung over us, too, like a dark cloud. Lodging with Miss Trott had been discounted; other options seemed evasive. But one day Norm took me to one side and held my hands, his blue-grey eyes darker than usual, and said, 'Nancy, maybe we could get married and then you can move in with me? We can ask if you can transfer to a grammar school over in North Shields. We'll have to stay there till we're both twenty-one. I will have finished my apprenticeship and you will have finished your teacher training by that time. Then we can go to London together, if you like, if you promise me that afterwards we can go and see the rest of the world.'

As ever, Norm was the one to think around and over the problem, and not just stand like a lemon at the metal bars at the front of it. Married at sixteen, though? We'd both need the permission of our parents, or in my case my grandparents, who were officially my guardians. A future for me where I was officially affiliated to the Mitfords … the snob in me recoiled at the thought, but I knew my heart would be with Norm forever. I felt conflicted; this was not quite the start I had been hoping for, but also possibly the beginning of another adventure – my future with Norm, who'd become as much a part of my being as anyone could.

Leaning forwards on my window ledge, I traced the layers of sooty dust with my fingertips, writing my name, and then following that with the words: 'Tell me what to do.' But the night was still, and held the answers in the darkness in a place I could not reach.

Chapter 4

Two weeks before my fifteenth birthday we received a telegram from Nana's niece. We all called her Cousin June, even though she was probably Nana's great-niece and some sort of relation to Aunt Flo. I had never met her but I had heard snippets about her over the years. I wasn't quite sure of her exact relationship to Nana or where this left me in the pecking order. Anyway, the telegram told of an impending visit and gave a date of my birthday, which was on a Saturday.

I spent much of the intervening time staring excitedly at the telegram, which was as foreign as a distant planet. I loved its worldliness, its officiousness, loved the fact that it had travelled all the way from London. It took on a higher state, became a hallowed parchment to be stroked and touched and smelled. I took it to bed with me, slept with it under my pillow and clutched it to me when I woke up in the mornings.

I begged Nana to tell me what she could about Cousin June, but all I got was that she was a flibbertigibbet who had married her way into what Nana called 'high society' – she'd met her husband, Richard, at a Christian camp out at Holy Island when she was fifteen – and had not given her home so much as a second glance when she had shut the door and run off to get married all those years ago. This intrigued me even more.

'How old is she?' I asked.

‘Let me see,’ said Nana. ‘She’ll be about twenty-five, I suppose.’

‘What does she do in London?’

‘She’s a mannequin,’ was Nana’s ambiguous reply. I imagined Cousin June standing statue-still in a shop window for hours. I wondered if I had misheard and asked for clarification.

‘She parades clothes on the catwalk,’ said Nana, crossly. ‘I think I heard she’s sometimes in the magazines. Half-naked no doubt. With paint all over her face.’ Ha, this was going to be an interesting encounter.

I encouraged Nana to tidy the house and do some baking in preparation for our illustrious big-city relatives, but all I got in return was a dismissive shrug. So I set about blitzing the house myself. I must have dusted up a good hundred flies from various corners of the house. I tidied the backyard and made sure that we had plenty of water. I picked daffodils from nearby fields to make a pretty arrangement in an old milk bottle, and even baked a cake for the occasion. Nana, as if to prove the point that she wasn’t going to be impressed by the likes of Cousin June, went out of her way to linger in town or at the bingo, uninterested in the condition of the house or my efforts to smarten the place up.

As the deadline drew nearer, the butterflies in my stomach increased. June and her husband, Richard, were coming from London by motor car, staying overnight in Darlington, and were due to arrive on Saturday morning. They would be staying at the Oslington Hotel in town. I suggested afternoon tea at our house followed by a walk, and perhaps a trip to the seaside on the Sunday.

Aunt Flo was invited too, which was a worrying piece of news. I had developed an almost pathological fear of them embarrassing me in front of my sophisticated, worldly cousin and her aristocratic husband.

As the morning of the big day arrived, Nana announced that she was off to wash her hair and doll herself up. She disappeared into the scullery and emerged half an hour later with alarmingly large hair, a most splendid bouffant that had the shape of a mature oak tree in the height of summer. It appeared to have the consistency of wire wool and had also turned completely white. Nana admired herself in the hallway mirror, announcing proudly that she had made an excellent discovery: not only was Persil amazing at getting clothes clean, it also had a very chic effect on hair. My embarrassment quota was reaching its limits and we hadn't even made it to mid afternoon.

'Hold up, it's Marie Antoinette,' said Grandad, roaring with laughter from his armchair.

Nana strode over to the window, ignoring him. 'The tankey's in, Bill,' she said, peering out through the netting. 'Go and give Aunt Flo a hand down the street will you.'

'So soon,' said Grandad, ruefully.

I put on my shoes and coat and left to collect our visitors.

***

June and her husband were waiting for me in the front parlour of the hotel. They smiled and jumped up when I walked in, both giving me huge hugs. Richard was a pleasant-looking man with auburn hair and freckles. He wore a wide, double-breasted suit. June was elegant and attractive but, like me, boyishly thin. Her hair was peroxide blonde and cut short like a boy's, and was worn swept over to one side. It had a sheen to it that reminded me of Grandad's Brylcreem. Her dress was like nothing I'd ever seen before: a pale mauve colour, in what I later learned was crêpe de Chine, it was belted at the waist and finished just below the knees to reveal long, slim legs in silky stockings. She wore pearl earrings which matched her long pearl necklace. Her smile was enough to tell me she was one of those lucky people who was born grounded, happy within themselves, their personality like a magnet to others. And in that split-second first impression I felt a rush of infatuation, and wished I could be more like her. My personality was like a deadweight in comparison.

'Nancy! I'm so happy to meet you finally,' she said, holding my shoulders and looking me up and down. 'Quite the Louise Brooks, aren't you? Wow, Richard, I told you I was from a good-looking family,' she added with a wink. She leaned over and kissed me on both cheeks in the European style, her pearls dangling across my waist. I could smell her perfume, which I later learned was Chanel N°5. 'Gorgeous,' she added, laughing. In spite of the compliment, I felt the drabness of my clothing.

Richard laughed, too. 'I hear it's your birthday today,' he said, shaking my hand. 'Many happy returns.'

'We brought you a little present.'

I sat down and peeled off the shiny wrapping paper. It was a silver jewellery box, with a pair of pearl earrings inside it. I was overwhelmed.

'Thank you so much,' I said, shyly, feeling my cheeks burn.

'Well, shall we go and meet everyone else?'

June pulled on her cloche hat and fur coat and I led them back to the house, feeling more and more despondent with every step.

***

What joys awaited our London guests? Behold the scene: the waiting tea party, featuring Aunt Flo as Queen Bee, Al Jolson's Dad and Marie Antoinette. The table had been set for tea by this weird teenage creature: she had somehow cobbled together a Victoria sponge, a Battenberg cake, some sausage rolls cut into smaller pieces, and earlier she had spread butter and jam over scones she had bought from the baker's. The gods of fat and sugar were smiling down approvingly on the scene and were happy to see her lowly but heartfelt homage. Next to the food were plates, cups and a teapot, all borrowed from the neighbours.

'It's so lovely to see you all again,' said June, with a breezy smile as they entered the front room. 'Here, I bought you some presents.'

'Aye,' said Grandad, nodding. No one got up, in fact Grandad didn't even put his paper down. His all-encompassing statement of welcome and appreciation over, he hid behind his paper and left the women to it.

Scarcely had our visitors taken off their coats and sat down, when Aunt Flo began to hold court like the true philosopher she was. Ah, yes. What glorious maxims, bathed in the misty light of octogenarian wisdom, spilled forth that afternoon? What gems of missing wisdom had Aristotle and Plato and Socrates turning in their graves, clicking their fingers, slapping their heads and shouting, 'Darn it! Why didn't I think of that?' What was said that had Moses thinking he must've dropped another slab of gems on his way back down from Mount Sinai?

Hark, the tea and cake were served, and the elderly oracle and her minion asked not one single question of our visitors but instead held court on their own topics, giving us life-changing advice such as the need to keep one's feet warm at all times, because if your feet are warm, all of you will be warm. More philosophy filled the airwaves during those precious inter-Battenburg moments. This time an insight about ageing: lo, cried the doily-clad preacher, take heed, for growing old is a curse and what does not go south will surely get hairy – Richard nearly choked on his sausage roll at this point. But what is this? Halt, I hear you cry. No more, for the history books will already need to be rewritten to take into account such new revelations. Linger a second longer, I beseech you, for the wise old owls had yet more in their arsenal. And in your haste, let's not forget: that it's nice to be nice; if you go to Edinburgh you will get to see the scotchie kilties on parade; and did you know that a visitor to the Oslington Hotel once asked for wine! And not just any wine either, it had to be the right colour! La-di-da. Maybe they were French? – sometimes true philosophy allows itself a humorous moment. I know, sire, you have hardly caught your breath or laid down your quill but still they come: you canna whack a bit o'liver and onions now and again, did you also know that men have 'needs', and, playing Aristotle to Aunt Flo's Plato, last but not least we had Marie Antoinette chip in to tell us that Persil is an under-valued domestic resource, with multiple hitherto undiscovered applications, all of which would be revealed to the world in next month's colliery magazine.

Presently, our visitors did manage to get a word in edgeways, but even then they were polite enough to ask questions about us and not talk about themselves. The room began to swirl around me and after a while I felt strangely detached from it all.

'Aunt Ada, you used to be a typist for the civil service, didn't you?' said June.

This was news to me.

'That's right pet. Loved that job. Such great fun there with all the other girls. God, we had some laughs. And nice having my own money, too. I ended up more than a typist in the end, you know, I got promoted and I was actually the one writing government documents. But I had to give it up when I got married.'

'What a shame, Ada. I remember you talking about your job when I was little. You loved it, didn't you. Why did you have to give it up?'

'Well, they call it the "marriage bar", pet. Married women aren't allowed to work. Some girls I know kept quiet when they got married so they could keep on working. Unfortunately, everybody knew in my case. Just my luck.'

I felt my ears start to burn. 'Does that law apply if you're a teacher?' I asked.

'Oh, yes – think about it, Nancy. Are any of your teachers Mrs not Miss?'

I considered this for a minute. 'No,' I admitted.

'Well, that's because none of them are married.'

'So if I want to become a teacher, I can't get married?'

'Hinney, I thought you knew. I thought you wanted to be a career woman. D'you know, she's *such* a brainbox, June and Richard. Honestly. Bright as a button, that one. Got into grammar school as easy as anything. Too clever for a life like this, to be truthful. Becoming a teacher really is the one thing William and I hope for her,' said Nana, her voice full of emotion. 'That's what her mother would have wanted for her. And our Neville.'

'*That* daft bugger,' said Grandad, peering over the top of his newspaper.

We all fell silent, and Cousin June took hold of Nana's hand.

'But you work, don't you June? Why doesn't the marriage bar apply to you?' I said, the temperature of my ears verged on volcanic levels.

'That's a good question. Different rules in London, I think,' said June with a nervous laugh. 'No one has ever mentioned that to me, I must admit. Have you heard of it, Richard?'

'No, definitely not. It's a new one on me.'

'Must be different if you're a mannequin,' said Nana.

'I'm not actually a model, Ada. I just get the models ready. Do their hair, their make-up and such. And all their clothes.'

'Oh, well, there you go. I had it wrong all these years.'

'The agency belongs to Richard's father. Richard managed the business with him but we've decided to give it up and do something completely different. That's one of the reasons we're here. Do you want to say it, Richard?'

He laughed. 'No point beating about the bush. Well, the news is that June and I have just bought a hotel in Whitby. We're moving away from London and we're going to run the place between us.'

'We got a bit fed up with the London life, to be honest,' said June, carefully, leaving the impression that there was probably a lot behind that statement that they would not be inclined to reveal to us.

'Good grief, that *is* a piece of news all right. What does your father think?' said Nana, turning to Richard. 'I can't imagine he's too happy about it.'

'I think he's getting used to it.'

'Well, you know what? At the end of the day it's up to you two. You've only got one life to live so why not,' said Nana, emphatically. 'Shy bairns get nowt. Good luck to you both, I say.'

'We'll have to pay them a visit, eh, Ada,' said Aunt Flo, rearranging her shawl. 'Go down for the weekend.'

'Aye, pet. And you two'll be getting yourselves a Yorkshire accent.'

By this point, Grandad had taken his teeth out, put them on the newspaper next to his armchair and fallen asleep. His only audible contribution to the afternoon had been four words and the loud gurgling of gastric juices as they reached the final furlong in preparing his digestive system for his weekly trip to the nettie for a painful bowel movement on Sunday.

It's great when you stop feeling embarrassed about things, and I moved to a new phase that afternoon: acceptance. Ah yes, acceptance. The younger brother of maturity. The disdain was still there, mind you, Norman. I'm not trying to imply that suddenly everything turned fluffy and rose-tinted. But the plans I had made lay dead on the floor with a stake through their heart. The marriage bar, a cruel law that was designed to keep us women in our place, even if that place was totally wrong for us, was the final *coup de grâce*. Emancipation? What a joke. Only if you're upper class, apparently. But there was no need for histrionics; the school in Hampstead, the boxing husband who looked like Norman Mitford, the interview with the *Daily Sketch* – it was simply over. I didn't want a future teaching if it couldn't be with Norm, and I didn't want to pick my future from the few unfulfilling local templates to just be Norm's wife.

'Shall we head out for a walk?' I said. It was almost a relief, in a way, to know how I stood. The struggle was over.

Our visitors nodded enthusiastically, and so we got our coats and headed out towards the rec.

***

The next day, Nana and I took a ride in Richard's motor car to the seaside. It was cool but sunny and breezy and I felt the occasional rush of salty moisture on my face as we drew closer to the shoreline. I felt refreshed after a deep, untroubled sleep. In fact, I felt happier than I had done for a long time. But a new hardness had grown in my heart, an unspoken rebellion that was spreading through my body. I felt duped. Society had gone to the trouble of educating me and preparing me for work, but the whole time she was waiting to hit me with that nasty sting in her tail. Marriage as an institution had never seemed less appealing. I was silently outraged. It's obviously a cliché but nevertheless it was still true: no one was going to tell *me* what to do.

We arrived at the seaside and began to walk along the long promenade. I strolled on ahead with Richard; June walked behind with Nana. I asked him all sorts of questions about the models, the agency and the photographers. It was fascinating – a picture of a life so different I could hardly comprehend that it was taking place in the same country as the one I also inhabited.

'Our photographer is a man called Dalglish. I'm sure he has a first name but that's what we all call him. He really is amazing, Nancy. You should see some of his work. But he needs to be, because he's really rather a pain in the arse in other ways.'

'Why's that?'

We stopped at an ice cream van and Richard treated us each to a cone of whipped ice cream topped with a chocolate stick and raspberry sauce – the sauce being a bit of a stretch for my anodyne taste buds. Nana and June sat on a bench on the promenade while Richard and I took off our shoes and wandered down to the water's edge.

'He insists on using all his own models. And … well, these people are a bit different to you and me, Nancy. Let's just say that working with them has put a strain on June, and on our marriage.

'What do you mean, "different"?'

'How do I explain? Well, basically, he and his crew don't conform to the rules the rest of society lives by. Dalglish … he makes his own rules up, so to speak. And everyone else follows them. They all live together in a large old stone tenement in Chelsea.

It's all tremendous fun, of course. We all belong to a private members' club, Club Gargoyle. Cocktails after work, dinner, and dancing to jazz music every night. The chap can be very charismatic,' he said, wistfully, and I wondered what he meant. Could Cousin June have had an affair with Mr Dalglish?

'It's been such a crazy, exciting few years. But June and I have outgrown that life. Ha,' he added, 'it's a good thing you don't live down there. Dalglish would have had you in front of the camera in a heartbeat.'

'Do you think I could be a model, Richard?'

'Oh, for sure.'

Suddenly, I had an idea. 'Will you talk to him about me? Dalglish, I mean. And show him my photo?'

He looked out to sea, contemplating this. We sat down at the water's edge and turned our faces up to the watery spring sun. Richard rolled the ends of his trousers up. The tide was heading out. The beach was busy. Next to us some children were excitedly building sandcastles and digging moats. 'I don't think so,' he said, at last. 'Your grandparents want you to become a teacher, don't they? And you are clearly a very clever girl. You've got yourself into grammar school, Nancy. That's a huge achievement. Don't waste those brains of yours on a vacuous career like modelling. My father, you know, he's very grounded in spite of the circles he moves in. He always says, you're not in the shop window forever. And that's true. Whereas you can spend your whole life teaching.'

I turned to face him. 'I've no intention of becoming a teacher any more. If you won't help me, I'll just run away,' I said, quietly. 'And then no one will know where I am.'

Richard looked at me, aghast. 'Take me with you,' I pleaded. 'There's nothing for me here. I hate this place. What's the point of any of it? Please, please just take me back to London with you. I'll live with you and June. I'll be your housekeeper. I'll go and see Dalglish and get some work off him.'

'I can't believe you are talking to me like this. You hardly know us. And you know we can't just take you with us, Nancy. We're only going back for a couple of weeks to pack our things and then we'll be gone, too. Look, I can try to put you in touch with him. I'll take some photos of you and show him and see what he says. You might be too young to go down there. I'm sorry I can't help more. I feel terrible now. I wish I had never said that you could become a model.'

'It's not your fault, Richard.'

'Nancy,' he said, frowning, 'please don't run away, all right?'

I looked at him for a long time, then headed back to the promenade. Nana and June were deep in conversation but I interrupted them with a smile, plonking myself right between them on the bench.

'Ladies,' I said, 'how often are we all together like this? Richard – you absolutely must take our photo!'

***

Richard was a good man. A good-natured man. I had put him in a very difficult position. He could have outed me and my intentions to my grandparents and to June, but I don't believe he told anyone about our conversation. Six weeks later I received a handwritten letter from Mr Dalglish. In informal tones, he told me that he had seen my photo and heard my story. He would love to work with me, he said, and gave me his address in Chelsea. He described me as an incredibly special person, possessing a liberty of spirit that not many people have. In closing, he added that if I wanted to join him in his 'ghetto away from societal repression', there would be a life there waiting for me.

Ha, I thought. A dreamy, romantic, quixotic letter but no clue as to how a fifteen-year-old girl whose possessions consisted of two dresses, an old bicycle, a school uniform with dubious panama hat and a jewellery box, and who had an excellent working knowledge of trout fishing, pheasant poaching and otter trapping but no knowledge of national transport systems, no knowledge of London and only five pounds to her name, was to achieve this.

Chapter 5

Grandad's impending retirement loomed over us like a dark cloud. He grew thin and was afflicted with lengthy coughing fits, and said he wasn't sure he could keep on working right up to the retirement date. Norm was true to his word, coming back every weekend to see me. He had started to pretty much live at ours during these visits, occupying the couch in the sitting room overnight. He went next door to give Elsie money for the children's food, but that was all. He could no longer stand it over there, he said. Five minutes was enough; he just couldn't bear the place, and seeing his parents and the way they went about things – or rather, didn't go about things – made him angry. Norm chatted animatedly about his job, and clearly loved everything about it. He talked about the inefficiencies in working practices he had spotted and how they could be improved. And he had the ear of the foreman, who had told him he would likely do very well if he continued like that.

I hadn't the heart to tell Norm that I'd gone cold on the idea of marriage, nor had I the heart to tell my grandparents that I no longer wanted to become a teacher. A solution would present itself, of that I was sure. For the moment, I had simply decided to plod on with a life that I had fallen out of love with.

One Sunday, Norm and I returned from Mr Turner's to find a heated argument taking place in our sitting room between my grandparents and Mrs Dobson, the Methodist Church Sunday school teacher. She was an attractive woman with delicate features and blonde hair set in a wave. She was wearing her Sunday best: a wide-brimmed hat, a patterned blouse, a mid-length black skirt, and patent strap shoes. I often saw her walking backwards and forwards between the chapel and her house – three visits every Sunday. She seemed embarrassed about her beauty, almost, as if it might detract from the seriousness of her Christian calling.

'So, let's get this straight,' said Nana, her face crimson. 'You're telling us we're both sinners?'

'Well, Mrs Thompson, it sounds harsh when you put it like that. What I said was you know that the Sabbath is the Lord's day. It's a day of rest. In Sunday school, for many years they didn't even let the children do writing on a Sunday as it was considered a secular art. I'm talking quite some time ago now, admittedly. However, I'm sure you'd agree that Sundays are a time for spiritual enlightenment. They should be spent in Christian reading and thinking. So …' Here, she paused and looked around her, perhaps checking the exits.

'Well, out with it, pet, we're all big and ugly enough to hear what you've come here to say,' said Nana, settling back into her chair and crossing her bootees.

'Mr Thompson has been spotted playing Pitch and Toss behind the pit heaps on Sundays. Not only is it immoral but I don't need to point out to you that it is also illegal.'

Pitch and Toss, Norman, was a simple gambling game using two pennies, the aim being to have both coins landing heads up. There was usually a lookout, a boy paid to alert the men to any polis or men of the cloth, who were liable to arrive at any time. It was indeed illegal, but that didn't stop the men playing it, and word had it that one or two of the local policemen were fond of an occasional bet themselves.

I felt a surge of anger at her. Grandad was clearly unwell; who knew how long he had left? If he wanted to spend his Sundays with his friends, tossing coins for a couple of pennies, who were she and her religion to judge?

'And you, Mrs Thompson,' our visitor continued, 'you seem to always put your washing out on a Sunday. This is at odds with what the Bible tells us about resting on the Sabbath. I'm sure you're aware of Moses' decree that the man who gathered sticks on the Sabbath should be stoned to death? Of course, we don't teach that any more, but it is still there for us to take heed of. Anyway, a few of us have noticed your Sunday activities,' she added, as if this lent credibility to the reprimand. 'You have the whole week to do your washing. Why must you always peg it out on a Sunday? It's almost as if you – I don't know – you're goading us in some way.'

'The last time I looked this was a free country,' said Nana, frowning. 'And anyways, I'm far too busy in the week doing other housework.' At this, Mrs Dobson looked around her and let out an involuntary laugh. Our house was not run quite as the proverbial tight ship but more along the lines of the ailing *Titanic*. I winced inwardly.

'And anyway, how dare you,' said Nana. 'This is your same God who sent our Neville head first down the mine, when he was a good lad who never did anyone any harm and loved our Vera dearly, and had a bairn on the way. And the same God who took my only daughter from me in childbirth, leaving our Nancy over there an orphan? He's no friend of this family, I can tell you that much.'

'God didn't send Neville down the mine and he didn't take your daughter either,' said Mrs Dobson.

'Well bugger me. This isn't making any sense. I thought he was all-powerful? Had he just taken his eye off the ball? Get your story straight,' said Nana, stoking the fire angrily. 'Do you understand it, Bill? When anything good happens, it's down to God, but when anything bad happens, it's nowt to do with 'im?'

Grandad shook his head. 'No, pet,' he said.

'We're all very, very sorry for your loss, Mrs Thompson. I cried for you and prayed for you both times when I heard the news. It's an unbelievable tragedy if it happens once, but to happen twice … well, I can't even begin to imagine how that might feel. And so close together, too. Minister Lewes gave you a special mention at both Sunday services when it happened, and asked us all to pray for you, even though you don't come to church. But that doesn't mean that forever more you can operate outside the laws of your community here. The point I am making, is that pegging your washing out on Sundays is a sin. It may not seem a very bad sin to you, but nevertheless it is one, and it upsets us, and we worry for you. If you came to the church on Sundays you might learn how to earn grace by confessing your sins and pledging to lead a Christian life, which will also earn you a place in heaven. And you might find comfort for all the suffering you've been through. The same goes for you, Mr Thompson.'

Grandad cleared his throat. 'Look around you,' he said, breathlessly. 'Are you honestly coming in here, telling me this house is a place of sin? The only crime round here is Ada's cooking. Mind you, pet,' he continued, looking at Nana, 'I will say that liver and onions you did for me the other day needs its own spot in the confessional. Ya bugs, it repeated on me for at least three days. The lads wouldn't come near me down the pit.' They laughed loudly, and Grandad began to cough. Mrs Dobson blushed and looked as if she would rather be hewing coal than standing in our sitting room. I could see my grandparents were entering a dangerous phase where they were not only angry, but also enjoying themselves.

'You leave my cooking out of it, Bill,' said Nana. 'I don't see any of the Ten Commandments being broken in here. There's nowt about cooking or pegging out washing in them as far as I know.'

Norm chuckled lustily at this, while I stood there, mortified.

'There's no chastising your neighbour's wife going on in *this* house,' continued Nana. 'No, I think you'll find that very few of the top ten have been broken here, pet. *Unlike some houses I could mention.*' She stood up and picked up a large piece of wood, throwing it onto the fire and stoking it vigorously.

'I think you mean coveting,' said Mrs Dobson, furiously. 'Any anyway, what do you mean by that?' I could see she was blushing and wondered what it was they were really talking about.

'For the moment, I have forgotten,' said Nana. 'But if I continue to suffer this *religious persecution*, I think I will suddenly start to remember again.'

The room fell into an uncomfortable silence, with everyone looking past each other and Grandad clearing his throat.

Eventually, Nana, who could not stand silences, decided to press on. 'Obviously,' she said, 'you know that we live next door to the Mitfords.'

'*Them* buggers,' said Grandad, shaking his head and laying his newspaper down. 'Present company excepted, that is,' he added, hastily, looking at Norm.

'Say what you like,' said Norm with a shrug. 'Doesn't bother me.'

'Them lot practise jumping out of the window on Sundays, the little'uns that is. While their parents are in the club. They leap out of the top window, land on the nettie, then jump off the nettie to the ground, do you mind. There's always loads of screaming and noise. Sometimes they add a little star jump, or maybe a turn, to spice things up even further. What does God have to say about jumping out of a window on a Sunday?'

'Well,' said Mrs Dobson, wringing her hands with the anxiety of someone who is not being taken as seriously as she would like, 'that's not something I've ever come across directly. But I would think that's also a sin. I can't imagine God would frown at writing in Sunday schools but condone jumping out of windows. I'm not sure what it's got to do with your washing, though. Can we stick to the point please?'

'All right,' said Nana. 'Let's say I stop pegging my washing out on Sundays and start going to chapel. Let's say I earn God's grace. Let's say my spot in heaven is booked, my ticket on the tankey to the sky is all paid up.' Grandad, over in his armchair, let out a raucous chuckle and reached over for a cigarette. 'And then, after ten years, I suddenly peg my washing out again one Sunday. Maybe I just forgot. Am I going to hell? Or will God let me off for one silly little mistake?'

'Well that *is* a ridiculous question,' said Mrs Dobson, firmly. 'I didn't come here to argue the nuances of God's grace with you.'

'But that's exactly what you're doing, pet. The truth is that you can't answer it, can you? Because,' said Nana, standing up and walking over to the anguished lady, 'it's all-a-load-of-tripe,' she said, poking her in the chest one word at a time. We all took a deep breath; Nana shrugged as if to indicate there was nothing more to say.

Mrs Dobson shook her head. 'You're entitled to your opinion, Mrs Thompson, but the way I see it, we're all answerable to Him at some point,' she said, after a pause, gesturing upwards. 'Anyway, I've said what I came to say, so I wish you a pleasant afternoon and hope that one day you do find God's grace. And as I said,' she added, piously, 'our church welcomes sinners with open arms. Goodbye.'

There was a silence of maybe a few seconds, and then Nana and Grandad looked at each other, shaking their heads. Mrs Dobson left and Nana reiterated her statement that they could all kiss her arse. I sighed, and went into the kitchen to make a pot of tea.

'Sinners, be blowed. I've heard it all now,' said Grandad, as I returned with the tea. '"Chastising your neighbour's wife." He, he. Wait till I tell the lads the morra.'

But Nana was indignant. 'Make no mistake. Religious persecution, that's what you just saw here.' She pulled out her sketch pad and started to look for pencils. 'Fancy a crumpet, you two?'

'*Colliery Magazine* headline: "Oslington Attacked by Marauding Crusader Disguised as Attractive Middle-Aged Woman,"' said Norm, indicating the words with his fingertips.

'Ee, stop it,' said Nana, laughing. The clock on the sideboard struck five. 'Good grief, is that the time? Norm, don't you need to be heading back now? Your train's in five minutes. You'd better get a shifty on, son.'

***

Although my teenage years were characterised by what you might call a blunderbuss approach to life, in the end the solution came to me. Maybe there is sometimes an argument to just let go of your fears and wait for opportunities to come your way, rather than forcing things. In any case, I could hardly believe my luck.

It was a Thursday and I was on my way to the institute library after school to get ready for the evening session. But I had to go the long way round and drop off a bag of coal at the Pearce's on my way. I walked slowly, enjoying being outside and away from the constant, exhausting natter of our house.

At some point, I walked past the Methodist chapel and paused a minute to rest on a low brick wall to catch my breath; the bag of coal was heavy and my arms felt like they'd been placed on a medieval torture rack. I looked up at the church noticeboard and a piece of paper pinned to it inside caught my eye. I noticed the word 'London' and suddenly I was on my feet, peering closely at the board like a hawk circling a dormouse.

'London (Hampstead) family seeks Nanny/Housekeeper for family of four. Mr and Mrs Matthew Clayton-Reid and their children Bella, 3, and Paul, a baby. Must be a Christian and of a God-fearing family. Please speak to Minister Lewes for further information.'

Ha hah, I thought delightedly. There it was – the stepping stone I needed to get myself to London. How easy, after all that.

And so it started, Norman – my charm offensive began. People have been lying about their religious beliefs for as long as religions have existed: sometimes to save their own skin, sometimes for personal advancement and sometimes because their holy book tells them that lying, if it happens to promulgate their own religion, is both acceptable and encouraged theologically.

The minister's daughter was in my class, a shapeless and dull girl called Patricia, with jam-jar glasses and a serious countenance. I took a very deep breath, put a smile on my face and made my way over to speak to her at break time. It wasn't long before I met the minister and his earnest wife, and had convinced them of my Damascene conversion, citing Mrs Dobson's visit as the 'turning point'.

I also began a fawning, sycophantic campaign to win over Mrs Dobson, who could not contain her delight at the thought that it was her visit that had prompted such a quest for grace.

I stopped going out with Norm at the weekends and went over to the Lewes' house instead – helping the church in whatever way I could. Their house was over at the coast, so I would cycle there after going to the library. I would sit for hours, helping out with various ventures and listening to the friendly but sombre chatter between the minister and his family.

The Lewes were a hive of industry; seriously, you never saw people work so hard. The wife, Lydia, was always out and about. She ran a Methodist sewing group, carried out extensive fundraising for both the church and its poor, and every afternoon she and her husband walked to the outlying hamlets and villages to offer the consolations of the Methodist religion to those at the lowest ends of society – the drunks, the gamblers, the wives who had been beaten by their husbands, the parents who had lost children. Together, the Lewes would put into practice the teachings of Jesus's Beatitudes and tell the locals about God's love. Lydia was a stout woman, with thick glasses and sensible, short hair. I'm not saying she had huge teeth, but I wouldn't want to offer her a bite of my apple.

She didn't so much walk, as romp around with a kind of serious purposefulness. The minister was, in contrast, comfortingly handsome, with pepper-and-salt hair, black glasses and a kind face. Their relationship was respectful but distant, especially from the minister's side. It was difficult to see what might have brought them together in the first place, so different were they physically. I imagined earnest church youth clubs, both of them invigorated with their belief and intent on their calling, a physical attraction happily absent. 'Avoid all manner of passions,' advised Wesley, apparently.

They joked about the wages for Methodist ministers; it was not a religion you went into if a comfortable existence was your goal.

They were kept one step away from penury, but seemed very cheerful about it.

Over the weeks, I learned about the interesting history of the Methodist Church. Its founder, John Wesley, was not afraid to speak out against things that other branches of Christianity kept quiet on, or even were complicit in. The Lewes had a painting above their fireplace of John Wesley baptising an African-American slave.

'So he was an abolitionist?' I asked.

'Oh, yes,' said Lydia. 'Way before some other strands of Christianity had anything meaningful to say about it. He spoke out against slavery in all its forms.'

'"Liberty is the right of every human creature, as soon as he breathes the vital air; and no human law can deprive him of that right which he derives from the law of nature,"' quoted the minister.

'Indeed,' said Lydia. 'They say he was friends with William Wilberforce. He was also critical of slavery in America and in the Arab nations.'

I looked at her quizzically. 'What do you mean, Arab nations?'

'Wesley lived through an age where both Africans and Europeans were still being enslaved in North Africa in their millions.' She picked up a book called the *Doctrine of Original Sin*, by Wesley, and began to leaf through it. 'He was critical of the Islamic faith, for the violence he witnessed of its followers to one another and to those of a different faith. Here you go,' she said. 'He wrote this in the eighteenth century.' I took the ancient text off her and began to read, silently losing myself in the text:

'An ingenious writer,' wrote Wesley, 'who a few years ago published a pompous translation of the Koran, takes great pains to give us a very favourable opinion both of Mahomet and his followers. But he cannot wash the Ethiop white. After all, men who have but a moderate share of reason, cannot but observe in his Koran, even as polished by Mr. Sale, the most gross and impious absurdities. To cite particulars is not now my business. It may suffice to observe in general, that human understanding must be debased to an inconceivable degree, in those who can swallow such absurdities as divinely revealed. And yet we know the Mahometans not only condemn all who cannot swallow them to everlasting fire; not only appropriate to themselves the title of *Mussulmen* or *True Believers:* but even anathematise with the utmost bitterness, and adjudge to eternal destruction, all their brethren of the sect of *Ali,* all who contend for a figurative interpretation of them.

'That these men then have no knowledge or love of God is undeniably manifest, not only from their gross, horrible notions of him, but from their not loving their brethren. But they have not always so weighty a cause to hate and murder one another, as *difference of opinion.* Mahometans will butcher each other by thousands… It is not therefore strange, that ever since the religion of Mahomet appeared in the world, the espousers of it, particularly those under the Turkish emperor, have been as wolves and tigers to all other nations; rending and tearing all that fell into their merciless paws, and grinding them with their iron teeth: that numberless cities are rased from the foundation, and only their name remaining: that many countries which were once as the garden of God, are, now a desolate wilderness; and that so many once numerous and powerful nations are vanished away from the earth! Such was, and is at this day, the rage, the fury, the revenge, of these destroyers of human kind.'

I put down the book, a little shocked. Lydia, who was wandering in from the scullery with two glasses of water in her hands, seemed to read my thoughts. 'He spoke out against injustices and ungodly behaviour, child,' she said with a shrug, setting the glasses down on the table. 'He didn't care who the perpetrators were. We all fall equally under judgement from the almighty when the day comes.'

***

I also learned much about the Lewes family. Lydia's great-grandmother had been a lay preacher, back in the early nineteenth century when, for a short period, they allowed female preachers. Hers was a typical story, of a sinful youth of drunkenness and sexual promiscuity, followed by a near-death experience on a boat. She had travelled from town to town, gathering huge crowds in the marketplaces with tales of being visited in her dreams by the ghosts of her past sins in ghastly form. She had swooned as she talked. She had feared dying without ever really knowing the love of Christ. She had captivated audiences, reduced them to tears, watched them in turn swoon with stories of how she begged God for forgiveness, and how he came to answer her. But then Mrs Lewes' face turned gravely serious as she revealed to me that the men in those town squares had widened their eyes when her great-grandmother had revealed that the Devil still filled her with sexual lust *each and every day*, and how that good lady had faced an ever-present temptation to fall back into debauchery. Eventually, this unfortunate lady had settled into marriage with a happy but no doubt exhausted husband. At this point, the sight of Lydia's earnest face and huge teeth and stories of the rampant relative were too much; I had to go and lock myself in the outside toilet for a good five minutes, where I sat, laughing silently at the wall.

I began to attend church on Sundays, something which was interesting from an anthropological perspective but did little to invigorate me with any kind of faith. I felt nauseated and exhausted on hearing that my salvation could never be assured. It was always under threat, like living across the bank from an army you knew would one day attack you, you just didn't know when. Over and over again, the need to remain sober and industrious was drilled into us, fire and brimstone being the predictable alternatives.

Norm, of course, shook his head at me and asked me what the hell I was up to. He didn't believe in my conversion story for one second. 'You might as well put yourself though old Archie's trout smoker,' he said, 'you'll come out the same. A dried-out version of yourself with all the spontaneity and passion bleached out, replaced by repression and fear, Nancy. Fear of all sorts of things: sex, laziness, making money – especially if you are poor.' I shook my head, guiltily, and told him that one day he would understand.

After only a few weeks, I asked the minister about the notice in front of the church. I was sick with nerves at the thought that someone else might have got there first, but luckily no one had enquired.

It turned out that Lucy Clayton-Reid was the minister's sister. She was a housewife, a Catholic convert through marriage, and now active in the local church. She was married to a lawyer and they had two children, Bella and Paul, aged three years, and six months, respectively. They lived in a beautiful old Gothic house in Hampstead, London. The baby was very sick, apparently. 'I love children and I feel a calling,' I said, lying through my teeth. 'And this is one way to care for others before I return permanently to give myself to God.' That's the only time, I think, that he questioned my motives. He looked at me quizzically for a long time, and said he would think about it.

***

On Saturday I went round to the Lewes' home as usual, only to find the whole place empty. This was strange, because there was usually always someone there at that time. I sat down in my usual spot at the kitchen table and decided to wait. To pass the time, I began idly to check through the letters lying on the table. The minister and his wife often had Patricia and I read through the letters and put them into categories: bills, letters from the Methodist Church, letters from churchgoers, etc.

But in front of me was a different kind of letter: a report from the coal company. It seemed very detailed, showing industrial output at Oslington per quarter, cost per tonne, and the equivalent cost from Polish coal which, it said, was produced at around ten per cent of the cost of British coal.

Along with the report was a handwritten letter:

Dear Minister Lewes,

I write as your humble servant, Edward Moreton. I hope that you and the family are quite well. Both the Trust and our colliery manager, Mr Shaw, are very pleased with your work with the men of Oslington Colliery since I last wrote to you back in June. Please find attached an economic report of the mine, for your information. The inspectors' findings are interesting; there is some clear over-staffing going on. Thirteen chargemen per shift. Nearly one hundred ponies. It makes for interesting reading. The board is deciding how to proceed, however, I am actually writing *this* letter to address pastoral matters.

As you know, I would never undertake to peddle gossip or try to manage the lives of individual miners, however, as I also mentioned at length in my last letter, we were having issues (shall we say) with the Hardcastles and the Bamfords, who both moved to Oslington and joined our church community back in January of this year. Both families are treading a well-worn path all the way up from Cornwall and, as you know, being new to our ways, they undertook to uphold Methodist vows of sobriety, frugality and industry.

Anyway, back in June I wrote to you to inform you this quest for God's pardon had sadly been of the temporary variety, and that unfortunately Mr Hardcastle and Mr Bamford had both been seen staggering home drunk after drinking in the Soot, singing songs of a lascivious nature, indeed on more than one occasion. I now further understand that Jonny Bamford had been late for work a couple of times, and although there was no discernible downturn in productivity attributable to Mr Hardcastle, the Lord moved in a more mysterious way than we could ever imagine. My sources tell me that he had gone to the Soot and was apparently having another lengthy drinking session with his cronies. Mrs Hardcastle became so incensed that she locked him out of his own home, then lay in wait like a snake in the grass by the scullery window, which she had left slightly ajar. I understand that she then locked the back door. Later that same evening as Ed Hardcastle was trying to climb back in, she apparently slammed the sash window down on his hands whereupon she managed to break several bones, resulting in Mr Hardcastle having to suffer the ignominy of having to be bandaged so that he was wearing what looked like giant white paws until his bones had healed. There was no 'industry' from Mr Hardcastle for over a month. This is no laughing matter, though I admit I have to stifle an uncharitable guffaw now and again at home, for Mrs Moreton has two rather delightful, proud-looking china spaniels who are dark in colour but for their lovely white paws. They sit above our mantelpiece at home in the front parlour and one cannot help but think of hapless Mr Hardcastle when one is eating one's tea, doing the crossword, etc. I believe this is what our Teutonic brethren refer to as *Schadenfreude*, and I am sure it must be a sin. Anyway, I digress. Back to our Hardcastles and our Bamfords. We spoke back in June about wanting to halt their downward trajectory into a life of sin, for the good of these men and their families. You will remember that Mr Bamford was turned down in his request to be moved to the Abbot district for hand-drilling, and both men were put back to doing coal screening, which even they surely recognised as a demotion.

No matter: following the requests I made to you in my letter, you and your wife have done excellent work with both families in the intervening months and also through your Sunday sermons in general. I particularly liked your diktat that the 'forgiveness of sin lasts only so long as the penitent maintain their avoidance of further sin,' and that 'forgiveness is conditional and provisory' – well put, sir! These piteous creatures cannot hope to maintain God's grace by even occasional ale-drinking and worse in that dreadful establishment they like to call the Soot. Please also pass on my thanks to your wonderful wife for working so closely with Mrs Hardcastle and Mrs Bamford, whom are both of excellent character and are active in the Methodist sewing circle. Sometimes we need to choose an indirect path to our fallen, no? The good news is that for the past two months both men have avowed to renew their attempts to win God's grace and renounce sin by eschewing the temptations of the Devil. During this period they have not been near that aforementioned establishment. The drinking of alcohol leads to the breaking of all Methodist vows, directly or indirectly, but especially for the meek. Last week we were delighted to be able to reward Mr Bamford by giving him the position of hand-driller, and two shillings a week increase in pay to boot. He is highly delighted, and so is his wife, though they complained about being dripped on from a hole in the chapel roof during last Sunday's service (I am sure you will remember the din of the incessant rain when you were trying to deliver your sermon and your wife will certainly remember having to empty the bucket that was placed below to catch the incoming rain). Mr Hardcastle is still coal screening while his hands heal properly, though the hapless fellow is now complaining that the constant din is wreaking havoc with his tinnitus and is driving him insane. My wife and I have said prayers that he receives the patience he needs to carry on for the next few weeks until he can resume his normal work.

However, there are a couple of other matters within our community for which I ask your help in solving. Firstly, there is the perennial issue of the boys' starting age down the mine; like a snowball rolling down a hill this one seems to be growing ever larger and gaining speed. After the accident with Albert Wiggs, God rest his soul, a number of the mothers have formed a sort of unofficial union and have written to the board, urging us to increase the starting age for boys down our mines to fifteen, and at the same time, to increase our safety practices. Mrs Wiggs is leading the charge, as you might imagine, but she is joined by Mary Phipps, whose son is undergrown and has poor lungs on account of the tuberculosis. Mrs Phipps is worried about his lungs underground with the coal dust. This kind of nervousness is understandable in a poor unfortunate such as herself, who has lost already her husband to silicosis.

Regarding the point about safety practices, I should point out that we have already made several changes. We have increased the training for the new lads and introduced a system whereby they must shadow a miner of skill and experience for several weeks. However, on the question of starting age, I'm afraid we operate within national guidelines. We look after our men and their families where we can but we are not a charity. We are always trying to compete with the Poles who, as you will see, are able to manufacture and distribute coal at a fraction of our costs.

The current starting age is beneficial to the poor for many reasons, not least that they need to learn work-discipline before any of the usual temptations that befall their kind can take hold. Please can you, therefore, in your next Sunday sermon emphasise the need for *industry* in a man's life and the need for it to start *early*.

Secondly, I have become aware of a relationship between Miss June Farrow and Mr George Falby which I believe to be of a sexual nature. I cannot reveal my sources in this claim, suffice to say that they are to be trusted. Apart from the practical implications, this contravenes the Bible's teachings in this area. I will trust you to guide the flock in the right way, as you always do. Additionally, I believe a woman's delicate touch may be called for; perhaps your wife could be prevailed upon in this matter to intervene in a subtle, feminine way?

Ha, I thought. And read on.

As my father, God rest his soul, used to say, 'Down the mine, the moral machinery of the workers is every bit as important as the mechanical.' We were a poor family, sir, our station in life vastly improved by following a Methodist way of being. God has an open heart, my dear minister, and I beseech you, therefore, to also take some time to consider how we may reach more of the unredeemed and bring them into our family. Methodism is a religion of the heart, but it is only once some of the natural human weaknesses have been tamed into submission that we can allow the heart its freedom.

On a more prosaic note, please be informed that Mrs Moreton and I will be departing for Nice, France, this coming Monday, where we once again intend to spend the winter months. Mrs Moreton is still suffering from a slight nervous condition of indeterminate origin and the warmer climate suits her very well. We have found a welcoming home in the local church there, where we are greeted warmly as *nos amis anglais*, which is indeed heart-warming. I will forward on our local address so that we may continue to converse. However, I feel that Oslington, left under your management, will be very well served in my absence.

A final point: I enclose a cheque for £5.00 for general costs and for the repair of the church roof. Leaking on the Bamfords, or anyone else for that matter, on consecrated ground simply will not do.

I bid you good day, sir.

Yours faithfully,

Edward Moreton

Chairman of Oslington Coal Company

I tossed the letter aside, feeling confused. I stood up and walked slowly round the room, aware that I was missing something key, that there was something taking place I didn't understand. The letter had left me with a sense of unease that I couldn't explain. I lifted Edward Moreton's letter up once more and noticed some handwritten notes underneath. Clipped, tight writing, left-sloping and austere, reflective of the good minister himself. I started to read:

Notes for Sunday sermon

Talk about why God exists – see Wesley's notes.

Refer to why he sent Jesus Christ to die in order that we might be saved. God offers mercy and has promised that he will look after those who are obedient to him.

Describe what constitutes Christian behaviour: loving God, inward conscience, letting the Holy Spirit guide us from sin in the form of ignorance, pride, unbelief, enmity, self-will, lust and covetousness. Perhaps here add slothfulness and the need for work-discipline, why God supports early industry in order to prevent this sin from taking root – perhaps refer to God's curse over Adam and how He compelled mankind to a life of hard labour, poverty and sorrow.

Talk about the sin of sexual promiscuity and why God supports sexual congress between a man and a woman only within the institution of marriage.

Talk about the sins of drunkenness and debt, and how we must beware of the corrupting power of money.

Explain how we know, with absolute certainty, that God loves us. This is not guesswork or wishful thinking but based on empirical evidence, i.e. God has told us in his divine revelation.

Invite them to partake in a new life journey to holiness.

End by mentioning the kindness of the Oslington Coal Company in its donation for mending the roof.

I finished reading and placed the minister's notes carefully back under Mr Moreton's letter. I moved the papers to and fro until I was happy they were in their exact original places. Uncovering this lovefest between the Oslington Coal Company and the church was like finding out that first cousins were planning to marry. I felt a bit queasy, and went over to the sink to get a glass of water.

The house, I decided, was bare and a little shabby. There were no ornaments; this was a house that bragged about its own frugality. The now-familiar painting of John Wesley baptising the slave hung gravely on the wall, an omnipresent and pious reminder of his anti-slavery stance and a nod to Methodism's egalitarian origins. The grandfather clock ticked industriously in the corner. Books of hymns lay scattered on the table. So many contradictions everywhere, it was hard to think.

It was only then that I remembered Mrs Lewes telling me last Saturday that she was taking her daughter to stay with relatives down in Durham this weekend. I had completely forgotten. I sighed and looked out to sea. There were white ripples on the grey water and the wind howled down, battering a small boat that was travelling southwards, carving up waves which crashed violently against the shore. The windows of the old house rattled with the wind and this only added to my sense of unease. The content of the letter had deeply unsettled me, for reasons that my fifteen-year-old brain could not really comprehend. I continued to stand, arms crossed, looking out to sea and a sky of ominous grey and hurtling white clouds, waiting for some sort of enlightenment to follow. I thought of Alfie Phipps with his tiny frame and his weak lungs, descending that cold, black mineshaft on his fourteenth birthday. Was it right that such cosiness existed between the Coal Company and the church?

I sighed again, wondering if I should perhaps wait on the minister, who was no doubt out on a pastoral visit. I would wait, I decided, and talk through with him my unease, though without directly referring to Edward Moreton's letter. Perhaps I had misunderstood. I sat down on a wooden chair at the kitchen table and began to leaf through the books of hymns.

Presently, I was aware of what sounded like a laugh: short, shrill, feminine. This startled me greatly, and I looked around uneasily at the empty room. I waited for some minutes. Nothing. Then I heard a groan, just as distinctive, most definitely masculine. I had entered some dream sequence, I was certain. My heart was thumping so violently I thought it would burst out of my rib cage. I stole as quietly as I could out to the passageway, and listened. There were more groans, then a definite rocking sound, a wooden headboard banging against a wall, the legs of a bed protesting squeakily at some unusual movement. I was utterly transfixed. I had no doubt what was going on upstairs, but in my befuddled state I had convinced myself – idiot that I was – that it must be June Farrow and George Falby who were up to no good upstairs. I imagined myself the heroine of the story, thwarting these two unwed lovers in their sinful act of sexual congress, revealing this terrible sin to the lovely, handsome minister, his admiring and thankful smile enough to light up my world for years to follow. I climbed the stairs as quietly as I could but then burst through the bedroom door like an out of control tankey.

The first thing I noticed was the whiteness of their skin. His buttocks were virtually translucent. The scene was not as I had in my naivety imagined it: dimmed lights, rosy skin, tender caresses. A feminine scene, in retrospect. This was about as opposite as could be imagined. Harsh daylight, hairy, snowy skin, feet everywhere. I stood there like a bloody stupid rabbit caught in a car's headlights, watching until she pushed her lover off and sat up to see who it was. She gave a little shriek when she saw me, then lay back down on the bed, staring furiously at the ceiling. He couldn't see who I was, and started fishing around for his glasses.

Minister Lewes and Mrs Dobson were both flushed and still panting as they adjusted to this intrusion. Mrs Dobson's blonde hair, usually so neat and prim, cascaded about her shoulders like a waterfall. Her breasts were small with tiny nipples. I glimpsed all this in an instant, before the Minister hastily pulled the sheet over them to cover their modesty.

Neither of them spoke, and I seemed to have lost my tongue too.

'I forgot Mrs Lewes and Patricia were going away this weekend,' I said, after a pause, and looking at the floor.

'Oh, damnation!' said Minister Lewes. I think both myself and Mrs Dobson found our first common ground in our shock. 'I'm finished,' he continued, shaking his head. I looked out of the window. There were so many thoughts in my head, and none of them were making sense. I didn't even know if I should be angry and disgusted with him, or apologise for the intrusion.

Mrs Dobson began to weep, and curled back down in the bed, pulling the sheets over her head.

'Go downstairs, Nancy, please. Wait for me in the front room. I won't be long.'

***

I sat with my back to the door and stared out at sea. The urge I sometimes felt to be free of myself, to be anybody else but me, was strong. Ideas zoomed left and right across my brain, like skaters on an icy pond. I lost track of time. Finally, though, the cognitive mists began to clear.

Presently, the door opened softly and the minister walked in and sat down opposite me.

'You're crying, Nancy,' he said.

I looked at the ground, embarrassed.

'Well,' he began. 'What you just saw was unforgiveable. Truly. But this thing between me and Mrs Dobson … if I could just explain it to you. It was like being hit by a train. It was like a meteor crashing into earth. There was just nothing I could have done to stop it,' he said, his brown eyes wide and pleading. 'Something clicked into place that just fitted. I – we – have had to learn that sometimes this happens between two people. Mrs Dobson feels it too, Nancy. She isn't a bad person. She has never done anything like this before, and neither have I.'

'All right, *Minister*,' I said, though the title now felt inappropriate and weird. 'I do understand that. But I have to ask you, why do you think God, who is omnipotent, made such a weak creature as mankind? Made creatures who are bound to fail? Why not invent a different species, one less weak?'

'God gave mankind free will. That's not a weakness, Nancy, it's one of the most beautiful things about the Christian faith. He appeals to us to do the right thing, to obey his instructions, but he does not force us. He doesn't control our fate; instead, the Bible tells us that we make our own fate. He asks us to work hard, be diligent, show compassion and charity. That's all I've ever tried to do …' he said, looking miserable. 'You're angry and you have every right to be. But don't lose your faith on account of me.'

'You're too bloody right I'm angry,' I said, shaking with fury as I turned to face him. 'Never mind what I just saw upstairs. You talk of my faith but you choke the life out of your followers, turn them into their own slave drivers; you spy on them, and then you laugh in their faces and tell them it is a religion of the heart. All of them, including your little bitch upstairs. Do you know she came round to my Nana's and told her off for putting washing out on a Sunday?' I let out an angry laugh, though I was still crying. 'My grandad is probably dying and she told him off for playing Pitch and Toss. You're the biggest bunch of hypocrites under the sun. God really was having a laugh when he put humans in charge of delivering his message. And in any case, from what I've just read, you work for the Oslington Coal Company, not God.'

'Nancy,' said Tim Lewes, quietly, his face ghostly white. My out of body experience continued – the whole scene like something I was dreaming – and I felt like I was present only in the third person. 'That is not fair of you. You've seen the work that Lydia and I do here. The Methodist Church is the only reason half the children in the country know how to read and write. Before state schools came along it was our church above all others that cared about educating the children of the poor.'

'Ah, yes, children. I've just been reading about that. You've not had so much to say about sending them down the mine aged fourteen though, have you? Knowing that some of them will die before they reach their sixteenth birthday? Because that might upset your relationship with the Coal Company.'

The minister stared at me, shaking his head. 'Well you may have a point, but this isn't about that though, is it Nancy? You're angry at what you just saw. Look, I tried to love Lydia, really I did. At the start, I do believe I loved her in a certain way. But it was more that we both felt a common calling to do this work together. We are an amazing team. It's just that, for many years now, I haven't loved her in what you might call a passionate way. A way that would lead to the procreation of more children. And however mad it might sound, I have to believe that God sent Mrs Dobson to tempt me to prove my love for him. I have failed the test, Nancy,' he said, shaking his head.

Inwardly, I uttered a sarcastic laugh. I suddenly saw us for the self-deceiving, irrational mammals we are. The minister was sitting in front of me in an oversized shirt, a pair of long black socks, and white underpants, close to tears. I looked at the dark hairs on his legs. I almost felt sorry for him. But I quickly realised that I needed to use the situation to my advantage.

'I need your help, Tim,' I said, recklessly dispensing with his title altogether. 'I can't stay here, knowing all this. It's too much,' I lied. We sat in silence for a few moments, listening as wind rattled the windows, which I suddenly saw as tired and peeling, instead of worthy. 'Tonight, you are going to write to your sister in London and tell her you have found someone for the position of nanny. You will ask her to sort out my passage to London and pay for it. She is to meet me off the boat at the docks and bring me to her house. I will go in two weeks' timc.'

'I can't do that,' said Tim Lewes, shaking his head. 'It wouldn't be right.'

'You can do it,' I declared. 'And once you've done it, I will forget I ever came here today and saw what I saw. I mean really, properly forget it. Blackmail isn't my style. I just want out of here. We can all come out of this well.'

'I don't know,' he said. Small white tidemarks had formed in the corners of his mouth and his hair was sticking out post-coitally all over the place. Out of the corner of my eye, I saw the silhouette of Mrs Dobson gliding like a wraith across the hallway, and out of the front door, which she closed gently behind her.

'You will make this happen, Tim. Or else I will not be responsible for my actions. I've already told you: I can't stay here.'

'All right, Nancy,' he said. He looked tired. I stood up to leave.

'You know, Tim,' I said, 'I think I do feel sorry for you. If this thing between you and Mrs Dobson is as unavoidable as you say it is, if this was meant to be, then what does that say about your supposed God, and how he has rewarded your lifetime of piety? Are you now to feel guilty for the rest of your life? I hand it all back to you on a platter. I am giving up my quest for grace. I won't let my loins rust over just because I am not married, nor will I submit to the life of a miner's wife and give up any career that I may one day have. You've always said that girls like Pat and me deserve a career, haven't you? No, I won't forsake a drop of beer with my friend Norm under your ridiculous threats of fire and brimstone. I won't keep my money locked under my bed until the day I die when it gets given to someone else – I will buy as many jewels and stay in as many expensive hotels and entertain as many lovers as I can, and sip from great vats of champagne and bloody well enjoy my life before you lot slowly turn me into the living dead.'

'This is ridiculous, Nancy. This is disproportionate. Don't abandon a whole religion because of my failings. Listen, think of it this way. Can you imagine people like Mr and Mrs Mitford, what would happen if they embraced the Methodist vows of industry, sobriety and frugality. Are you honestly trying to say that wouldn't benefit their family? The children would be fed and looked after. The Mitfords would find a purpose to their lives that they don't have today. We help families stay away from temptation. We teach them that serving God and looking after their own families is the most important thing.'

I considered this statement. 'Fair enough,' I said. 'But what about someone like Mr Pearce? He has gone through so much tragedy and he doesn't believe in God, but he's tried to make the best out of his circumstances. He's built a library for the whole town. That wouldn't have happened if it wasn't for him. You don't have a monopoly over teaching people about ethics. People have always understood what is good and bad. Mr Pearce says there's more sensible teaching about ethics from the Greek philosophers than you'll find in the Bible. And he says that during the Renaissance, Christianity started to look back to the Greeks to define its ethics because there was so little in the New Testament. He told me all about Thomas Aquinas, and how he borrowed ideas from Aristotle.'

'But that doesn't make Christianity wrong, does it? It means that it is open to change, and that has to be a good thing, no?'

'It also doesn't mean it's the word of God.'

'Fair point. But there's the rub: not everyone can find the inner strength to behave ethically by themselves, Nancy. Not everyone is that strong. It looks like Mr Pearce is, but Mr Mitford isn't. Anyway, I'm not sure right now is the time for us to be having this conversation.'

I turned on my heel and walked over to the door.

'True, but right now I'm not sure you and Mrs Dobson are the best people to be the judge of what constitutes ethical behaviour. Right now, I just feel more confused about it all than ever. Goodbye, Tim Lewes,' I said. 'I will take your secret with me when I leave and once I am on my way to London, you will never hear from me again. Oh, and by the way, you can tell Mrs Dobson not to come near our house again. I will pay Pearl Mitford to beat her up if she does.'

He smiled, in spite of himself. 'All right, Nancy, goodbye it is. I don't think I have ever come close to understanding you, for you are as deep as the ocean. But I wish you well and I know that God loves you.'

We smiled at each other for the last time and then I walked out of the house. I continued walking out onto the cliff, the wind blowing my hair across my face. I sat by a tree near the edge, picking at the yellowing grass and smelling the salty sea air and watching the boats sail away into the distance. The events of the day had drained me. Before too long I began to feel that my words to the minister may have been a little harsh. I lay my head on my shoulder and leaned against the tree. In spite of the cold and wind, I fell asleep.

Whichever way you care to slice it, part of my fury and disappointment was fuelled by the fact that handsome, eloquent Tim Lewes had not chosen me to conduct a passionate affair with. I am only human after all.

In any case, my liberation was imminent. I rolled the names of my new employers over my tongue: Mr Matthew and Mrs Lucy Clayton-Reid. Gothic house in Hampstead Heath. Daughter Bella and son Paul. I'd never met anyone with a double-barrelled surname before. I imagined golf courses and riding lessons and cucumber sandwiches and home-made lemonade. Already I felt removed from my life in Oslington, like a cloud that once passed overhead but has now been blown far away.

Chapter 6

Islington, July 1999

Nikki Clayton-Reid was checking the updates from the Asian trading desk on her BlackBerry when she heard the growl of the car outside. It was just after six in the morning. Sometimes there was confusion, as a radio presenter who lived diagonally opposite in the conservation square also travelled to work by private car and so the sound of the engine was ambiguous. But this time the vehicle was there to pick her up.

She stepped out into the morning with a relieved sigh. A light drizzle was falling and a warm, summer's mist hung about the square, highlighting dew-covered spider's webs chained across the black railings.

The limo pulled away and a couple of turns later they were already scooting along Upper Street. The vehicle smelled strongly of air freshener and aftershave. Nikki looked out of the window and mentally checked through the day.

For the past year, she had been heading up a team of quants and traders tasked with coming up with a new trading strategy, a fresh flavour for statistical arbitrage – buying and selling the same stock over and over, hundreds of times a day, using a combination of the average price for the stock or index and deviation levels therefrom, overlaid with fixed trading ranges for the day based on the level of the opening call, several different moving averages and about twenty other factors. The idea of the new strategy was to automate the trading process by having the computer make the trading decisions in milliseconds rather than rely on a team of expensive traders and their armies of support staff working from knowledge, experience and spreadsheets.

Statistical arbitrage itself was nothing new but, as ever in the trading world, the idea was to get in and make your money before other market participants worked out your strategy and began to employ it themselves, at which point it would start to behave like a virus that had grown immune to medicine. The new process had been given the thrusting name of 'Sprint'.

So far, the results had been promising. After months of testing in a demo system, followed by small real-world bets, they'd moved up a gear and had generated nearly two hundred and fifty thousand pounds of profit the previous Friday. Nikki opened her BlackBerry again and looked through her diary for the rest of the week. US government results in on Friday afternoon; time for a pre-emptive trading halt in the US indexes – the Dow Jones, NASDAQ and the S&P 500 – from lunchtime onwards. Images of the whole team spilling down the pub came to mind: something to look forward to. Nick would be okay with the kids; in fact, he was much more popular than her at the toddler music classes and church play sessions. The other mums cooed round him like mother hens, his male sexuality acknowledged but disarmed by the presence of his children and official role as house husband. *Well, good luck to you,* she thought, *rather you than me.*

The BlackBerry flashed up a reminder: *Aunt Bella hip replacement – send flowers to hospital*. Poor Aunt B – nervous and fretful at the best of times, in spite of being the mother of five grown men and owner of two gorgeously boisterous springer spaniels (the most compelling reason for any visit, in Nikki's opinion). She forwarded the message on to her personal assistant with the words: *Please action.*

In truth, she'd never actually forgiven her aunt for perceived transgressions against womankind; this was a woman with a PhD in electrical engineering who'd met her husband during her final year, was married and pregnant within six months, and who had spent the rest of her twenties and thirties popping out babies and ferrying them to tennis and football and rugby and rowing and god knew what other improving activities. At Christmas she created home-made wreaths for the front door, and in the summer she held charity coffee mornings. She made her own jam with plums from her garden. She seemed happy, and that annoyed Nikki as well. All the women's magazines said you shouldn't judge other women and their life choices, but such thoughts didn't just evaporate, they got pushed down to the basement of your mind, where you had to lock them away so that no one else could find them.

The limo travelled on past the Angel, Islington, where commuters holding takeaway coffee cups descended into the bowels of the tube station. The morning journey was time to reflect on a few 'Noteworthy Items of Catholic Guilt': the state of her marriage; her abject lack of interest in her own children and guilt at a growing panicky feeling that she should never have had them but no one could ever know; and a lesser, yet still tangible, environmental guilt at the knowledge of the non-recyclable coffee cup and whole bag of plastic that would be generated from her breakfast alone. Locking these items into this 'worry time' meant that she could put them away for the day once they had been dealt with, like ticking off items on a to-do list. And so, guilt trip over, as the car pulled into Canary Wharf, she suddenly felt much brighter.

The anticipation of coffee, so strong she could taste it; the early-morning meeting for all the team to get together to talk through the day ahead; Brad Quattroci, her American sales director with his clubless golf swings, implausibly white teeth, unshakeable optimism and strange Yank metaphors. God, she loved it all, in all its loud, fake, meaningless, capitalist, master-of-the-universe loveliness. An addictive gambling game of who has the best quants – those pointy-headed gnome people who sit by the side of the trading desk and work out not just the profit and loss, but also the risk you are taking with each trade. Paid by the millions to spot patterns that repeat and are, with some degree of certainty, repeatable. Chelsea and Mayfair were full of gnomes on six- and seven-figure salaries.

She didn't even mind that they all called her Yummy Mummy to her face and Darth Vader behind her back; she got the job done – trading paid for all the other feeder fish in the bank and sent millions of pounds in tax back to the exchequer each year, therefore she was providing a social service, was she not? And she wasn't going to fall into that clichéd female trap of needing to be liked – not necessarily, anyway.

The diary showed that the run-up to Friday did not look so hot, however. Gunther had booked in a 'graduate bonding session' up in the rooftop dining rooms after work on Wednesday – less said there the better, but summed up in one word: excruciating. And as the youngest ever managing director, and the first ever female head of the equities trading desk in the firm's one-hundred-and-fifty-year history, she was due to give a talk to the company's Women's Forum on Thursday. Look at me, she mused, I'm amazing at my job, but the rest of my life is a fucking car crash.

But in terms of low points, the *pièce de résistance*, right there in a black and white calendar entry, was the school mums' night out on Thursday. Lorna had stood over her, frowning, and had made her put the entry into her phone. An opportunity to reflect on Reception class's Easter project on airports, no doubt. A chance to hear the inverse boast-fest: the more they bigged-up their children, the more they bragged about their sporting achievements and musical gradings, the worse they painted themselves as mothers, with Nikki interested in neither side of it. An evening of listening to women talking about lives lived vicariously through their children, while she felt like the weirdo in the corner for wanting her own life too. Modern parenting was tedious claustrophobia wearing a Prozac smile.

Q: A couple of lines of coke might make the evening a little more bearable?

A: Unlikely, but it might be worth a try.

The only takeaways from the evening would be a mouth like a hamster had slept in it and lingering, multi-way guilt. And, speaking from extensive experience, the only way to get through the *next* working day would be a bottle of Lucozade and a midday sleep in the disabled toilet.

To be discussed, she thought: *I think I feel a forward-dated headache coming on which may reach its peak on Thursday afternoon*. But then the European markets opened, the coffee tasted great, the bag of breakfast rubbish was in a bin which was not in a direct line of vision. Suddenly the misanthropic mist lifted and all other thoughts drifted away. It was time to make money.

***

Lunchtime. Four missed calls, all from Aunt Bella calling from hospital. Polite messages in a voice still slow and groggy from a general anaesthetic; please do call back as soon as possible. Nikki frowned and retreated to the stairwell. Mobile phones were strictly forbidden on the trading floor. She called her aunt's number.

'Hi, Bella,' she said, wondering how long the signal would last in a windowless stairwell. 'How was the operation?'

'Oh, Nikki,' said her aunt, in a weak voice. From the background came the sound of trolleys clanking and distant, cheerful nurses. 'It went well thank you, and thanks for getting back to me. I'm so sorry for disturbing you at work. But it's …'

Nikki waited. Each word sounded like such a struggle. Was she supposed to say something helpful and encouraging at this juncture?

'Take your time,' she said, rolling her eyes and looking at her watch.

'Oh, I'm so sorry,' her aunt whispered. 'Bear with me. I'm in a lot of pain still.' Silence followed, until Nikki checked that the call was still active.

'Nikki?' said her uncle's voice, finally. The word was strongly delivered, infused with middle-class stoicism and a no-nonsense delivery that he prided himself on, a delivery that stopped the whimperers and malingerers and repeat offenders who plagued his doctor's surgery dead in their tracks. It took Nikki by surprise. 'It's Jim here. Nikki?'

'Yes, I'm here. Glad to hear the op went well. Is she okay, though?'

'Hang on, let me put you on loudspeaker so Bella can hear. There we go. Can you still hear me?'

'Yup.'

'Your aunt's not feeling up to speaking right this moment. Totally to be expected. Look, it's about Grandma Lucy. She was taken into the Royal Free last night with pneumonia.'

'Oh?'

'Yes. Bella had been phoning the house for a couple of days but couldn't get through. She was really worried. Then she had to come in here for the operation. Terrible timing. In the end, I called Mrs Thomas next door and asked her to go over and check,' he said, clearing his throat. 'Anyway, to cut a long story short they rushed Grandma in but basically we don't know how long she'd been in that state. Nikki, you know I wouldn't say this lightly, but the old dear is *really* poorly. The pneumonia has really taken hold. They're giving her morphine. Well, I presume an intelligent woman like you can guess what that means; unfortunately, at her age it only goes one way from here on in. Bella, as you can imagine, is devastated she can't get there.'

'I can imagine.'

'And as you might also expect, your aunt is not allowed to move. Not one inch. They even come to the bed with the bedpan … she tells me she's lost all her dignity. I felt it my duty to remind her she has given birth five times, at least one of which was witnessed by a roomful of medical students.'

'The bedside manner is as soft and fluffy as ever, I see.'

Jim laughed. 'Yes, well. You know me. Anyway, I've told her she mustn't even try.' Nikki scanned through the latest emails on her BlackBerry.

'Can you go and visit her please?'

Nikki flinched. 'Come on, Jim. What about your boys? And why can't you go?'

'Love, I am working today and tomorrow and there's no one else at the surgery who can cover. I'm also trying to come in and visit Bella in between working. And I'm looking after the dogs. The boys would go, as you know, but they are spread all over: Ed's in Australia, Max is in New York, Jake is still down in Montpellier, Ben is up in Edinburgh and Gavin's in Cornwall – and he's on call for the next few days, though he says he might be able to get there by the weekend.

'You can be in London from Edinburgh by train in about five hours, Jim. You can be back from Cornwall in, what, six, seven, hours?' *Ah, the faithful cousins*, thought Nikki, *at least two of you cowering behind insignificant geographical distance like the big babies you are.*

'I know. I'll ask them, but they've got work commitments too. You're the only one who's on the doorstep. Oh, god, you'll have to tell your father too: when *is* Paul next back from Dubai?'

'I've no idea. He's just been over at Easter, as you know, so not in the near future I wouldn't think. Although I guess he'll have to come back now. Anyway, look, guys – you know how the situation is with Grandma and us.'

There was a feminine sigh from the other end of the phone, followed by a long pause. 'I know, Nikki,' said her aunt, slowly. 'I do know how you must feel.'

'Do you?' asked Nikki. 'Do you really?'

There was a pause on the other end of the phone. 'No,' admitted her uncle. 'No, I don't think we do. But you of all people know how your aunt and I tried to talk her out of it.' That much was true; after Grandpa's death, when Grandma Lucy arbitrarily decided to cut Paul, her own son, out of her will, and by proxy Nikki and her own children, no one had been more vocal than her aunt and uncle, even visiting the old bat in person several times to try to talk her out of it. Grandpa would have been turning in his grave.

'What kind of a person cuts their own son out of their will?' Nikki asked, feeling this was now the 'cards-on-the-table' moment she had been waiting a long time for. 'And me and the kids? It's not like Dad even fell out with her or anything, is it? There's no logic behind it. It's just hateful and spiteful. Look, you've always been her favourite, I get that. I could tell that even from being really young. It's true in every family but with Grandma it went much further. It was almost as if she'd rejected my dad. I could never work out why. No one ever explains anything in this family.'

From an even more distant planet, her aunt started to speak. Nikki strained to hear. 'I know, Nikki, I know. But …' she added in her sluggish voice, 'there *is* more to it than I can tell you right now, over the phone.' So many secrets, thought Nikki miserably. The whole family rendered immobile from the venom of its pointless, poisonous secrets. Each one treated like first prize in a county show.

'Why don't you try me?'

'I promise you that I will see your father right when the time comes. You have to trust me on this one, Nikki. Please, just do it for me, if not for Grandma.'

'Okay,' said Nikki, sighing. 'But for the record, I just want you to know that it's not about the money. I just want the truth, Bella.' Her BlackBerry was flashing to indicate new messages had arrived. 'Anyway, look, in terms of visiting … I'll think about it. I've got to go. Get well soon, okay? Take care of yourself.'

'Will you go tonight, Nikki?' said her aunt, her voice wavering again. 'I don't want her to die alone,' she added, melodramatically.

'Goodbye,' said Nikki, ending the call and looking again at the BlackBerry. The FTSE index had broken through the expected theoretical price range for the day and Sprint had started throwing out some suspect – and loss-making – trades. The strategy had been suspended. Nikki hurried back down to the trading floor, to where a group of programmers and quants were standing, frowning at screens above them.

'What the hell's going on?' said Nikki. 'We back-tested against breaches like this. We've been over this scenario loads of times. Why didn't we switch to the breach model? This is 101, guys.'

***

After the London markets had closed and the flash profit and loss had been calculated and signed off, Nikki wandered over to the meeting room area. She leaned against the coffee machine at the far end, her eyes looking furtively around the room.

'Look, I'm going to have to cancel tonight,' she said, in a quiet voice into her mobile phone.

'No way,' said a male voice on the other end. 'What's up?'

He's so young, thought Nikki. Even his voice is young. Twenty-five. Christ, what on earth did she think she was doing? But even as she heard his voice, something tightened almost painfully deep down inside her and prompted a sharp intake of breath.

'It's my grandma. She's in hospital with pneumonia and she's very ill, apparently. It's a long story; we're not close, but my aunt has asked me to pay her a visit, so I'm kind of doing it as a favour to her.'

'Shame,' said the voice on the other phone. 'Because I'm very, very ready for you.'

Nikki laughed. 'Me too,' she whispered.

***

The hospital was a sea of fluorescent lighting and smelled of chemical disinfectant. The receptionist had helped Nikki identify the location of Mrs Lucy Clayton-Reid with practised efficiency and an undertone of detached suspicion that comes from working with the public for a long time. A lifelong snob with a mordant fear of the great unwashed, the old woman had lucked out in getting her own room. Not that it mattered, apparently, because she was clearly out of it when Nikki arrived and sat down on a chair next to the bed. A husk of what used to be Grandma lay on the bed, her breathing as shallow and as rapid as that of a hibernating dormouse.

For all the problems between them, it was still sad to see her reduced to this. A small, neat woman with more than a hint of old-school glamour, she had been so proud of and careful about her appearance. When Nikki thought of her it was with coiffed hair, a dash of red lipstick and a twinset and pearls. How many years had it been since Nikki had seen her? The last time was shortly after Grandpa's death, so that made it about three years ago. She had never even met Nikki's youngest, her own granddaughter. Grandpa's passing had definitely been a turning point; it was almost as if Grandma had made a decision that whatever charade had been in place up until that point – *to keep Grandpa happy,* Nikki thought – no longer needed to be acted out, and that she could make her last act one of publicly rejecting her own son. That was the point, Nikki reflected, when the relationship had shifted from ambivalence into downright hostility.

For the next hour, Nikki ignored the patient, fetching cups of takeaway tea – more environmental guilt for the next morning – and checking her emails. An aura of anti-climax hung about the room. She was bored. What was she actually supposed to do?

A passing nurse seemed to pick up on her indecision and helplessness, having no doubt seen it many times before. 'I know it seems like she can't hear you,' said the nurse, breezing into the room with a smile, 'but she might well be able to understand that you're here, and that will give her a lot of comfort. Just talk to her like you would normally, hold her hand, that kind of thing.'

'I don't want this to sound bad, but how long do you think she has left?'

'Hmmn,' said the nurse, gently. 'You can never really tell, but if I were you, I wouldn't be planning on leaving tonight.'

After the nurse had left, Nikki sighed, leaned forwards and picked up a tiny, clawed, hand covered in the liver spots of old age.

'It's Nikki,' she said, leaning over the bed. 'It's Nikki here. I've come to see you,' she added, obviously.

The lips twitched, she was certain of that. Grandma was trying to speak.

Talk to her, the nurse had said. But what about? Words and ideas rolled around in her head but none made the neural journey down to her tongue. Everything she wanted to say felt controversial, tinged with accusation. You couldn't do that to someone on their deathbed. She sat back, holding a cup of tea with her free hand, wishing it was a cigarette, or a large vodka. She thought regretfully about the evening she was missing.

'Do you remember, Grandma, that time I won the school prize for maths?' she said, finally, in what she hoped was a friendly voice. 'I would have been about ten? You came to school with Grandpa to watch me collect my trophy. I remember how excited I was to see you all in the audience. And do you remember, for my speech, I recited the numbers of pi to fifty decimal places? To the whole school. How embarrassing! I bet you would never believe that I can still do it. I learned it like a song, but in my head it feels like patterns on a graph. And so it's easy to remember. D'you want to hear it again? Okay, here goes. Three point one, four, one, five, nine, two, six, five …'

Outside the room, the nurse looked in through the window, relieved to see the visitor finally engaging with the patient. She would perhaps have been surprised to hear that the loving conversation she imagined was actually a list of numbers being read out in a slightly menacing manner. The nurse looked relieved and continued on her round.

'Shall I tell you about Sprint?' Nikki continued. 'You won't believe what has gone into it, Grandma. The quants, well they can tell you all the theories in the world and they can reel off all the Greeks and all that, but they can't *feel* the patterns like we can.' She proceeded to give a cheerful synopsis of the project to date. Lucy's mouth twitched occasionally. The breathing really was quite off-putting. 'Nancy,' said Grandma at last, after much effort. 'Nancy …' The words were almost inaudible.

'No, Grandma, it's Nikki here.' There followed a tiny but perceptible shake of the head, just a few millimetres, but enough for Nikki to realise that Lucy knew exactly who was there. Grandma was trying to tell her something; she repeated the same name: Nancy. Nikki gripped the old woman's hand tightly.

'What are you trying to tell me, Grandma? Why couldn't you tell me this before? Why all these secrets, for all these years? You waited till Grandpa died to carry out your cruel trick, didn't you, Grandma,' Nikki said, louder than she intended, suddenly feeling a surge of both personal and vicarious grief that was tinged with three years of unresolved anger. 'You know he would never have agreed to it. But it was never about your money, you know. I want you to know that. I only want to know why.'

But then Lucy seemed to retreat into a place right on the edge of life; the sentient being had already checked out and just the fading mechanics remained. Her grandma's breathing had accelerated and turned into desperate little rasps. *What do you do now*? thought Nikki, with alarm. *Just wait for it all to be over?*

'Grandma,' she said, taking hold of the old woman's hand, 'I'm here with you.' But she couldn't say the words that a dying person needs to hear. After checking her BlackBerry once more, Nikki yawned and laid her head down on the bed. She fell asleep, holding Lucy's hand. Some hours later, she awoke to feel the hand beneath hers was cold.

'Wait!' she said, still groggy from sleep. 'Don't you *dare* cark it now, Lucy. Who the hell is this Nancy? This is like a scene from a bad movie.' But the elderly lady had gone, her mouth still open, mid gasp.

Nikki turned around. The nurse stood, looking horrified, at the end of the bed. They looked at each other for a long moment. Nikki realised she was shaking. She wondered if she was definitely awake, and not just in some horrible bad dream.

'You have to understand the context,' she said, haughtily, after several millennia. God, she could do with a cigarette. What time was it anyway? Jeez, the clock was showing just after two in the morning.

The nurse shot her an evil glance. She walked up to take Lucy's pulse and make a few other checks.

'Mrs Clayton-Reid has passed away,' she confirmed, refusing to look at Nikki. *One thing is for sure*, the nurse thought, bitterly, *you meet all sorts doing this job. Look at this Morticia Addams over here: designer handbag, blood-red nails and diamonds galore – this woman is completely immaculate, and yet apparently just another fruit-and-nutcase*, as she liked to call the crazier members of the public, *except that this one is proper nasty with it.* She had half a mind to check the old dear for vampire bite marks on her neck. Reining in a half-chuckle, the nurse took a deep breath and put on her game face. 'I'll fetch the doctor,' she said.

'Have I got time for a cigarette?'

'Yes,' said the nurse, looking straight ahead. *Straight out of charm school, this one,* she thought. 'I expect you've got a few minutes. And then when you're ready, you can speak to the doctor and we'll make a start on some of the paperwork.'

Nikki pulled on her jacket, grabbed her bag and strode off down the corridor, fighting the urge to run. The whole thing felt deeply unreal, but whatever barrage of emotions she was feeling, grief was conspicuous by its absence.

***

'Nancy,' said Nikki out loud to the crisp night air, feeling the word on her tongue. 'Nancy Drew. Nancy Reagan. Nancy Sinatra. Who are you and what have you got to do with our family? What an effing tragic bunch we are.' She shook her head, then took out a cigarette and lit it, inhaling deeply and watching the white smoke blow away gently into the blackness of a huge night-time sky. Then she made a mental list of all the calls she would need to make later on that day. Grandma's death was already fading from her thoughts and a tiny wave of excitement rose up in the back of her throat as she wondered how the Asian trading desk was doing in its morning session.

Chapter 7

The *Colchester* stood, majestic, in the dock. Out to sea the waves crashed white and grey over the bay, flattening into a slate-coloured horizon. It was a squally morning, although perhaps it was always like that over at the coast. The ticket man looked at me sympathetically.

I stood at the front of the queue, looking up at the boat, trying to get my head round the scale of it all. The railway track ran right along the edge of the dock. A train was stationed there and row after row of railcars full of coal stood on the track. A crane lifted each car up individually, and then the coal was tipped into huge containers within the ship, emitting both an ear-splitting cracking noise and huge clouds of black, sulphurous dust. The crane was operated from a raised hut, perched on top of steel girders at the water's edge.

'Ten thousand tonnes of coal, this'un,' said the ticket man. He was sweating profusely. The ticket machine hung round his neck. He mopped his brow with a hankie. 'Seven-hundred-foot long.'

I shook my head in disbelief.

'We're just getting the last few cars on now. Should be away soon. Hop yourself on and take a seat. And no trouble mind,' he said with a wink. *If only you knew,* I thought, grimly.

I turned to take a last look at the North East. My only goodbyes had been a short letter to my grandparents and another one to Norm. I simply couldn't face it all, the anger, the recriminations, my grandparents' pleading and cajoling, Norm's disappointed but stoic shrug. It was easier just to run away. That morning I had done the fire, fetched some water, pretended to eat some porridge and said goodbye as normal. But instead of heading off to school, I had sneaked into the nettie, got changed out of my school uniform, stuffed my school clothes into my army and navy bag, and slunk off down the street to the railway line. I had my copy of *Jane Eyre*, my tobacco tin full of money and a nicely matured steak pasty which had been busy sweating some of its fat onto the brown paper packet overnight. Feeling like an escaped prisoner, I had boarded the train to North Shields. I had been terrified I might see Inspector Bray or Norm, but that was a chance that I'd had to take.

***

The boat rolled out slowly, sounding its horn as we laboured out onto the open sea. We were accompanied by noisy, pasty-stealing seagulls. I should make an effort to get over that incident at some point … mental note to speak to Sarah … anyway, Norman, moving on …

The smallish passenger bay was located on the stern of the ship; there were about fifty passengers, including another girl who looked absolutely terrified. She said her name was Charlotte and she was only fourteen. She was also on her way to London, to become a housekeeper. Sensing a kindred spirit, she stuck to me like glue. We bagged some seats, then stood by the railings, looking back at the land as it faded slowly into the distance.

Soon there was no land, just sea all around us, and lots of time to contemplate it all. While Charlotte cried hot, homesick tears, my mind was a symphony of contradictory emotions.

But as the journey unfolded I could think of nothing but my seasickness. We spent a whole day and an uncomfortable, cold night laid out on long wooden benches with our coats wrapped over us, until, with the warm morning sun on my face, I felt a new lightness of being as we sailed into the mouth of the Thames. At some point through the night, Charlotte's sobbing had subsided into the occasional shudder, but once we were fully awake she began to cry and clung to my arm once again.

After a while, the river narrowed and we sailed into Docklands. The scene turned into something from H. G. Wells' *War of the Worlds*. The scale was unimaginable. Both sides of the river were flanked by rows of tall, steel, alien-insect-like structures with legs and cranes and booms all lined up as far as the eye could see. It appeared that earth had already been invaded by Martians. Our noses were filled with petrochemical fumes and smog, and beside me Charlotte began to sneeze. The passengers jumped to their feet and pointed, and then my new friend pressed a piece of paper with her address into my hand and made me promise to visit her.

The boat spent what seemed like an age carefully manoeuvring itself into its bay in West India Quay. Even as we disembarked, a boom had already swung round to start to collect the coal and pour it back into rail cars, where it would be taken to factories and heavy industries and homes. I thought of my father, and all the others, who had given their lives for this.

***

It took me a while to find the Clayton-Reids' driver, who was waiting for me by the manager's office as agreed. He ushered me back through the hordes, for as well as the coal boat there were all sorts of other cargo boats, too, and the docks thronged with literally hundreds of men scurrying around, wearing cloth caps and braces, cigarettes hanging out of their mouths, carrying goods on and off the boats onto the waiting trolleys below. Oh, the thrill of hearing the East End accent for the first time!

We drove through a London I never imagined could be so big nor could have so many different personalities, winding our way north until we reached the streets of Hampstead. The car pulled into a driveway that belonged to a vast and imposing Gothic mansion, nestled in a copse of mature trees and covered in climbing plants. The house swept upwards gracefully, seeming taller than the neighbouring buildings. Each window was framed with ornate, decorated arches; there was detail everywhere. Little Juliet balcony railings across each of the windows, multiple chimney breasts. The property and grounds were so large they even had their own street lamp within the front garden. A little girl stood, excited, at a bay window; she jumped down and ran to the front door when she saw me walking up the driveway.

'Hello,' she said, looking up at me.

I smiled and patted her on the head, as I walked through a pointed archway into a large, open-plan hallway, covered in mahogany panelling. At a glance, I took it all in: large chandelier, paisley carpet, red walls and curtains. It was like something from a film. The parents were already waiting, and they all stood together in the hallway. The master was small and almost bald, except for a mousy ridge that wrapped itself round the back of his head. His wife was equally petite, dressed in a tweed skirt and twinset and pearls. She might have been considered attractive in a neat sort of a way, but her nose was wrinkled into a kind of a sneer, and that was the first thing I noticed about her.

The master of the house shook my hand vigorously and welcomed me to the house and family with a broad smile. 'How was your journey?' he asked.

'Oh, fine thank you, sir. Although it would appear I have yet to find my sea legs.'

'Ha. Please, call me Matthew. And this is my wife, Lucy. What an adventure, though. Bella,' he said to the little girl, 'did you know that Nancy travelled down on a boat carrying huge containers full of coal for our fire?'

The little girl looked at me then looked around her. 'Where is the coal?'

We all laughed and the girl leaned into her father in embarrassment. 'It's still on the boat,' I said, bending down and placing my hands on her shoulders. She had a cute, round face with mousy hair, cut in a fringed bob. She wore thick glasses and was a little plump. 'But don't worry, they're going to bring some over for you very soon.'

'Bella,' said her mother, sharply. 'Stop clinging to your father's leg like that.'

I fancied I saw Matthew roll his eyes, just a shade or two, but the smile stayed in place.

'Where's your suitcase?' said the little girl.

'This is all I have,' I said, pointing to my army and navy bag.

'Travelling light, best way to travel,' said Matthew, breezily. 'Well then,' he continued, taking his daughter's hand. 'Let's introduce our new nanny to baby Paul.'

Bella regarded me shyly, but then hung back to walk with me, looking me up and down as we went. Lucy also watched me, tight-lipped. 'The last girl we had from up your way was hopeless. It took us three months to even understand what she was saying. We hear from Tim you're a grammar school girl so I just hope you have a better grasp of the King's English, and I also hope the good Lord has given you as much common sense as he did brains, because the last girl had neither.'

'I'll do my best,' I said, taking an instant dislike to my new employer. After my initial surprise and annoyance, I made a mental note to line up Pearl Mitford as my replacement when the time came. A little parting gift from me. Two people for whom the phrase 'you deserve each other' was clearly invented.

They led me to the drawing room, an impressive chamber with paisley carpet and a Queen Anne chair in the middle, set against a large fireplace and huge bay window. The ceiling was outlined with highly ornate Victorian coving, a sort of leaf pattern at the top and egg shape below. Above the fireplace was a large painting of a fox hunting scene. I had never seen anything like it, and tried not to gape. The baby was asleep on his back in his cot, his arms up in a U-shape above his head. He had a sweet little face and a serenity that babies have when they sleep. Looking down at him, I was sure that his spine looked to be slightly twisted, and I wondered if this was one of the health issues I had heard about.

'This is Paul,' said Matthew. 'He has a few problems but we love him just as much as we could, and we're grateful for every single day that God grants us with him.'

'He's lovely,' I said, feeling genuinely moved.

We wandered in and out of all the other rooms. The house was as big as the Oslington Hotel, possibly bigger. I could hardly comprehend it all. It even had a separate staircase on the west side, leading up to some guest suites at the top. My own room was in the basement. It was beautiful: huge, light and airy, with more arches and ornate coving, and French doors leading out onto the back garden. I even had my own indoor bathroom. Little waves of delight rose up in my throat. I felt like a queen.

After I had unpacked – an act which, given the paucity of my possessions, took about two minutes – we all wandered down to Hampstead Heath. Mrs Clayton-Reid appeared at the front door in a fur stole. I had a wry smile and took a closer look to see if I recognised it as one of mine, but it was too difficult to tell. I wandered along wide, tree-lined paths through the groves, drunk with the beauty of it all. Finely dressed ladies and gentlemen, children dressed in Sunday best. I had spent years imagining this, and now I was truly here, perhaps not quite in the capacity I had imagined, but nevertheless, I had made it happen. We wandered over the huge area of the heath, through woods and past outdoor swimming pools. I couldn't believe how warm it was compared with the North East. I wiped my brow; I was sweating.

Matthew bought us all ice creams and then I played tag with Bella through the trees. We threw bread into the lakes for the ducks. She took my hand after that; I had a sinking feeling that the little girl had already thrown her lot in with me in that guileless, trusting way that young children have, and I began to feel horribly guilty. Though the wife was probably going to be a giant pain the backside, I could see that Matthew and his daughter were nice people; they did not deserve someone like me.

'Let me take your photograph,' he said, smiling. 'First day and all that.' And so I stood, holding baby Paul, with Bella to one side, and tried to smile through the mists of an awful guilt, a self-loathing that had descended on me. His wife looked away, as if to say, 'What an indulgent folly.'

***

And so, Norman, my life at 34 Westfield Drive began. I spent most of my time either with Bella or cleaning the house. Lucy tended to take care of baby Paul, as his needs were complicated. This suited me fine; I think I would have been quite terrified at the responsibility of looking after him, too.

Bella and I fell into our own routine through the week. We started the day with breakfast together, then did 'classes' for a couple of hours. She had an amazing concentration span for someone so young, and sucked up information like a sponge. During the lessons, we played at schools – I pretended to be her actual teacher and was strict with her and had her call me 'Miss Thompson', which she absolutely loved. I taught her all her letters and numbers, surprised at how quickly she picked it all up. And because she caught on so quickly, I started to teach her French nursery rhymes. I thought I had toned down my pitmatic accent but when I explained how there were hundreds of different languages in the world, she replied, quite innocently, 'Which language do you speak, Miss?'

After morning classes, she would rest and have a sleep, which freed me up for a couple of hours of housework. Then we would have a light lunch and head off into the heath or further afield, roaming around for the afternoon. We ventured down to Highgate Cemetery, where we played hide and seek among the gravestones. Her mother hit the roof when she found out we'd been there, complaining that such antics were disrespectful to the deceased, as well as being unladylike. After that she banned us from going further than the heath. Other days, I took Bella swimming in the outdoor pools, again finding those times I knew the mistress would be away for the afternoon, as I knew she would not have approved.

Lucy seemed obsessed with the baby, and had very little interest in her daughter, which I thought was a shame. Bella was a real daddy's girl, and his arrival home after work was a hotly-anticipated event. She would spend hours making sure her hair was neat and her dress tidy, and we sometimes compiled mental lists of amusing things she could tell him about her day. She was desperate to be interesting for him, although there was no need for that, really, as he doted on her, too. However, there was an agonising wait after daddy arrived home when he nipped off to the smoking room at the front of the house for his post-work drink – fortification to help him handle his sour-faced wife, was my own personal reading of the situation.

On Saturdays, I was expected to keep away from the family areas unless I was babysitting or cleaning, and so I roamed around like a wild animal, heading into Belsize Park and down into Camden and along the Regent's Canal. Sometimes I met up with Charlotte, and went for walks with her. I usually had Sundays free, too, but was expected to go to Mass on Sunday evenings with them all.

Catholic Mass was a revelation all of its own. 'It's a little different from what you as a Methodist will be used to, but you'll soon get used to it,' said Matthew, optimistically. During my very first visit it was with horror I realised I had to take my own turn at confession. Lucy pointed to a large wooden box with two compartments separated by a thick purple curtain. I could see the priest's cassocked knees sticking out of his side. When my turn came, I sidled in, petulantly, and waited for him to speak.

I could smell mints, wafting under the curtain. The priest cleared his throat, and said, 'With true sorrow, are you ready to acknowledge your sins before me, child?'

I thought about this, staring miserably in front of me. 'How long have you got?' I asked, picking at one of my fingernails. In the next compartment, the priest burst out laughing, his loud chuckles resonating all through the church. Unfortunately, I was told later that the whole congregation had been able to hear, and a red-faced Lucy chided me on the way home for making a spectacle of them in church. It was not the best start to my new adventure, though I fancied I saw Matthew trying not to smirk as we walked back through the heath with the breeze on our faces.

***

At night, I dreamed about school. Sometimes I was simply late, sitting on my bed back in Acacia Street reading *Jane Eyre.* Sometimes I was out, roaming up in the fields with Norm. Other times I was waiting down at West India Quay for a boat to take me back home. Thus, once again, I felt very conflicted. Also, I had grown very fond of the little girl, and I could sense that I filled a maternal gap in her life as well. I'd also grown fond of Matthew, and of the baby, and the house was beautiful and charming and huge. I had a comfortable existence. But this had always been a stepping stone to something else; this was supposed to be the bastion of convention, of 'societal repression', that I was running from. The paradox was that it was nice, and comfortably upper middle class. Hampstead was interesting, and the heath satisfied my free-range nature but my life here was, in its own way, just as oppressive as life in the North East. If I went back home, I'd be facing the same old thing I had been trying to escape from: dirty backstreets, marriage and babies, pea soup, liver and onions, the chapel and the institute. I needed to move on, to contact Dalglish and see what he had to say. The problem was, every day I was awoken by a little girl who had grown to love me unconditionally, who trusted me implicitly, who sometimes just came into my room with her book and sat, reading quietly by the bed until I awoke. The happy smile on that round, freckled face was the first thing I saw each day. I felt sick at the thought that she would be added to the list of people I had betrayed.

And so the weeks and months rolled by, and I still had not contacted Dalglish. I turned sixteen, Bella turned four and Paul had his first birthday. He was not well, though no one ever explained to me what his condition was. The doctor was often at the house, and Paul was often in and out of hospital. Much as I hadn't really warmed to Lucy, I did feel sorry for her. She had all the worries of a sick child and she didn't seem to have any friends, or anyone to confide in.

'Are you having guests over?' I asked, once, when she wanted me to bleach all the crockery.

'No, child. We keep ourselves to ourselves, here,' was the curt reply.

Intellectually though, I was bored to death, and I hated the daily two hours of monotonous and menial housework, the pointless repetition of it all: dusting the bronze artefacts and polishing the silver cutlery, washing clothes and clearing out fireplaces. This was made worse by the mistress hovering suspiciously and often finding fault with my mediocre attempts, sometimes even finding me asleep in a room I was meant to be cleaning.

I felt a constant sense of guilt when I thought of everything and everyone I had left behind in Oslington, and this guilt hung over me constantly, clouding my thoughts. I wondered how my grandparents were getting on, with Grandad ill and retired and them no doubt having moved in with Aunt Flo. I wondered if they missed Oslington, and if they felt cut off over at Barring Tye. I couldn't bear even to think about Norm. I wondered if they all hated me. I imagined Mrs Mitford raging around with an indignance she had not earned the right to feel. But this guilt was the catalyst for me to decide what I should do. Staying put was no longer an option in my mind. What remained was for me to go back up north with my tail between my legs and beg the school to take me back, then continue on to teacher training college. Or, Norman, I could resurrect my original plan, and step off the 'conveyor belt of convention', as I had pretentiously labelled it. So, almost exactly a year after I had arrived, I sent a telegram to Dalglish, telling him I would be over to visit the following Saturday. My intention was to check the situation out, return to make a decision one way or another, then serve notice and continue working for the family until they could find a replacement.

Chapter 8

I took the underground train to Sloane Square and with the help of my home-drawn map walked along the King's Road before turning south and weaving my way down towards the river. It was around the middle of the afternoon when I arrived at the address, which was located about halfway along a pleasant, tree-lined street with a large church at one end and a small square at the other. Before me stood a slightly scruffy three-storey stone tenement, with iron steps leading down to a basement and more steps rising up to a front door.

I walked up to the main door and knocked. After a reasonable wait, the door was opened by a tall gentleman with black hair worn long to his ears and down the nape of his neck, turning out gently at the ends. A thick moustache and beard made it difficult to determine his age. His clothes were sober – plaid jacket, white shirt, country-green necktie. I introduced myself and said I was looking for Mr Dalglish. The man smiled, and said, 'I'm Dalglish. You can dispense with the 'Mister', though.'

He had a handsome, open face with striking brown eyes. Something in the turn of his eye spoke of a quiet, liberal countenance. In fact, you could be forgiven for thinking the local minister had popped by while in lay clothes, or perhaps some highly-regarded visiting academic.

The entrance hall was like something from a bad dream. On the walls were painted a number of gaudy, picaresque murals: on one side was a tropical jungle scene of striking primary colours complete with pecans, birds of paradise and a happy black man dancing in a grass skirt; on the other side was a circus with staring clowns, a helter-skelter in the background and a frightening Gypsy Rose Lee with missing teeth.

'We were starting to think you'd forgotten us.'

I smiled politely, but in truth, I was starting to question my decision to come but did not want to lose face. I did that English thing of smiling while simultaneously expecting a sledgehammer to clobber me across the back of the head, basically anything to avoid embarrassing myself.

'No one's going to eat you,' said Dalglish, grinning. 'Here – this way.' We descended creaky stairs to the basement where there was more sense-assaulting art: a *trompe l'œil* plant pot and plant painted on the wall, with a window painted above it.

Real plants grew everywhere, up and down like stalactites and stalagmites in an underground cave. The window ledge facing the street was a colourful riot of potted pink and red geraniums set alongside milk bottles full of white gardenias. A musty smell assaulted my nostrils, a mix of unwashed bodies and dirty surfaces and a decades-old divan, its once-rich hues having now faded to a generic moss colour. In the centre of the room was an easel and a table laden with paint, oil pots, water-filled jars and brushes. An artist was at work, and turned to look at us as we descended the steps. He was exceptionally old, as translucent as a jellyfish, with a narrow head, thin dried-out features and a shock of white hair. A red and white spotted necktie peeped out from under his generous artist's smock, and the paint patches on the cloth bore witness to the longevity of his career. The material was now effectively the same colours as the painting in front of him, suggesting a 'style' of sorts: blues, greens, burnt orange … which contrasted with the bright red corduroy trousers which cocooned the legs of his skinny, almost concave frame. The trousers were turned up at the bottom to reveal a pair of orthopaedic sandals, from which peeped out a set of thin, hairy toes.

The low divan spanned the length of the entire room and was covered in various African and Far Eastern printed cloths. On it lay a naked woman facing away from us, her upper half covered with a blanket so that we could see only from her backside downwards. I blushed at the sight of her, but Dalglish didn't give her a second look. A glance at the painting on the easel revealed that her top half had already been painted. Some liberties had been taken by the painter, giving the woman's Rubenesque curves that her slim frame did not possess in real life.

'I'd better introduce you to our resident *artiste*,' said Dalglish. 'This is Queenie. Queenie, this is Nancy, the one I was telling you about.'

'Ah, yes. Nice to meet you, my dear,' said the artist, nodding briefly in my direction. 'It's always good to meet one of Daggers' new muses,' he added, cattily, turning back to his canvas. 'Although they seem to get younger each time. Anyway, Daggers, I am bleached out with hunger, quite frankly. I can barely stand up. When did Arthur say he would be back?'

Dalglish sat down on the divan and motioned for me to do the same. He looked at his watch, frowning. 'He should be back by now.

He was only off to fetch some bread and cheese, the useless swine. And beer, if there's anything spare.'

'I haven't eaten since yesterday and that was only a packet soup. Really, I'm quite faint.'

Dalglish looked at me and winked. 'Yes, I've long admired your packet soup and absinthe regimen, Queenie, I must say. When is your dealer coming round? I'm short of cash too, and the rent's due this weekend.'

'Oh, he said he would be here on Friday. Should get five shillings for this one. The oils are doing well at the minute. You'll get it all of course, Herr Oberführer.'

'Appreciated, Queenie,' said Dalglish. He stood up and stretched upwards, yawning loudly, and strolled up behind the artist. He laid a friendly hand on his shoulder. 'It needs some apples in a bowl, to the right, I reckon. A touch of Cézanne.' They stood, looking over the painting intently. Both of them seemed to have forgotten my presence and I waited awkwardly, like a child summoned to see the headmistress to discuss some missed homework.

'Eroticised Cézanne, even,' he continued. 'Your dealer from Fitzrovia said that, remember, last time he was here? He has that customer who loves that look. Hasn't he bought about five already for his country manor or something?'

Queenie shot him a long-suffering look. 'You know, it really is getting a bit boring to keep hearing you asking me basically to plagiarise Cézanne and jumble a load of his paintings into one of mine. Horrible. I might as well just be another performing monkey drawing caricatures on the Spanish Steps, or up on show like a circus animal in Piccadilly. I need to be true to my own instincts. If I was painting to be fashionable I would be trying out Surrealism or some such nonsense, for God's sake. I've said it a thousand times and I do wish you would listen: stick to photography, Daggers old fellow, and leave the fine art to me.'

'Ha. An old ferret like you doing a Dali. Now *that* I would like to see.' He stroked his beard, pointing at the painting. 'How about a two-dimensional packet soup dripping across Eva's backside? But seriously – it's all very well allowing yourself the luxury of being true to your ideals when there's someone else to worry about the rent, old chap.' His voice was quiet; I had to strain to hear it. 'I would go for some apples, personally.'

The old artist grumbled a little, and said he couldn't bear to paint any food when he felt so hungry. They began a lengthy discussion of Cézanne and post-Impressionism, most of which I was not really interested in enough to follow. I picked up a newspaper called *Industrial Worker* and began to read, idly, wondering if I were still part of the same world I had woken up in that morning.

'Are you actually still painting?' came a voice from under the blanket. 'I'm freezing.'

'It speaks,' said Queenie, in clipped tones, dipping his brush in a pot of murky water. 'Two minutes, my darling. Nearly done. You have done marvellously today. Your bottom looks like a wonderful, fleshy white peach.'

'Ah, yes,' said Dalglish. 'Nancy, meet Eva.'

'Hello, Nancy,' came a muffled voice from under the blanket. The bare backside stared back at me, unmoving.

'It's always nice to put an arse to a face, I find. Though in this case, it'll have to be the other way round,' said Dalglish, in the same mild tones, as if he were discussing the weather or some other such triviality. He stood up and pulled on his coat. 'Let's go out for a coffee, Nancy, while these chaps are finishing off.'

'All right,' I said, relieved and feeling a rush of latent puritanism. Pulling on my long grey coat, I felt every bit the conventional grammar school girl and cursed my knee-length school stockings.

We walked down to the Thames, into a gentle wind. I stopped for a second, looking out across the low, grey river to the tree-lined streets over on the south side of London. I remembered my first journey up the river on the coal boat and inhaled sharply again at the scale of it all; everything seemed much bigger and wider than up north. A lone boat headed past, eastwards, sounding its horn. Children from a Lowry painting played on the flat, wide banks on the other side. Dalglish smiled and said how amazed he'd been, too, the first time he saw this view of the Thames. We continued to stroll along the embankment walk, past wrought-iron piers, moored boats and pastel-painted bridges.

'So, then, what are you looking for, Nancy?' he said. 'Literally, I mean. Not figuratively. Or perhaps I do mean both.'

I looked at him, feeling self-conscious. 'I wanted some work. My cousin's husband said I might be able to work as a model.'

'Did he explain the way I work?'

'Not really,' I admitted. 'He just said it was all rather unconventional.'

'Good old Richard,' he laughed. 'He and June loved their life here, but I think that Richard's family put pressure on them to head back into the fold, so to speak. Back to a life of unthinking tradition and repression. Shame.'

Running a hotel in Yorkshire could hardly be described in those terms, I felt, but said nothing; Dalglish was clearly passionate in his views.

Presently, we turned off the pleasant riverside walk onto a side street to find my new benefactor's favourite Italian cafe – a high-ceilinged building of generous proportions, with walls covered with gilded mirrors. I was introduced to the owner, a swarthy looking fellow with a checked shirt, who greeted me with a kiss on both cheeks like I was an old friend.

I wasn't sure what to have so Dalglish ordered some coffees and pastries for us. Although I was a fussy eater, I did possess a sweet tooth, and helped myself to a generous selection of cakes. The coffee was strong and bitter; it smelled better than it tasted, in fact, I wasn't sure I liked the taste at all.

'Thank you for bringing me here,' I said, at last, relaxing a little.

'You're welcome. Have you ever been to a cafe before?'

I shook my head, my mouth full. 'They're called tea rooms where I come from.'

'Ha, I thought not. You know, I think I'm quite good at reading people,' he said, slicing into a warm *pain au chocolat* which oozed plentifully onto the plate. He traced his finger through the chocolate and licked at it slowly. 'Do you know what I see when I look at you? I see someone who is running away from the shackles of ordinary life. How else does someone from your background and gender end up here? And,' he continued, 'you are absolutely breathtaking, Nancy. When I first opened the front door to you, I thought I must be dreaming, and I'm still wondering if you are actually real, or if you're really a wraith that has decided to move among us and give the appearance of being real, until one day you'll simply disappear back to your supernatural realm.'

I was uncomfortable at such directness and my cheeks flushed, but I was also flattered.

'Well anyway, the simple answer is, I would be very happy to work with you. But listen,' he said, pausing as a waitress brought us some glasses of water, 'how do I put this so that it doesn't come out wrong? Basically, when you work for me, you must also belong to me. I don't mean that in any kind of slavery sense.'

'Phew,' I laughed.

'No, that's really the antithesis of what this whole thing is all about. I mean artistically. I work for magazines like *Vogue*, and I take photos of models on the catwalks and such like. But I can only work closely with someone if I understand their soul and if their spirit is free. I can photograph my friends all day long, but I can and will only photograph about four different models in the whole country. So,' he continued, 'it's a paradox of sorts. You need to belong, in order to be free. Do you understand, Nancy?'

I do not think another living human being could have impressed me more; I was intoxicated with the Italian cafe and the romantic promise of unshackling myself from the rest of society. I was terribly special, the fifth element of an elite set of models – although, at that moment, I would have happily clawed the eyes out of the other four. Coffee coursed through my veins and my heart thumped in my chest.

'I'll be honest with you, Nancy; you have a very unusual look. A lot of women I meet are quite beautiful in person but that does not always translate into someone being photogenic. But I can see from just looking at you.' Here, he traced a finger gently across my cheekbones. 'The proportions of your face, your bone structure … I can see that it will work with you. You'll probably be more stunning in photographs than in real life, funnily enough. Ha! Don't take that the wrong way, of course. But more importantly, there's a free spirit in there; there's something that's really quite defiant. And that comes out in photographs. You can't hide it.

'The agencies will want you and they'll try to pay me off to get hold of you. I've seen it before. Totally unscrupulous, but then that's what you get with companies motivated by profit alone in our capitalist world. You need to ask yourself: do I just want to make money or do I want my soul to be free? And if the answer is the latter, then I can promise you an authentic life with fellow artists, because the fact is that we would love to have you if you want to stay.'

I didn't know what to say. The door to the cafe opened and a man in a long trench coat walked in, tipping his cap to Dalglish. They greeted each other warmly, and Dalglish asked him how he was finding life in Italy.

'That's Ezra Pound,' said Dalglish under his breath when the man walked off, as if that name should mean something to me. 'I hear he's thrown his lot in with Mussolini these days. Better not tell Arthur I've been speaking to him. Bit of a pinko, our Arthur.'

I nodded, trying to look as if I understood, and we put on our coats and headed back out onto the street and down to the embankment. The sun was waning in the sky and the light shone in sparkling beams across the river. Some seagulls settled themselves noisily on the lamp posts that flanked the wide walkway.

'I'd better be heading back now,' I said.

'What, to your family?' he said, and a dark cloud passed across his face. I felt my cheeks burn; I wanted more than anything to please him. I thought for a second he might turn angry but he seemed to collect himself and smiled once again. 'But why wait? If you want to be free, then take your freedom. It's right here, on a plate. Think of it as an early Christmas present from me.'

'What about my things? And the family? I can't just leave. I'm their nanny. The little baby is sick. The little girl has grown very fond of me. And, well, I'm very fond of her too.'

'You can never truly be free when you are shackled by possessions,' he said, with a shrug. 'The family will be okay – they don't own you. They'll find another girl in no time. It's time for you to start to think of yourself.'

The man exuded quiet but heady persuasion, and I felt myself being drawn in inexorably, like a fly to a sticky spider's web. Fate tossed a coin with heads on both sides, winked at me, then told me to choose heads.

Dalglish fished in his pockets and took out a guinea. 'Send them this,' he said. At the back of my mind I thought this a little odd, given he had made a big deal of suggesting earlier that cobbling together the rent money might be a bit of a challenge, and the poor artist was clearly on the verge of starvation back at the house. We walked quickly to catch the post office before it closed, and Dalglish told me to send them a telegram announcing my resignation and cheque to the value of one guinea covering the cost of finding someone new. He waited outside, smoking, while I went in and sorted it all, as if the details of such a transaction were more than he could bear. But I was glad in a way that he did not want to know anything about the Clayton-Reids, though I couldn't explain why at the time.

I wondered if it would be terribly bourgeois to ask whether there was a bed for me. And it was only at the very far reaches of my mind, right out at the misty edges of my cerebral universe, that I could dimly make out the theoretical protestations of my grandparents – people who had never had the luxury of choosing the kind of life they led. In this grainy vision, Grandad was sitting in his chair, holding the newspaper open at the horse-racing page, shaking his head and muttering about lambs to the slaughter, and Nana was waggling her finger and proclaiming, 'What a load of old tripe. Divven't get sucked in, hinney, it'll all end in tears.'

***

This is the point in the story, Norman, isn't it, when you expect some sanctimonious crawling platitude about them being right? Everyone loves it when the bad girl gets her comeuppance then tells you she's sorry she was ever bad in the first place. But Mr Moreton has already told us that *Schadenfreude* is a sin, and I have already told you that the only way I can explain things to you is via my story. If there is humility to be found, it is in the pile of typed up chapters sitting on my desk, and in a wastepaper bin full of discarded sheets full of typing errors and changes to the prose and mistakes caused by the vagaries of a sometimes-epileptic typewriter.

Trotting out a platitude at this juncture would be an act of extreme vulgarity; honestly, I've no stomach for it. Let's move on …

***

The basement was in a state of excitement when we returned. 'Pinko Arthur' was back. He was a tall, intellectual-looking chap with little penny glasses and a lock of blonde hair that continually fell across his face and which every minute or so he patiently pushed aside, unaware of how irritating this might be to both himself and onlookers.

Queenie looked to be on the verge of tears. He lay mournfully on the shabby old divan in the arms of Eva, who had now grown a top half and had poured it all into a charming emerald gown. With her blonde curls and splash of red lipstick, she exuded the mesmerising charm and exquisiteness of a film star. I stared at her, open-mouthed, until she caught me at it and smiled. Her beauty was immense and I wondered if you had to be either attractive or intellectual to join this set, and how long it would be before I was found out to be rather ordinary.

'What's wrong, Queenie?' said Dalglish, taking off his jacket.

'Ask Arthur,' came the breathless reply, a theatrical voice fading into oblivion. Eva stroked his hair, as impassive as a Persian cat.

'Well? Where's the food?'

'Who's she?' said Arthur, nervously strumming the table, and looking at me out of the corner of his eye.

'We'll come to that. Where's our food?'

But Arthur had the look of a dog who had just snuck into the kitchen and eaten the family Sunday roast.

'They were just there, in front of me,' he said. 'Leather-bound. I've been looking for them all my life, and then suddenly there they were, right in front of me.'

'My tongue is leather-bound, you bastard,' said Queenie. 'Leather-bound with crusted packet soup. That's what they'll put on my tombstone: 'Here lies Quentin Falmouth, déclassé. His last meal was packet soup.'

'You love being déclassé, you old pansy,' said Arthur, with a snort.

'What did you buy?' said Dalglish, peering over Arthur's shoulder. 'I suppose Allah told you to do it, did he?'

Arthur ignored this. '*The Anatomy of Melancholy*,' he said, his eyes shining with delight and guilt. 'One of the original editions. Just eight shillings. Can you believe it? Seriously, I don't think the chap knew what he had there.'

'Goodness me,' said Dalglish. 'What a find.' He picked up one of the books and began thumbing through, emitting a cloud of centuries-old dust in the process. 'Well, seeing as we've got to eat wind pudding tonight, why don't you read to us instead?'

We settled down for the evening. I felt guilty that my belly was full. Arthur and Queenie continued to trade insults; Queenie made a cutting remark that it was a sad day indeed when a book like *The Anatomy of Melancholy* was preferable to Arthur's terrible homespun Fabian poetry, and Arthur responded in kind, saying that Queenie was an old has-been painter who should return to the aristocratic, bourgeois life of butler-buggering, and so on. But presently, even the resident squabblers fell silent. Eva and Dalglish moved around the room, closing the heavy oxblood curtains and lighting candles. Arthur positioned himself cross-legged on the floor, wrapped himself in a musty blanket, and began to read. I, too, found myself a spot on a heap of old blankets on the floor and relaxed into the evening, listening to Arthur's soft, earnest tones. After a while, Eva unwrapped herself from Queenie and sat down next to me, pulling me to her and kissing my head maternally. She smelled of sweat and expensive perfume. I wondered if she and Dalglish were lovers and felt a momentary stab of pain.

Dalglish managed to find his last bottle of vodka – or so he maintained – so we all shared from that, using a few miniature milk bottles that Eva found in the scullery. I got the feeling that there were several unspoken rules: in true communist style, whatever we had must be shared, or sort of shared, or maybe not really shared at all, depending where you fell in the domestic hierarchy, and, clearly, there was a pecking order when it came to choosing between art and food. I felt guilty about the Clayton-Reids, especially when I thought of poor Bella. I wondered about Cousin June and her husband Richard – difficult to imagine them here. I also resolved to send my grandparents a letter, though I could not face thinking about them right now, or that great, heavy block of Norm-shaped guilt that continued to lodge in my stomach.

But the disquiet soon became overlaid with the intoxicating feeling of being part of something utterly different; a place where the need for literature and art was elevated such that it looked down condescendingly on more prosaic needs like food. I felt properly free, for the very first time in my life. I doubt the gates of heaven could have impressed me more.

Arthur continued to read the depressing subject matter and we sipped slowly at vodka from the miniatures. An aura of sadness and gloom hung about the room, but around its edges was a frisson, akin to those final moments when the fireworks have been lit and are about to go off. Queenie began to whimper properly, reminding me of Sid the whippet; Arthur began to laugh cruelly, and finally we ran out of vodka. A most bizarre evening had come to a natural end.

Eva led me upstairs to my bedroom, a lightless, box room at the top of the house, nestled beneath a creaking roof. She left me there with a lingering kiss on the mouth that tasted of vodka and cigarettes and was just the wrong side of ambiguous. I crashed into bed fully clothed and, in spite of all the excitement, fell asleep immediately.

***

The next morning, I awoke early in a sweaty cloud of panicky disorientation. A bitter taste lurked accusingly in my mouth. I dreamed that I had taken Bella and Paul to Highgate Wood and had embarked on a game of hide and seek with them. After a while I had somehow managed to lose both of them and had begun a feverish search of the woods. I sat up in bed feeling sick with guilt. But at the same time, a sharp thrill licked its way round my stomach and the euphoria that comes with new-found freedom returned. I had liberated myself from all the constraints and conventions and disappointments of my life to date. It was as if my whole life had been leading up to this moment. There could have been rats crawling across the floor and open sewers and I would still have been blissfully happy. As it happened, there were quite a lot of damp corners in the house where fungi grew openly, and you wouldn't have wanted to go downstairs barefoot early in the morning while the slugs were still out and about, leaving their silvery threads all over the threadbare carpet or lino. In those early days, it just didn't matter to me.

The attic room was chilly, and in the daylight I could see it was larger than I had first thought. Its sloping ceilings were covered in a multitude of clashing African prints, and the walls below were painted a dusky orange and embellished with paintings and sketches. The bed was also low, divan-style, and covered in what looked like a hand-knitted patchwork quilt of brightly clashing coloured squares. On the floor sat a bronze statue of Buddha that bore an unsettling resemblance to Aunt Flo. Some joker had mounted a Harlequin doll onto the Buddha's shoulders in a vulgar manner. Spider plants hung from the ceiling and cheese plants burst upwards from the floor. In the corners of the room were wicker baskets of various shapes and sizes, out of which spilled ladies' clothing and accessories. A bevelled mirror stood on a small dresser at the far corner of the room, under a dormer window. On the dresser also stood a couple of burned out joss sticks, a pile of necklaces, earrings in little blue crystal pots and a pair of huge sunglasses with tortoiseshell rims.

Everything was beautiful in its own right; in theory the decor clashed deeply, but somehow it all worked in a sort of shabby Ali-Baba-cavern way. My heart beat fast at the gorgeousness of it all; I was as excited as a child at their own party. I felt hugely ridiculous in my grammar school outfit, though. Almost without a thought I began to rummage through the baskets of clothes for something else to change into. Most of the clothes either had a costume feel or were extremely opulent-looking, but eventually I found a matching outfit – plaid flannel trousers, and a knitted white-collared blouse with matching green tweed jacket – and decided to help myself to it. I picked out a green beaded necklace from the dresser, which I thought matched the jacket rather cleverly. Suddenly I was a well-heeled if slightly under-nourished farmer's wife and I laughed out loud at my transformation, face-to-face with myself in the mirror. Something told me that assuming possession of such garments would not be a problem; the whole house had a cheerfully communal feel. I wondered vaguely why Queenie hadn't been up here helping himself to stuff to pawn for the money he so desperately needed. That's what I would have done in his situation.

A trip to the lockless bathroom revealed further plant infestation in the form of cactuses lined up along the window ledge, and a few hole-ridden towels of exceptional vintage that smelled like mature cheddar. A framed print above the lavatory read: 'You should make a point of trying everything once, except incest and folk-dancing.'

The quote was from someone called Arnold Bax, apparently. I'd never heard of him.

I performed the most perfunctory of ablutions then decided to nose around. In an oversized, musty-smelling cupboard I found a pot of moisturising cream and some rouge, which I experimented with on my cheeks and lips. A hairbrush provided the last touches and I decided to go and fetch some breakfast for my hosts, as a gesture of thanks for taking me in. I stepped out into a chilly Chelsea morning and wandered around till I found the shops I needed.

The scullery was at the rear of the basement, facing out onto the garden. I had a fright when I first wandered in, to see Arthur's legs sticking out from a broom cupboard off the garden end of the room. This must be his 'bedroom'. But the noise of my cooking didn't seem to disturb him at all. In fact, Queenie was the first to arise. He almost trembled with joy when he wandered sleepily in and stared at the pan full of scrambled eggs, back bacon, plates piled high with toast and a pot of tea on the side. He looked close to tears.

'Marvellous,' he said, shaking his head. 'What a girl. Most kind. You spent your own money on these?'

I smiled. 'Have a seat,' I said. 'Let me get you a plate.'

He thanked me again profusely and began to eat with the vigour and seriousness of an arctic wolf who has made his first kill after a long, barren winter.

'You're like a Flemish angel, my dear. I would love to paint you. Do tell me about yourself,' he said, presently, taking a sip of tea.

The door opened and Dalglish wandered through in a long, scruffy white shirt. Arthur also came to life, looking around the kitchen as if he had wandered into the wrong house. After a few seconds, Eva also poured herself in, smiling sleepily. She refused all food but took a cup of tea and wandered back into the basement room and fitted herself into the divan, legs curled up beneath her.

'Breakfast,' I said.

'Can we keep her, please?' said Queenie, with a smile.

'I am hoping very much that she decides to stay of her own accord,' said Dalglish, staring at my outfit.

'I hope it was all right to just help myself to these clothes?'

'Yes, fine, Nancy. They belonged to a woman who used to live here,' said Dalglish, still looking a little shocked.

When I'd served up and everyone was seated in the basement room, I began to tell my story but I hadn't got very far when Queenie interjected.

'My dear,' he said, with a worried look. 'Don't take this the wrong way but … is that even English? I'm afraid I only got every fourth or fifth word. Do you think you could start again, more slowly and without so much dialect, for an old dog like me?'

***

So in love was I with my new-found freedom that it was not for several months, or years even, that I attempted to put any sort of context to my situation. Young, enraptured and drunk on the novelty of it all, I never questioned why they accepted me so readily or so quickly into their home and their hearts. I was little more than a child myself, Norman, with limited cultural or other references to bring to the table. Dalglish I will come to later, but the others welcomed me not just as an equal, but as a shining star to be revered, worshipped almost.

I had never even heard of the word 'bohemian' and I knew absolutely nothing about the history of the movement or the kind of people it attracted. But, of course, with hindsight, I can see that this is exactly the milieu my new flatmates inhabited. I met scores more over the years and worked out that, except for Arthur, these were a group of people fleeing from privileged upper-middle-class backgrounds to consciously pursue a life of poverty in order to promulgate their ideals regarding art or socialism or poetry or sex, or whatever happened to pique their interest. Arthur's case was different: he came from a family of wealthy progressive liberals who sent him to a co-educational Steiner school where he was allowed a lot more freedom than most of his contemporaries.

But, Norman, different backgrounds or not, they all idolised the same things – the working classes, poverty, beauty, friendship unencumbered by family ties, and especially the free-range child, à la Rousseau. And there it was in a nutshell: to them I was the embodiment of all these things. I entertained them in the evenings, huddled round the fire down in the basement with stories of my wild and uncorrupted childhood spent hunting and gathering. I talked at length about catching otters, pheasants and rabbits, and how we kept my friend Norm's family fed by fishing and hunting and weren't afraid which side of the law we ended up on. I also described finding the dead bodies and fetching the police – they thought this hilarious.

They could all literally quote passages by heart from a book called *Emile* by the aforementioned Rousseau, and so, just by luck, in their eyes I happened to represent an incarnation of that revered fictional character, that embodiment of every single value they held dear. It instantly classified me as a true bohemian. They also had the grace to be suitably humbled by the fact that, unlike them, I had never had the luxury of choosing a life of poverty.

Add to all that the fact that when faced with the choice of a future defined by dilemma – either submit to imprisonment within the anachronistic institution of marriage, unable to work due to English law, or become a spinster teacher – I basically ran away, they shook their heads and told me I was a true refugee, and that it was my free spirit that had led me to them. I could attain no higher accolade.

***

A few days later, Dalglish and I travelled in his motor car to Mayfair, to Richard's father's agency. Dalglish explained the set up: he was one of a number of photographers allied to the agency, which itself passed on (with appropriate commission) his skills and services to magazines and the film industry. As Dalglish insisted on using his own models, the purpose of the trip was to gain their acceptance for him to use me in his shoots. To 'get you onto the books,' as he put it. And, as he had predicted, they tried to buy me off him, shaking their heads at him and his lucky streak. Everyone at the agency was beautiful or at least looked like they had been once upon a time.

I spent a hugely enjoyable day in the centre of my new, shiny, technicoloured life. I was taken first to a salon for hair and make-up, then back to the agency for the photo shoot. They curled my hair and gave me false eyelashes. They plucked out then drew back in eyebrows like Marlene Dietrich's. They put me in a brassiere for the first time – itchy beyond belief – and a girdle by Kestos, and I then spent several hours trying on various outfits and having my photo taken by Dalglish. And all the time, as if contradicting the intensity of his dark gaze, he chatted easily and asked me questions and flirted in such a way that I felt entirely at ease, and ended up flirting back at the camera.

Richard's father, and his chief of staff – a woman who, in retrospect, I realise had the look of Mrs Simpson of Edward-and-Mrs-Simpson fame – took us to the Ritz for lunch, something I was too frightened and over-awed to enjoy. The whole hour passed as a gilt-coated nightmare. I had no idea what to order and which cutlery to use. It was not until the end of the meal that I worked out you have to put your napkin onto your lap, and at some point I cut my tongue on a knife – I could feel the blood gathering in my mouth – but managed to hide this from the others.

I was relieved when we returned to the offices. I tried on dresses by Balenciaga, Molyneux and Norman Hartnell, a white, backless evening gown by Vionnet, and then they put me in what they called 'Paris beach fashions': halter-neck navy-and-white swimwear, wide-legged trousers, and beach caps.

By late afternoon, the fashion editor from *Vogue* had been summoned and I had my very first assignment, booked in for the end of the week: an on-site shoot modelling Aquascutum trench coats at the Windsor races.

At the end of the day, I reluctantly changed back into my farmer's wife outfit and tried to hand back the brassiere and girdle, which made them laugh. They also gave me a bag full of new Max Factor make-up, and a gorgeous green Cloverdale crochet dress, and white platform shoes. Dalglish told me that I was going to be the new darling of the fashion world. My throat was so constricted with excitement that I could hardly breathe, but I was also acutely aware of the things I had got wrong, like having the table manners of a goat and trying to hand back my used knickers. I felt like a genius and a fool, all at the same time.

On the way home, we made a stop at a friend's house for Dalglish to buy some cocaine for the weekend. I thought initially this might be another clothes designer and was quite confused when he came out grinning, holding nothing. In any case, he made me promise not to tell the others.

'The household finances are complicated, Nancy,' he said, shaking his head. The car headed back to Chelsea, along a road parallel with the Thames. As we stopped at traffic lights, the smell of roast chestnuts wafted into the open window of his car. A mournful-looking street vendor with an over-sized cap sat behind his stall, poking the chestnuts around in a pan.

'Want some?' said Dalglish, and as soon as the lights turned green he pulled the car in to the side of the road a little way ahead and jumped out without waiting for an answer. He had already bought a bag of the steaming bronzed beauties by the time I had got out of the car. We sat down on a bench and looked out over the river. A peach coloured dusk was falling and the sun cast long shadows across the pavement. Out of the sun it felt breezy and cool. My stomach was not ready for more food after the heavy lunch, and I also was feeling carsick, but I forced myself to eat.

'Delicious,' he said, taking a handful and throwing a couple into his mouth. 'Anyway, as I was saying. I'm already carrying everyone else financially, as friends do.'

'That doesn't seem quite fair.'

'My friends are my family, Nance. No difference. I don't covet material things, and I don't really care about money. But even so they expect me to spend every last penny on them, and sometimes … well, sometimes I just need to keep a little back for me. Does that make sense?'

I nodded, thrilled at this little confidence between us. It confirmed the opinion I had already formed having witnessed the conversation between Dalglish and Queenie the day before, and I was pleased with my own astute reading of the situation, though I still had no idea what cocaine was.

'You can't put a price on liberty,' he said, looking directly at me.

I nodded, thinking how beautiful his brown eyes were, in an understated kind of way. 'I agree. A conversation I had with a Methodist minister, a while back. It keeps coming back to me. He talked about free will. I think about that a lot.'

He grimaced. 'Be wary of the clergy lecturing you about free will. Religion is the antithesis of that.'

'Maybe,' I said.

'Free will is allowed for those parts the church doesn't control. Like emptying the bins.'

'Ha!'

'Do you know, in Ireland, the priests even tell the people when they're allowed to have sex?'

I blushed, in spite of myself. We fell into a silence, watching the steady flow of river traffic following the tide out towards Essex and Kent.

'Arthur's flirting with Islam,' said Dalglish, presently. 'He met this chap at one of his rallies, some Muhammadan fellow whose family come from India originally. The father came over on one of the trading ships, worked as a cook I think. Anyway, this chap is off his head on hashish a lot of the time, then lecturing Arthur for drinking ale. Religious hypocrisy at its best.'

I shook my head.

'It just reminded me when you mentioned free will.'

'How come?'

'Well, from what I've gleaned from Arthur, Islam doesn't have the same notion of free will. You want to become a Muhammadan, you need to submit to the faith. You accept it all. You can't question it. And once you're in that's it, you're not allowed out. Allah decides everything. I've told Arthur what I think about it all, because at the end of the day he's playing a dangerous game, an ironic game in my opinion, in light of what he's had to sacrifice to have the freedoms he has. That's what I say to him. Arthur, I say, what else do we have but our freedom?'

'True,' I said, wiping my fingers on a hanky. 'I feel like I've spent my whole life fighting for my right to exercise free will. But I also worry about it. Can there ever be too much of it? Look at me, I've had to abandon my family and friends in my quest for free will. Society couldn't function if everyone acted like me. In a way, I liked the time I spent with the minister's family and the church. It gave me boundaries. Certainty. Seeing what they did with the poor, and helping out a bit myself. I'm sorry – I'm just rambling now. But it's so confusing.'

Dalglish laughed. 'Ah, you need to read Freud, Nancy. *The Future of an Illusion*. Absolutely terrible translation, but you need to see beyond that. Explains why societies concoct religion. Freud says, since the dawn of time communities of people have created sets of rules or arrangements that allow them to live among each other, ethics included. He calls it culture, or sometimes civilisation. Religion is just the emperor's new clothes in that respect, an illusion. Just another way of getting people to behave in a way that allows us all to live together as a community, except that in order to make these laws more palatable, they're elevated to a position above human society,' he said, gesturing upwards before taking another chestnut. 'These laws are extended over nature and the universe. Born, he says, of the need to make tolerable the helplessness of man. It's usually of the greatest benefit to the rulers of those societies, not your common man. For the rulers, the obvious benefit is that you can use it to control people. And offer people a lie that they can also control the forces of nature and that there is a higher power that will protect them if they obey a new set of rules. You must read it one day.'

I looked out over the river, contemplating this. The water was steel-coloured, but dappled spots of light twinkled on the surface. I understood what he was saying, but it didn't explain to me why, in taking my freedom and to hell with everyone else, I felt so guilt-laden. In front of us a wealthy couple strolled past; the lady wore fawn coloured furs and shiny, patent stilettos and the man wore a suit and bowler hat.

'Off to the opera, those two,' Dalglish continued, nodding at the couple. 'I do love to see the bourgeoisie out and about. Let *them* worry about the nuances of free will, I say. You're just a few days into your new-found freedom. Isn't it a little early to be questioning it? Do you think you would have had to run away if religion and society hadn't put so many rules in place to effectively rob you of your future and leave you no choice? Here we have our own society and our own rules, albeit you might find they are rather on the lax side. Heck,' he whispered conspiratorially, 'I once spent an evening with Augustus John when he was on a bender.' He gave a long whistle. 'That was messy. But I'll save *that* story for another time. I don't know who was more long-suffering, his wife or his girlfriend. Anyway, young lady, this conversation has become far too serious. We only stopped to have some celebratory chestnuts! Just be glad that you of all people have won the right to exercise free will. Outside the constraints of community, religion, gender, whatever. You should be proud of yourself.'

I smiled, wondering if he was going to kiss me. My heart pounded in my chest. But he nudged me in a brotherly way and chortled again. We got up and headed for the car, and all at once I felt foolish, like a child on their first day of school who has stumbled into a lesson of advanced mathematics when they don't yet know how to read and write.

Once home, I went up to the attic room to divest myself of my acquisitions. On the bed was a packet with a translucent rubber ring inside and the words 'Dutch cap' on the front. Next to it was a book called *Married Love* by a sensible-sounding woman called Marie Stopes and a piece of paper with a heart drawn onto it and the words: 'You don't have to be married to enjoy love. It's free and it's wonderful, but be careful. Yours, Eva xxx PS if you want some help fitting it just let me know.'

This place is wild, I thought, laughing out loud.

I opened the book and began reading Mrs Stopes's gentle but no doubt scandalous assertion that if sex did not always have to lead to procreation, it *might* also be considered a pleasurable activity in its own right and not just something to be endured for the proliferation of little darlings.

Then I wondered about Freud.

***

It seemed bourgeois to ask too many questions, so I resisted my natural analytical urge to pry into everyone else's situations. As such, I was constantly surprised by things. The first instance of this was when Eva accompanied us to Windsor on the Friday for the fashion shoot; up until that point I hadn't worked out that she was a model too. She laughed at my naivety, in fact for everyone it simply became part of the narrative they put together for me, and something to be expected from someone who grew up *Emile*-style, living on their instincts. We all had our oddness and quirks, though; there was some sarcasm, but generally these traits were celebrated because they made us individuals.

The four-page shoot for *Vogue* showed Eva and me posing at the Windsor races and appearing every bit the conventional English roses, peering through our binoculars at the racecourse, looking at each other through the gaze of benevolent and wholesome friendship, and so on. And yet, Dalglish somehow was able to capture a hint of something darker, less obviously conventional, something of the free spirit in the way we tilted our heads up and smiled, something more daringly sexual in the way our heritage jackets fell open to reveal low cut dresses underneath.

It goes without saying that I had never been to the races before; there were so many firsts in one week that I wondered what would be next. I felt pangs of sadness throughout the day that Grandad could not be there to share the experience; how he would have loved to see horse racing properly, rather than just on paper and in the betting shop.

After the shoot, we drove back into London. It was late by the time we arrived at the Mayfair agency offices, probably around eight o'clock. Eva and I waited outside in the car, while Dalglish ran inside to collect our wages. He was away quite some time, and seemed to have grown wild-eyed and manic upon his return, handing Eva and me a guinea each and telling us he loved us.

'C'mon ladies, it's Friday night and we're rich,' he shouted, turning on the car's engine. 'Let's go and celebrate. Why worry about the rent when there are private members' clubs to visit and bottles of champagne that need drinking.'

'In that case, it has to be Club Gargoyle,' said Eva, laughing.

A short while later, we pulled up outside a large art deco building with a limestone facade, lit up by brass lamps. My chaperones were greeted like royalty and welcomed on first name terms by the door staff. The doorman took our coats and someone took the car keys to go and park the car for us. Dalglish put his hand on the concierge's shoulder, like a best friend, and said, 'Bona nochy, Stewart, my good man. I'm relying on you to look after these beautiful ladies of mine tonight, all right?'

'Of course, sir,' said the concierge. 'Hello, Miss Eva, and Miss …?'

'Nancy.'

Inside, there was a large, open area with a plum carpet, and fresh lilies in a huge glass vase. Off the central area, large arches led to a restaurant to our left, a bar to our right and a wide curved staircase to the middle. The walls were half-covered with dark, mahogany panelling. Eva led me by the hand off to the bar area, in which an impressive jazz band were playing. The musicians were all black; I'd never seen a black man before and was absolutely fascinated. Let's just say, Norman, they made me wince at memories of Grandad dressed in blackface as Al Jolson. The band members were all dressed to look as smart and as alike as possible: matching black suits and bow ties, white shirts and handkerchiefs, slicked-back hair and small, neat moustaches. My eyes were drawn, in particular, to the trumpeter. After a few bars he caught me watching him and winked.

The bar room was filled with interesting creatures: a large, stern-looking lady wearing a man's suit and a monocle; a frightening creature with long hair and a flat, hairy chest and a beard, wearing a ballgown; art students with short spiky hair wrapped in bandanas; a woman in full Tyrolean attire, with blonde plaits, hat, dirndl skirt, embroidered peasant blouse, kerchief tied at the neck, the whole works. Flapper girls flirted with jazz boys. Plumes of cigarette and cigar smoke furled their way upwards, settling into the air.

The proprietor came over and chatted to us for a while. Dalglish spoke of his worries about the rent increases in Chelsea. Soon, he said, there will be no more artists left, and the whole place will be full of Arabs and merchant bankers.

Waiters crowded round with trays carrying glasses of champagne. I was introduced to scores of weird and wonderful characters; being on Dalglish's arm conferred an instant status to me that I would certainly not otherwise have had. The band played, glorious in their suits and black ties. I became aware of couples quietly disappearing upstairs together and returning some time later; Eva explained to me what was going on. I grew tipsy and lost all track of time. Eva and I danced together, and I think she may have tried to kiss me again.

‘Here,’ she said, as one song ended. ‘Let me introduce you to another of the group.’ She tapped the arm of an Asian woman clad in purple and lilac Indian veils, with diamanté jewellery across her forehead. The woman wore a lot of eye make-up in the same shades as her clothing, and had long, curled eyelashes. She was, I thought, almost unspeakably beautiful, doll-like. I tried not to stare.

‘Ayesha, meet Nancy.’

‘How do you do,’ she said, nodding at me. Her accent had a slight lilt to it.

‘Hello,’ I mumbled. ‘Where are you from?’ I couldn’t think of anything else to say.

‘East India … Docks,’ she said, and laughed with Eva. I shrugged, feeling foolish.

‘Ayesha is another runaway, aren’t you darling?’

‘I’m afraid so.’

‘Her family run a hotel over in the East End, isn’t that right? And one day she spots the Cobra over there,’ said Eva, nodding to the giant bass player in the band, ‘who’s staying in room number four with his band. They’re from New Orleans, by the way. And he spots *her*, of course. By the end of the week she’s in a van hiding between double basses and trumpets and is fleeing with him to Chelsea to live happily ever after.’

‘It’s a bit more complicated than that, Eva.’

‘I know, darling, I’m trying to give Nancy the abridged version as I’m dying for another glass of champagne. Ayesha, just remind me – we met here, didn’t we, about a year ago?’ She turned to me.

'Dalglish has got Ayesha into films. How's it going up at the Farnham, by the way?'

The woman rolled her eyes. 'Oh, God. *The Prince of Punjab* is coming along just fine, thank you. If you ignore the fact that the story is utter dross.'

'Needs must.'

'Actually, I just came straight from the set. I don't usually dress like this,' she said to me, pointing to her jewels and elaborate attire.

'You look very beautiful,' I said.

'Doesn't she? I did some work up at the Farnham last year as an extra. Looks like an old factory from the outside but then you get inside and it's just *amazing*,' gushed Eva in typically exuberant fashion. 'What a shame the film has to be in black and white – no one will get to appreciate that beautiful purple outfit. And your make up is divine too. Anyway, darling, great to see you. Would you like a glass of champagne? Oh, no, you don't drink, do you. Listen, do bring the Cobra over to meet Nancy when he's finished, all right?' Eva took hold of my arm and pulled me towards a waiter holding a tray of glasses.

The band stopped playing and the room thinned out. Couples sat kissing on the leather sofas, the paisley carpet beneath them a sea of intermingled shoes. I couldn't see Eva or Dalglish around. I began to chat with Ayesha again and was introduced to the Cobra. Then to my delight I began chatting to the trumpeter, Baz, who was also American – how exotic! – and at some point in the evening we started kissing. His lips were soft and his kissing was slow, and after a while I felt a new kind of urgency. I dragged him upstairs by his tie, and he followed behind, shaking his head and laughing.

'Nancy, you are one gorgeous lady. And feisty. No messin' with you when you've got an idea into your head,' he said, whistling under his breath. 'What's a man to do?'

***

We tripped out, tipsy and loud, Dalglish, Eva, Ayesha, the Cobra, Baz and I, arm in arm, just as the first waves of a wan morning light were reaching the cold shadows of sleepy London streets. Giggling and dishevelled, with loosened ties and smudged kohl, we stumbled down the steps, helped by heavy-eyed doormen. On the other side of the street was a man standing against a lamp post, a man whose form was lost in a lumpy jacket and whose face was shaded out by a huge cloth cap. He stiffened straight as we emerged, shielding our eyes from the light. He watched us intently for several seconds, arms folded, then walked off into the distance.

'Did you see that man?' I said.

'Which man?' said the others.

'I saw him,' said Ayesha, and a frown passed across her face. She was even more beautiful in the daylight, I thought. She exchanged a glance with the Cobra.

'Time for a greasy fry up and fifteen mugs of tea, each with two spoonfuls of sugar,' said Dalglish, ignoring us. 'Sausages and eggs, black pudding and bacon. Covered in brown sauce. Fried bread. I know a wonderful little place in Soho. God, I can taste it.'

'Oh, man,' said the Cobra, shaking his head. 'You tryin'a kill me?'

***

Of course, Norman, the freneticism of the first week belied the fact that it wasn't like that all the time. Workwise, there would often be nothing for weeks, then we could be off on assignments every day for a fortnight. We all had a fair amount of time on our hands and slowly I got to know all my flatmates individually. People came and went constantly at the house and so I was also getting to know a wider circle of friends and acquaintances, more inhabitants of the *haute Bohème* spheres in which Dalglish and Eva moved.

The local pub was a big feature in our lives and it would have been easy to spend all my free time there – many did – but I tried it a few times and just felt either terrified or bored. At the end of the evening a fight would usually break out – and not just between the men – or someone would take all their clothes off, or be found under the table weeping over a long-standing syphilis affliction. Clearly there was more of a Methodist in me than I cared to admit, but I found sobriety more appealing than drinking oneself to death. This was no exaggeration, I saw it many times. Bohemians did nothing by half.

I was earning really good money and no longer needed to live a subsistence existence, but to pass the time, and to divert myself from my increasing infatuation with Dalglish, I bought a wire box for trapping rabbits and enlisted Arthur's help to go out late at night to see what we could get hold of. We didn't have the luxury of a Sid to help flush the rabbits out of their warrens, but I remembered some other techniques Norm had taught me over the years, one of which involved digging-in the trap under the soil, so that the top was flush with the ground. The rabbit would run over the top of the box, trip the trap and fall into the box. The act of triggering the trap caused it to shut and lock, and the rabbit couldn't get back out.

I also decided to buy a fishing rod and tools and teach the household to fish. A book on fishing from the library informed me that the Thames had many weirs and a steady supply of pike and roach. My housemates, though encouraging, were uninterested in such a pursuit. One by one they made their various excuses, all except Arthur, who from his years at Steiner was imbued with a passion for roaming around outside, building things, and self-sufficiency. And so we pored over a map and located our nearest fishing spot, and began to cast our lines there regularly, with fairly good results.

I enjoyed watching Queenie eat, enjoyed seeing him becoming slightly less concave and his breath become a little less like mouldy cheese mixed with white spirit. I had grown quite fond of him. With a better diet in the household, the general mood improved, too, and they praised me as their saviour while sometimes mockingly calling me 'Dr Kellogg.'

It was Queenie I grew closest to in those first few weeks and months. He was often melodramatic and cantankerous, but he had a warm side and a terribly catty sense of humour that I loved. We were quite wicked to each other, in fact we became quite the double act at times. For example, Arthur often cooked ratatouille, but try as I might I could not bear the smell of garlic. I couldn't even be in the same *room* as people when they were eating it. And so, when this dish was served I would slope off to the square with a cream horn that I had picked up from the bakers. When I returned, Queenie would accuse me of having had a 'Northern moment' and talk loudly in a ridiculously poor Yorkshire accent – unconcerned with the trifles of geography, apparently. In turn, I loved to mimic his never-ending sense of melodrama, creating scenes worthy of a Shakespearean tragedy to convey such life-changing decisions as, 'Should one make a cup of tea?' and, 'Is it ever all right to wear socks with one's orthopaedic sandals?'

Perhaps we recognised each other as kindred lost souls. In any case, we talked for hours and I watched him paint, sometimes even posing for him if we had no work.

He was from a wealthy family, landed gentry. His father was an earl, from a long and illustrious line of military men dating back to the Raj. His mother was an Austrian beauty, lovely but unhinged, and spent her life on lithium and living in and out of institutions. His father was cold and distant, and so Queenie and his brother had derived love from their nanny, a long-serving lady of a kindly disposition who doted equally on the boys and spoiled them with treats from the kitchen.

The way Queenie told it, he was basically disinherited once he revealed his intention not to go into the military like the rest of his family, but to become an artist. And although he didn't directly allude to it, it was apparent that his father could not come to terms with his son's homosexuality.

And so, déclassé and penniless, Queenie had gravitated to bohemian London to begin that exhausting tightrope walk of being true to one's ideals but not slipping too far down the tracks into penury and starvation. Somehow he had ended up at a place of uneasy dependency, with Dalglish as his sort-of benefactor.

He did not like to leave the house – I could not entice him further than the square at the end of the road – and even then he was nervous about going outdoors. During those few steps between our house and the square he would cling to me, as if letting go might mean he would spin off into oblivion. He refused to go to the pub with us, or anywhere else except when I bought him tickets for the ballet in Covent Garden for his birthday. Then he opened up and talked for hours about the good old days of watching Diaghilev's Ballets Russes before the Great War. I remember him holding on for dear life to the rails on the underground train, eyes wide with fear. But he loved the ballet and his eyes filled with tears as the curtains opened and the performance began.

One day, when we were strolling round the square under the shade of the lime trees, Queenie stopped and turned to me.

'Whatever you do, Nancy my dear, don't get involved with Dalglish,' he said, out of the blue. I was surprised. I didn't think my feelings for Dalglish had been obvious. Certainly, I'd gone to great pains to hide them. 'You do know his first wife killed herself, don't you?'

I was shocked, and shook my head.

'Yes,' he continued, 'it's all her stuff you've been wearing.'

'Oh, my God. I never knew. Why didn't anyone tell me? What happened?'

'Well, she bought into this whole lifestyle but in the end she was consumed by jealousy. She couldn't stand his constant infidelities, I think, even though they'd agreed to have an open relationship.'

'Did you know her well?'

'Yes,' he said wistfully. 'Lovely woman. Loretta, was her name. Another model, of course. Nowhere near as smart as you, though. Did some acting, too.'

Next to us in the park, a mother played ball with her toddler son, and the air was filled with the sound of laughter.

'So, my dear, all I am saying is, don't get sucked in to all that. Because he's never been the same, you know? Well, of course, one wouldn't be, after something like that. But these girls, they always try to change him. Always think it'll be different with them, somehow. He comes on strong and they fall in love, and then he says he feels claustrophobic. When he's moody, they spend their time fretting over how to please him. When he's content it's like Christmas Day and they rejoice. Keeping him happy becomes their *raison d'être*. He has this knack – quite uncanny, if I may say so – of making them feel like wanting a proper relationship is a sign of *their* weakness and not his. Their bourgeois folly. I hate watching it, if I'm honest.'

'How many have there been?' I said, feeling quite sick.

'Oh, not too many,' said Queenie, quickly. 'But still.'

In front of us, the game was over and the boy flung himself happily into his mother's arms. She smiled, and bent down and kissed his head.

'You are young and beautiful. Find someone who will cherish you. You'll never be happy with him.'

'Oh, I don't have any feelings for him,' I lied, blushing. 'Anyway, isn't he with Eva?'

Queenie sniggered. 'That's a very interesting notion. And I wish I knew the answer. They are together sometimes in a physical way, yes, but even I can't work out what the set-up is between them.'

'Oh,' I said, nonchalantly. 'Maybe she's right for him, then. Gives him the space he needs. Doesn't make any demands on him.'

'Let's go back,' said Queenie, suddenly, looking around him. It was as if he'd caught himself gossiping in the third person and felt ashamed. 'The dog has officially been walked for the day and would like to return to its basket.'

***

Although Arthur had a girlfriend, a serious art-student type, I could tell he had fallen a little in love with me. This made things somewhat awkward. Nevertheless, I spent many hours with him as my new fishing companion, consciously ignoring the pain of unrequited love that was written very obviously across his face. I found him serious in countenance, but clever; his mind was always way ahead, probing and questioning. He would sit by the water and read Shakespeare to me and then we would discuss what we thought it meant. His parents were incredibly liberal, but even they could not understand why he did not take a 'proper job', and therefore steadfastly refused to fund his lifestyle of trying to sell his socialist poetry to *Industrial Worker* and similarly sympathetic publications. I sometimes wondered, with a wry smile to myself, what someone like Norm would have had to say about this.

Arthur was fascinated by mining – certainly more interested in it than I had ever been – and grilled me for hours about it. I don't even know how we got on to the subject, but one day we were down at the weir when he asked me if there had been any accidents at Oslington. I thought back to my lamplight conversations with Mr Pearce in the institute library and felt a pang of guilt – I'd never even said goodbye to him when I left. I sighed and looked out over the river.

'I do know about an accident,' I said. '1922. If you mention the word "accident" to anyone in Oslington they'll immediately know what you're talking about.'

'So, what happened?'

'Well, let me try to remember. If you can imagine that in a mine, men travel down to the pit bottom, and up again at the end of their shift, in a giant cage, using a winding system. Mr Pearce was the winding-engine man at our pit. The two cages are connected to each other by a cable,' I said, using my hands to demonstrate, 'each cage travelling in the opposite direction.

'Apparently it was a normal Friday morning and the first cage of the morning shift was descending, full of men. Friday mornings were a happy time – the men got paid and there was usually a lot of joking and banter. They waved a good morning to Mr Pearce as they got into the cage. Mr Pearce's brother-in-law was in there too.

'It's normal practice for the winding man to start applying the brakes when the cage gets about three quarters of the way down. Mr Pearce started to apply the brake as normal, but this time, nothing happened. He tried it, over and over, getting more and more frantic each time, shouting for help, desperately trying to gain some traction from the lever, but still nothing happened. The brake was completely dead. The cages were moving at full speed and Mr Pearce had no way of stopping them. There was a large, red button on the control panel in his booth, with the word "Emergency" on it. Mr Pearce had been trained to press this during emergencies, of course, but it turned out it was absolutely the worst thing he could have done, because it killed all power in the system and therefore all means of slowing the cages down.

'Luckily the ascending cage was empty, else things would have been even worse. There is a sort of safety system in place whereby, if this sort of thing happens, once the other cage has reached the top and is secure, it immediately cuts the rope between the two cages. But once it had been cut, the rope fell heavily all the way to the bottom of the shaft and, during that process, managed to dislodge woodwork and iron piping and all sorts of metal rivets and so forth, which then all fell down on the already crushed cage at the bottom, full of men. Twenty-five men were in that cage; I seem to remember that seventeen died immediately and the other eight died from their injuries afterwards.'

Arthur turned towards me, his face red. He pulled angrily at the line. 'Go on, Nancy,' he said, shakily. 'I want to hear the rest.'

'If you're sure. Anyway no sooner than that had happened, but Mr Pearce immediately had to join the rescue team. When he got there, he said he'd never seen anything like it, bodies mutilated and crushed down to half size, limbs and blood everywhere, most of the men already dead or dying, but some still in the crush, begging for help. His brother-in-law was one of the ones who lay dying when he arrived, and he later died in hospital.

'I cannot even begin to imagine what that must have been like.'

I nodded. 'Well, Mr Pearce was eventually exonerated; the cause of the accident was found to be mechanical failure due to metal fatigue. But he was also told that lives could have been saved if he hadn't pressed the emergency button.

'He tried his best after that, and I don't need to give you all the details. He transferred to a different job, but the guilt of what had happened never left him. Money was tight; you don't turn up for work and you don't get paid, right? He was off sick with his nerves the whole time. And just a few years after that, all miners were told they would be getting a fourteen per cent pay cut and would have to work another hour each shift for it.'

'And all the while the bosses are growing fat and rich on the misery of the workers.'

'Indeed. I read a letter once from Mr Moreton, the owner, planning his next trip to the south of France with his wife and leaving the Methodist minister in charge of the men's morals while he was gone. Off to Nice for a nice little winter break, no less.'

'Oh, yes. That doesn't surprise me. Get the church to help keep the workers oppressed. Makes me so angry. Anyway, go on.'

I put a conciliatory hand on Arthur's back. 'In 1926, as you know, there was a national miners' strike. They ended up reliant on the Salvation Army and soup kitchens. Mr Pearce spent his time putting together, and then running, the local library, reading and learning what he could. You can ask Mr Pearce a question about anything – anything at all – and I guarantee you he will have read a book about it, and will spend time to give you his honest appraisal of it, or patiently teach you about it if it is a new subject. His nickname down the pit was "Books".

'A few years after he set up the library his son passed his eleven-plus exam and started going to the boys' grammar school in town. That year, though, Mr Pearce had a relapse and struggled to work at all. When it came to the second year, they couldn't afford the grammar school fees and his son had to leave and return to the senior school, to be churned out as mine-fodder and sent to work down that very same mine, aged fourteen.

'We used to talk about religion a lot; I know that Mr Pearce lost his faith in God, though he never came right out and said so. He'd had his doubts for a long time, I think, probably all his life. But the accident, and its aftermath, confirmed it for him. He talked to me a lot about it all, but it was all quite abstract. He didn't want word to get out, I think. We were friends. I'm a bit different, though. I never had faith, and I'm certainly not going to now.'

I realised I had got lost in my story, and looked over to Arthur. He was looking out across the river, and I think he was crying.

'This is why I do what I do, Nancy,' he said, presently, his voice angry and full of emotion. 'People don't understand. All they hear about is greedy miners, always unsatisfied, always on strike. They don't hear the truth.'

'People see and hear what they want to,' I agreed.

'Thank you for sharing that story, Nancy. I can honestly tell you that I'll never forget it.'

***

Arthur was affected by the story for quite some time afterwards. It made him even more passionate about workers' rights and even more sure that he had chosen the right path in life. He went out on more marches than ever, and kept on churning out his angry poetry, which to be honest was an acquired taste. He began to withdraw from life inside the house and locked himself away for hours in his sad little broom cupboard off to the side of the scullery.

One day, he emerged looking energised, wearing a smart white shirt and waistcoat. A small book poked out of his trouser pocket: a collection of Shakespeare's sonnets. Eva and Dalglish were playing gin rummy in the basement, Eva sprawled out on the divan looking as beautiful as ever. I was wearing a white, backless gown and was being painted by Queenie. I was cold, moaning frequently to Queenie to hurry up and finish.

'Can I borrow your bike please?' Arthur said to Dalglish.

'Of course, old boy. Looking very smart today, I must say. Where are you off to? Haven't seen you about much recently.'

'I've got a job,' he said, then disappeared to the back garden and returned with Dalglish's bike. He tried to manoeuvre it past the detritus of the basement, but eventually gave up and lifted it up and carried it to the top of the stairs. Then he wandered back down to the basement, looking for his cap.

Dalglish whistled. 'Well, well. Arthur's got a job! What are you doing?'

'Washing the dishes at a hotel. In Hampstead. Doing a bit of bartending as well. Mekhi got me it. He's a chef there.'

'Your Muhammadan friend?'

Arthur nodded.

'Good for you,' said Eva, looking over the top of her cards. 'Seriously, you have dealt me the worst hand, here, Dags.'

'Oooh,' said Queenie, mockingly. 'Arthur is going to have his *own* money to spend, folks. I thought you socialists were only happy wasting everyone else's.'

Arthur shook his head and fiddled idly with his cap. 'Says the man who's lived off handouts all his life,' he said.

'How's the poetry coming on, Arthur?' I said.

Arthur confirmed he had been locked away working on a new piece, and after much persuasion, we managed to get him to agree to recite it to us. Initially, he wanted Queenie out of the room, but Queenie promised to behave himself. We always looked forward to Arthur's poetry not, it has to be said, for the most noble of reasons. It was defiant in its anti-cosmopolitanism and unflinching in its intention to appeal to the common man. Eventually, he gathered himself up before us, and took a deep breath.

'It's called "The Crush of Capitalism",' he said.

'Sounds uplifting,' said Queenie, setting down his brush. He sat down on the divan and clasped his hands together. 'Get ready for death by iambic pentameter.'

'Do you even know what that means?'

'Quiet, everyone,' said Dalglish, putting down his cards. I pulled a blanket round me and sat down next to Queenie.

'The Crush of Capitalism,' said Arthur in a loud voice, an angry voice that carried in its chords and cadence the anger of every wrongdoing, not just to Mr Pearce, but to mankind, ever, at the hands of a private company:

It began that Friday just like all the others
Husbands kissed wives, sons waved to their mothers
Men who were uncles and fathers and brothers

Off to the coal mine, the winding shafts turning
Men worked to death to keep home fires burning
The greasy wheels of capitalism keep on yearning
To keep workers oppressed
Every year working longer, for a little bit less

And the owner grows rich off the toils of the poor,
Strolls down a boulevard on the Côte d'Azure

That Friday, a shaft hurtled out of control
The safety equipment was worn, frayed and old,
And just as the other shaft rose to the top

A button was pressed called Emergency Stop
But it could not avert a most deadly drop
To a place down the mine, a place worse than hell
Where bodies were crushed as the mineshaft fell

And the owner grows rich off the toils of the poor,
Kisses his wife on the Côte d'Azure

'Is that a euphemism?' said Queenie, taking hold of my hand. 'Dear God, give me strength.'

'Shush,' said Dalglish, winking at Eva and me. 'Go on, son.'

'You'd better shut up, old man,' said Arthur, with a menacing look. He composed himself and brushed his hair to one side. We waited to hear what was coming next:

Bodies twist and sinews snap
The blood of the innocent spurts out like a tap
Human flesh crushed, the world out of kilter
Mashed up and squashed like tin cans at a smelter

And the owner grows rich off the toils of the poor...

Next to me, Queenie roared with laughter. 'I know, I know,' he said, pointing an old claw at Arthur. 'Strokes his wife's pussy on the Côte d'Azure.' A huge quarrel ensued, and Queenie was banished to his room. I closed my eyes as an attack of giggles tried to infiltrate my chest. 'I heard better limericks at school,' muttered the old artist as he floated up the stairs like a puff of steam.

Alas, I cannot remember all the poem, Norman, suffice to say that it seemed to go on as long as one of Grandad's shifts. Queenie re-emerged to daringly shout, 'Shoves a baguette up his Côte d'Azure,' and the last couplet used the words 'cataclysm' and 'Capitalism' in a somewhat awkward pairing. As the final words were spoken, relief filled the room in waves.

'Phew,' said Dalglish, letting out a whistle. 'Strong stuff, Arthur. I think I need a drink.' He got up and headed into the scullery. 'Whisky, anyone?'

'Capitalism is a difficult word to rhyme,' said Eva, kindly, reaching for a cigarette. 'Yes, please, Dags.'

'It's really good, Arthur,' I said.

At the top of the stairs Queenie peered down. 'Well that was uplifting, wasn't it, folks? Heart-warming. Excuse me while I throw myself off the nearest bridge.'

'I'm fucking sick of you,' screamed Arthur, scrambling suddenly up the stairs with his fists clenched. We heard the sounds of metal clattering against walls and wails of pain as it banged against human flesh; Arthur had got tangled up in the bike.

Dalglish leaped up after him and had to restrain him from punching Queenie, who shouted 'Oh, oh,' then barricaded himself in his bedroom.

And thus, Norman, Mr Pearce and the accident featured heavily in Arthur's new work, giving him unlimited means to depress people in new ways. We saw very little of Arthur after that – he was either at work or away, pursuing his new religious zeal with his friend Mekhi. But occasionally we would still spend an evening listening to him reciting one of his poems, with Queenie courting violent retribution by mocking openly in the background.

Chapter 9

It was around six in the morning and I was swimming naked in the Serpentine with Eva. We had been to a dinner party in Bloomsbury, and had stayed up drinking absinthe until the sun rose in the sky. We were more than a little worse for wear. Dalglish was climbing out of the lake. His naked frame and white skin created a luminously surreal silhouette against the damp morning light. Geese swam nearby, oblivious to our presence. Through a clearing in the trees we suddenly saw two figures cycling towards us and, when they grew closer, we could see that it was Arthur and his friend Mekhi. Arthur slowed and looked across at us. A dark cloud passed over his face, the shame of being associated with such a louche bunch of reprobates. He seemed to deliberate whether he could get away without stopping, but ultimately remembered who his benefactor was and reluctantly alighted near Dalglish. His friend looked away.

'That looks fun,' shouted Arthur, unconvincingly. 'Sorry we can't stop – we'll be late for work.'

Dalglish threw on his pants and chatted for a while, running up to shake the friend's hand. Then the workers turned and rode off, fast. I floated up onto my back, looking up at the grey clouds, searching for familiar shapes and faces. Eva swam up behind me and stood upright, cupping my body underneath and holding me up at the surface. Then she began to move me around slowly in the water, singing a few bars from a popular song, as she swayed me in a slow figure of eight. 'What was Arthur like as a lover?' she whispered after a while, and I wondered if she had noticed his discomfort moments earlier. The kohl was smudged down her cheeks and her breath had a faint whiff of liquorice. A light dusting of raindrops began to fall on my face, making dimples on the surface of the lake.

I laughed, and shook my head. Arthur was one of many lovers that came and went but, unfortunately for him, I wasn't taking anyone with me in those days. *Ménages à deux, ou à trois …* whatever, whenever and whoever. My life was baked in the sunlight of newly-acquired freedom and I was determined to enjoy every second of it.

'A bit like his poetry,' I said, and Eva giggled. 'Anyway, doesn't matter, does it? He's ashamed of us now. Doesn't even want to come fishing with me any more.'

'He's changed,' she agreed, and let out a yawn. 'We should get out, I suppose. I came down with bronchitis last time I swam in here after drinking absinthe.'

***

What else can I tell you, Norman, about those first couple of years? Hiding from the landlady, a Polish Jew whose family had fled to London to escape the Nazification going on over there. Trying not to giggle from our hiding place in the broom cupboard as she did the rounds of the house, cursing in Polish.

Drinking to the thought that there is no such thing as immortality, that religion is there to hold you back and keep you in your place, and that this is it … so you'd better make the most of it and raise your glass to now.

The time I had a Club Gargoyle soul-crushing, bile-tasting, existential hangover and had to do modelling for The Women's League for Health and Beauty. I just about made it through the shoot, which featured us all sitting in a rowing boat on the Thames in our swimsuits looking chaste and healthy. What you don't see is me throwing up off the side of the boat as Eva screamed with laughter and the other women looked on in disgust.

Wearing a *Letty Lynton* sateen evening dress with huge ruffled shoulders to a masked party in Fitzrovia, which ended up with singing and dancing and nakedness.

Fashion shows, modelling shoots for *Vogue*, *The Lady*, *Tatler*, *Vanity Fair* …

Surrealist hat parties.

Reflective times: poetry readings by candlelight; Arthur's angry poetic tirades, interrupted only by the sounds of stomachs gnawing with hunger.

The feeling that as soon as one had any money, it was terribly, terribly important to spend it all straight away, as if it might literally burn a hole in one's pocket.

My first ever trip in an aeroplane.

Modelling assignments in Paris and Monte Carlo, where men strolled around in blazers and linen shorts, and women wore navy-and-white halter-necks and stylish hats.

Childish and irresponsible, quixotic and romantic I know, but so, so much fun. This was life in technicolour, perhaps not as I had originally imagined it, but a whirlwind of circus and harlequin prints, of hats shaped like Saturn, Chinese porcelain and Japanese blossoms.

Visits from families with bands of feral children with wild hair, modelled on *Emile*, and who ran around naked in our back garden, shooting and fighting each other – and the sigh of relief when they left.

Dark times, too. Eva's friend who died having an abortion. An acquaintance of Queenie who died literally of starvation and wasn't found for weeks. Poets whose hearts and livers gave up after years of heavy drinking.

The frisson that existed between Dalglish and me and, underneath all my bravado, the hours I spent retracing his fingers across my cheekbone from that very first afternoon in the cafe.

Elsie Mitford ...

I was eighteen by that point. We were up in Hampstead, doing a shoot at Kenwood House. We always shot a season ahead, and so although it was midsummer and warm, Eva and I were dressed in Digby Morton woollen tailored suits and I could feel rivulets of sweat running down my back. It was a little close to the Clayton-Reids' house for comfort, but I decided it would be very bad luck to actually bump into them.

We often attracted a little crowd when we were shooting; it was just something I'd learned to ignore. But this time I heard a girl saying my name, over and over. I turned to see Bella holding hands with Elsie Mitford. Elsie looked as shocked as me, to be fair. She was somehow taller, much slimmed down, prettier than I remembered, and strikingly similar to her brother. Bella was also taller and slimmer, her hair now long and in pigtails. I took a deep breath, made my excuses to Dalglish and Eva, and walked over to the girls.

Bella was excited to see me, and ran over, wrapping her arms round me and shrieking. Elsie stood, arms crossed, stony faced, looking at me.

'Elsie,' I said, finally. 'What are you doing here?'

She looked at me as if I were mad. I waited for an answer, but she simply continued to stare at me.

'Where's Paul?' I said, to Bella.

She looked across at Elsie, as if for approval. 'My brother is in heaven with the angels,' she said, blinking up at me.

I took hold of her and wrapped my arms round her. 'I'm so sorry, Bella.'

'Come away from her,' said Elsie, frowning. 'Remember your mother says we don't talk about that. It's nearly teatime. We'd better get back.'

I stood and watched as they turned to leave. 'Wait,' I shouted. 'How is Norm, Elsie?'

'Norman is fine,' she said, and I noticed that she, too, had begun to lose her Geordie accent. 'They're saying he'll make foreman, no problem, once he finishes his apprenticeship. He's getting married as well.'

'That's great,' I said, gulping.

She took hold of the little girl's hand and turned to leave. 'By the way, your Grandad died last year. Your Nana is living with her aunt out in Barring Tye.'

I stared at her, each word stinging with shame and recrimination.

'C'mon Bella, we really need to go now.'

'Why did you run away from us?' said Bella, with childish innocence.

'She spends her life running away from things,' said Elsie, simply. 'She doesn't care about anyone but herself.'

I stood and watched as they walked away, up the hill, and disappeared into a dense copse of trees.

***

Norman, I still find it difficult today to articulate how I feel about things, or how that afternoon made me feel. Sarah's son once told me that all the cells in your body replace themselves at least once every seven years. So, technically, you are not the same person you once were. And that's how I feel about her, the person I was back then. I don't know her at all. I don't know how she could have behaved like that, to have let down so badly those who loved her, cared for her. It's not a cop out, a ruse to stop me from taking responsibility for what I did. I take responsibility every single day. And that's why I'll never ask for forgiveness.

But we are not who we once were – it's simply a fact.

Chapter 10

Hampstead, July 1999

It was an uncomfortable truth: Grandma Lucy's dying words had begun to nag at Nikki, to penetrate her thoughts at the most inopportune times. Her daydreaming had even caused her a couple of concentration failures at work. On one occasion halfway through a detailed conversation where she had suddenly been unable to remember what on earth they had been talking about. Brad had given her the oddest look and suggested, with a nasty undertone that was meant to sound jokey, she cut down to half a bottle a day. Nikki wouldn't be able to get away with that kind of mistake for long. After these episodes she had felt empty and drained and scared: her life was a non-stopping high-speed train and she wanted to get off. Not forever, maybe, but long enough to sort out this business with the now pervasive 'Nancy', and work out what the hell was going on in her marriage and with her kids.

From a meeting room on level thirty-three, Nikki watched the window cleaners suspended outside in their cage. Even the glum London daylight was magnified up at this level. The city crawled by below in miniature. The wind tugged at the window cleaners' clothes and hair; nearly every piece of equipment was locked down. She wondered what it would be like to fall from there, to have that brief moment of freedom before the whole circus ended.

At work Nikki avoided her lover, and at home she avoided her family. Even her therapist was bored with her first-world, middle-class, partly self-inflicted problems. The final straw had been when Nikki had described watching the window cleaners with envy – for theirs was a real job, unlike hers which involved moving vast sums of money between globalists. Even as she had spoken, Nikki heard how ridiculous the words sounded.

The therapist had thrown out a few platitudes, then taken off her glasses and pretended not to look at the clock. 'I think we have successfully concluded our sessions,' she'd said, in a falsely cheerful voice. 'A friend is all you need now.'

Sacked by a hundred-pounds-an-hour therapist. She would laugh about that one day, maybe, if she were to learn the art of self-deprecation.

***

The black and white porch tiles of 34 Westfield Drive were now cracked with age, and the large stone blocks above the doorway were no longer visible, lost many years ago to the thrusting forces of wisteria and ivy, which had blanketed the entrance and embroidered the walls. Opening the front door, Nikki was hit with a faintly mouldering smell of age, of walls that had never known the words 'damp-proof course'. The burgundy curtains in the hallway still spoke of old-school glamour and the umbrella stand was still there, but they were now coated in a film of light-grey dust. Only the mahogany panelling looked as imposing as ever. Turning left into what they guilelessly called the smoking room – *Who still has a smoking room, for God's sake*? thought Nikki – revealed entire walls covered in bookcases full of old leather books: first editions, legal reference books, the Old and New Testaments, several books about the Catholic catechism. On the floor were a large aspidistra and a daybed near the window with a small mahogany table next to it. Nikki felt a lump in her throat when she realised that some three years after his death, Grandpa's pipe and a box of tobacco were still on the table. Family photos adorned the shelves – her Aunt Bella as a child, and her cousins. Even one of the springer spaniels, but none of Nikki, her children, or her father, Paul.

Still, returning to the house alone like this brought back happy childhood memories. Nikki wandered in and out of rooms, enjoying the associations that seeing the house's old artefacts produced. She peered out of the kitchen window, remembering glorious afternoons during the summer holidays when Grandma Lucy would be called upon to look after Nikki and her cousins. This was a task the old lady performed with a begrudging tight-lippedness, an expression which fell into a proper sneer when she was prevailed upon to cook proletarian food such as fish fingers, oven chips and baked beans en masse at lunchtime. Such wonderful memories, though: clad in seventies attire of brown corduroy flares or denim dungarees, Nikki had fought her cousins, rolling around in the mud at the back of the garden, fighting until one of them begged for mercy. She still remembered the screams as they sprayed each other with the garden hose, then the excitement of needing to not be the last one down to Hampstead Heath for a game of cricket or football. All played out against a backdrop of tacit disapproval from pursed lips watching through the kitchen window. Small acts of cruelty: Grandma Lucy giving all her cousins ice lollies from the freezer, but then shaking her head when it came to Nikki's turn, saying she'd run out. Ridiculous, really. Grandma Lucy was hugely outnumbered, though, remaining housebound as Nikki and her cousins had conducted their operations outside, and so becoming nothing more than a side note to these memories.

Nikki wandered back to the smoking room. Grandpa's return from work had been an event to be looked forward to, but it was in this so-called smoking room, this no man's land between the outside world and the rest of the house, that he had expected to relax and wind down with a gin and tonic and a smoke after a long day at work. Children had not been allowed in there, except to carry drinks. They had looked forward to that job, Nikki and her cousins, had fought over it, even. Grandpa had been treated like a celebrity, revered and allowed some 'breathing space' to unwind when he had arrived back home.

Since Grandma's death, the initial conversations had all been about telling everyone the sad news, but things had quickly moved on to the logistics: registering the death, contacting the solicitor and the funeral companies. Nikki had taken it all on, feeling both resigned and angry, but sensing that close involvement might perhaps now lead to an opportunity to get to the bottom of things.

It was only then, a couple of days on from the death, that she had felt it okay to raise the issue of the mysterious new family member with her aunt. 'So, then. You better tell me who Nancy is,' she had said to her aunt over the phone. A tedious to and fro had followed: What exactly had Grandma Lucy said? Tell me again exactly what she said. Are you sure she didn't say anything else? Her aunt had been palpably relieved when she realised that Grandma had told Nikki practically nothing.

'There's a box in the smoking room,' she had said, in a thin, exhausted voice. 'That box contains everything you need to know. It's probably best for you to read it first, and then for us to talk. You might want Nick to be there with you. You must promise me you won't call anyone else until we've spoken. I'm so sorry, Nikki. We haven't gone about this the right way at all.'

***

The large black box was inconspicuous and not easily accessed up on the top shelf. Grandpa, with typical brevity, had simply labelled it 'Nancy Thompson'. Nikki pulled down the dust-coated box, set it on the floor and opened the lid.

On top of the pile of papers inside was a photo of a teenage girl, standing with a young Aunt Bella, and Nikki's father as a baby. She laughed, and stared at the photo for a gratuitously long time. She'd never seen any early childhood photos of her father. The girl was very attractive, tall and slim with short dark hair, stunning really, like a film star, though she looked horribly awkward in the photo. Aunt Bella looked about three or four, still tiny and cute, though already wearing thick glasses. The nanny – she presumed? – was holding the baby; he was tiny, not even one year old by the looks of it. Yet there were six years between her aunt and her father, Paul. Nikki was perplexed. On the back of the photo Grandpa had written 'Nancy, Bella and Paul, First Day. July 1935.'

Then there were a couple of cuttings from magazines, featuring modelling shoots. Nikki skimmed over these at first, but then on closer inspection she noticed that they all featured the same teenage girl, now looking older: confident and worldly, somehow. There was also a wildness about her, a hardness. You had to look closely to see it, but it was there all right.

Her grandparents had never mentioned having a nanny who went on to become a famous model, but that was typical really, especially of Grandma. She'd been born with an innate ability to simply block out anything she didn't like, and pretend it had never happened. Or in this case, lock it away in a box and let someone else deal with the aftermath. Her therapist had said, 'Unfortunately, Nikki, that's exactly what you tend to do too.'

Underneath the cuttings was a thick, weighty manuscript, tied up in ribbon, addressed to someone called Norman. Nikki's heart began to beat fast. She pulled out the papers and held them to her chest. This was it. But she wanted to read it uninterrupted. She called next door to chat with Mrs Thomas, then wandered slowly to the corner shop to pick up bread, milk and a few other provisions. After that, she made a coffee and called in to work, taking the rest of the week off.

Amit was keen to come over for some divertissement, and this was definitely an opportunity wrapped in a huge, shiny Christmas bow topped with flashing neon lights, but Nikki felt the same gnawing unease she had come to expect since Grandma Lucy's death, so she sent a text back telling him she would not be able to see him again this week. Then she settled down on the daybed, thought about ringing Nick again and asking him to come over, but decided against it. She relaxed into the divan, covered herself with a blanket that still smelled rather wonderfully of tobacco, lay back and closed her eyes. It was great, in a way, just to slow down, to rediscover her thoughts and feelings, to take some time out for contemplation. It felt like such a luxury.

Sacked by her therapist, she contemplated calling Lorna but worried that she would come out with some more rubbish about window cleaning when actually what she wanted to talk about was, 'Why can't I love and appreciate my husband and my kids?' or the even more profound, 'Who the hell am I?'

It was now up to Nikki to work out her own feelings. Her marriage was crumbling before her eyes; her children were not even school age yet but already they barely even asked for her any more. The other week, when Nick had been ill, she'd gone to the nursery to collect them and the staff hadn't even known who she was. She'd had to go through a humiliating wait in the office while her identity was verified. And the fact remained that she had brought two small people into the world but was unable to connect with them. Weekends were simply tedious time-traps until the working week could begin again. She felt the loneliness of not being able to recognise herself in any other kind of mother she knew. Once again, her unshakeable energy sapped away and she just felt tired. Motherhood was something she had fallen into without much thought. Everyone else was doing it, so it must be the right thing to do. 'Why didn't you tell me?' she wanted to scream. She felt duped.

What part of this horror show is meant to be fun, is meant to be fulfilling?

Nick had been distant with her for a while. He felt the same way as her about their relationship, she was certain, and she couldn't blame him in the slightest. They were both just treading water, caught up in the all-encompassing maelstrom of life with babies and young children and the demands of her job. But before long, some difficult conversations would have to be had. She wondered if he suspected her affair. If someone had asked her why she was even having the affair, she would not have been able to answer them. She had just done it because she could. But for the first time, the guilt was creeping in. This was much more than just finding out the answer to a family puzzle. Her crisis was of the existential kind. Things could not go on as they were. She switched off her BlackBerry, opened the manuscript, took a deep breath and began to read.

***

The daylight had started to fade to dusk when she was interrupted by a call to the house phone from Nick.

'Hi,' he said, coolly.

'Hi hon. How are the kids?'

'Oh, you know. They're good. Off to bed soon.'

'Okay. I'll probably head home shortly. Hopefully I'll get to see them before they go to sleep. I think I've found out who Nancy is, by the way. She was my dad and Aunt Bella's nanny. She's sent her memoirs to someone called Norman, though, who appears to be the boy next door. I mean, *literally* the boy next door. But they're from the North East. All very confusing.'

'Okay,' he said, distractedly. 'You know, it's really great that you would rather sit on your own reading at your grandma's house – the same grandma you couldn't stand, by the way – than come home and put your own children to bed. Fabulous. The kids don't need their mother at all. I don't need a break. I've only had them all day. All night. All fucking *week*.'

Nikki was shocked. She looked at the receiver for a long time. *I know*, she wanted to say, *I know … but …*

'Listen, Nikki,' continued her husband, 'I didn't want to have this conversation over the phone, I just need to know the truth. You're seeing someone else, aren't you?'

Nikki paused. 'Yes,' she said. 'I am. Nick, I'm sorry. It doesn't mean anything …'

'Okay,' he said, flatly. 'Thank you for being truthful. Don't bother coming home.' Then he put the phone down.

***

Half an hour later, Nikki returned from her second trip to the 7-Eleven that day with two bottles of red – *seems excessive,* she thought, *but you never know* – and some toiletries. She opened the wine and poured as much as she could into one of Grandma's old crystal glasses. It was so heavy! And small! Nikki's wine glasses were oversized and contemporary. They came from Germany via a household shop on Upper Street. Hadn't the older generation heard of binge drinking? Nikki sat down with a sigh onto the daybed. Sometimes the answer *was* heavy drinking.

‘You can fucking fuck off, the whole fucking lot of you,’ she said, raising a toast to no one in particular. Then she flicked back to the page she had reached previously and took a long drink of wine, clearing out half the glass in one go.

Chapter 11

I wonder if you're already thinking ill of me, Norman. I couldn't blame you if you were. I thought about the encounter with Elsie Mitford for a long time afterwards. Memories of baby Paul flooded back in nostalgia-crested waves, as irrepressible as high tide. The little tea party we had had for his first birthday: Bella and I had spread out a picnic rug on the lawn in the back garden. We'd baked fruit scones and shortbread biscuits, and a chocolate cake which we'd decorated with candles. Paul had been propped up in his pram, sucking on a biscuit, trails of shortbread-drool running down his chin. Bella had dressed all her dolls in their finest hats and clothes and arranged them on the rug with their own china tea set. I had lifted Paul out and held him upright on my lap as I'd rested on my knees on the tartan blanket. All those months, he'd never managed to sit upright or move his legs and I remembered looking at his sweet face and tufts of ginger hair and wondering if he would ever be able to move around like other children. He had been happy, that day, gurgling and waving his arms around madly. There was a swing at the bottom of the garden and later, I had sat on it with him on my lap, rocking him to and fro, listening to his giggles as Bella had pretended to be a monster each time the swing approached her. To hear that he had died was heartbreaking, and it sounded as if Bella was not even being allowed to talk about it. But even *that* paled into insignificance when I realised I would never see Grandad again. He would have died not knowing where I was, and if I was all right.

I retreated from life at the house, sick of myself once again. I fell back into the old unhealthy habit of staring out of my bedroom window, though this time the view was a terrace of shabby tenements. I felt a strong need to grieve and lament my own shameful part in the story. I decided that this prodigal and newly penitent daughter would have to make the trip back home and stay for a while – a month or two, maybe longer. That's if they would have me back at all. Just imagining the diatribe from Aunt Flo made the hairs on the back of my neck stand on end.

Luckily, I had been savvy enough not to have joined in with the hot-coal approach to the ownership of money exhibited by my contemporaries. There's no way you can come from near-poverty, Norman, and not give a fig about money. I had a sizeable pot of savings, even in spite of helping out with the household bills, food, and so on. Once home, I would be able to stay at the Oslington Hotel if necessary. I checked my finances: over £300 stuffed into my various tobacco tins and in the Buddha, my makeshift giant moneybox. £300 – a small fortune really. I might even be able to help Nana out by finding her a place of her own and giving her money. How shameful to know that I could have sent money home a long time ago and eased whatever hardship she might be facing.

It was a typically busy Saturday, with people coming and going all day. Ayesha turned up in matching carmine red coat and hat, looking every bit the glamorous film star. She had brought over some outfits for me, beautiful jewelled full-length Indian saris in cerise and teal and purple from *The Prince of Punjab*, robes that I had admired on her on drunken evenings in Club Gargoyle, and once when the make-up artist who worked at the Farnham had been sick and I'd spent a fascinating day on set filling in. We enjoyed a pleasant hour in my bedroom, with me trying the outfits on in front of the dresser mirror.

'I don't know why they care so much about the colours when the film's in black and white but I do love wearing them. You'll have to take them in though, Skinny Lizzy,' said Ayesha, folding back the shiny teal material around my waist so that it fitted me. 'Or eat a few more of those cream horns you seem to live off.' I laughed – I didn't have her curves, and the material hung off me. The image was one of little girl playing dress-up. But at the back of mind, all I could think of was Nana stuck out at Barring Tye with Aunt Flo. I sighed and looked at my reflection. 'What's up?' Ayesha said. 'Something on your mind?'

I turned to see my figure in the dress from behind. 'Just a little homesick.'

She gave me a sympathetic smile and quick hug. 'I know what you mean. I really miss my mother. All the time. D'you know, I have a strong feeling that this place is just a stage in your journey, Nancy. It won't be forever. Follow your heart.'

I felt comforted by this and was about to reply when Ayesha continued, 'Yes, we'll not be around for too much longer, Nancy. That's why I brought you the outfits. Cobsy and I are off to New Orleans after the film.' I felt a pang of sadness that my new-found confidante was leaving so soon after we'd begun to nourish our friendship and was about to say as much when Arthur popped his head round the door.

'Hello, ladies. What are you doing? I'm bored. Can I come and join you for a bit?'

'Of course. Fetch us some tea though,' said Ayesha.

A short while later Arthur reappeared carrying a tray with teapot and an array of our chipped, old cups on it.

'There we go,' he said, setting the tray down on my dresser. He settled himself down on the overflowing clothes basket in the corner of the room, stretched his long, skinny legs out and yawned. It struck me at that moment that there was something quite vulnerable about Arthur I hadn't noticed before. 'Gosh, this takes me back to when my sister and I used to dress up. My mother found me in one of her dresses once and became apoplectic.'

'Always a deviant, eh Arthur?' Ayesha laughed, pouring out the tea.

'Oh yes. That's me. Anyway how are things with you?' Arthur had become quite friendly with Ayesha since being enlisted to help her and the Cobra move between friends' houses on occasion. He'd also done some casual work up at the Farnham as a sort of stage hand, moving parts of the set around and setting up the props between scenes.

'I was just saying to Nancy that we'll be leaving for America soon.' Once again, I wanted to tell her how sad that made me feel, but somehow the words would not come. However, hearing about this impending departure emboldened me to have the necessary conversation with Dalglish about my own. A little while later, Ayesha left (collected by the Cobra, who came in, smiled and tipped his hat). Arthur and I played gin rummy half-heartedly for a while and then I decided it was time to open up to Dalglish about my plans. I invited him to one of the quieter pubs nearby; we ordered our drinks awkwardly and I sat down to outline my intention to head back up north. He was very supportive and agreed that, most definitely, I should take a trip back and not to worry, no one was going to take my place in the house, they had all grown very fond of me, I was part of the family, and so forth. Just let him speak to the agency, he said, and work out when the last booking was. After that, I would be free to go.

We sat drinking ale in the warm summer's sun and watched the light fade into long shadows across the table. I began to feel tipsy in a sleepy kind of way; the evening had passed and we had been chatting about everything and nothing and suddenly it was quite dark outside and the landlord had started to light candles. I felt Dalglish's hand creep across the table and take hold of mine, a pained expression on his face. And then we were kissing, and our warm lips tasted of summer and beer. We left and began to embrace again against the wall of the pub, passers-by whistling mockingly at us. His lips were soft and inviting, and I began to feel myself falling into a deep tunnel.

Everyone was in bed when we got back, and Dalglish led me straight to his room, which was much larger than mine. Piles of books sprouted everywhere and in the middle of the back wall was a large fireplace.

'Nancy,' he said, his voice wavering. He held my face in his hands. 'Don't ever leave me.'

***

Afterwards, he lay in my arms, oddly subservient, and began to cry. I understood why he was crying. He knew he was bad news, he knew how he'd treated all those girls before me, and it became clear that he'd been keeping his distance for fear of hurting me the same way.

I felt a rush of something deeper than love, almost maternal. I wanted more than anything to fix him, to make him happy. And I no longer cared about my family or my redemption; I had someone new to try to save.

He fell asleep on my chest and although it was uncomfortable, I lay there like a corpse, scared to breathe in case it woke him up.

The next day we checked into a small hotel near Sloane Square; he wanted us to be away from prying eyes back at the house and to discover each other at our own pace. We didn't leave the room for three days, except for the occasional trip to buy food and beer.

At the end, I began to grow restless, in spite of my feelings for him. I simply wanted a change of scene, maybe to go out for a walk. But he grew fretful, convinced I had tired of him already, and I backed down. We spent a fourth night at the hotel.

By the time we returned to the house, all thoughts of travelling back home to the north had been wrung out of me and memories of the Clayton-Reids were fading, replaced by the first flushes of all-consuming, passionate, complicated love.

***

As if to anchor me further in his London world, Dalglish got me a part as an extra in the next Farnham production (following the critically unacclaimed *The Prince of Punjab)*. The film was called *Prehistoric Terror*, and the cinematic enactment of the title was to be achieved with a mix of suggestion, a great deal of painted cardboard and the requirement that the viewer should willingly suspend disbelief throughout. Eva and Ayesha had been enlisted too – we played a group of multi-tribe flibbertigibbets wearing skimpy loincloths. I envied Ayesha her beautiful brown skin – my own legs stood out like a couple of milk bottles under the harsh studio lighting. After drinking copious amounts of champagne our job was to run away screaming from an unconvincing cardboard cut-out of a woolly mammoth. It was not, Norman, the most demanding role an actress has ever faced.

Over at the studios in Limehouse, the scene was set to mimic a typical evening in primordial London, which had a swelteringly tropical climate. To that end, large paraffin heaters had been brought in to give off heat and light. Next to them the director had placed large buckets of water, hoping the evaporation would make the scene more lifelike. We stood among plastic palm trees dripping with condensation, leaning over papier mâché rocks, sipping on the champagne between takes, ready to run from dangerous cardboard. The thick, strange-coloured make-up they had plastered all over my face began to melt and trickled down my face into watery beige rivulets that ran down my neck. When I eventually saw the film, the undemanding nature of the role sadly could not detract from the fact that my acting was less animated than the rocks that provided cover from the rampaging cardboard beast. *Prehistoric Terror* did not herald the start of my glorious film career. It was also famously described by a critic writing in the *Daily Sketch* as 'A blundering, moribund mess of a film in love with its own sense of irony.' Nevertheless, Norman, you might stumble across it one day. Look out for me if you do, won't you.

After filming one day, we fell into a tired little pub that smelled of urine round the corner from the studios. Dalglish bought drinks, and we found a table in the corner, next to a rather half-hearted fire. We slumped, exhausted, into the rickety wooden chairs as best we could. Dalglish regaled us with stories of films he'd worked on previously. Eventually, Eva left.

'So,' said Ayesha, 'we were far too busy trying on my old outfits last time I saw you and I never got to hear how you came to be down here, Nancy. Tell me your story.'

'I'd rather hear yours,' I said, truthfully.

'Huh,' she said, with a shrug. 'My family wanted me to marry my cousin; something neither of us wanted. They wanted me to stay at home and have babies. My mother threw her hijab in the sea when they came to this country, but my father and brother want us to pretend we're all living in a country I've never even been to.' She began to play with the candlewax that was dripping down the side of the candle in the centre of the table. 'My father wants me to go back to the family and marry. I've dishonoured them. They call me a whore. And so now my brother follows me everywhere.'

'Can't you go to the police?' I said, taking a sip of gin.

'And say what? That's naïve, Nancy,' she said, shaking her head. 'They won't help.

I realised that it must have been the brother I saw waiting in the shadows after that very first visit to Club Gargoyle. Just then, the Cobra appeared in the doorway, smiling. He was a giant of a man, well over six feet tall, with broad shoulders. 'There's only one thing keeping them away,' she winked.

'I see,' I said. 'Hence the move to America.'

'Yes. After this film we'll be leaving,' she explained to Dalglish. 'It's no longer safe for me here. I think I told you already: we're heading to New Orleans. Cobsy is sick of the weather here too.'

I nodded, though I wondered how an Asian woman and a black man in an unmarried relationship would fare over there – we heard the odd story, even from the Cobra himself, about how blacks were treated. 'What do you mean, not safe? Will they force you to go back?'

She looked at me and shivered, pulling her shawl over her shoulders. She was about to speak when the barman appeared, his lips pursed. 'No coloureds in here,' he said to the Cobra, pointing to an imaginary sign above the door. 'The Spanish lady's okay though.'

We all stood up silently and walked out. We had got a couple of streets away when Dalglish told us to wait for him; we saw him turn round and run back towards the pub. Presently we heard the sound of glass breaking in the distance, lots of shouting and then footsteps running towards us. 'Move it,' he muttered, out of breath, ushering us away quickly.

'You shouldn't have done that,' said the Cobra, shaking his head. He pulled Ayesha to him protectively. 'I appreciate what you done, but believe me it's not worth the trouble.'

***

It was a week or so later when Dalglish and we *Prehistoric Terror* girls were driving up to the Farnham for a day's filming, and we got stuck in a traffic jam that slowed into total gridlock. Eventually we abandoned the car and walked up to Commercial Road to see what was happening. We could smell burning as we drew closer to a large crowd of Asian men dressed in brown smocks, gathered round a tall firepit, shouting and pointing at a pile of books which were smouldering on the top of a pile of coals and logs. The pages burned first, leaving half-chewed black covers melting like tar into the flames. Tendrils of grey smoke curled upwards in thin spirals where they hung in the air briefly before evaporating into the damp mist. And then, quite unexpectedly, we saw Arthur in the throng, his white skin making him stand out instantly.

'What's going on?' said Dalglish, to a reporter in a long mac who was leaning on some railings, smoking a pipe. A large camera was slung round his neck.

'They're burning copies of an H. G. Wells book,' said the man.

'What? Why?'

'He's offended their prophet or something. Crazy, isn't it?'

Dalglish shook his head at me, speechless, his eyes full of fury. We looked over at the crowd, who were punching the air and shouting loudly in protest. As we watched, a man installed himself at the front and began to herd the crowd into a line behind him. Slowly they began to walk as a group southwards down the street. They continued to point and shout as they began their journey, walking down the middle of the road. 'Where are they going?' Dalglish asked the reporter.

'They're marching down to India House. Aldwych. Indian High Commission. Sorry, pal, can't stop. I need to go with them. Read about it in the paper tomorrow.'

'Thanks, my friend.'

Dalglish leaned against the railings and took out a cigarette. I noticed that his hands were trembling. 'Let's get out of here,' he said. We headed back to the car, clouded in a disturbing feeling that we weren't quite sure what we had just witnessed. Dalglish backed the car out, turned it around and drove off at speed.

'I saw my brother in there,' said Ayesha, sadly. 'Next to that white man.' The streets grew poorer as we headed out to the east, but in a way seemed to grow more full of life as we slowed to pass: large and colourful fruit stalls that bustled and thronged with people; broken-faced women with prams; dirty-faced children running around barefoot trying to steal an apple. Sights of Depression-era London that were usually just flashes of colour as we sped past them in the car; this was a world from which we were usually shielded.

'Let's think about this.' Eva said. 'Pull over, Dags, we need to think this through. How did Arthur meet Mekhi again?'

Dalglish turned into a side street and parked up. He was silent, lost in thought. Then he pulled himself up straight, his face grey. 'It wasn't Arthur he met at first, it was me. I had parked up to drop

Arthur off at a rally, and my car wouldn't start. Suddenly this chap appeared from nowhere, friendly as you like, and offered to give me a push. He and Arthur gave me a running start, and I managed to get her going again after that.'

We let this information sink in. 'He recognised *you*,' I said. 'He'd seen you with Ayesha. He couldn't get near you so he went for Arthur instead.'

'Oh, God,' said Eva. Up close her eyes were a feline shade of pale green.

That day we were actors, playing actors. Life carried on in the third person, out of our control.

***

Arthur was washing his clothes in the scullery when we returned, standing in front of the metal tub in a string vest and oversized pants. A chemical smell of soap suds filled the room. We explained to him what was going on with Mekhi, how his agenda may be about more than simple friendship. He listened, shaking his head occasionally.

'Unbelievable,' he said, when we had finished. His face was grimly inscrutable. 'If what you say is true … and it does make sense … then I had no idea. I've been completely duped.'

'It's very, very important, Arthur, that you do not have anything more to do with him, and that you do not tell him where Ayesha is staying,' said Dalglish, sternly.

'I wouldn't know that anyway, would I?' he said, wringing out a shirt. There was a hint of aggression in his voice.

‘And anyway, Arthur, what the hell do you think you’re doing out in the streets, burning books? Remember what your friend Shakespeare said about art made tongue-tied by authority? Religion loves to be the authority that circumscribes art. Always has done. This is a dangerous path, Arthur. For all of us.’

Arthur was silent. He picked up a new shirt, threw it into the tub and began to wash it. ‘He wasn’t talking about art in that sense,’ he said, pedantically.

‘He was talking about his writing and H. G. Wells is a writer too, you fool. I met him once, Wells, that is. Down in Sussex. He was onc of us, Arthur.’

‘That’s by the by, wouldn’t you say? You look at things with colonialist eyes. Yes, in spite of everything you tell yourself about being so bloody open-minded. You don’t even attempt to understand someone else’s point of view. That’s called bigotry. I mean, overall, it’s just racism, pure and simple.’ The words came from nowhere, like a sudden gust of wind on a calm day. They fell on us, and after a sudden intake of breath, we all understood that the dynamics of the house had shifted permanently, like the earth’s plates moving to reveal a new geography.

Dalglish leaned over, grabbed hold of Arthur by his collar and yanked him out roughly from behind the tub. Smoke-coloured water spilled from the vessel, splashing all over the scullery floor. ‘What did you say? You think I don’t have the right to question what you’re doing because your friend’s skin is brown? Are you honestly standing there, and calling me, of all people, a racist?’ he shouted, just inches from Arthur’s face. He suddenly punched the wall to the left of Arthur's head. Eva rushed in, quickly pushing the men apart. Dalglish turned away, anguished, holding his hand in pain. 'I don't hate brown-skinned people, I just have a problem with people burning books. Anyway, I'm not going to lower myself to this. You've read Freud, Arthur. "The time has probably come to replace the consequences of repression by the results of rational mental effort." Remember? This Muhammadan religion you've got yourself embroiled in offers you the same old false promises of divine protection by demanding you play by its rules. Our freedom is all we have, Arthur. Don't you see that?'

Arthur flung his shirt onto the floor and pointed at Dalglish. 'Oh, yes, and we can see the results of unbridled freedom, can't we?' he shouted, sarcastically. 'Remind me once more how that worked out for Loretta? You stand there and lecture me. Quoting from Shakespeare, no less!' he said, with a horrible laugh. '"And maiden virtue rudely strumpeted," I'll think you'll find in the same sonnet. So then, Dalglish, what about all the girls you've dishonoured? What about your wife?'

Dalglish turned white. Until very recently Arthur had been quite happy to take part in the libertarian approach to love that pervaded our society, he just happened to be less successful at it than his benefactor. I looked at Eva, and in a single glance we wondered whether a proper fight would indeed break out. But Dalglish composed himself. 'I will ignore that,' he said, quietly. 'This is not about me. You can live by the rules mankind needs to live among one another without turning those rules into a fairy tale. Without adopting religion's totalitarian cloak. Every inch of our freedom has been fought for, Arthur. Every inch of it is drenched in the blood of men and women who have died fighting for it. And here you are just blindly willing to hand all that back? I mean, seriously, Arthur. You're openly burning books, out in the streets, because the book in question offends the Muhammadans? You don't believe in the right to free speech any more?' He shook his head. 'My enemy's enemy is my friend? Is that what's going on? You're drenched in this colonial guilt, my son, and it's going to be your undoing. I don't think you're welcome here any more, Arthur, if that's how you feel.'

Arthur seemed to calm himself, or maybe he just needed to be reminded who was paying his rent. 'I'm sorry,' he said, in a strangled voice, as if the words had been wrenched out of him. An uneasy truce fell upon us as he grabbed his coat and announced he was going out for a walk. Yet again I had the strong feeling that my life had left me behind, was travelling at a speed I could only ever try to catch up with. I wandered up to Dalglish's bedroom and sat on the bed, looking out of the window. Only in a bohemian household could people conduct an argument using a Shakespearean sonnet and Freud as reference points; one day I might find that amusing, but right at that second I had the urge to walk out, there and then, to head off back to the docks and get on a boat home. It no longer mattered who was right and who was wrong; I just wanted so badly to see Nana and try to make things right. Maybe I would find us a place together. And I wanted to know that Ayesha and the Cobra were on a boat, sailing off to my rose-tinted vision of their future together in America. Both instincts were felt keenly, a physical sensation, an ache in the pit of my stomach. But then Dalglish came in and put his arms round me and gradually I began to feel anchored again.

'Arthur's right,' he said. 'I murdered my wife, in that sense.' Then he said it over and over, that awful statement about murdering his wife, until I began to feel quite frightened.

'I don't ever want to hurt you, Nancy, my love. Arthur's right about me. And you … you're too good for me …' Now it was my turn to comfort: I held him in my arms and worried for him, my flawed, licentious lover, and his state of mind. The shock of feeling his tears on my face dried my own away, instantly. Presently, the need to restate our deep emotional connection took on a sexual manifestation. Desire flared and we began to come together once again, as we had many times before. And I pushed all thoughts of leaving away.

***

Life with the bohemians, Norman, was never black and white, never about absolutes. It was only ever lived in shades of grey and conducted under the knowing guise of impermanence. Even the status of my relationship with Dalglish was never certain. A few months after our affair had begun, Dalglish and I took Eva to a garden party in Richmond. Loud and brash and typically bohemian, it was the usual riot of colour and style and cross-dressing – followed by undressing. At some point a limbo frame appeared and people began to try their hand at limbo dancing, shimmying under the frame while the other guests clapped them on in encouragement and hooted with laughter. The day was hot and we had been drinking all afternoon. Dalglish was deep in conversation with the owner, a well-known actor called Gavin Winterfield and Eva were talking to the owner's wife, Hettie, who was an artist. I felt a headache coming on, so I decided to take myself off inside for a few minutes and drink some water. I lay down on a generous chaise longue in a sunroom just off the kitchen and closed my eyes. I think I must have dropped off to sleep, but presently I heard Eva's voice from the kitchen. 'Where do you keep the gin, Hettie darling? I can't drink any more wine.' There were the sounds of cupboards opening and glasses chinking.

'It's in the drinks cupboard. In the pantry. Here, let me get it for you. I'll have one too, if you're making one.'

I was about to sit up and ask for a gin and tonic, too, our when our hostess continued in a low voice, 'So, Daggers has a new girlfriend, I see. Very easy on the eye too. And young. How do you feel about *that*?'

Uh-oh. I sank back down prostrate onto the seat and held my breath. 'Oh, you know. We've been here before, haven't we?' said Eva, lightly. 'I know that it'll eventually burn itself out and he'll come back to me. It's always the same.'

'The voice of bitter experience speaking there.'

There followed the sound and smell of cigarettes being lit. 'You know what, I'm all right about it. It takes a whole new way of looking at things to be able to give someone up for a while,' she said, pouring the drinks.

'I know what you're saying. I don't really have you down as the jealous, long-suffering type. You do cope with it admirably, even so.

It isn't easy. James and I have been through it all a couple of times, you know. To be honest, he was worse when I had my affair with a woman. That really riled him.'

'Ha,' said Eva, laughing. 'Who could've predicted that? Lemons? Ah, here we are.'

'Exactly. Here's the tonic, by the way. James was beastly at first but then when he thought we might let him in on the action he seemed to come round a bit.'

They chuckled at this. 'And did you let him?'

'Now that would be telling. C'mon on, let's join everyone. Let me find my hostess face. And do *not* let me anywhere near that limbo.'

***

Round about the same time, Queenie took me on a walk to the square, his brow furrowed. A path lined the edges of the square, from which benches flanked by delicate pencil conifers had been set back. He sat down on one of the benches, then tutted at me.

'You know, I'm very disappointed you haven't heeded my advice about Daggers, Nancy. I know you think me just a crazy old man who doesn't know what he is talking about, but I can assure you that I have lived through this before, and I do *not* want you to turn out like his wife. I'm talking to you as a friend. This is not an auspicious situation. It's like watching a slow-motion version of *Little Red Riding Hood* being gobbled up by the Big Bad Wolf.'

I felt anger welling up inside, burning out through my ears. 'I love it how everyone round here has an opinion about this. *Little Red*

Riding Hood? Seriously? I'm eighteen, not six. And how about acknowledging that it's possible for a person to change. You don't know all the facts. Maybe you'd like to know that Dalglish kept away from me for the last two years because he was frightened of hurting me.'

'Is that what he told you?' said Queenie with a snort. 'Forgive me but I don't think he's been busy in the church choir all that time.'

'Your cynicism is very sad,' I said, shaking my head, with the self-righteousness that only exists in the young.

We walked in silence back to the house. My life had become a merry-go-round, with no chance of the ride stopping long enough to let me off.

***

The last few weeks of filming *Prehistoric Terror* were greeted all round with sighs of relief. Ayesha was happy to be able to have a date to leave for America, away from the ever-present threat from her family. Things had become quite uncomfortable between Eva, Dalglish and me, and she was subdued around us. She had taken on a new lover herself – the dreadful monocled creature – more out of boredom than desire it seemed to me. When we weren't filming, Eva went to great lengths to keep out of our way.

Filming took longer one Friday, and it was later than usual when we left the studios. Ayesha remarked, brows furrowed, that she could not see her brother anywhere.

'It worries me when I don't see him. Do you mind if we drive around for a while?' she said to Dalglish. 'I want to know where he is. Head for the mosque, it's nearly time for Friday prayers.'

The building was not easy to find and we ended up stopping a couple of times for directions. As we drove up, Ayesha pointed to group of men standing outside the domed building, chatting. 'Look,' she said, flatly. 'There he is. That's the men's prayer room. The women's entrance is round the corner.'

I couldn't make him out from the others, and peered out of the window, craning my neck to see. 'He's second from the front. Look, he's on his way in now.' As the figure disappeared, behind him a line of men dressed in smocks threaded into the building.

'My parents used to bring me here when I was young,' she said, in a voice that was choked with memories and loss. Our stories were different and yet the same, and I felt it throttle itself right through my body, that familiar need to be able to exercise free will. It was a fight that came from our very bones, an instinct that was so strong it caused us to cause pain not only to those who deserved it, but also to our guardian angels, and to ourselves in a way.

'What will you do?' said Dalglish, turning to face us from the front seat.

Ayesha stared ahead for a long time. 'Let's go,' she said eventually, in a whisper.

***

The next week it was just Ayesha and me, and we found the building straight away; in fact, it was a just shortish walk from the studios through the sorry East End streets. There was a new resolve about her, though she wouldn't explain why she now felt it was the right time to confront him. I wondered if something had happened during the week. 'I've had enough of this, Nancy,' she said, as if confirming my thoughts. 'I'm going in after him.'

'Ayesha,' I said, staring at her. I grabbed hold of her arm as she turned to walk off. 'Do you really think it's a good idea to gatecrash a male prayer session? Let's just think about this for a while.'

She shook her head reluctantly, but allowed herself to be walked over towards the back of the building. We pulled our coats and hats tight and huddled in together, leaning on the cold railings, talking through the pros and cons.

'This can't go on, Nancy. I don't really think you understand what's going on. I'm going in,' said Ayesha determinedly, and suddenly walked off towards the entrance. I trailed reluctantly behind. Inside the mosque were rows of men, all kneeling on crimson prayer mats. Mekhi was about halfway down, bent prostrate to the floor.

Ayesha walked calmly to the front. 'You are all witnesses,' she said, pointing to Mekhi. 'Including you, Imam. My brother will kill me unless somebody can stop him. You have to help me.'

There were gasps from the men and even Mekhi looked shocked. 'What is this intrusion?' said the Imam, shocked. 'Ayesha?' he said, peering at this unwanted guest. 'Is that you?' He had a short, neat beard and was dressed in brown robes, with a white cap. 'You cannot be in here. Please wait outside for us and after prayers we will talk more.'

We trooped out, with rather less self-assurance than when we had entered, and stood once again at the edge of the building, smoking. After a while, the men started to pour out, all except Mekhi. We waited for a long time, nearly an hour, until the Imam appeared and gestured to us to follow him back in.

'Your brother has already left,' he said to Ayesha, his voice echoing round the empty chamber. He nodded towards the back exit. He was younger than I had first thought, perhaps only late-twenties but he looked stressed and tired. 'I will talk to him for you.'

And so we returned as promised the same time the following week. This time, we were ushered to a back room where the Imam began to describe his conversation with Mekhi.

'Your brother believes,' he began, 'that according to the scriptures of sharia, you are a whore who should be stoned. He's also concerned that he has now been in the same room as a woman during prayers. This is strictly forbidden and, he says, will lead to judgement by Allah.

'I told him: there is nothing about stoning in the Qur'an, Mekhi. And so he referred me to the verse of the Rajam. This verse should have been in the holy book, he said, but it was eaten by a goat just after the holy Prophet died. He was adamant, all right: many significant figures have confirmed this, he said. Muhammad's favourite wife and the second caliph. And so I had to explain. The rule exists in sharia law, but not in the Qur'an, and in this mosque,' he said, 'we follow only the Qur'an and the Hadiths. But your brother is now unhappy that I do not believe in the application of sharia law within the faith. Our conversation was not good. Mekhi thinks that, to be a true Muslim, one must aspire to live within an Islamic caliphate, and this necessarily includes sharia law. Your brother got so angry and – because my family is Turkish – well, Mekhi pointed out to me my own "traitorous Jew-loving leader Atatürk". According to your brother, he killed off the last European caliphate like it was a leftover meal to be thrown in the bin.' The long-suffering Imam shook his head.

'I'm sorry,' said Ayesha.

'Well, I told him he has done me and the Islamic faith a great dishonour, especially in a holy place. Don't come back here, I said to him. Mekhi then argued that I am a poor Muslim because, at the very least, disobedient women must be beaten. He even gave me the chapter: Qur'an, 4.34. But, you know, I really had had enough by this point. That ayat is just about wives, I said, not sisters. I threw him out. Allah will decide the fate of your sister, I told him. Allah's word is final,' he said. 'He is the only one who can judge us.'

The Imam dabbed his forehead with a handkerchief. 'The relationship between sharia and our holy books can sometimes be … problematical. And there are some debatable verses in our most holy book,' he said. 'Especially in the later suras. I teach from the early ones, when the holy Prophet was in Mecca and taught peace and kindness. The way some suras deal with women and those of a different faith are … difficult. But we are on the verge of our own Enlightenment, I am sure. And then we will have clarity on these matters and I will have … how do you say … *ammunition* against those such as your brother who do not favour a reinterpretation.'

It all seemed very theoretical, very theological. 'Hang on,' I said, feeling suddenly furious. 'We're talking about a death threat here. We're not talking about religion.'

The Imam looked at me quizzically, as if this were something I could not possibly hope to understand. The room fell silent.

'So,' said Ayesha. 'Will you help me?'

The Imam shook his head. 'Your brother is all full of the fire-words of youth. I have told him not to hurt you. But you must go back to your family now. Every day you dishonour them is a day longer you will spend in hell when the day of judgement comes.' Ayesha looked around the room hopelessly. That didn't sound particularly enlightened to me. There was nothing else to do but leave.

On the way out, Ayesha turned back to the Imam. 'I remember now,' she said, 'one of the Hadiths. I think it was Sahih al-Bukhari. Hell is full of disobedient women.'

The Imam looked down at the floor. 'Please go now, sister. I have done all I can.'

During the long walk back I mused at my own response to everything I had just heard, which as ever was one of anthropological curiosity rather than inspiration to faith. I could not fathom that mankind believed it morally sound to channel every earthly decision, every pronouncement, every thought and deed through the prism of religion, to view as gospel ancient texts whose ethics were cast once, many hundreds of years ago, and thereafter forever preserved in aspic. To be forever searching for analogy and approval – to say, not, what do *I* think is the right thing to do, but what does *my ruler* think is the right thing to do. To never be able to revisit ancient texts within the context of the prevailing moral zeitgeist and say, look here old chap, this may have been cutting-edge thousands of years ago but these days, well, it doesn't sound quite right. Can we perhaps discuss some changes? I saw the hope in the Imam's eye, but he was facing resistance from people like Mekhi. People who were determined that their religion be as locked in time as a photograph. I marvelled, with the awe and wonder of a child, at those whose lives worked in that way.

***

And so, Norman, we worried for Ayesha, even more so when we heard she had been persuaded to do a final film up at the Farnham. But the Imam's words had consoled us, and of course, aside from all that, I was in love, and the bond between Dalglish and me continued to grow. Passion blazed day and night; Dalglish was by constantly my side and true to me. A couple of months later we were invited to a dinner party in Bloomsbury. A banker turned publisher, with a penchant for all things bohemian. His wife was from aristocratic stock and they were both learned and cultured, and yet as the evening progressed I felt increasingly tired and bored. Dalglish glanced over as if to say, what's wrong?

I began to eat the steak and sipped at a glass of red, but the more I indulged, the worse I felt. Faces became red and ugly and picaresque, like drawings from some Victorian caricature. Our host's laughter turned into a cruel honking. The fire began to die down and the room turned chilly. For the first time, I began to find the whole gig a little childish and I wondered if bohemianism was just a stage in your life, rather than a destination.

Halfway through the main course I excused myself and ran to the bathroom where I was sick into the toilet. As I washed my mouth and faced myself in the mirror, a horrible thought dawned on me. I could not remember the last time I had had a period. I considered it bourgeois to keep track of such things. We had been scrupulously careful about contraception, in fact Dalglish was even more solicitous than me about it all. And yet …

I returned to the dining room. Dalglish was in his element and grew loquacious as the wine flowed, though his voice remained quiet. He proposed toast after toast, to our hosts, to art, to friends, to a life removed from the constraints of social convention. The hours dragged on and on, and the conversation became tediously circular; the same old points were revisited every couple of hours as everyone got so drunk they forgot what had been said. Dawn was breaking as we left, Dalglish staggered around trying to find his car keys. I had switched to water after being sick and was now stone cold sober.

'Let me drive,' I said.

'All right,' he said, rubbing my arm affectionately, as we stepped into the car. 'You were quiet tonight, my darling?'

I looked through the glass of the windscreen out onto the street. The gas lamps were beginning to click off. 'I think I might be pregnant.'

Dalglish said nothing for a long time. I wondered if he had fallen asleep. A postman walked past and a scruffy dog ambled by, sniffing at the tyres. 'Oh, God,' he whispered. 'Are you sure?'

'No, I'm not,' I admitted. 'I've been feeling weird and I can't remember the last time I had a period.'

'That's true. I can't remember the last time you had one either. Hang on. Wasn't it over Christmas?'

I looked at him. 'You're right, you know. I'd completely forgotten.'

'And it's now March.'

'Yes.'

'Fuck. I'm sorry, Nancy,' he said, in a strangled voice. 'This is my fault. But don't worry. I know someone who can take care of it for us.'

What if we want to keep it, I thought, but said nothing. I turned on the engine, pulled out onto the road, and drove home slowly, deep in thought. Dalglish's head lolled and he fell fast asleep.

***

My breasts and belly swelled. My aversion to certain smells became even more heightened and I felt like Grandad on a Saturday afternoon after he'd just finished five and a half days down the pit. Dalglish took me to see his doctor, a French fellow whose surgery was located just off the King's Road. The doctor asked me lots of questions and prodded me around a bit. There was no definitive way to tell, he said. Well, there *was* a new test which, naturally, wasn't widely available and was expensive. It would involve injecting my urine into a rabbit and watching for certain symptoms – as well as sacrificing the rabbit – but that was not necessary, he said, as he was pretty sure that I was pregnant.

'Are you planning on getting married?' he asked Dalglish, with a frown.

Dalglish looked at me then looked away. 'No,' he said. 'We don't want that.'

'Well then, as Nancy is unmarried she will have to go to a hostel to have the baby. There's a very good one not too far away. It's run by the Sisters of Hope. You go in three weeks before your due date, and you'll stay there for three weeks after.'

'Why can't I just stay at home?'

The doctor sighed. 'There's more to consider here than just your comfort, my dear,' he said, curtly. 'The sisters will help you consider your baby's future too, and what's best for him. Or her.'

We thanked the doctor and left. As we walked back, Dalglish took my hand and said, 'I won't put you through all that, Nancy.' My heart beat fast, wondering if he'd changed his mind about marriage.

'I know someone who can take care of this for us. I'll pay for it all. This is my doing.'

I looked at him coldly and wondered, for the first time, if I actually knew anything about him at all.

***

The abortion would cost over a hundred pounds. I felt sad, thinking that there was no question of us keeping the baby, and that he would rather pay a huge sum of money and put my life in danger than embrace the situation. The mists of love began to clear for the first time, leaving a heavy base of resentment. I thought of Eva's friend who had died having an abortion a year or so earlier.

Ayesha visited me at the house and told me not to go through with it, turning the air blue with her thoughts about Dalglish and how he was behaving towards me. But Dalglish organised it all and simply told me when he would be taking me. Conveniently, his earlier diktat about me exercising my right to free will did not appear to apply in this case, I thought bitterly. But I was young and confused. I couldn't seem to verbalise these angry thoughts. When the day came, we headed off in his car to Bethnal Green in the East End. The streets grew narrower and dirtier, until I was back in Oslington, but then much, much worse – poverty like I'd never seen before, and I realised we'd actually been living the high life up north. Row after row of slums, with emaciated children running around naked, covered in mud and filth. We parked outside a shabby end-of-terrace house. I was about to ask Dalglish about the wisdom of leaving his motor car in such a place, when a hard-faced, undergrown teenager walked up and demanded a shilling to watch the car for us while we went inside. And did we want it cleaned for another shilling? There was a proper, organised little industry going on here.

The house was filthy inside and out. A cheerful old crone showed us to a back room and offered us tea. The cup had huge tidemarks round it and the teaspoon was dirty. From the room above we heard a woman's cries, deep and elemental, and all of a sudden it all felt too adult, too serious and real. I lowered my eyes and began to cry.

'I can't go through with it.'

'Nancy,' said Dalglish, trying to smile. He moved close and put his arm around me. 'It'll be ten minutes out of our lives. I'll stay with you, I promise. We'll be out of here after that. We'll be more careful in future. I'll be more careful.'

'You don't understand,' I said, and I felt a strong sense that in that very moment I had suddenly done a lot of growing up. 'I'm not going through with it. Eva's friend died doing this. And you haven't even asked me if this is what I want. Why can't we try to make the best of it? Make a little family together?' Dalglish gave a horrible laugh, then began to implore me to change my mind.

Eventually, it became clear that his strategy was not working. 'So, you're trying to trap me,' he said, coldly. That was the first time, I think, that I truly felt hatred towards him. It came in a flash and left soon after, but it was there. We sat in a charged silence, facing away from each other.

After a few more minutes, we heard the incumbent patient sobbing as she moved slowly down the stairs. Each step was agonisingly slow and accompanied by a cry of pain. Then the front door shut and the crone returned to collect us. Dalglish looked at me, pleadingly, one last time.

'I'm sorry,' I said to the woman. 'I've changed my mind.'

'That's no problem, my dear,' she said, wiping her hands on a bloody pinny. 'That must be the right decision for you, and I wish you both all the best.'

***

We drove back in silence and I went straight to Dalglish's bedroom and lay down on his bed, staring at the wall. Dalglish went out, probably to the pub. Later, I heard the latch click and Dalglish entered the room and sat down next to me on the bed.

'Nance,' he said, holding his head in his hands. I could smell beer on his breath. His eyes were unnaturally bright and he seemed agitated. I sighed inwardly; I had worked out by now what was going on when the eyes were open wider than usual, and suddenly he had so much to say and everything was all right with the world and he was full of love for me again. We never spoke about it, but I knew all about his white, powdery friend who was most definitely not a clothes designer.

'I'm sorry about today. I've been thinking about it. You're right. We need to make the best of this, and we will. I will try, all right?' But then I realised that he wanted to make love, which he did, more insistently than ever.

And truth and lies and obfuscation all bled into each other until it was impossible to tell them apart.

***

Over the next few months, my feelings intensified. I hated Dalglish and I loved him at the same time. I felt I could rescue him from himself. I covered up for him at work when he was wired and unable to string a sentence together; in truth, both Eva and I were actually becoming reasonably proficient at photography and sometimes even took over the shoots ourselves.

Although I was dimly aware that my dream of us becoming a conventional family was further away than ever, I convinced myself it was simply a matter of working harder at it, of concealing my pregnancy and subjugating my personality and needs to his until he had the space to work this out for himself. The more I did this, the worse I felt about myself.

I was also scared he would abandon me for Eva. Beautiful, charming, sweet Eva, who was secretly devastated at my pregnancy but who was still trying to be nice and remain my friend. Eva who, unlike me, was not growing fat, whose face was not puffing out and who was not now empathising with her grandad and his single bowel movement a week.

And so, when I started to feel those first ripples and movements, and later on when those small movements turned into a whole body moving around inside me, it was not an amazing and joyous time for me, because I was too worried about what Dalglish was feeling about it all. I was consumed with a horrible jealousy and lack of trust, and for every minute that he was not with me I fretted that he was off with someone else.

I was also incredibly angry and disappointed in myself. I'd turned into the very cliché Queenie had warned me about. No amount of intelligence or grammar school education had been able to immunise me from the power of Cupid and his twelve-bore, as old Archie Turner had once put it. Though, what was 'it', exactly? Love, lust or just plain old maternal pity? Marriage was not even discussed, but when I reached the latter stages of pregnancy, shopkeepers refused to serve me because of my lack of wedding ring. I took matters into my own hands, and found a suitable proxy up in the attic in the form of a large dress ring. Arthur obligingly sawed off the gold flower petals and in the process liberated the huge green emerald set within – which we gave to Queenie to pawn for cash – leaving a more sober if slightly wonky gold ring. My housemates, including Dalglish, found this hilarious.

'Why do you want to bow to such bourgeois conventions?' he said, loftily, one evening, sipping from a glass of claret. 'Marriage has done nothing for women except entrap them and confine them to a lifetime of subservience, childbearing and domestic drudgery.'

Nevertheless, when you can't get served at the butchers, conventionality doesn't look quite so bad. You suddenly realise that the alternative might even be worse. I was heavy and tired, and I had gone cold on the idea of changing the world. I wanted certainty, not shades of grey. I began to regard bohemia as a petulant, spoiled child, concerned only about its own right to unbridled hedonism.

***

I managed to go on working until six months through my pregnancy. Up until that point we had managed to conceal what was actually a fairly small bump by a mixture of clever camera angles, loose clothing and lighting. Six months in, Norman. That was exactly when Ayesha disappeared. One day the Cobra turned up at our house at four in the morning, inconsolable.

'Have you seen her?' he sniffed, between sobs. His suit was dishevelled and his hair, which was usually gelled back, was sticking out. 'She didn't come home last night. She came to say goodbye to you, Nancy. I've been walking the streets all night. Been up to the studios – everywhere. We're supposed to be leaving tomorrow.'

Then he sat in the basement, crying and telling us over and over how he'd failed her. But he couldn't be persuaded to go to the police under any count. Eventually, he admitted that he was already legally married (though separated) back in America. We all had our own reasons for not being the ones who went to the police and so nothing was done. The Cobra wiped his eyes, picked up his hat and left. That weekend he got on a boat and sailed back to America as planned. One day Ayesha was there, and the next she was gone.

I cried for my friend, but my grief was tempered by my own worries. The merry-go-round continued as did the feelings of unease and sadness, which were with me now all the time. A cloud of unspoken suspicion about what may have happened to Ayesha, a kind of guilt by association, fell on Arthur, though once again there was nothing to say because nothing could be proved and it seemed to us that since our previous argument, Arthur had made a conscious job of distancing himself from his new friend.

Arthur was still collecting glasses to try to earn a few bob, and Queenie continued his painting. Dalglish and Eva began mysteriously to procure lots of assignments in far flung places – Paris, Monte Carlo, stately homes in the West Country. And shoots that we used to do in a day now somehow required overnight stays. A mudslide of jealous dread washed over me, and remained in place more or less permanently. The week before it was time for me to go into the hostel, Dalglish and Eva were abroad again – in Le Touquet this time. It was a weekend assignment which was unusual in itself. I was expecting them back by the Monday or Tuesday at the latest, but by the following weekend they had still not returned or sent any kind of message. I travelled alone by taxi.

'Ah, the home for Naughty Girls,' said the taxi driver with a chuckle, rousing me from my thoughts. The streets scooted past in a blur, a bad dream come to life. Every time I saw a woman with dark hair walking down the street a well of hope sprung up inside me – this time it might be Ayesha. But in my heart I knew she was gone.

Suddenly, I missed Norm. I could no longer deny what was going on between Dalglish and Eva. Norm wouldn't have treated me like that. I cried tears of regret, finally acknowledging that I had made a huge mistake. I sobbed and sobbed, inconsolable, until the taxi driver slowed the cab to tell me he was sorry for having made fun of my situation.

The home was a drab, squat building with mean windows. I heaved my bags across the front drive, which was an uneven area of paving slabs. A nun opened the door, her face expressionless. She led the way up linoleum-covered stairs to a dormitory where I was to sleep. The place had that sanitised institutional smell, a place where the servants of the Almighty used vinegar and bicarbonate of soda to try to wash away the sins of us Naughty Girls.

'Pull yourself together,' she urged, as I wept onto my new bed. 'You're not the first and you sure won't be the last. I'll give you half an hour to unpack then you can come and pray with the others. We give every girl here the chance to repent of her sins, and you'll be no different. Then you'll start work.'

And so, a mere half an hour later, I found myself on my knees in a long row of sorry-looking girls with large bellies, repeating the humiliating verses of repentance bestowed on us by stony-faced nuns. And shortly after that, they set me on scrubbing the staircase I had walked up just a short time before.

On Sunday we were marched to church in crocodile formation. The shouts and whistles of the local street urchins confirmed – in a less formal vernacular – our fallen status. The other girls were sweet, and many of them made light of our situation, but humour had deserted me. I befriended one girl: a tiny, chameleon-featured creature called Tania who lived with her mother in a run-down flat near Waterloo. After she had had her baby, the vicar came twice a day to tell her she was a sinner and to persuade her to give the child up for adoption. The nuns kept a close eye on the baby to see if she had any congenital defects or other obvious disabilities; these would have made it more difficult for her to be adopted. Eventually, Tania conceded defeat. I will never forget her cries as they took her little girl away.

I wrote a note to Queenie to tell him I was terrified they would take my baby away, too. With only a week to go, Sister Agnes came to tell me that I had a couple of visitors. My heart leaped, thinking that Dalglish had come to visit me. There was an austere common room on the ground floor where visitors could be received. It was a bare little room, with a few chairs, a side table and a picture on the wall of Jesus looking remarkably uninterested in proceedings. As I walked in, I saw Queenie and Arthur waiting nervously for me. My heart sank, but I tried not to let it show. Queenie, as usual, looked ill at ease to be away from the house. Arthur just looked startled.

'I suppose you're going to tell me this is your grandfather, and this is the boy who got you into trouble?' said Sister Frances, disdainfully, peering round the door. Not waiting for an answer, she continued, 'Well young man, it's not too late to make amends for ruining Nancy's life like this.' Then she slammed the door shut and we heard her footsteps disappearing off down the corridor.

'Good God, I didn't realise this place was run by the nuns,' whispered Queenie, shaking his head. 'Really, Nancy, I am so angry with Dalglish. No sign of him or that gangster's moll for three weeks now. To treat you this way, well quite frankly it's disgraceful. Have the nuns already tried to put pressure on you to give the child up for adoption when it arrives?'

I nodded, not trusting myself to speak. Arthur looked down at his hands, which he twisted nervously.

'Look, my dear, Arthur and I have been talking,' continued Queenie.

Arthur looked at the ground. His voice was full of emotion. 'Yes. It's just that … it's not fair that they'll make you give the baby up, Nancy. What I'm trying to say is that I'm offering to marry you, if that would stop them.'

I looked at Arthur, who could not meet my eye. I felt a rush of deep gratitude towards my friend for his selfless actions, though at the same time my heart sank. The disappointment that he was not Dalglish was so complete, so intense, and was matched with a new-found hatred of the man who had abandoned me. A clamp pressed against my throat, making it hard to speak. We sat in silence for several minutes.

'Thank you, Arthur. And Queenie. You have been such good friends to me,' I said, looking at the floor. 'Let's just pretend, shall we? If we say we intend to get married but want to wait until after the birth then they might just leave me alone.'

'All right,' said Arthur, relieved.

'Will you come back and see me after I've given birth?'

They promised they would return, and we whispered our plans to each other. Twenty minutes later they hugged me and left, and went to speak to Sister Agnes to outline our fake intentions. And I was left with nothing but loneliness in that shabby room. I lingered much longer than I ought, staring out of the window. I thought about the marriage bar. Norm would have worked things out. He would have got round it somehow. Maybe we would have had to move abroad, or maybe we would have just cohabited – and you can bet your life Norm would have shielded me from society's harsh judgement if we had. He would have found a solution. Norm never let anyone stop him, even though plenty of people made it their business to try.

I stroked the bump, the life that was growing inside me. 'If you're a boy, I'm going to call you Norman,' I said, as it moved and squirmed and wriggled. Because that's who your father should have been.

And that's what I did, Norman, when you were born, a little over two weeks later, and I fell in love with you instantly, with a deep, primordial, overwhelming, one-way, lifetime-lasting thud.

This thing that I'm writing. These words. Each and every one is for you.

Chapter 12

Once again we were in autumn and the days began to cool and the rains fell on dried earth. The large oak tree on the street in front of the hostel began to loosen, then shed, its yellow and red leaves. The vicar turned up to take down the details for the birth certificate, and it was then that I realised I didn't even know Dalglish's first name. And so, Norman, that most important document holds a fictitious first name for your father, inspired by a panicked glance at the *Daily Sketch* that was lying on a coffee table in that hostel visitors' room.

The time I spent at the hostel after the birth was actually quite useful in teaching me the basics about caring for a baby. Sister Agnes and the other nuns showed me how to make up bottles of watered-down evaporated milk, change and wash nappies, how to hold the baby correctly so as to support his neck, how often to feed him and when to let him sleep. At night all the babies were taken off to their own dormitory, so I managed to rest fairly well and get my strength back up and prepare for the time when I would have to leave.

The nuns were made of steel, except that even steel may bend a little after a while. This was with the exception of those times when the vicar came round and they turned into blushing, bashful girls. And in the same vein, they were similarly impressed by Queenie and Arthur – two of the least masterful males you could ever meet.

The day arrived when the vicar had to make his final assessment of the fate of the baby. 'Sister Agnes tells me you want to keep the child,' he said, wearing the distasteful look of a man who could no longer be shocked by the appalling behaviour of your average fallen woman. 'You have no husband and therefore no income. I would strongly advise you give him a future by giving him to a decent Christian family. We choose the families very carefully, you can be sure of that. I would not normally allow an unwed mother to keep her baby, Miss Thompson.'

He and the sisters sat opposite us in the visitors' room; I was flanked by a nervous Arthur and an agitated Queenie.

'Before I start I'd just like to say thank you so much for looking after my darling granddaughter,' said Queenie, ignoring the vicar. He looked like a mad old professor with his shock of white hair and red neckerchief. He dabbed at his eyes. 'One little mistake,' he said, shaking his head, gesturing at Arthur and me. 'I leave them alone after Sunday school just one little time. They were supposed to be peeling potatoes for lunch but then … well, they got carried away. Oh, yes, I was young once, you know vicar. I had feelings and passions. One little mistake. Seems so dreadfully unfair.' He took hold of Arthur's hand and held it in his ancient, freckled claws. 'But, vicar, this wonderful gentleman here, this *Theodore* Dalglish, well, it doesn't matter, does it, if people think he's slow now, vicar, does it? Remedial is just a word, and we all know about sticks and stones.'

I looked over at Arthur, who had turned pale. He looked back at me with dead eyes.

'This young man has decided to do the right thing, the Christian thing,' he said, making the sign of the cross on his chest and looking upwards. 'Theo, I cannot wait for you to become my grandson-in-law and make everyone happy again: the supernatural judiciary,' he continued, pointing up to the heavens, 'this lovely vicar and these *marvellous* ladies.' Arthur looked straight ahead, expressionless. 'So, vicar, no need to send baby Norman away. He will have a happy home, one that is run by a legally married man and wife. And, if I may say so, God has blessed this baby. Made, as they all are, in his image. Created in joy on the sabbath from the loins of a simpleton bartending socialist poet and …'

It went on endlessly. Or at least that's how it felt, Norman. The nuns all flinched at the word 'loins' and the vicar flinched at the word 'socialist'. The air curdled with Queenie's Stilton-tinged breath. I didn't know whether to laugh or cry. When he finally paused for breath, Queenie had delivered his part with the confidence of the lead actor in a Shakespearean tragedy. He was in his element, so toe-curlingly theatrical that I swear even the old carpet in the visitors' room started to curl up at the edges. In the end, I put my head down and tried not to giggle. But after those fifteen cloying, treacle-soaked minutes, Queenie had talked the vicar into submission. It no longer mattered whether they believed us or not, they just wanted us gone, with much the same urgency as one has with blocked drains. And the right outcome had been achieved: with the promise of respectability around the corner, I was allowed to keep you.

***

The atmosphere in the house felt flat; it had become a dank, mouldering place filled with pockets of stillness, and cramped energy. Even the plants had wilted without Eva's attentions. There had been no sign of the doyens of *haute Bohème* for nearly two months and we all wondered if they would ever return. Queenie had been raiding the Buddha in the attic on my instructions, taking just enough to keep the rent paid and to buy food for Arthur and himself.

We strapped my beautiful new baby into a home-made sling made of a torn up old blanket, then Arthur and I walked up to the King's Road and bought a pram and some clothes and bottles. Norman fell asleep as we walked back. Once home, I decided it was time to clean the house a little, but I was facing years of neglect. Over the next few weeks, I was suddenly seized by a new zeal – namely to protect my newborn from the grim horrors of a house where cleaning was considered almost as bourgeois as asking your lover their first name. Progress was tediously slow but once you lowered your expectations it was a case of removing the dirt layer by layer.

We couldn't rid the house of its sad feel; it had simply lost its heart. My own abandonment had turned into a low, constant angst, but this was tempered by tending to the constant demands of a baby. But while baby Norman was sleeping my thoughts often turned to Ayesha and how everyone had failed her. It was a pain that seemed to grow daily. I began a habit of wandering up to the loft bedroom, where I would lie on the bed, curl myself into a ball and nestle my face into Ayesha's garments. Tears followed, as I finally allowed myself to feel proper grief for my friend.

But as autumn stretched into winter, as well as all the other jobs, we now needed to sort out the fires every day. Queenie was happy to have a new subject for his art, and there are several paintings of you and me, Norman: mother and baby in Queenie's trademark post-impressionist style, that are now littered throughout Fitzrovia and beyond.

Just as I was getting used to the idea that I would never see Dalglish again, one day in early December the door opened and there he stood, a real-life ghost, his face full of ersatz guilt. His dark hair was long and unkempt and his skin was slightly bronzed.

'Nancy … I'm so sorry.'

I shook my head then shrugged, and returned to the basement where Arthur and Queenie were quarrelling over grammar. Norman was asleep in Queenie's arms. Dalglish followed, standing tentatively halfway down the stairs.

'I think you'll find that "it" is an impersonal pronoun, old chap,' said Arthur, over the top of his *Industrial Worker*. 'Like teacup. Or testicle. See these here babies, awful nuisance so they are, but the pesky little chaps tend to have what we call a *sex*. I think the phrase you're looking for is "How should I hold *him*?" It's not too difficult once you get your head round it. You'll find you've only got the three to choose from: he, him, his. Give it a while, I'm sure you'll master it.'

'Oh, do give over. What does it matter, anyway?'

They looked up and saw our visitor.

'Well, well, well,' said Queenie with a sigh. 'It's the prodigal musketeer. You never fail to surprise, Daggers. Right, well, Arthur, let's go and take a walk round the square. You can tell me all about that nice Mr Pearce getting squashed again.'

'It wasn't Mr Pearce who got squashed, Queenie. How many times.'

'Whatever,' said Queenie. He handed baby Norman back to me then they left for the square. I could see they were conflicted; Dalglish was their benefactor, and they existed in a state of economic dependency with regards to him. There was only so much they could have said. I looked at Dalglish, definitely musketeer-like, a picture of mock penitence and a glint in his eye.

'I bet you weren't expecting to come back and find a baby here,' I said, calmly. 'You hoped the nuns would pressure me into having him adopted. Do you know, I only worked that out when I was leaving? I didn't need to be there in the first place. I have to hand it to you and your doctor friend. Nice try.'

He looked at me mournfully.

'But when I had him, Dags, well … something's changed in me now. I'm different. I can't imagine life without him. And we don't need you, in fact, we don't want anything more to do with you,' I said, flatly.

I picked up the sleeping baby and went upstairs. For the next three days, I refused to speak to him, but eventually his presence, always larger than his physical persona, started to subsume us all. The energy in the house changed and became charged and full of possibility, something I have never been able to resist. I was sitting on the divan feeding the baby when he wandered in and stood over us, arms crossed. All Dalglish had had to do was wait a few days; he knew it and so did I.

‘So … are you going to introduce me?’ he said, and I realised just how much I had missed that quiet voice of his.

‘His name is Norman.’

‘Good God, how terribly northern! After your old boyfriend?’

‘I’m not interested in what you think.’

‘I know, darling. I let you down. I don’t think I can ever make it up to you, I know that. I just … couldn’t cope with it all. I was scared of being trapped.’

‘Where’s Eva? Did you get bored with her again, too? Must be marvellous, having her standing by like that. Waiting for you to shower her with a few crumbs of interest when you’re not having fun elsewhere.’

Dalglish ran his hands through his hair. ‘It’s over between us,’ he said, quietly.

‘That’s a shame.’

‘Don’t you want to know where I’ve been?’

I shrugged.

‘I have been down in Monte Carlo, working for the French magazines. Eva left after two days. We had a blazing row. She said she didn’t want to be second best to you. She’s moved back in with her mother down in Dorset.’

‘You’re mistaking me for someone who’s interested.’

Dalglish hung his head, suddenly looking vulnerable. He looked red-eyed and hungover, but still disgracefully handsome, and already I felt my hostility and anger falling away, giving way to relief and the over-arching need to save him from himself.

That's right, Norman. I, who had been given away to the nuns for repentance, who had given birth alone, who had had to fight to keep my child. I pitied him for feeling trapped. Already I could see that his cocaine habit had spiralled to new levels, even in the two months he'd been absent. In those few days since his return I'd watched the ups and downs play out in the house: I'd heard him laughing uncontrollably and sharing champagne with Arthur and Queenie, then suddenly become full of fury, irritable, shouting and slamming doors. The whole household was on edge: grateful for the highs, frightened of the lows. But for me he was the ultimate drug, and though I spent as much time despising him as I did loving him, I was seemingly powerless to stop him coming back into our lives.

If there is enough delusion, bad behaviour can always be forgiven or explained or denied, just as when you are dealing with explosives you might be able to convince yourself that with careful management, the whole thing won't blow up in your face.

We became lovers once again, and I tried to kid myself it wasn't tinged with shame. But just a little while after that, during one of the lows, I returned from shopping one afternoon to find my beautiful baby with a black eye – he'd managed to fall off the bed by himself, said Dalglish. I had no evidence against my lover, but the story didn't add up – tiny babies can't just move around by themselves. I decided there and then we would leave, Norman, you and I. We would just get Christmas out of the way first.

***

'By the way,' said Dalglish, 'we're throwing a party tonight.' It was Christmas Eve. I was on my way to the washing tub with a load of nappies.

I shook my head at him, yawning. 'You're crazy. I just want to sleep.'

Arthur walked past. 'There's a letter for you,' he said, handing Dalglish an envelope.

'Thanks,' he said, opening it up. He looked over it briefly and frowned. 'It's about the rent. Two crowns a month increase. All we need eh, chaps?' He folded the letter away and put it in his jacket pocket. He was a fairly effective liar, as liars went, but even he had fallen short of usual standards this time. I looked at him, coldly.

'I'm off to Hyde Park to a workers' rally,' said Arthur. 'But I'll be back to give you a hand later. Leyla will be round about seven. She's made us some costumes.'

Dalglish laughed. 'Excellent news. There's nothing like a Leyla costume to brighten up a do.'

'Am I the only person who didn't know about this?' I said, suddenly furious. Arthur looked sheepish and hurried off up the stairs.

I'm not quite sure what happened next. Dalglish and I ended up having a blazing row, which on my part came out as a hideous litany of his failings as both a partner and a father, and on his part became childish accusations that I had 'changed' since having the baby. These circular arguments dragged on with a sort of perpetual motion, growing more and more accusatory. Out of sheer frustration, I threw a cup at the wall, and then he slapped me hard across my face. I remember going into a state of shock. I ran upstairs to his bedroom and started to pack Norman's and my things into a bag. He raced up the stairs behind me, slammed the door shut, pushed me roughly to the bed and pinned me down by my arms. He slapped me again, and then slowly leaned right over, so close that I could see every hair of his beard and feel his breath on my face. His cheeks were flushed with emotion. 'Do not even think about leaving me,' he whispered, menacingly. 'Now get up and help me get the place ready.'

***

At seven o'clock, Dalglish and Arthur went out to buy alcohol for the party; Dalglish insisted on taking the pram with the baby in it. It would act as a trolley to hold all the beer and whisky, he said breezily, and the baby needed fresh air. It had been snowing since midday, and large flakes continued descending through a charcoal evening sky. Outside, the night was eerily silent and the wind had dropped away, bringing a picture-postcard stillness to the scene.

I watched them disappear down the street, worried sick. Dalglish heaved the pram backwards through the snow, twisting left and right in order just to make a few inches of progress. The decision to take it at all was plainly ridiculous, though none of us said so. As soon as they were out of sight I dived into Dalglish's jacket and grabbed the letter. I recognised Eva's right-leaning, energetic sprawl immediately, written on attractive, cream Basildon Bond writing paper. My heart sank:

Dearest D,

Where are you? Beastly man. There are only so many times a gal can listen to her mother drone on about the parlous state of the village hall accounts or Mrs Powell's secret drink problem or the nasty stink we're going to cause in Dorset's most small-minded village by our audacious decision to cohabit. I swear I'm going insane. You must come home soon, if for no other reason than to help avoid a rather ugly matricide.

I do hope you're not playing with the children again, naughty boy. You must let her be and not give her false hope this time. Women get very funny about these types of things after they've just had a baby.

You were wondering how big the area is out the back of the house. We walked around it so many times over the past month – and explored it nocturnally in other ways, you may recall – but we couldn't quite work out the acreage, because there are so many walled areas. Well, I checked with Taylor, and there is at least an acre here, all in all, and there's a huge space next to the orchard that I reckon would be the right size for a good old-fashioned party. We already have a huge gazebo in the garage and we can get Taylor (lucky for you he is no Mellors to my Lady Chatterley – perish the thought!) to set up chimeneas around the perimeter. Let's ship Mummy off for the weekend and get Gavin and Hettie down with their limbo thingy. We'll invite all the old crowd, and throw the most wonderful New Year shindig outside, with mulled wine to celebrate the start of our new life in the country and to welcome in 1939.

The pillow on your side still smells of you and I won't let Mrs Taylor wash it, sentimental old fool that I am. Hurry back, my love.

Yours always,

Eva

I put the letter back inside the jacket and plodded slowly back down to the basement, where I lay on the divan. Strangely, I no longer felt jealous; all I felt was the realisation that I knew nothing about this man and carried the primeval fear of a mother who senses that her baby is in danger. For our own safety and sanity, it was time for Norman and me to leave.

I ran my hand across my cheek. Nearly four years ago Dalglish had used his hand to flatter me into embracing the life he wanted to share, and now that same hand had been used to slap me into place. It was an act that could never be undone. I heard the front door click and the sounds of the pram being manoeuvred into the hallway, then the clinking noises of bottles being decanted. Relief flooded over me and I bounded up the stairs and took the baby into my arms, trying to appear nonchalant.

Arthur's art student girlfriend, Leyla, arrived at the same time, carrying a huge sack. We wound our way back down to the basement, where she revealed their outfits for the evening. For Arthur, she had created an oversized jacket made of tassels of brightly coloured crêpe paper. It made a dry, crinkly sound as he pulled it over his skinny frame.

'It's my project for this term,' she said, proudly, pulling on a matching hat. Then she took out some theatrical make-up and set about covering Arthur's face in chalky, pastel strips.

Queenie arrived, clomping down the stairs in his sandals. 'Ah, look at you,' he scoffed at the sight of Arthur before him. 'Your mother would be so proud. Let me guess. You're going to the party as a piñata? I do hope there aren't any cricket bats lying around.'

'Haven't you got any arses to paint?' said Arthur, wearily, lifting his arms up and down, trying to establish what range of movement he still had. The jacket rustled as he shifted around.

Queenie began to laugh like a hyena. It was a few moments before he could compose himself. 'I would love to hear you read *The Anatomy of Melancholy* dressed like that. Seriously. It would be a much more cheerful affair when I'm forced to listen to that drivel. Perhaps you could add in some maracas for added poignancy during the really depressing parts. Or a little tambourine.'

Arthur sighed and shook his head. 'Go away, you sad man.'

'Gladly. I've just come to collect my last few things. They'll be safer with me tonight, I fear.'

'Need a hand?' I asked.

'That would be kind, thank you, Nancy. Can you pick up my easel over there? And don't worry about what anyone thinks, Arthur, *amour propre* is overrated anyway,' he said, chuckling his way back up the stairs.

I left Norman on the divan and carried the easel up the two flights to Queenie's tiny room.

'I need to talk to you,' I whispered, closing the door. 'I'm leaving. I'm taking Norman back to Oslington.'

Queenie sat down on his bed and sighed. 'What's the Big Bad Wolf done now?'

'Oh, God, Queenie, where do I start? He's still with Eva. That letter he got, you know? The one he said was about the rent increase. It was from her. He was with her down in Dorset all the time he was away. She thinks he's only here to collect his things and then he's moving back down there to be with her.'

Queenie shook his head. 'Dear God. And yet … I wish I could say I'm surprised. He's a monster.'

'And, well, there's something else too. He hit me today. And Norman has suddenly developed a black eye. I'm worried sick.'

'Oh, that is simply dreadful, my dear. You must go. In fact, why not go right now?'

'He's told me I can never leave him. Ever since he hit me, he's been patrolling around, watching me like a hawk. He even took Norman with him to the shops just now; I think he suspects I'm planning to just disappear. Anyway, we'll head to the docks in the morning. I'll stay here tonight, go through the motions at this damned party, and then just creep out early tomorrow when he's sleeping off his hangover.'

'Christmas Day tomorrow, my dear. No boats till the New Year now.'

In my panic, I hadn't thought of that. 'I'll have to find a guest house somewhere. I'll think of something. Perhaps I could stay at the hostel for a few days.'

'Let's hope so. So, what will you do back in Yorkshire?' he said, stacking the easel in the corner of the room along with all his other art materials. I had given up trying to explain that there were in fact other regions than Yorkshire in the north-east of England.

'Try to somehow finish school and do my teacher training, probably. That was always my dream. There must be a way, even for a fallen woman like me.'

'Darling, one piece of advice. Reinvent yourself as a widow by the time you get back home. No one can argue with that. Use my name if you like. The way I'm feeling, it'll probably be true anyway by then.'

'Don't say that, Queenie! But you know what? That's a great idea,' I said, brightening a little. 'I'd be proud to have your name. You and Arthur are the only reason I've still got Norman with me at all. And I'm luckier than most, you know, I've got enough to live on for a few years while I go through school and college. Though if we're at war again who knows what will be going on.'

'Well, if there's a way, I'm sure you'll find it,' he said, with a weak smile.

I handed him a small bag with a drawstring top. 'Forty guineas. For you and Arthur. You need to get away from Daggers, too. It's not safe being near him anymore. Will you promise me you'll find somewhere else if he doesn't go back to Eva?'

Queenie sighed. 'I hope so. I'm so bloody old though, Nancy. I'm tired of it all. But listen, I will keep an eye on things tonight. If he comes anywhere near Norman when you're at the party, he'll have to get past me first. And thank you.' He wiped away a tear. 'I'll miss you. Both of you. You've brought light and joy to this house. But in a way, I've always hoped you would escape.'

My eye fell on a painting on the wall, of a woman in a white, backless satin evening dress, her back to the painter. A black fur cascaded over the seat she was sitting on. It looked like coal, in a way; I wondered if that was deliberate.

'Is that me?' I said. 'Looks like me wearing a Vionnet.'

Queenie looked up. 'Oh yes, that one is you. It's one of my favourites. Such serenity. That, for me, is the essence of your beauty. Listen, when you get settled, send me your address and I'll post it to you.'

I looked at him. 'I can't send anything here that might have my address on. But I'll never forget it.'

I hugged him for a long time, though he was so thin and brittle I felt he might snap under the pressure of my arms. I could feel his bones under the smock. His breath smelled like oranges mixed with nail polish. We shed a tear together, until there came the faint sounds of the baby crying.

When I returned to the basement, Leyla had finished putting up crêpe paper garlands all over, and one of Dalglish's friends, a banjo player named Carl, had arrived and struck up a rendition of a popular song. An aura of excitement hung about the house in expectation of a huge, bohemian party – a revelry with no food but with a whole smorgasbord of debaucheries. I took hold of Norman and was heading upstairs when Dalglish appeared. 'Where are you going?' he said.

'Just putting the baby to bed.'

'Put something nice on, all right? How about that little white dress? Tonight is about us. I'm sorry about earlier, Nance. It won't happen again. I need to lay off the snow for a bit. It's not good. I'm going to make a new start tomorrow.'

Guests had started to arrive; the stern-looking monocled lady, and the Bloomsbury publisher and his wife were already descending the steps to the basement in a cloud of whoops and welcome hugs. Smoke filled the air, and the sweet smell of hashish. A group of musicians sat at the far end of the divan. 'I'm dying of thirst, Dalglish old chap,' shouted one of them. 'Can you fetch me a beer? Actually, don't worry – the clown can get it,' he said, nodding at Arthur, who rustled off obligingly to the scullery, leaving strands of liberated crêpe paper in his wake. His piñata jacket was already falling victim to a rapid onset of alopecia. 'Anyway, Dalglish, you're looking as dastardly as ever if I may say so. Come and tell me what, and more importantly *who,* you've been up to, you gorgeous big bad hound, you.' Dalglish laughed and nodded, and I quickly exited up the stairs.

I decided to pack as little as possible. I threw a few possessions – just enough to get us through the journey – into a couple of shabby old knapsacks. I shoved them under the bed in my old garret bedroom, then I emptied the Buddha of the remaining money and filled up my tobacco tins, which I also thrust under the bed. I would keep everything hidden upstairs until the moment we left. I didn't dare take the pram, so I fiddled around with a thin, multicoloured blanket to make a baby sling, which I tied tightly once

I'd got it to the correct length. What a look. We'd probably have to prove we weren't gypsies before they would allow us onto the boat.

***

The party was like a bad dream. The dress was too tight – my body was bigger all over and my belly was still stretched and loose. I was sick with nerves and exhausted with the effort of keeping a smile in place. Whenever I tried to move away for just a second, Dalglish would appear with another drink for me. He would not even let me go upstairs to check on the baby. 'Tonight's for us,' he said, over and over, his eyes like saucers. The musicians were in full swing, and though it was too early for clothes to be shed, the writing was definitely on the *trompe l'œil*'d wall. One man was already shirtless, and another woman was down to her brassiere and girdle. I wondered if you were cold, upstairs, Norman, as it was freezing outside. The fire was banked, so it would not be throwing out much heat. I waited and waited, counting out the minutes listening to gossip and innuendo and singing. I tried to join in with the dancing. I looked up at the clock. Nearly eleven. The song ended and I heard distant baby cries from upstairs. Dalglish was nowhere to be seen, so I crept up the stairs, looking carefully around me at each step.

I opened the bedroom door to see Dalglish standing over the cot with his fist raised. He turned to me, his eyes were red and blurred. 'He won't shut up,' he slurred.

I screamed and ran towards him, and in that split second he caught me, and flung me down. I hit my head on the side of the fireplace and then the room began to swim around me, and everything faded into a deep black nothingness. I passed out for a few seconds, but aching and a horrible burning smell brought me round; my own arm being held in the fire by Dalglish. Agonising canons of pain shot through my arm and I whimpered to him: 'Please,' I said. 'Please …'

All of a sudden, he seemed to come to his senses, and pulled away. I crawled up into a ball and began to weep tears of shocked pain. 'Just let us go,' I begged.

'You've got this all wrong,' he said, kneeling beside me, stroking my hair. 'I still want you. But if you go together, I will find you. At the hostel with your little nun friends. In the hospital. Down the police station. At the docks waiting for your little boat. I'll find you Nancy, and I'll teach you not to leave me. It doesn't have to be like this, you know? If we get rid of him, it can just be you and me again … like it was before.'

I looked at my left arm in horror. It was no longer smooth, but right from the elbow to the wrist had opened up like the charred, rocky coolings of some violent molten outpourings. Waves of nausea washed over me and I felt weak. I lay, panting on the ground, as Dalglish stood and picked up a poker, which he twirled in his hand. He walked over to the cot.

'Stop,' I pleaded. 'Don't do this. I'm begging you.'

Dalglish held the poker up, ready to strike. 'You and me,' he said softly, looking up at the ceiling. He closed his eyes.

I screamed out with all my might, but my cries were drowned out by the music and laughter coming from below. *This is it,* I thought. He's going to murder our child. I tried to pull myself up, gagging with dizziness. Suddenly, there was a loud thwack, but when I looked up, I saw that Dalglish had crumpled to the ground. Behind him stood Queenie, thin and pale in a long white nightgown, shaking, like some benevolent, post-apparition Ebenezer. He held a cricket bat in his hand. Dalglish had taken a blow to the back of the shoulder, and blood began to trickle through his shirt. He started to groan.

'Quickly,' said Queenie, trembling. 'Get out of here now.' I looked at him plaintively. 'Now!' he screamed.

Dalglish began to pull himself upright. 'Ah,' he spat. 'You've broken my fucking shoulder, Queenie. After everything I've done for you. I'll kill the lot of you.'

Queenie looked at me angrily, as if to say why are you still here? 'Come any closer and I'll hit you again,' he said to Dalglish. 'And this time you'll get the bat right through your skull.'

I picked up the baby, who was now screaming at the top of his lungs. I grabbed a blanket, then ran down the stairs, throwing on my boots and ignoring the drunken folk lining the hallway. I didn't even stop to pick up my coat.

Holding the baby as best I could with my right arm, I clomped through the snow back up to the King's Road and flagged down a taxi I could not even pay for.

***

The taxi driver was a proper East Ender, who was shocked by my plight and willing to waive his fare. 'Snakes alive, you need to get yourself straight to hospital right now, young lady. You smell like a bacon sandwich,' he said, proving, it seems, that there is always a time and place for East End humour.

'No,' I said. 'We're going to Hampstead.' It was the only thing I could think of, the only place Dalglish wouldn't be able to find, and somewhere Norman could be safe while I went for treatment. Though it broke my heart and went against every maternal instinct, I knew we couldn't be together until I got better, until I had a better plan to escape. If Dalglish found me in the meantime, so be it, I was resigned to my fate. But I was determined he could never find you.

Eventually the cries abated and Norman settled into an exhausted sleep, lulled by the motion of the cab. I couldn't bear to look down and see what sort of damage Dalglish had done. And so I looked backwards at the road, checking that we were not being followed. It was slow going through the snowy roads, and it was nearly midnight when we pulled up at 34 Westfield Drive. I looked up anxiously at the house, magnificently Gothic against the cold, wintry night, the snowflakes whirling round the chimneys and gathering on the railings.

The cold hit me again as I waded through the snow up the driveway to the front door. The blanket trailed through the snow. I banged hard several times on the door and waited for what seemed like an eternity until finally the door opened.

'Nancy,' said Matthew, ever the embodiment of bourgeois tradition, standing in the doorway, hastily tying his paisley smoking jacket. 'What on earth is going on? What are you doing here?' He looked at me closely and took a gasp. I saw his wife trail up behind him, looking fearful. When she saw it was me, her eyes narrowed.

'You're hurt. Oh, my God, look at your arm. Come in,' he said.

But Lucy stepped in front of her husband. 'She will not step foot on my property again, Matthew.'

'I need your help,' I said. The pain in my arm was becoming unbearable once again and I gagged in response to the waves of agony that washed over me.

'She's drunk,' said Lucy in disgust to her husband.

'He's yours?' said Matthew, peering over the blanket at the baby.

I nodded. It was difficult to speak. 'His father tried to kill him. He said he's going to find us and come after him.' The statement sounded ludicrous; childish and silly. I found myself unconvinced at its veracity.

'A likely story,' said Lucy, shaking her head. 'More likely you hurt him. Why should we believe a word you say? And how long have you been working as a prostitute?' she said, looking at my tiny dress and bare legs.

I didn't know what to say. I handed Norman over. 'Can you take him in for a while and keep him safe here? Matthew, can you help me get to hospital?'

'He's been beaten, Nancy. Oh, my good God.' They looked at each other, shocked. 'What have you got yourself mixed up in?' But then Lucy seemed to be filled with some new purpose and pulled herself up straight. 'We'll take in your bastard for you. We will give him a Christian life here. But you, you're pure evil. You're on your own.'

'Go, Nancy,' said Matthew, 'before I call the police. Don't come back here. They'll string you up for attempted murder.'

I looked at them both. I was starting to feel weak and my thoughts were taking a long time to process. But then I realised what they meant: this would be a permanent arrangement. I could find no strength to fight them, and right at that second I couldn't think of a single reason why what they were suggesting wasn't a good idea.

'His name is Norman,' I whispered.

'No,' said Lucy. 'He doesn't need anything more from you.' She looked down at the baby and her eyes had a curious shine to them. 'His name will be Paul.'

I was beaten. I moved forwards to give the baby a kiss and say goodbye but Lucy was too quick for me. 'Go to hell,' she hissed, and slammed the door in my face.

I stood there, swaying gently. I looked at the door for a long time. The drama was done, those few moments that would decide the rest of all of our lives were already consigned to history, and the peacefulness of a snowy Christmas Eve had returned to Hampstead. A few streets away, drunken revellers were returning from the pub, happy with ale and companionship, and red-faced from the warmth of the fire. In Victorian tenements and modernist blocks and Gothic sprawls, parents were checking that their children were asleep, then putting out Christmas stockings filled with presents. Out of the nearby church, Christians were emerging to return home from midnight Mass. In a party in Chelsea, a very old man – our own kind of saviour, Norman – had just drawn his last breath.

I turned towards the street and pushed through the snow back down the drive. The gas lamp threw long, stick-man shadows of my silhouette across the front lawn and suddenly I became nothing but particles of light and shadow, weightless and empty.

***

I became aware of a presence kneeling next to me. 'Look who it is,' said a voice. I opened my eyes to see a blend of shimmering images that put together looked a little like Mekhi. 'I did not expect to see this after a long shift at the hotel.' He bent over me, looking me up and down, blocking out the light. 'Technically, my right hand now possesses you,' he continued. 'It is written in the holy book: I have the right to know you, as a husband knows a wife. But it's late and cold and – what a sight you are – you look like you're full of disease. So I will leave it up to Allah to decide your fate, though it seems to me from looking at you that he has already done that,' he said, standing up to leave. 'Just as he did for my sister,' he whispered, under his breath, and the deep blue light of the snow-filled sky reappeared to the crunching sound of his footsteps as he retreated quickly from where I lay.

I tried to speak to him, but the words would not come to my lips. *Why can't you help me?* I wanted to say. *Where is your free will?*

Snowflakes fell on my face, melting into tiny rivulets of water which ran down my cheeks and into my ears and onto my neck. My body grew completely stiff, and I could no longer make any sound. I drifted off to a frozen sleep.

In the end, I was not saved by a divinity but by a milkman dressed as Father Christmas on his horse and cart out doing a special Christmas morning delivery to the local hospital. I was vaguely aware of a man shouting for help, and a woman's scream.

I drifted to a different place, in fact I was back in the pictures in Oslington, arm in arm with Nana, watching a silent film, with the pianist playing a mournful tune to accompany the black-and-white tragedy that was unfolding on screen. I felt sad that they were taking me to hospital. Our time together could be measured in weeks, Norman, but already I could not imagine life without you. I wished, simply, that it would all end.

'Tired with all these, from these would I be gone, Save that, to die, I leave my love alone.' The fluid eloquence of Shakespeare: the antithesis of my jumbled life.

Chapter 13

After that fateful night back in Christmas 1938, I had a broken rib and third-degree burns on my arm; the only relatively 'good' point being that the fire had destroyed all the pain receptors in that area and so overall it was not the agony one might imagine. Additionally, I was suffering from hypothermia and, as if that wasn't enough, pneumonia decided to come and join the party. The milkman had taken me to the Royal Free in Hampstead. They did skin grafts to my arm, a pioneering technique in those days and only the second the hospital had ever performed. They kept me hydrated and filled me with painkillers.

Those first few weeks were touch-and-go for me, and I floated in and out of consciousness like a drowning woman who keeps on coming up to the surface for air. I saw grotesque, multi-dimensional visions. But I also entered a state of peace that went deeper than the areas touched by the morphine being dripped, steadily, into my veins. Because, ultimately, Norman, I knew that you were safe from your father.

Have you ever had an extended stay in hospital, Norman? Two months into my stay and I'd already become well and truly institutionalised. At the beginning, or at least when I'd stopped saying crazy stuff and had remembered what was going on, time seemed to bend in two, and then bend in two again. Time was cruel, mocking me with its endlessness. Time lodged itself inside me as a physical pain, cruel and taunting, something to be endured. The days stretched out ahead of me interminably. I watched the hour and minute and second hands of the clock opposite, above Mrs Butler's bed, except when she was asleep or they closed the curtains to go in with the bedpan.

Mrs Butler, as a side note, was an incredibly naughty old woman. She had spent at least twenty years in a state of incipient death, always on the cusp of its moribund jaws, but somehow always eluding it. She was blind and struggled to hear, but still managed to gossip mercilessly about her visitors to me as soon as they had left. It was a pleasant kind of background noise, if I'm honest, with no reciprocation from me being necessary and in any case unable to be heard due to her deafness.

Time dragged by, Norman, I swear those clock hands above Mrs Butler's bed slowed down when they were being watched. But then I fell into the rhythm of the place, and my own body clock moved in sync with the temporal shape of the day. First, were the early morning cleaners, and, after the initial flush of disappointment that I was still animate, I felt grateful for their cheerful good mornings, and for the rattles of their tin buckets and mops. I came to expect the smell of vinegar as they washed the floors. Then there was the woman who called me dear and pulled back the blue curtain at eight to bring in a cup of tea and slice of bread and jam. She came again at twelve for lunch and at six to deliver the dreadful slop they called dinner. These punctuation points took on almost biblical significance in the day, even though I had no appetite. The nurses and doctors treated me well enough but could not categorise me at all – I had no visitors, no name, no money, no history, and the dress I'd arrived in was indecently short, short enough to arouse suspicion as to my moral standing at a time when beds were being required for more worthy candidates.

Actually, on the visitor front, that's not quite true, Norman. I had a short note from Arthur – God only knows how he found me. 'Queenie didn't make it,' said the note. 'The police have closed up the house. Dalglish has fled. Take care of yourself.'

I had not even seen my arm at that point, they made sure of that, but of course I was in pain the whole time and heard their mutterings to the effect that it was a miracle I had made it that far. The chaplain came by but I sent him away; the consolations of his faith held no interest for me. Queenie didn't make it – never have so few words conveyed so much. I imagined him, distracted by my hurried departure, checking over his shoulder; and in that split second Dalglish seeing his chance at revenge. A few minutes later Dalglish leaving the house forever and disappearing under the radar – easy to do when those who know you don't even know your first name.

Queenie's death, the loss of my baby and the guilt I felt on both counts were simply too much for me to deal with. Emotionally and intellectually I resigned myself to a quiet state of vegetative withdrawal, and dreamed of the day when my body would give up and I would no longer hear that early morning clanking sound and smell the disinfectant that signalled the start of a new day.

One afternoon, when the boredom and Mrs Butler's inane wittering had become intolerable, I dragged myself along to the little hospital library. This was really nothing more than a few shelves in a room full of medical equipment. A book on psychology caught my eye and piqued my interest. I had a new urge to better understand the circus that was my life: my motivations, Dalglish, the Clayton-Reids... I thought back to that day, when Dalglish and I were sitting on a bench, overlooking the Thames, eating roast chestnuts. I thought about you, Norman, realising that my own redemption would be the only possible way back to you, and that I needed to do this for both of us. Having already become adept at using just one arm I nudged the book out, sat down on one of the benches and began to read. I became engrossed in the book. After a while, a woman walked past: shortish in height, clipped brown hair, glasses, dowdy clothes. In other words, fairly nondescript. She glanced at me and our eyes met, briefly, then she seemed to frown and walked on to speak to the ward nurse about someone else. I thought nothing more of it and resumed my reading. Hours later, she walked past again. I was still compulsively devouring the same book.

A few days later she appeared again and this time she came over to my bed area. By now I had two or three books on psychology by my bed. I had spent the intervening time iteratively reading the contents of those books – the same chapters over and over - as if these were my last hours before being sent to the gallows. 'Hello,' she said, peering over the top of her glasses. 'I'm Dr Sarah Mead. I see you're interested in psychology. Would you like some company?' I shook my head at her and felt a surge of anger; I didn't want to be interrupted by anyone in my now manic quest for understanding.

'Would you like me to get in touch with anyone for you?' she said, sitting down tentatively on the edge of the bed. 'I've not seen anyone visit you the last few times I've been here. Friends? Family?'

'No, thank you.'

'Are you in pain?'

I shrugged. I glanced over at Mrs Butler in the opposite bed, who was tunelessly singing 'Pack Up Your Troubles' to no one in particular.

She smiled sympathetically. 'Would you like to talk about what happened to you?'

'No, thank you.'

After she left I regretted my petulance and was cross with the doctors and nurses instead, as if it were somehow their fault I'd tossed aside the only opportunity that had come my way in months. I threw my plate of dinner onto the floor and screamed so loudly that even Mrs Butler stopped singing and shouted at me to shut the devil up.

But the next day Dr Mead came back. 'You've probably gathered that the reason I'm around from time to time is that I work at this hospital. I'm a child psychologist. Once every couple of weeks or so I come here for a few days at a time from Cambridge where I live. If you're interested in psychology, if you're looking for answers to something, then maybe I can help out just a little. There are some other books you may be interested in.'

I looked at her, a small inconsequential woman in drab clothes, a faded-out pixie. Someone you wouldn't notice if they walked past you in the street. Everyone I knew was either glamorous or quirky and I'm sorry to say I was rather judgemental about Sarah during those early conversations. To be honest, I was more interested in the thought of new books rather than striking up a friendship with this woman.

'You never know,' she said. 'You may be able to help me too. We've all had different experiences. We all bring different perspectives to things. I get caught up in my academic world. Sometimes I over-intellectualise things.'

'I don't think so. I don't know anything about it.'

'Let's just keep an open mind,' she said, in a way that implied I did not have a choice in the matter.

Later that week she returned. She brought a pile of books by Sigmund Freud and put them on the tallboy next to my bed. 'Perhaps we could venture outside too, for a little walk?'

The fresh air on my face felt invigorating, in more ways than one. Outside I could see that spring was already changing into summer. The air felt full of hope. I had the sense of my past life drawing to a close, and a strong feeling that a big change was taking place. After Sarah had gone I stared at the books for a long time, then summoned the nurse to pass me over *The Future of an Illusion*. A tiny spark of excitement and a wave of sadness both assaulted me at the same time.

And that was how it started. Sarah didn't mind that I had nothing interesting to say. In fact, I had become so unused to speaking and had lost so much confidence (I was consumed by a hideous self-loathing every time I tentatively ventured out from my self-imposed vegetative state) that I developed a stammer for a while. I wanted so badly to impress her intellectually with something, anything at all, but there wasn't much, back then. Nevertheless, Sarah saw something inside me she was prepared to fight for. She offered me her humanity, in that quiet way she has.

***

I'm lucky, Norman. I now get to spend every working day with my guardian angel. And as she talks more and more about her retirement, she has made sure I have my own wings for the next stage of this journey. I hope there is another Sarah Mead somewhere, looking out for you.

***

At some point during those feverish first few months, I had the strangest dream, more of a vision, really. I was waiting at the docks at West India Quay with Minister Lewes. The coal boat was there, filled with new cargo, ready to head back up north to exchange its load for the next collection of coal. The sweat-prone ticket man was at the head of the queue, and in front of us was the Imam. When it came to his turn, the ticket man smiled and proclaimed, 'Well, this *is* a turn up for the books. Delighted to see you here, sir. You won't regret this journey.' Suddenly Mekhi and Arthur appeared and started shouting at the ticket man.

'Stop trying to impose your white, imperialist agenda on him,' Arthur said. 'He doesn't need to do this.' And they bundled the Imam away, continuing to rant and rave at the ticket man, calling him a bigot and worse.

I grew angry with Arthur. 'Why are you stopping him—' I shouted, but suddenly the air was filled with white noise and my words were lost. Then they all left peacefully; the Imam seemed to have given up his fight.

The ticket man mopped his brow and shook his head. 'I get this all the time,' he said. 'I try to ignore it, but it gets to you after a while. Shout first, ask questions later. They're all the same. Anyway, Minister, this is a journey of Enlightenment, a journey to discover where you stand on the question of free will. And you, sir, have a dubious record in that department yourself, if I may say so.'

'This is a journey God has told me I must make,' said Tim Lewes, and the ticket man grudgingly handed him a ticket.

When we were on board, the minister also began to rant and rave: 'The Bible is the final word of God,' he said, 'and should have complete authority in all matters of theology and ethics. It should be interpreted literally.' I argued vociferously against this, citing the horrors of a literal interpretation: condoning of slavery, treatment of homosexuals, burning of witches and so on, but the minister was adamant that he was right.

After a few hours, he turned to me and I saw some doubt on his face; it seemed as if he was no longer so sure. 'Perhaps I have been too hasty,' he said. 'We can respect Christianity's Holy Scriptures and know that they faithfully represent God's word, but perhaps we should agree to interpret them as part of a much wider context?'

Thomas Aquinas was passing, and he nodded in agreement. 'Reaching out to the polytheists for help in defining a wider set of Christian ethics is a strength, my friend, because mankind has exercised free will,' he said, before disappearing from sight. The minister sighed, wistfully, and fell silent. After a while, Martin Luther walked past us, tipping his hat.

'Perhaps it is all right to see the Holy Scriptures just as witness to the word of God,' said Minister Lewes. 'Some of the better stories in the holy books need to become *allegorical* and the uncomfortable ones *apocryphal*.'

'I don't know what that means,' I said, so he explained it to me.

We were way past halfway into the journey by this point, and I began to think of the future, which was defined by the past. The minister was silent once again for a long time.

I looked over to the bow, where a tall gentleman was standing, looking out to sea. I recognised him from the painting in the Lewes' house: it was John Wesley. He turned to us and shook his head. 'Life without free will is just slavery,' he said, frowning. 'Find your voice and speak out.' Then he turned and walked off, too.

After that the setting changed and there were just the two of us on the boat and Minister Lewes turned to me once more. 'You know, Nancy, I am ashamed at how the church has behaved at times in its past,' he said. 'I believe we need to implement our religion as part of a much wider system of beliefs and ethics. Our holy books are only partly useful; we should not be afraid to operate within the world in which we live today, to change if we need to. My belief is a living organism; it thrives on being fed a diet of challenge and discourse.'

I could see land ahead and turned to the minister. 'Do you think, Minister, that we can be friends, and put our differences behind us, even though I do not believe in God?'

'I am sure of it, Nancy,' he said, with a smile. 'And in terms of our ethics, you know, now that I have made this journey, I think that we are much closer than you think. But you must also learn lessons from this. You swapped one kind of slavery for another when you let Dalglish into your life. And you abused your free will though a life of excess. Now you have a chance at redemption. Goodbye, my friend. The time has come to make the right changes and lead an ethical life. I know you have repented of your sins, so now it is time to forgive yourself, just as I know God has forgiven you. And as I believe he has forgiven me too. Look to the future. If I cannot persuade you to join me, well then use your free will to set your own parameters to help you in this quest.'

'I will, Minister,' I said. 'But let's not forget what the others said too. We must find courage to speak out.' But the scene was fading by this point and if he answered me, I was not able to hear it.

Just as I am no longer physically lying in the snow in that strangely quiet street, I know that my soul has never really left that place. In the same way, the dream has never left me: it has entered my soul and become part of me.

***

And so then, Norman, how should a non-believer live? How should we behave towards others? Are we allowed to change our minds about ethics and morals if a case can be made that we are wrong? What constitutes an ethical life? I am reminded of that old statement from Minister Lewes: 'What about those of us who are not strong enough to do this on our own? Do we need some kind of rationalist church for us all to go to on a Sunday?'

I'm not sure I'm ready to go that far, but it's an interesting thought. In my own case, I have come to accept Freud's thesis that every culture is based on compulsory labour and instinctual renunciation and so the only way I can find peace within society is to live a life of discipline and hard work. It's not a terribly sexy message, in fact it's like finding out that your after-dinner treat is not actually the Turkish delight but rather the over-strong, hard-boiled mint that has been stuck for several weeks to a paper bag that you found at the back of the drawer. Nevertheless, that maxim works for me.

I'm lucky because I was able to find that inner strength with the help of people like Sarah and her husband. An ethical life in terms of my own personal sphere means that I've stopped doing irresponsible and hurtful things 'just because I can'. It means big things, like having a job that tries to help the most vulnerable children you could ever meet recover from traumas. It means joyful things, like when one boy who'd witnessed his mother's murder finally spoke after over a year of not being able to. It means small things, like taking the family next door a chocolate cake and an apology when I have been typing too long or too late at work. It means thoughtful things, like those which encourage a plurality of views, such as respecting the choices of others – including their right to be religious. It means difficult things, like standing up for our rights as human beings when they are under threat – including the threats to our free will that come from religion.

More recently, Karl Popper warned us about the Paradox of Tolerance, which is the idea that unlimited tolerance must lead to the disappearance of tolerance. If we extend unlimited tolerance even to those who are intolerant, if we are not prepared to defend a tolerant society against the onslaught of the intolerant, then the tolerant will be destroyed, and tolerance with them. We must fight these threats with courage, you and I.

Living in an ethical way also means sad things, like taking responsibility for my own actions, Norman, including my cataclysmic failure towards you. And my grandparents, and the other Norm, and all the others. There were times when I hid in a broom cupboard to deprive my landlady of her rent when I had hundreds of pounds to my name. This was a woman who had fled from the Nazis. Sometimes you go past the point whereby apologising for your actions or forgiving yourself is appropriate, or even relevant. You have to look forwards, and decide how you would like the rest of your life to look.

Dalglish has stayed locked away in my memory since that fateful night. I simply cannot go there, and I wish I could give you a better story about your father. Perhaps, you will argue, Norman, that I should not have given you the burden of this story. If that is the case, then I am truly sorry and for that, at least, I hope you can forgive me.

My life now resembles that of Miss Trott. No, the irony is not lost on me. I live alone and rent an ancient stone farmhouse with a ramshackle garden on the edge of town. I sing for the church choir, where they accept my now very open rationalist views. I grow sweet williams in the summer, tend to my greenhouse and keep three chickens which I've named Eva, Ayesha and Elsie. Eva is always on the hunt for a mate, and will sometimes turn to the other girls in desperation/boredom. Ayesha is serene and composed, and Elsie just wants a quiet life.

I hope that Matthew and Lucy have given you the kind of life I never could – not back then anyway – and that it has been a happy one. You are still a young man, just twenty-three. It's not too late for us to find each other. And so, to my very first point, what is *this*, this manuscript? It's neither an apology nor a confession, but an act of taking responsibility, and of hope.

Chapter 14

Hampstead, July 1999

'Knock, knock,' came the cheerful voice, accompanied by some actual token knocking. 'Alcoholics Anonymous ground force here. Nikki? Are you still alive in there? I come bearing gifts. Fear not, Berocca and Lucozade are on their way.'

Nikki lay asleep on the daybed in the smoking room. Sunlight streamed in, lighting up the manuscript that was strewn all over the floor. She came slowly to consciousness, her head throbbing. She attempted to sit up gradually, feeling decidedly nauseated. Her lips were chapped and her tongue was glued to the roof of her mouth.

'Oh, dear,' said Uncle Jim, standing in the doorway. 'A proper casualty.' He walked over to the side table and picked up one of the empty wine bottles. 'Only the two bottles was it? Quiet night in, then. And I bet you don't remember phoning your aunt at three in the morning either, do you?'

Nikki closed her eyes. 'Oh, no,' she said. 'I'm so sorry. Is that why you've come?'

'We will help you sort this all out. You've just had a massive piece of news. Bella and I have been guilty of keeping your grandparents' secret all these years. The least we can do now is help.'

'Do my cousins know?' said Nikki, miserably.

'No. Only your aunt and I. And neither of us has read the weighty tome in there, so we only know a little of the story.'

'Jim?'

'Yes?'

'I'm sorry for being such an idiot and phoning you in the middle of the night.'

He chuckled and disappeared off, returning a few minutes later with a tray full of tissues, a mug of tea, a large glass of Berocca, a bottle of Lucozade and some slices of toast. 'No Marmite, I'm afraid. And didn't think you looked like a marmalade kind of a girl. But the Berocca should help with your vitamin levels,' he added, cheerfully.

'Thank you for coming, Jim. I really appreciate it,' said Nikki, taking a sip of the vitamin water. She shuddered. 'I'm not sure I can face this yet.'

'It really was the least I could do. I should have come up here as soon as Lucy died. I owe you an apology. Anyway, you'll still be in shock from the news and you're going to need to take it easy while you process it all. And that's even before we come to what's going on between you and Nick. One thing at a time, though.'

'Did you bring the dogs?'

'Indeed, I brought the dogs, madam. I thought I'd check you were still alive before I brought them in. Let me go and liberate them from the car before I am reported to the authorities. Finish your breakfast, then take a shower, and after all that we'll take the dogs out onto the heath for a walk. You might want to clean your teeth as well before your breath flattens that aspidistra over there.'

'That sounds like such a good idea. I've got no clean clothes, though. And there's a serious chance I may chunder in public.'

***

After the walk, they wandered down to Haverstock Hill. Nikki bought some emergency clothes and underwear from the Gap there, and then they sat outside a cafe, drinking coffee.

'Feel better now?'

'A bit, thank you. So – can we just go through this again? The real Uncle Paul died when he was just two. *You* think he probably had spina bifida. A few years later, Nancy's baby Norman gets dumped onto Lucy and Grandpa, and then Norman is given Paul's identity. But what I don't understand is why? Why pretend?'

'Well, the truth is that your grandma couldn't stand the shame of bringing up someone else's bastard, as she saw it.'

'Not terribly Christian of her.'

'No. That it was not. But *she* would say that she did behave in a Christian way – she took in someone else's child and brought him up when she was still grieving for her own. Only a few people knew about Paul's death – she couldn't bring herself to tell anyone about it and they weren't a couple who socialised much. She saw an opportunity, especially with war probably coming on and all that. They were away for years, up in Cumbria.'

'But she was resentful. Every single day. I can see that now. My poor father.'

'Yes. I must admit I did often think that, privately at least. What a mess.'

'How on earth can I explain all this to him? I don't know where to start. Our whole lives have been built on lies.'

Jim shook his head. 'Let's have a think this afternoon, okay? One step at a time. You know – I do just want to say, for the record, that I will always regard you as my niece. So will your aunt. Nothing has changed, for us at least.'

'Thank you, Jim. I appreciate that,' said Nikki, taking a welcome sip of coffee. 'Ah, that's better. So, I think this helps me understand Bella better too. She went through such a lot. She had so much loss in her young life. It explains, in a way, why she wanted such a big family of her own.'

Her uncle nodded.

'Do you know if Nancy is still alive?'

Jim looked sheepish, and sighed. 'I believe she died in the eighties. Cancer. There should be an obituary, a newspaper cutting in that box somewhere. Didn't you see it?'

Nikki shook her head, not trusting herself to speak.

'She was quite an activist in the end, I believe. Wrote a book about free will and religion. Which is, let's face it, never going to win you first prize in a popularity contest. Made a *lot* of enemies doing it. But Bella said the surprising thing was that she was either castigated or ignored by the people you'd think might have supported her. She ended up being rather more infamous than famous, but she battled on with it all, right to the end. Got to hand it to her: very strong character.' Jim looked at her sideways. 'That's where you get it from.'

'Belligerent is probably the word you're looking for,' said Nikki, with a sigh. 'Do you know, Nancy spent nearly six months in the Royal Free? I was only there last week myself with Lucy.' Just then, her phone pinged to signal a text had arrived: *Just about to board the flight. Sent you the details on an email. Can you pick me up from Heathrow? I will help you with the rest of the funeral arrangements. Not fair you've had to do it all by yourself. Anyway, looking forward to seeing you, Nick and the girls. Lots of love, Dad xxx*

Nikki sank back into the chair and covered her eyes. The traffic of Haverstock Hill roared past. Emotions washed over her and this time she could not be consoled by the sensible, grounded tones of her uncle.

***

What did it mean to live an ethical life? Nancy had explained what it meant to her personally, and now it was up to Nikki to face up to it, unpick it, layer by layer, mentally plot it all out on a graph and work out what it would mean to her, too. She was never going to be like Aunt Bella, or all those other women who were content to stay home and play mum. But that didn't mean she couldn't at least try to sort her life out, to give more of herself to the people who needed her. Her grandmother had lost her child; it looked like Nikki was heading the same way.

'Your feelings towards your children are actually more common than you might think,' said Jim. 'We can work on all of this once we get this week out of the way.'

So many other things to consider. Was her marriage worth saving? *Yes,* she thought. *Of course.* She missed Nick, and actually she missed her kids. Was it already too late? Uncle Jim thought not, and the next morning he made a call to Nick on her behalf. But her husband was not yet ready to forgive or even to talk to her. Behaving badly, just because you can. *In the end, not terribly rewarding, is it,* she thought.

She started to write a text to her father. *Got your email and will be there to pick you up. Can't wait to see you. We have a lot to talk about. Love you. Nikki xxx*

Already the loneliness of being who she was had begun to evaporate, and in the reflected light of Nancy's story she began to understand herself for the first time. Empathy flooded over her, channelled towards the woman who was her real grandmother, and the tragedy that, on a personal level, Nancy would never have the same chance at redemption. Nikki stared out of the window and mentally made her grandmother a promise.

'Ready to go?' said Jim, checking his watch. 'Heathrow here we come.'

Nikki picked up the car keys and they headed outside.

Epilogue

Cambridge, June 1964

In a small side room at the top of a building which lists and sags with age sits a middle-aged man. He is sweating after climbing three flights of stairs and then finding the room airless, in spite of the open window. He wonders if Dr Mead is going to offer him some water. He is nervous, too; this feels odd because he is not that kind of a person. In any case, he cannot quite believe that he is here. An aura of anticipation hangs about him.

Six months ago, he had received a letter from a Dr Sarah Mead, a Cambridge academic and practising child psychologist. Sent all the way to his office in Hong Kong, addressed simply to 'Mr Norman Mitford, Chief Executive Officer, Mitford Haulage, Hong Kong.' His secretary had a good laugh at that one. A miracle, really, that the letter had ever made it.

Dr Mead wrote that she had read the article about him in the *Sunday Times*, the fascinating rags-to-riches tale of the miner's son who ended up creating one of the largest and most successful shipping haulage companies in the world. She offered condolences for the untimely death of his wife, and announced that there was someone from his past who, if and when the time was right, she thought it would be beneficial for him to meet. Although, she had said, it was probably best to keep it between them.

He did not respond, initially. Too soon after Anne's death. They were all still reeling from it, the grief coming in waves. He was realising he would probably need to move back to the UK to be nearer to his teenage children at their boarding school in Rutland, and wondering what on earth that would mean for his business. Delegation had never been his strong point but maybe now was the time to start working on it.

Initially, he had read and reread Dr Mead's letter, mulling it over. All those years ago when Nancy had done her disappearing act people had asked him how he felt. He had only been able to shake his head and shrug. He'd known it was coming, somehow, in that weirdly instinctive way that he has, from the moment he had seen her the weekend before she skedaddled off into the sunset. Her face was full of a guilty intention that she couldn't even confess to herself. But then, Nancy had always been absolutely rubbish at hiding her feelings. He had, as the saying goes, seen her coming before she'd arrived. He couldn't even feel anger towards her. Sometimes you get too close to people for that.

The only other time he'd seen her was when he was at home one day, distractedly leafing through a copy of Anne's *Vogue*. He can still remember how shocked he had felt, wondering if old wounds were going to be opened up just from seeing her looking implausibly beautiful and more remote than ever in that magazine. But he was a practical man and not given to paroxysms of emotion. He had simply put down the magazine and went on with his day.

Kids though, weren't they? Just kids. Living on their wits. He has a reputation at work for being tough to the point of belligerent but it doesn't feel like that now. His heart is thumping boisterously in his chest. He stands up, shifting from foot to foot. Sarah is just as he'd imagined her, quietly spoken and composed and academic. Over dinner at her house the previous evening she had revealed to him that Nancy never got over what she did to him and even named her child after him. He is still reeling from the shock of this information and right now he simply does not know what to think.

Presently, the door opens, and a tall, slim woman walks in and looks at him, expecting him to be her next patient, not understanding at first. He recognises those fierce blue eyes – behind Hank Marvin glasses – and the dark hair, longer now and softer than the severe fringed bob he remembers from their last encounter. The face is slimmer than it was, but the body has filled out a bit. Suddenly, she understands who he is and shock fills her face. She turns to her colleague, but Dr Mead has already begun to make her excuses and is retreating, closing the door behind her.

They stand in that airless room and look at each other. 'Hello, stranger,' he says presently, with a sad smile.

THE END.

Printed in Poland
by Amazon Fulfillment
Poland Sp. z o.o., Wrocław